# A COMPLEX SOLUTION

## by
## Kurt Gerstner

authorHOUSE™

1663 LIBERTY DRIVE, SUITE 200
BLOOMINGTON, INDIANA 47403
(800) 839-8640
WWW.AUTHORHOUSE.COM

*© 2005 Kurt Gerstner. All Rights Reserved.*

*No part of this book may be reproduced, stored in a retrieval system, or transmitted by any means without the written permission of the author.*

*First published by AuthorHouse 08/01/2005*

*ISBN: 1-4208-3788-5 (sc)*
*ISBN: 1-4208-3787-7 (dj)*

*Library of Congress Control Number: 2005904318*

*Printed in the United States of America*
*Bloomington, Indiana*

*This book is printed on acid-free paper.*

**For my wife, Jane**

# PROLOGUE

College can be hazardous to your health!

This little tidbit of information is not generally known to the public. The marketing gurus in college admissions offices certainly don't tell you about potential hazards in those glossy bulletins they send out to lure prospective students to their schools. I guess they don't like to scare away their customers before they get them in the door.

So when I drove up to my new college for the first time, and saw the stately, ivy-covered brick walls, I wasn't considering the dangers that might be lurking behind its ivory towers. Instead of hidden perils, I was thinking about hedonistic pleasures. My parents were going back home to Seattle and I'd be remaining behind in Cambridge, Massachusetts – an entire country between us. I'd be on my own for the first time in my life and I can tell you I was looking forward to my independence. I would make the campus my playground and enjoy my new-found freedom, blissfully ignorant of any menace that might await me.

My parents, both college graduates, also seemed to be oblivious to any potential dangers at my new home for the next four years. They just wanted me to enjoy myself and experience everything college life had to offer. Before my folks left for the airport, my Dad took me aside and gave me a final pep talk.

"Jerry, I have one word of advice for you."

"Plastics?" I asked, smirking.

"Very funny. No, the one word of advice I have for you is – try everything."

"That's two words, Dad."

"All right, two words. Stop interrupting, wise guy," he replied. "Just listen."

He removed his glasses and began polishing them absentmindedly, something he always did just before he lectured me.

"Jerry, I did pretty well in college. I studied hard and I got good grades. But do you think I can tell you anything that I learned in my classes in the four years I was there?"

I shrugged my shoulders.

"Not a lick. The things I learned in college that have stuck with me my entire life are the practical things I learned outside of class, mostly in my fraternity. You know, things like getting along with people that are really different from you, or how to stay up all night playing cards and still function the next day. Oh, and how to get by without doing laundry for three weeks – the secret is turning your underwear inside out." He winked at me. "You don't learn stuff like that in class, Jer."

"No. I guess not," I agreed.

"Now don't get me wrong. Mom and I want you to do well academically. But we also want you to get an education. Understand? So go out and seize every opportunity that comes your way – carpe opportunem, or whatever it is. Take advantage of all the great things school has to offer." Then he glanced over at my Mom, who was fiddling with a suitcase, leaned close to me and whispered conspiratorially, "By the way, I know Mom doesn't want you to join a fraternity, but go ahead and check 'em out. If you find one you like, I'll run interference for you," and he winked.

How could I argue with advice like that? I decided to follow my Dad's advice and experience college life to the fullest. As it turned out, following that advice would nearly get me expelled and killed in the very first semester of my new college career. But hey, I sure got an education.

# ONE

The clue to two across read: 'The reason why a Frenchman will eat only one egg for breakfast.'

I pondered this for a while, but came up empty. My four years of high school Spanish, under the tutelage of Señora Washington, left me ill-prepared to solve crossword puzzle clues that required knowledge of French eating habits. I mean, how was anyone other than a Frenchman supposed to know what motivated his appetite?

I sighed. Here I was, seated in the last row of a large lecture hall, attending my very first Chemistry 101 class. In row upon row before me were the backs of countless heads, attached to the bodies of countless students, all trying to unravel the mysteries of chemistry. But the only mystery I was trying to unravel at the moment was the answer to two across.

My class was scheduled to run for forty minutes and there I sat with well over sixty crossword puzzle clues remaining to be solved. I was already stuck on the second one. At this rate I'd never finish the puzzle before class ended. I decided I needed help.

Seated next to me was my new friend and fellow freshman, Randy Bradford. Tanned, clean-shaven and wearing a threadbare Texas Rangers baseball cap that contrasted with his green Brooks Brothers polo shirt, crisply-pressed white pants and topsider shoes, Randy was engrossed in a video game he was playing on his Game Boy. An enormous wad of chewing gum swelled his cheek as though a bee had just stung it.

I had met Randy the week before while attending a rush event at one of the fraternity houses on campus. In case you're wondering, the term 'rush' is short for 'rush smoker.' I don't know who coined the term, but it sounds like it may have Jamaican origins. It describes the process used by fraternities to recruit new members.

It was a fairly simple process. Eligible males (mostly freshmen) attended a series of rush parties hosted by the different fraternities on campus. The rushees and brothers met each other. After a short courtship period, the brothers selected the rushees they wanted to join by giving them 'bids' – offers to pledge their fraternity. Randy and I had gone through that process and each of us received bids to pledge several different fraternities. But we both decided to pledge Sigma Epsilon Chi. So we were going to be pledge brothers together.

I liked Randy from the instant I met him. He had an easy, laid-back quality about him, with a self-deprecating Southern charm. At first I thought that he was just displaying false modesty, particularly about his intellect, but as I got to know him better I learned there was a good reason for his humility. Randy had the mental capacity of a biscuit. Well, that's not really fair. Let's just say that the CPU in his brain worked more like a 286 than a Pentium 4.

Randy's view of his mental prowess was realistic. He told me he'd always been a mediocre student at best. The only way he had gotten into college was through his family connections. And what Randy lacked in gray matter he certainly made up for in green matter. Randy was from Texas – most of the time. When he wasn't living in Texas he was living at his family's other home, on Bradford Island in Maine – named after his great grandfather. His family was rolling in dough – old Yankee money and new oil money. He also had all sorts of political connections in his family. His relatives had been governors, Congressmen and ambassadors to half the banana republics in the world, including some French protectorates. So I figured it was worth a shot asking him about the clue.

"Hey, Randy," I whispered. "Do you know anything about what Frenchmen have for breakfast?"

"French toast?" he replied hopefully.

I didn't think that was what the puzzle master had in mind but I checked the available spaces.

"Doesn't fit."

"How many letters?" he asked in his Texas Brahmin drawl. I counted.

"Six."

Seated next to Randy was his valet, Cheever, a proper British butler. I had seen Cheever with Randy at the rush parties. As always, Cheever was dressed in an impeccably neat black suit, starched white shirt with dark tie, and a bowler hat, which was now resting on a chair at his side.

"Hey Cheever, you know somethin' about Frenchies, don't ya? See if you can help Jerry out. He's stymiediated."

"Indeed, sir?" Cheever responded with a British accent that was right out of the movies. "Might I be of some assistance?" he asked, addressing me.

"Uh, sure. I guess so," I replied, never having spoken to a butler before. "I'm trying to figure out the answer to this crossword puzzle clue – the reason why a Frenchman will eat only one egg for breakfast; it has six letters."

One of Cheever's eyebrows rose slightly.

"I believe the appropriate response to your query would be 'un oeuf'," he replied almost instantly.

"Excuse me?"

"Un oeuf," he repeated. I thought about that for a moment but it still didn't register.

"What's enough?" I asked.

"One egg," he replied.

"One egg is enough?"

"Precisely," he responded.

I continued staring at him blankly and he sprang forth with the explanation.

"If I might explain, sir? In the French language, the word for 'one' is 'un' and the word for 'egg' is 'oeuf.' Consequently, 'one egg' pronounced in French, is 'un oeuf.' A Frenchman has only one egg for breakfast because one egg is 'un oeuf.' Coincidentally, 'un oeuf' sounds similar to the English word 'enough.' Therefore, the creator of your crossword puzzle undoubtedly was employing a play on words or pun with this clue, sir."

3

I smiled admiringly. This guy was good.

"Thank you, uh ... Cheever?" I said. "That's gotta be it." Now that he had explained it, it seemed simple.

"We endeavor to provide satisfaction, sir," he replied humbly with a slight bow of his head.

"Did you hear that great answer Cheever gave me?" I asked Randy as I wrote 'un oeuf' in the appropriate squares. Randy nodded while continuing to play the game.

"Yep," he replied vaguely, then added, "I let Cheever do all my serious thinkin' for me. He's ingenuous."

I looked at the next clue, but decided it was equally impossible unless I had more help. Rather than continuing to bother Cheever I retired the puzzle as a hopeless cause and began scanning the lecture hall.

Hutchins Hall was a large lecture hall, located in the Chemistry Building. It could easily accommodate 200 people with its many rows of seats. Stairs descended from an elevated doorway at the rear of the room down to a small raised lecture area at the front. The students who occupied almost every seat were principally freshmen, most of whom were concentrating on the lecturer down in the front as they scribbled notes furiously.

The lecturer, droning on about different chemical reactions, was Professor Ronald Harnash – reputedly a brilliant Nobel laureate who brought millions of dollars of government research grants to the university. But his appearance sure didn't match his reputation. He was a non-descript man in his late-50s, of average height, balding, with a blotchy red face that was adorned with a ragged salt and pepper mustache. His ample belly hung over baggy wool slacks, and the tie he wore over a wrinkled white shirt looked like something he might have obtained by mugging a supermarket bag boy.

His speaking style was no more impressive than his appearance. He stood behind a podium at the lecture area, almost inanimate except for occasional trips to the blackboard when he needed to write down an equation. He was equipped with a wireless microphone into which he mumbled, making the gibberish he was saying louder gibberish but no more intelligible. I could tell very quickly that with this guy at the podium these lectures were going to be murder. I

4

would need a large supply of easy crossword puzzles to get through this class.

I daydreamed for a while, half-heartedly taking notes, checking my watch every few minutes. At about the 35-minute mark, Prof. Harnash mercifully concluded his lecture so that he could introduce his graduate teaching assistants. These are the people who do the real teaching; they supervise lab work, meet with students in small groups to answer questions and translate the professor's lectures into English. Each of us was going to be assigned to one of his three teaching assistants. Based on the quality of the lecture I had just experienced, I figured that I'd need to spend a lot of time with my T.A. to make any sense of this class.

The graduate T.A.s were assigned to students alphabetically by last names, with letters A through G going to Laura Wellman, H through Q assigned to Nikesh Rastinjani and R through Z assigned to Percy Jordan. My last name being Taylor, Percy Jordan would be my T.A.

As each grad student was introduced, he or she rose and turned to face us. Harnash told us a little about the background of each. Percy Jordan had done his undergraduate work in England and was now in his second year as a graduate student. He was also Prof. Harnash's research assistant, so I figured he must have something on the ball.

There was something very familiar about Percy, but I couldn't put my finger on it. Had I seen him before somewhere? He was about 5 foot 10 inches tall, of medium build, with short, wavy brown hair. Wearing a pair of faded jeans and a red plaid shirt, he appeared to be younger than the other two grad students, maybe in his early 20s at the oldest. He wore glasses with tortoise shell frames and he struck me as being a very handsome guy.

I continued looking at Percy but I still couldn't place where I had seen him. Then I heard a gasp to my right. I looked over at Randy, alarmed that he might be choking on that gargantuan wad of gum. But Randy wasn't choking – he was just staring intently at Percy Jordan, his mouth agape.

"Damn!" Randy exclaimed. "He looks like you, Jer."

"Who? What are you talking about," I replied, not understanding.

"Percy Jordan," Randy said. "He looks jist like you. This is fantastical!"

I looked from Randy back to Percy Jordan and then I noticed that there was a slight resemblance. I was also about 5 feet 10 inches tall and had a medium build. I agree that we had some similar facial features, and I also had wavy hair, but my hair was lighter in color – more of a dirty blond – and longer. And I didn't wear glasses.

"He doesn't look like me – at least not much," I protested.

Randy shook his head, looked back at Percy Jordan and then at me again.

"You're on peyote, buddy. Look at him. You're the spittin' image of that guy. Cheever, doesn't Jerry look jist like Percy Jordan, the grad student down there?"

Cheever looked at Percy and then at me.

"Indeed. There does appear to be a rather striking resemblance if one ignores some of the superficial characteristics of their physiognomy and grooming."

"You hear that? Cheever said it's striking if you ignore the supercalifragil ... well, whatever he said. And Cheever's never wrong. He eats lots of fish." I looked at Percy Jordan again, but I wasn't convinced.

By that time class had ended and the students had begun filing out. We rose and joined the exodus shuffling toward the exit in back of the room. As we reached the doorway, in walked one of the brothers from the fraternity we'd be pledging, a good old southern boy named Steve Lorey, whose nickname was Redneck. As he entered the lecture hall for his class he recognized us.

"Wassup?" he greeted.

Before I could even say hello, Randy blurted out, "Hey, take a look at that feller down there," and he pointed toward Percy Jordan. Steve followed Randy's finger with his gaze.

"Doesn't Jerry look jist like that guy?" Randy asked.

Steve looked a little more intently at Percy Jordan, and then turned to look at me.

"Well, they're both purty ugly," he replied, grinning and winking at me. "But I do declare you're right. Jerry and that guy could be two cheeks from the same butt. That's interestin'."

"I don't think we look that much alike," I said.

He turned to Randy, ignoring my comment. "What's Jerry's brother's name there?"

"Percy Jordan."

"If I were you, Jerry, I'd go down and tell Percy that you two were separated at birth and you're his long lost evil twin."

"We're not related," I said, irritated.

"No? That's not how I see it. You might be more related than you think," Red Neck responded, laughing ominously. Then he gave us a wave goodbye and proceeded down the steps of the lecture hall to take a seat.

"What did he mean by that crack?" I asked Randy as we left the building.

"Beats the shit outta me," Randy replied. "I s'pose we'll find out at the pledge meetin' tonight."

"I guess," I said as we walked out of the building. I sure didn't like the sound of that laugh.

# TWO

The Sigma Epsilon Chi Fraternity house was a large brick Greek Revival affair, located smack dab in the middle of the Fraternity Quad. From the outside the house looked impressive. It was stately and elegant, with ivy snaking its way up several exterior walls, the green leaves contrasting with the red bricks and the white ornamental trim and columns. Looking at the outside of the house gave me a feeling of clubby tradition and gentility. I could almost picture a young Peter Lawford, nattily dressed in a tweed suit, pipe in hand, walking out of the house on his way to a sorority mixer.

But looks can be deceiving. Like Christmas presents from my Aunt Betty, the health food nut, what you saw was not what you got. Every year for Christmas Aunt Betty gave me an exquisitely wrapped gift that I couldn't wait to open. But invariably, after tearing off the beautiful wrapping paper and ribbons, and flinging open the box, I'd find something like tree fungus or organic moose dung inside.

If the exterior of the house was like a beautifully wrapped present, then all I can say is beware of Greeks bearing gifts. Because the interior was more akin to a Mad Max post-nuclear holocaust movie set. At one time, many, many years before, the inside of the house must have been gorgeous. The walls in most rooms were covered with richly stained wainscoting and intricately carved paneling. The cream colored ceilings were criss-crossed with dark wooden beams. Bedrooms featured built-in bunk beds, also constructed of woods stained to match the paneling covering the walls.

But the bloom had definitely left the rose. The paneling and wainscoting now revealed missing or blemished panels. Initials and other messages had been carved into the walls and on the bunk beds. Spirited football and hockey games within the house left un-patched holes in the walls, and the whole place was badly in need of a good paint job, or two, or three.

The furniture and other house decorations, too, had seen better days. Think Salvation Army rejects. All of the common rooms of the house contained rich, oversized leather furniture. While this furniture would have flattered a London men's club when it was new, it was now showing its mileage. Legs on chairs and sofas were missing, with bricks and stacks of old magazines occupying the vacant spaces where the legs had been. Many pieces bore stains or contained burn marks and holes with springs protruding from them like snakes from Medusa's head.

The thick, once elegant damask drapes covering the windows appeared to be original issue and hadn't been cleaned in years. Resembling Lorraine Swiss cheese, they harbored many well-fed moth families. In place of curtain rods many of the drapes were suspended from old broom and mop handles.

Adorning the walls were composite photographs of the fraternity brothers dating back to the early 1900s, and other fraternity memorabilia. The glass over many of these objects d'art was broken, having also fallen prey to errant football passes and slap shots. Pictures now rested crookedly within their frames, having slipped from their discolored and water-stained mats.

But what the brothers of Sigma Epsilon Chi lacked in decorating skills, they made up for with poor housekeeping. These guys weren't going to win any Good Housekeeping awards for general cleanliness. The stainless steel kitchen sinks were stained and filled with dirty dishes. New species of plant and animal life grew on those dishes like science experiments. And the bathrooms were indescribable.

The basement was the nerve center of the house, a.k.a. the fraternity party room. It contained a massive carved wooden bar and a stereo system with speakers the size of refrigerators, each of which had outputs that could rival jet engines. There were several dilapidated ping-pong tables located in an alcove off the main party room. The tile floor was missing a lot of its tiles owing to the fact that spilled beer made the old tiles stick to the bottoms of people's shoes. At the rush parties I saw several people clopping around like tap dancers with tiles stuck to the soles of their shoes.

The living room of the house was affectionately called the Thunder Dome. That's where members of the fraternity would go to wrestle during parties. The living room was the venue of choice for wrestling because its old sofas and other furniture generally were located around the periphery of the room. This afforded a relatively large open space in the middle and the carpet in that room had been replaced at least once in the last thirty years. It wasn't quite as threadbare as the carpet in other rooms and it offered some modicum of padding to the combatants.

After drinking copiously at parties, it wasn't unusual for a number of the brothers to gravitate to the living room and before long find themselves grappling with each other on the rug. This wasn't without certain casualties. The next morning after a party, those brothers would awaken to find their bodies covered with rug burns of unrecalled origin. And invariably the fraternity would lose a few lamps and items of furniture. But the entertainment value more than made up for the minor collateral destruction and injuries.

I can truly say that I had never before been in any place quite like the Sigma Epsilon Chi house. You may be asking yourself, if the house was such a wreck, then why had I decided to pledge this fraternity? That's a good question – one that I had been asking myself.

My dormitory roommate thought it was because of the fraternity's name – Sigma Epsilon Chi. The Greek letter for Chi is an "X," making the initials read SEX. I suppose there's a certain cache in being able to say, "I'm pledging the SEX house," but that wasn't why I chose this fraternity.

I'd also seen that they threw great parties and knew how to have a good time. That was obvious by looking at the condition of the house. Having a place to party was a nice benefit, but I think that most of the fraternities on campus could also claim that distinction. So that wasn't what attracted me.

To tell you the truth, I'm not entirely sure why I pledged Sigma Epsilon Chi. But I think it had a lot to do with the way they ran their rush. I liked the fact that the Sigma Epsilon Chis were such a diverse group, allowing everyone to feel welcome and at home. And unlike some of the other fraternities, they didn't brag about themselves. They had a quiet confidence and they seemed genuinely friendly and interested in me. In the short time I'd been exposed to the fraternity, I could see that it had a lot of great guys. They certainly weren't saints, and I could tell that some of them might be real pains in the ass if I pledged. But when it came to brotherhood I could see that they really cared about one another. If the going got rough they seemed like the kind of guys that were going to be there to support each other, just like brothers should.

Surprisingly, they also took their fraternity mumbo-jumbo – ideals, history, purposes – really seriously. I would have expected them to be irreverent when it came to corny things like that. But they weren't. To a man, they all seemed to be into that stuff.

Why they were like that I didn't know, but it certainly made this fraternity different from what I'd expected and kind of refreshing compared to other fraternities on campus. These guys intrigued me and I intended to find out what could bring and keep such a ragtag group together when they appeared to have so little in common. I was looking forward to beginning my pledgeship and hopefully solving this mystery.

There were five of us who were going to be pledging the fraternity this semester. Four were freshmen – Randy Bradford and me, Sam Fillippo and Brad Chan. The remaining pledge was a junior, Arnie Rosen.

Our pledge class mirrored the diversity of the brothers. Although a freshman, Sam Fillippo was older, having served a stint in the Army as an enlisted man before starting college. He was now enrolled in the Marine ROTC program here at school. I could tell that he loved being in the military – maybe too much! At the rush events he regaled us with macho man stories of his days in the Army and instructed us as though he was a drill sergeant and we were in his basic training class. At one rush event he spent a good ten minutes lecturing me about the 35 ways to kill someone using only your thumb. At another he instructed me on edible insects including ants, maggots, beetles and worms – just in case I got shot down behind enemy lines with no provisions.

Brad Chan was our international delegate to the pledge class. He lived in Hong Kong. Although coming to school here in Massachusetts was his first visit to the United States, he was very Americanized. Brad's greatest interest was martial arts – of every type. The first day that I met him he showed me the picture of Bruce Lee he carried in his wallet. That was just after he gave me his review of the "Kill Bill" series, which he contrasted with "Crouching Tiger, Hidden Dragon" and the Japanese samurai film genre.

"I liked the movies, but they're really not anything new or innovative. The Japanese have been making samurai films with similar styles and themes for years. The 'Kill Bill' movies were just an imitation of samurai slice and dice movies, like the series about Zatoichi, the blind swordsman. And even 'Crouching Tiger' had fairly typical elements. You know, searching for enlightenment through martial arts and perfection of swordsmanship. Now if you're keen to see a smashing series of movies like that you should see the Samurai Trilogy by Inagaki. Those are dashed good films. Of course, you'll need about ten hours to watch them all."

Brad wanted to find and join a martial arts club here at school so that he could also search for enlightenment. I couldn't wait to see that. Brad was about five feet five inches tall and about five feet five inches wide. I would estimate that he weighed in at a good 250 lbs. He looked more like a very large jack-o-lantern than a Jackie Chan.

Arnie Rosen was born and raised in New York City. He was the consummate New Yorker, exuding New York City out of every pore. He had the requisite 'tick New Yawk City' accent and used New York City expressions when he spoke. He perpetually wore a Yankees cap and made disparaging remarks about the Red Sox. He complained about the pizza available in Boston, which he said could never compare to a good New York pie. In fact, as far as he was concerned, everything about New York was the best. Of course, if that were the case, it didn't explain why he had chosen a college in the Boston area rather than attending college in New York.

Arnie was a pre-med student with a staggeringly high grade point average. He was definitely a bright guy and he studied his ass off. He'd been friends with a lot of the brothers and he'd been asked to pledge before but had always declined for fear that it would interfere with his academics. Now, in his junior year, he'd changed his mind. He said he was now confident that he could handle pledging and academics at the same time, and he'd accepted the fraternity's bid to pledge. Of course, some people thought Arnie was just looking to add an outside activity to his resume to make himself look better-rounded.

Whatever the reason, Arnie was going to be pledging along side me, Randy, Brad and Sam. And tonight was going to be our first pledge meeting.

I arrived at the fraternity house about 6:45 pm for the 7:00 meeting. I was wearing a suit as requested by Todd Weinberg, the Pledge Trainer. My pledge brothers, also sporting suits or jackets and ties, had already arrived. I found them lounging in the T.V. room of the house.

The T.V. room contained three T.V.s, and all of them were in use at the same time, each with a different program or activity. But I was able to discern a definite military theme in the selections. One was tuned to ESPN which was running a program on the Army-Navy football rivalry. The second had an XBox connected to it. Four of the brothers were playing a death and destruction video game in which the army battles aliens. The third T.V. was tuned to an old re-run of Gomer Pyle, U.S.M.C.

The cacophony of three different T.V. offerings, along with the grunts, cusses and cheers of the brothers playing Xbox didn't seem to faze anyone except Sam Fillippo. Everyone else in the room focused on one of the T.V.s and tuned out the others. But not Sam. He was such a military junkie that he couldn't focus on any one T.V. alone. I could see his head swiveling from one T.V. to another like he was watching a tennis match. I kept waiting for him to pull an "Exorcist" routine with his head spinning completely around. Sam kept yelling advice to the Xboxers while providing ongoing color commentary on the Army-Navy game and Gomer Pyle.

I was afraid Sam was going to blow a gasket or fall into convulsions from sensory overload, but at that point Todd Weinberg came into the room and said, "I need all the pledges in the library."

We all got up and started to move.

I asked Randy, "Where's Cheever?"

With a dour look Randy replied, "Weinberg told me I couldn't have him at any of the pledge meetings. I hope he doesn't expect much outta me if Cheever's not around."

I looked at Randy. At first I thought he was joking, but I was wrong. He was really upset at not having his butler at the meeting.

"Don't worry, you'll be fine without him," I said, trying to raise his spirits. I felt a little sorry for him because of his lack of confidence in himself.

We entered the library, a small paneled room with a sliding door situated just off the living room. I guess it was called the library because it had some built-in bookshelves across the back of the room. The shelves were filled with old, dust-covered books that probably hadn't been cracked open in forty years. In the middle of the room was a large oak desk where brothers occasionally pulled all-nighters studying or finishing up papers that were due the next day. The drawers of the desk were crammed full with piles of photographs of the brothers – usually taken at parties or other events worthy of remembering, like the time one of the brothers had thrown up and then passed out with his head in a toilet. Or the time that another brother passed out and was stripped to his underwear, then covered with masking tape before having graffiti written on him in marker pens.

Chairs had been set up in a circle around the room for the meeting. We all sat down, careful to avoid impaling ourselves on the springs that protruded dangerously from the seat cushions. Sam, who had been bending Arnie's and Brad's ears since we left the T.V. room continued his commentary.

"And the way Gomer got to socialize with Sgt. Carter and his girlfriend was bullshit, too. I mean, if I had tried socializing with my sergeant when I was in the Army I would have found my ass kicked from here to Beirut. When I get my commission, if an enlisted man tries to socialize with me I'll ..."

Just then Todd Weinberg came into the room, slid the door shut, and mercifully silenced Sam.

"O.K., knock it off. We have to get started with our meeting."

Todd Weinberg was a senior. He was about five feet seven inches tall and soft-spoken with wild, unkempt hair the color of straw. A rabid U2 fan, he was always humming one U2 tune or another. He perpetually had a benign, friendly smile on his face, even when he was angry. As far as I could tell he hadn't even begun to shave yet. He looked like he was about twelve years old and his nickname was Toddler, which he hated. He was a popular guy whom everyone seemed to like.

Toddler rummaged around through his papers, humming "With Or Without You" all the while. All eyes were on him as he finally got himself organized and began to speak to us, a big smile on his face.

"All right, men. Welcome to the Sigma Epsilon Chi Fraternity. We're all glad to have you aboard as pledge brothers. Tonight at this first meeting I'm gonna cover the basics of the pledge program and let you know what the brothers expect of you. First, I want to give you your pledge manuals."

He took a stack of booklets and passed them out to us. Each was about 100 pages long and on the cover was the title "SEX Manual For Pledges."

Arnie commented, "Hey, a sex manual. If I'd known what kinky stuff yous were into I would have pledged years ago."

"Very funny," Toddler said. "This manual describes the founding and history of the fraternity. It contains the various standards, ideals, mottos, purposes, government organization and other details about the fraternity that you'll need to know before you can become a brother. You'll be tested on the material at the end of the semester and you have to pass the international exam to be initiated. But don't worry. You'll learn the material over time. Every week there'll be a pledge meeting at which you'll be quizzed on the material for the test.

"Now, as pledges you'll be responsible for meeting and getting to know all the brothers. I'm gonna give each of you notebooks and you'll have to interview each brother and get basic information about him. You'll also need each brother's signature in your notebook to prove that you've interviewed him. You should get that done in the next three weeks. Try to come by the house and hang out here as much as possible to get to know people.

"Let's see ...," he said, flipping through his notes. "You're also responsible for doing house clean-ups during the week and every Saturday and Sunday morning with the brothers. In addition, your pledge class is expected to do at least one community service project of your choice this semester. You're also expected to maintain your grades and to attend study halls in the university's main library twice a week. You should attend all parties, all fraternity activities and you should participate in at least one activity outside of the fraternity during the semester. That could be a sports team, a club, the school newspaper, student government – whatever you want. Any questions?"

We all looked at each other. Randy moaned, then said, "Let me get this straight. Y'all want us to do all this stuff in one semester?" Toddler smiled again.

"I know it sounds like a lot. But every one of us has done it. With a little organization you'll be able to get it all done."

"Yeah, if we don't take the time to sleep, eat or take a shit," commented Sam under his breath.

"Why the outside activity?" I asked.

"Because we don't want our pledges to just bury themselves in the fraternity without experiencing other things on campus. We're a part of the campus community, not apart from it. Same with the Cambridge and Boston community," Toddler replied, then continued, "I almost forgot. Each of you will be assigned a special project or task this semester to demonstrate your interest and devotion to the fraternity. It won't be illegal, destructive or dangerous in any way. But you'll find it to be ... challenging." He placed special emphasis on that word.

"Each assignment or task will be specially designed for each of you. The fraternity will be deciding on your assignments in the next few weeks.

"Now, I'm gonna get Waldo Schnapps. In case you didn't meet him before, Waldo's the President of the fraternity. He wanted to say a few words. I'll be back in a minute." Toddler stood up and left the room. We all looked at each other again.

"I don't know about you guys, but this sounds like a lot more work than I was expecting. I don't know if I can do it," I said. Randy laughed a mirthless laugh.

"No shit. If they expect me to do all that stuff they'd better let Cheever help me out or I'm dead. I'm not that organizational."

Brad Chan sounded enthusiastic.

"I wonder if the outside activity can be martial arts. I've heard they have a Tae Kwon Do club here that I'd like to join. If not maybe I could start a martial arts film club."

Arnie was less enthusiastic.

"This fraternity is my outside activity. I'm pre-med. I already have too much to do. I'll give it a few weeks, but if it starts taking up too much time I'm outta here."

Just then Toddler returned to the library with the President of the fraternity, Walter Schnapps, in tow. Walter, a/k/a Waldo, was a senior and insufferably straight as an arrow. He was also the consummate diplomat and politician. The Dean in charge of fraternities loved him and I heard Sigma Epsilon Chi often got away with things that other fraternities didn't because Waldo was such a smoke blower with the university administration.

Waldo, tall and lanky with short, curly carrot-colored hair that had been wetted and combed straight, stood before us. He was wearing a tan suit with a white button-down shirt and a rep tie for the occasion. His fraternity badge was pinned to his shirt and just visible under his suit jacket. He cleared his voice loudly.

"Gentlemen, good evening. I just want to let you know that we're really pleased that you've decided to pledge our fraternity. Welcome." He said this in his best rah rah voice.

"By now you've seen some of the social aspects of our fraternity, but there really is a lot more to Sigma Epsilon Chi than just the parties. One of my responsibilities as President is to remind you that your pledgeship is a probationary period. We take our fraternity seriously and if you want to get initiated then we expect that you will, too. In fact, it's especially important to take things seriously this semester. I was just speaking with Dean Houser the other day and he told me something that's going to have a profound impact on Greek organizations this semester."

We waited expectantly to hear what he had learned from the Dean, but Waldo just stood there beaming at us.

Finally, irritated, Toddler asked Waldo, "Well, what did he tell you?"

"Oh, Dean Houser gave me the information in confidence; I promised that I wouldn't reveal it to anyone. Sorry, but I can't say!"

Toddler, with an uncharacteristic frown, looked at Waldo as though he was going to slug him. But Waldo just ignored him and turned back to us.

"I also want you to know that you're going to have a great time this semester. You'll accomplish a lot and I can guarantee you that by the time you finish the program, assuming that you complete it, you'll be different and better men than you already are.

"Now then, if there are no other questions, I'd like you all to stand up and get in line, single file." We complied and he and Toddler handed us blindfolds, which we all stared at. "Now, put on your blindfolds and then put your hands on the shoulders of the person in front of you," Waldo ordered. I thought this a weird request, and my anxiety level went way up, but I did as I was told. I stood at the front of the line and Toddler moved in front of me. He took my right hand and then my left and placed them on his shoulders.

"Follow me," he instructed. Then he began moving forward and we all followed, in single file, creeping along, each with hands on the shoulders of the one in front of us.

We moved slowly through the first floor of the house. The customary noises of the brothers watching T.V., arguing or playing were absent. There was utter silence as we snaked our way through the house, save the shuffling sound made by our shoes. It felt kind of eerie. I could tell that something was up and I didn't know if I liked it. What was I getting myself into?

Toddler led us to the basement stairs and slowly we began descending the steps, moving down them like a chain gang. He kept the pace slow so no one would trip. As we got about halfway down the steps I heard the muffled sound of humming coming from the basement, quiet and melodious, like a far off Gregorian chant.

At last we reached the bottom. Toddler led us about another ten feet and then stopped. I could tell that we were in front of the door that led to the basement party room. Toddler knocked on the door. I heard the door handle start to turn and then the door began to creak open. As it opened the humming became louder and more distinct.

It was a beautiful melody being hummed softly by a large number of male voices.

We shuffled forward into the room, and the humming continued. I had the sense that there were many people in the room with us.

At last we stopped and Toddler turned and removed my hands from his shoulders. Then I and my pledge brothers were turned 90 degrees so that we were all facing the same way, side by side. At that point the voices behind us very softly began singing the lyrics to the song they had been humming.

"...and sing the praises of dear Sig Ep Chi. We'll raise our glasses high and give a toast, Sig Ep Chis we'll be until we die." After singing that last lyric the voices went silent.

We stood there for about ten seconds in complete silence, anxiously waiting for something to happen. Then I heard the voice of Waldo saying, "You may now remove your blindfolds."

We took off our blindfolds and saw Waldo and Toddler standing before us at a lectern, next to which was a large candleholder containing a white candle with a brightly flickering flame. Waldo and Toddler wore serious expressions on their faces. Even Toddler had been able to wipe the smile off temporarily. He began to speak.

"Honorable President and brothers assembled. Tonight I present to you the following individuals who desire to become pledged to our fraternity. They are: Bradford Lee Chan, Samuel Salvatore Fillippo, Randall Dewhurst Urquhart Bradford, Arnold Neil Rosen and Gerald Robert Taylor."

Then Waldo stepped forward, accompanied by Toddler who held a black velvet pillow containing five little round pins bearing the letters "SEX." Waldo stood in front of me, took one of the pins from Toddler's pillow, and pinned it to my jacket. Then he gave me a wink and a smile and moved on to Randy, whom he also pinned. He repeated the process with each of my pledge brothers and then stepped back to the lectern.

"Gentlemen, if it is your desire to become pledge brothers of the Sigma Epsilon Chi Fraternity, then raise your right hands and repeat after me." I raised my right hand and out of the corner of my eye I saw my pledge brothers do the same. Waldo continued.

"I, say your full name, being of sound mind and with no one twisting my arm, desire to pledge the Sigma Epsilon Chi Fraternity."

He paused there to let us repeat what he had said, which we all did, filling in our own names, except for Randy who repeated, "I, say your full name, being of sound mind,..."

Waldo continued the oath. "I understand that my pledgeship is a probationary period and that as a pledge brother of Sigma Epsilon Chi I will be expected to comply with all the requirements of pledging. I will take seriously and embrace the slogans, mottos, creeds and ideals of the fraternity. I make these promises willingly, and with knowledge that if I violate this oath I will be considered a stinking no good loser. I make this, my solemn oath, on my honor as a pledge."

As we said the last line in the oath and pronounced the word "pledge," a yellow rose was placed in each of our upraised right hands. Then a roar went up behind us, the lights in the room clicked on and we were surrounded by forty brothers, also dressed in suits, slapping us on the back and congratulating us on having officially become pledges. They explained that the song they had been humming was one of the well-known fraternity songs and the yellow rose was one of the symbols of the fraternity, which had been founded in Texas.

I can tell you that at that moment I felt great. I had never seen this side of the fraternity members and I was really impressed. This ceremony reminded me of the fraternities of old that I had seen in movies. I felt so close to these guys and to my pledge brothers, and I decided that pledging this fraternity was about the best decision I had ever made in my life, right up there with my decision to remove the screwdriver from the electrical outlet when I was five.

I looked around at my pledge brothers. Sheer delight registered in all of their faces. Whatever was to come, we would face it happily, together.


After some general socializing and joking around, Waldo rapped his gavel on the lectern and called for order. The room quieted down.

"Brothers, the time has come for a second but no less important event in the lives of our new pledge brothers," announced Waldo.

He was interrupted by some cheers and catcalls from around the room. Waldo continued.

"It's now time for us to bestow upon our pledge brothers, their new nicknames." More roars of agreement.

"I want you pledge brothers to know that great thought was put into creating nicknames that captured the essence of each of you, nicknames that you will be proud of and nicknames that will probably remain with you for the rest of your natural lives."

Although I was still euphoric from the earlier ceremony, at these words I began to feel a few butterflies start to kick their way out of the cocoon and begin to flit about in my stomach. What type of nickname were the brothers going to give me? They hardly knew me at this point. How could they come up with a nickname that captured my essence or that of any of the other pledges? But then I thought, "Since they know so little about me, how bad could it be?"

Waldo was still talking.

"Brothers and pledge brothers, we have had a committee working on this task for some time. They've worked diligently on this project to create nicknames for each of our new pledges, and I would like to call the Chairman of that Committee, Brother Steve 'Red Neck' Lorey, to announce the new names. Red Neck?"

Red Neck sauntered up to the lectern, a mischievous smirk on his lips. Now I was really starting to get anxious, particularly in light of Red Neck's comment to me earlier in the day as I was leaving Chemistry class. Red Neck began.

"Brothers, as Waldo said, my committee has been busy as a blind dog in a meat locker, tryin' to come up with the perfect nicknames for these boys, here. We've spared no expense, buying numerous pitchers of beer to loosen up the creative juices, and I think we've come up with some winners this semester." Applause all around.

"Now I'm now gonna announce our choices. Let's begin with Pledge Brother Bradford Lee Chan. Pledge Brother Chan, we could not help hearin' of your great interest in martial arts and your search for Divine enlightenment. We've attempted to devise a name for you that'll take into account these elements of your background as well as one other obvious characteristic. Before I announce your nickname, I want to do somethin' that will give me a little luck with the hope that you'll like the nickname we've picked for you."

With that, Red Neck walked up to Brad and rubbed his hands on Brad's ample belly.

"For luck," Red Neck said. Then he added, "Brothers, I'd like you to meet Pledge Brother Buddha."

Howls of laughter rose from the crowd. Brad blushed, but then grinned and said to me above the din, "Some people used to call me that in my secondary school."

Red Neck then turned and looked at Sam.

"Pledge Brother Samuel Salvatore Fillippo. Having observed you over the past few weeks, and having conversed with you, our committee came to a quick and unanimous decision for your nickname. From now on you'll be known as Pledge Brother Mad Dog."

We all laughed at that one. If anyone fit the part of crazed postal worker it was Sam Fillippo. And true to form Sam seemed pleased with the new nickname. It must have fit in well with his self-image.

Randy Bradford was up next.

"Pledge Brother Randall Dewhurst Urquhart Bradford, there was some disagreement among the committee members as to the most appropriate nickname for you. There were many choices that we considered and then rejected. But fortunately, your names gave us a perfect nickname that is short, snappy and to the point. Taking the first letter from each of your two middle names, D and U, and the first letter of your last name, B, we get 'DUB'. And that's your new nickname, Pledge Brother Dub."

There was some chuckling around the room. Randy had a vacant look on his face, as if he was trying to figure out what Red Neck had meant.

Red Neck then cleared his throat.

"Next is Pledge Brother Arnold Neil Rosen. Now many of us have known Arnie for the past three years. In attempting to come up with a nickname for Arnie we knew that we had to focus either on his cutthroat attitude toward schoolwork and studying, or we had to choose a name that reflected on his great devotion to his hometown, New York City. We decided on the latter.

"Arnie drives us nuts with his talk about how great New York is all the time. Frankly, we're sick of hearin' it. So it's only fitting that a die hard New Yorker like Arnie should have the same nickname as one of the great New York ballplayers who is, no doubt, one of his heroes. Therefore, brothers, I present to you Pledge Brother Yaz."

"Yaz? You can't call me Yaz. You made a mistake. Yaz isn't a New York player," Arnie explained nervously.

"He's not?" Red Neck replied with a wink, feigning surprise. "Oh, well, too late to change."

"But I can't be called Yaz. He was a stinkin' Red Sox player. I can't have the name of a stinkin' Red Sox player," Arnie whined, shaking his head in disbelief as the rest of the crowd laughed and pounded Red Neck on the back.

Now Red Neck's gaze was resting on me. He waited for the room to become silent. Then he said, in an ominous tone, "And now, last but not least."

I gulped, dreading what I was about to hear.

"Pledge Brother Gerald Robert Taylor presented a bit of a challenge to the nickname committee. In fact, we devoted most of our creativity budget to the dilemma of finding a nickname for old Jerry here. He hasn't been around the house as much as some of our other pledges and we haven't gotten to know him quite as well as we should. But we'll make up for that soon enough." He laughed and then continued.

"In fact, we were at our wits end tryin' to come up with a nickname that would truly capture who Pledge Brother Taylor is. But just this afternoon, we received some inspiration. We found out that our pledge brother is not who we thought him to be, but someone else entirely. So we have selected a nickname that captures who Pledge Brother Taylor really is." He paused there for effect. "Brothers, I present to you, Pledge Brother Percy."

I groaned, but throughout the rest of the room there was stunned silence. Then several of the brothers started asking, "Percy? What does that mean? Why Percy?"

With a smile Red Neck explained the so-called resemblance between Percy Jordan and me. After hearing the explanation the brothers expressed their approval by snapping their fingers. But I didn't approve. I didn't even think that I looked much like Jordan, and now I was going to be saddled with that stupid name for the rest of my college career? Sometimes life just sucks.

But then a reassuring thought bored its way into my brain: "Look on the bright side.  Things are bound to improve from here on in.  It can't get any worse than this, right?"

# THREE

Brrring, Brrring, Brrring. The silence in my dorm room was violated by the insistent ringing of the telephone.

I cracked open one eye and looked at my alarm clock. It was 6:00 am. Who could be calling me at 6:00 on a Thursday morning? It was still dark in my room. I groped for the phone, knocking the receiver off its hook, and then struggled to find it again. I got a few fingers on the receiver then clutched at it and brought the receiver to my ear, my eyes still closed.

"Hullo?" I mumbled.

"Jerry, dear. It's me, honey. Am I calling too early?" The sound of my Mom's voice penetrated my brain.

Some people might describe my mother as a ditz. There's no doubt that she's an intelligent woman. She earned a Bachelor's degree in psychology from Stanford University, and then a Masters in Social Work from U.C. Berkeley. She became a Social Worker and has practiced off and on, taking some time off when she got married and after I was born.

But despite all of her education, or maybe because of it, she didn't quite stay in touch with reality. Don't get me wrong, she's a great Mom, but come on – who in their right mind would call a college student at 6:00 on a Thursday morning and ask if she was calling too early?

I thought about how to respond. I suppressed my initial thoughts about what to say and instead replied calmly, "Mom, why in God's name are you calling me at six in the morning? Of course it's too early. I didn't get to bed until two."

Based on the sound of her tongue clicking I could tell that she was giving me a disapproving look right over the phone line.

"Two in the morning on a Wednesday night? Young man, you should be ashamed of yourself. Why were you up so late?"

"Remember how I told you that I was thinking about pledging a fraternity?" I replied.

"Don't remind me," she said sharply.

"Well, I did pledge, and we had our first meeting last night. Then there was a celebration afterwards. We ended up driving to Chinatown for a late night all-you-can-eat buffet. It only cost $4.50 per person. Cheap and the food was great. But we didn't get back until about 1:30."

My mother sucked in her breath. "Jerry, you know I don't like the idea of you joining a fraternity. But I'm not going to get into that with you again now. And the reason why I'm calling you this early is because you're never around. We offered to get you a cell phone so we could always reach you and you didn't want one. I call you in the afternoon and you're not there. I call you at night and you're not there. Calling you in the morning is the only time I can get you."

"O.K., O.K., you've got me," I replied. "So why are you calling?"

"To make sure you're getting enough sleep. And to see how you're doing. Do you need anything, sweetie," she said brightly.

"You called me at six in the morning for that?" I said incredulously. "Isn't it 3:00 there in Seattle?"

"Yes. And some boys would be happy that their mother was interested enough in their welfare to get up at 3:00 in the morning to call them," she remarked.

"Mom. I'm very happy that you cared so much about me to wake me up and ask if I was getting enough sleep."

"And whether you needed anything," she added.

"O.K. And whether I needed anything. I don't need anything right now," except sleep, I thought. "But thank you for calling. Tell Dad I said 'Hi'," I replied.

"All right, darling. I can tell you're tired. Go back to sleep. I'll call you again when you're more awake. And be careful at that fraternity. I told your father that I didn't want you to join a fraternity. Now you're not getting enough sleep. You should try to get at least eight hours a night, you know? Go to bed earlier at night. Good bye, honey." And with that, she hung up.

As you've probably gathered, my mother doesn't think much of fraternities. Where she went to graduate school and among her peers, fraternities were shunned. My mother and her social crowd considered fraternities elitist, exclusionary, anti-intellectual, intolerant and chauvinistic. And those are what they considered to be the best points of fraternities. I'm sure that there were some fraternities like that. But my Mom would have no basis to know because she and her friends were focused on the stereotype of fraternities that existed in the media. In her own way she was equally intolerant – of fraternities – and she never got close enough to a fraternity to see past the stereotypes.

As much as my mother disapproves of fraternities, my father loves them. He's a fraternity man to his core. My Dad attended Georgia Tech where he studied aerospace engineering. After getting initiated during his freshman year at Tech he went on to hold an office in his fraternity every semester, and served as both Treasurer and President of his fraternity in his junior and senior years. After graduating from college my Dad attended grad school and while there he became involved in his fraternity alumni organization. Since that time he has served as a fraternity alumni officer and he's an advisor to one of the undergraduate chapters of his fraternity at a college near our home. And he's done all of this while married to a woman who hates fraternities. Go figure!

My Mom claims that she never would have married him if she knew how devoted he was to his fraternity. Of course she's joking – I think. But it all comes down to the fact that I have a couple of weird, very different parents who complement each other in some bizarre way. I don't know why it works for them, but it does. And it gives me something to talk about with my friends.

As you can imagine, the idea of my wanting to join a fraternity created a bit of controversy in our home. Of course my Dad was completely in favor of it, although he wanted to personally check out all of the fraternities on campus and give me recommendations when I told him I had been rushing. My Mom, on the other hand, was dead set against it. We had a few family "discussions," a.k.a. knock down, drag out fights on this topic. But in the end my view and my Dad's view prevailed. After all, when I told my Mom, "Look how well Dad turned out, despite being in a fraternity," and when I reminded her of how nice many of his fraternity brothers are, she had to admit that there were exceptions to her jaded view of fraternities. After many telephone conversations I was allowed to pledge on the condition that if my grades ended up being poor I wouldn't be permitted to get initiated. Nonetheless, my Mom was still troubled by the thought of me pledging.

After hanging up the phone I glanced over at my roommate to see if the call had disturbed him. Fat chance of that! He was lying in bed, inert, his mouth fully open, his eyes half open, snoring softly. The drugs he regularly ingested assured him of uninterrupted sleep regardless of noise, light, nuclear explosion or any cataclysm that would disturb a normal human.

My roommate, Jeff Bliss, was from Scarsdale, N.Y. I discovered that Jeff thrived on large quantities of drugs and alcohol the first night we roomed together. I learned that Jeff slept with his eyes half open, like some reptile, on the second night we roomed together. Jeff had been out somewhere and returned to the dorm room about 1:00 am more loaded than a new Mercedes. He lay down on his bed reading a magazine. I was listening to tunes, still unpacking when he returned. I went out to the bathroom to wet a sponge to clean off some dusty bookshelves. When I returned Jeff was lying there on his bed with his eyes half open. He appeared to be relaxing, just listening to the music.

Thinking that Jeff was still conscious I began talking to him, telling him about places I had visited on campus, activities that were available, and a host of other things. I probably spoke to Jeff for a good ten minutes before it dawned on me that he wasn't moving.

I got scared. Maybe he was having an overdose or something. This was just great. I was going to have a dead roommate, whose belongings were probably loaded with all sorts of illicit substances and I was going to have to call the police or at least campus security. This might be the end of my college career before it even started.

I walked warily over to Jeff, looking for any sign of movement. He looked so creepy, staring straight ahead with his two bloodshot eyes half open, like an alligator on a riverbank in the Everglades. As I got next to him I gave a sigh of relief. I saw his AC/DC T-shirt rising and falling slightly as he took each breath, so I knew that he must still be alive. I shook him.

"Jeff?" I said tentatively. No response. "Jeff, are you all right?" I said again, in a much louder voice, shaking him hard.

I saw his gray shadowed eyelids begin to flutter and he groaned. "Wassamatta?"

"Are you O.K.?"

"Waddayou mean, am I O.K.? Of course I'm O.K.," he said groggily.

I looked at him. I could see now that he was perfectly fine. Or at least he was as fine as he was ever going to be.

"Sorry," I said. "Just checking." I returned to my unpacking and a few minutes later I glanced over at him again. The same thing had happened. His eyes were half closed again as he lay on his bed. Now, a few weeks later, I was used to it.

After looking over at Jeff and seeing that he was still out cold, I also tried to go back to sleep. But I did have plenty of homework to do that I hadn't gotten to the night before and I started to worry about that. In a few minutes of thinking about when I was going to get my homework done, I was too whipped up to sleep. So I got up and started work on my chemistry problem sets. What a way to start off a morning.

After my morning classes I walked to the dining hall. I was looking forward to lunch. The fraternity didn't have a meal plan and most everyone in the chapter was on the university meal plan. They would generally go to the main dining center for lunch and dinner and sit together at the same tables everyday. I learned about this after the pledging ceremony and Toddler had suggested that all of the pledges try to eat with the brothers at meal times. It was a good way to conduct interviews for our notebooks.

I arrived in the main dining center a little after noontime and looked around for the fraternity table. The dining center was a large room with old chandeliers sprouting like upside-down mushrooms from its twenty foot high ceilings. High windows scattered around the exterior walls of the room rose almost to the height of the ceiling, allowing beams of sunlight to penetrate deep into the room. Long tables stretched from one side to the other in neatly ordered rows. At one end of the room were doorways leading into a cafeteria area where the food was served.

I saw the fraternity table and walked over.

"Hey, it's Percy. How ya doin'?" Sam Fillippo greeted me exuberantly. I cringed.

"Not bad, Mad Dog," I replied testing the nickname. Mad Dog grinned approvingly as did some of the others present. Only Mad Dog, Randy Bradford and a few of the brothers were at the table so far.

I staked out a seat at the table, dropped off my books and then went into the cafeteria portion of the dining center to see what gourmet fare they were serving for lunch today. The main courses were an overcooked pasta dish, rubbery looking fish filets and watery chicken chow mein. Instead I opted for a double cheeseburger, cooked to order at the grill by a large oafish man who looked like an axe murderer. He had a greenish-blue spot on his middle front tooth. I studied the spot to see if it was a piece of food caught in his teeth. I decided it was more likely some form of mold. I wasn't real hungry today anyway.

I returned to the table. Mad Dog was gone but Randy was still there, so I plopped down next to him and across from several of the brothers.

"Hey, everybody," I said. Greetings were exchanged all around. "Where's Cheever," I inquired of Randy.

"Oh, he just went to get my lunch for me. Should be back here in a few. God, I hope they have somethin' worth eatin' today. I'm sick of those burgers cooked by the Creature from the Black Lagoon."

I looked over at the two brothers sitting across from me. One was heavy-set, with black hair and very thick bushy eyebrows. I had seen him before at the house. The brothers had called him J.D. or T.C. or something like that, I recalled.

The other one was thin with dark, somewhat unkempt hair, and glasses. He looked a lot like the cartoon character known as Sherman. You know, the dumb kid sidekick of Mr. Peabody, the dog – from the Rocky and Bullwinkle Show? I couldn't remember what his name was either.

I hadn't spoken with either of them before. Both were tucking into their lunches pretty well and I figured I might as well get started on the interviews for my notebook.

"Excuse me. Would you guys mind letting me interview you? And would you sign my notebook?" I added.

"Good idea," Randy jumped in. "Can I get some info, too?"

The two brothers looked at each other, then at us.

"Sure," they said, somewhat reluctantly.

I began with the heavy-set one who had initials for a name.

"Now I think I'm supposed to get your full name. And can you spell it for me so that I get it right in my book?"

"Fred Burdick, F-R-E-D-B-U-R-D-I-C-K," he responded.

"O.K.," I said, writing it down. "Do you have a nickname?"

"C.P."

"C.P.?" Randy and I both said simultaneously.

"C.P.," he said again, with a broad smile on his face. The other brother was smiling as well.

Randy and I looked at them and then at each other. Then Randy said, "Is that like the gold robot on Star Wars?"

"That's C3PO, not C.P.," replied the other brother who looked like Sherman. Then he began humming the Star Wars theme absent-mindedly.

"How do you get C.P. out of Fred Burdick?" I asked.

"Think about it," C.P. responded. He pronounced the word "about" like it was spelled "aboot."

Randy and I looked at each other again. I had no idea what he was talking about.

"What does C.P. stand for?" I asked.

"Tell you what. Figuring out what my nickname means can be another pledge class project, eh? I'll give you a hint. It's a take off on my last name. Think about my last name," C.P. suggested.

I gave it some more thought but I guess my brain wasn't working. Randy didn't seem to have any more luck than I. After about a minute we moved on. We learned that C.P. was a junior from Halifax, Nova Scotia, in Canada. He was majoring in mechanical engineering and liked to play hockey. He refused to sign our notebooks after we had finished the interview.

"I'll sign it when you tell me the meaning of my nickname," he said. I intended to ask every brother what his nickname meant. No doubt one of them would spill the beans.

We then turned to the other brother, the one that looked like Sherman.

"Sorry, but I don't think I actually got to meet you before. I'm…," I began. But before I could say my name he interrupted.

"Percy. I was there the night you got your nickname. I'm Chuck Reagan, but everyone calls me 'Tuney'."

I had expected him to say Sherman, but I assumed the name had something to do with the fact that he looked like a cartoon character. I asked my next question.

"And where are you from?"

He burst into song. "Oooooklahoma, where the wind comes giving me a pain," he sang. "Tulsa."

"Hey, that's pretty close to me," Randy piped in. "My Daddy has some oil businesses in Tulsa. It's a pretty good party town."

"Used to be," Tuney replied. "But the economy's not so good anymore." Then he burst into song again. "The party's o-ver, it's time to call it no way," he sang.

We continued interviewing Tuney. We learned that he was also a junior. He was a theatre major (no big surprise there) and a member of the men's acappella singing group on campus – the Monotones. Tuney reverted back to song three more times during the interview and then it dawned on me that his nickname wasn't 'Tooney' as in 'cartoon.' It must have been 'Tuney' as in 'sing a tune,' because he was always singing. He was an odd fellow but I liked him.

Tuney signed Randy's and my notebook when we finished the interview. Then he and C.P. left.

Brad Chan had shown up at the table when we were about halfway through our interviews with C.P. and Tuney. His tray could have been called a groaning board by itself. He had two double cheeseburgers, an enormous mound of chow mein, three desserts and four glasses of Coke. He sat a ways down the table and seemed content to work on his repast while the interviewing was going on. But he moved over to the seats recently vacated by C.P. and Tuney after they left.

"Hey, Brad. How's it going?" I asked.

"Oh, call me Buddha. I like the name. Things are great. I see you fellows were getting a few interviews?"

"Yup," Randy replied. "You interview those two yet?"

"Yeah. I got them right after the pledging ceremony. They seem pretty nice."

I chimed in. "Did C.P. tell you what his nickname meant?"

"Negative. But it was some type of joke name, I gathered. One of the other guys said it was based on where he lives," Buddha responded.

"That's weird. C.P. said it was a take off on his last name."

"Maybe it means Canadian Prince," Randy suggested.

"What does that have to do with his name?" Buddha asked.

"Uh, maybe he's like the singer, Prince?" Randy replied. I was doubtful.

"When you say 'where he lives', did he mean the fraternity house or his hometown?" I asked.

"Gee, I don't know. It wasn't clear. I assume he meant Nova Scotia."

Yet another mystery to be solved, I thought to myself.

"If anyone gets any more information be sure to share it with the rest of us, O.K.?" I asked. Randy and Buddha both nodded.

Randy and Cheever left, and a few minutes later I started to get up. I had another class starting in 15 minutes and it was all the way across campus. As I was collecting my belongings Buddha said, "Hey, Percy?"

"Don't call me that, O.K.? I hate that name."

"O.K. Jerry. Have you found an outside activity to do yet?"

"No. Got any suggestions?"

"Well, the Tae Kwon Do Club has a practice tonight at 7pm. Why don't you try that? I'm planning to attend."

Hmmm, I thought to myself. I didn't want to admit it, but I had always been a little intrigued by martial arts myself. When I was in high school a friend of mine had convinced me to go with him to a Karate tournament in which his sister was participating. It was really fascinating. I loved watching the fighting, which was almost like a choreographed dance. The action went back and forth as first one person attacked and then the other responded. It was fluid and more graceful than I could have imagined.

Back then I'd said to myself that I should start taking lessons. But inertia set in. I got involved with other things and I had never done it. This might be the perfect opportunity for me to try it.

"How often do they practice?" I asked. "And what if I don't have one of those uniforms?"

"I think they practice three times a week and you don't need a uniform when you first start. If you like it and decide to stick with it you can buy a uniform from the instructor."

I thought about it a little more, then decided I'd give it a try. Watch out, Bruce Lee!

"O.K., I'll go. Where's the practice?"

"Smashing," said Buddha. "It's in the wrestling room of the Alumni Gymnasium, at 7pm. They said we should get there about 15 minutes early to stretch out. It ends at 8:30."

I told the Buddha-meister that I'd see him there and headed off to class. This was going to be fun. I could feel it in my bones.

# FOUR

I finished classes about 3pm and returned to my dorm room. I was beat from waking up so early and I knew that I would need energy for the Tae Kwon Do class so I took a refreshing little nap. My roommate Jeff never showed up so I had a couple hours of uninterrupted slumber. Sometimes there's just nothing better than a siesta in the afternoon.

I had an early dinner. I didn't want to blow chow at the practice. Then I did a little homework until 6:30 pm and headed over to the gym.

I didn't know what the well-dressed neophyte martial artist without a uniform was wearing these days, but I figured that a pair of sweat pants and a Sigma Epsilon Chi T-shirt that I had been given should fit the bill. I was lighthearted and really looking forward to this.

I changed in the locker room and then asked for directions to the wrestling room. It was on the third floor, up a rickety flight of stairs. Between the second and third floors there was a balcony off the staircase overlooking the main gymnasium. Warfare was being waged below me in the form of intramural basketball games.

Several people wearing martial arts uniforms were standing at the balcony watching the hoops action while stretching. One was a beautiful Asian girl, her long silky black hair tied up in a pony tail. She wore a snow-white uniform that fit her trim body as if it had been custom-tailored. Cutting across the narrow waist of her uniform was a dark purple belt. I didn't know the ranking of the different colored belts, but I figured that purple must be pretty good.

She had rested her leg high up on the rail of the balcony and she was lowering her nose to her knee, stretching. I was staring at her in appreciation when she glanced over my way and saw me watching her. She had beautiful brown eyes. I gave her a goofy smile – I didn't know what else to do – and said, "Is the Karate class up this way?" She gave me, my old sweat pants and particularly the T-shirt a disapproving look.

"The Tae Kwon Do class is up the stairs, if that's what you mean."

She jerked her head toward the flight of stairs going up. I thanked her and left quickly.

The wrestling room, where the class was being held, was a relatively small square room, maybe 40 feet by 40 feet. There were four pillars in the room, each located about ten feet from a corner of the room. The pillars went from the floor to the ceiling and were covered with padded material. The floor was completely covered by blue mats. Alternating blue and yellow mats also covered the walls. It was certainly a festive, if cramped room.

As I walked into the room I saw about a dozen people wearing uniforms and another half dozen or so wearing sweats and gym clothes like me. Among the latter was Buddha, sporting a tent-sized T-shirt containing a picture of a shirtless Bruce Lee in a fighting pose, cut marks across his chest. On Buddha that T shirt was about as incongruous as it could possibly be. Buddha looked more like a moving billboard than a martial artist.

Buddha saw me and called me over, gesturing.

"Hey, Jer, you made it. Isn't this great?" he said beaming. "I've been checking things out. They have one promotion every semester. There are five belt colors before black. So at one color advancement per semester we can be black belts by the time we're juniors."

"How do you know that we'd get promoted every semester?" I asked skeptically.

"Oh, no problem. I've been watching them warm up. It doesn't look too hard."

Just then, a tough-looking guy wearing a uniform with black pants and a black belt, came up to us. He looked to be in his mid-thirties and was about my height, with short brown hair and a mustache. I could see his muscles bulging under his uniform jacket. This was not someone to mess with, I decided.

"You new guys. I'm Ray Harper. Stretch out and get warmed up. We're gonna get started in a few minutes," he said. He had a slight New York City accent.

I looked around at what other people were doing and started copying them. Buddha did the same. At that moment the beautiful Asian girl with the purple belt appeared in the doorway, bowed, and entered the room. She looked at me and then Buddha stretching together and frowned. I smiled at her and she looked away.

"What's the order of belts?" I asked Buddha while gazing at her purple belt.

"Well, everybody starts out as a white belt. Then you go to yellow." He pointed over to a couple of people wearing yellow belts. "Then green, purple, brown and black." He pointed to people wearing each of those colored belts as he mentioned the colors.

He had just finished educating me on the different color rankings when Ray started the class. He stood at one end of the room and had everyone line up in front, facing him. The brown belts were to the far left in the front row. Next to them were the purple belts. At the far left in the second row were the green belts. To their right were the yellow belts. In the third row were the white belts in uniforms. We were directed to stand in the third row to their right.

"This is Tae Kwon Do – a Korean martial art. For you new people, we do some of the same things at every class. First we're going to stretch out. Then we do our 14 basic moves. When we finish those we'll work on forms or patterns of moves combined together. The last thing we'll do is spar. You're in the back so you can watch the people in front of you. Follow what they do. O.K.? Let's go, stretch." With that Ray began stretching and everyone else mirrored him.

We finished stretching and began doing the basic moves. Like any athletic activity, when done by well-conditioned athletes that train regularly the moves looked easy. I watched Ray leading the class and he did the basics with power, speed and precision. I watched the female purple belt do them. She was good, too, making the moves look very graceful and fluid.

When performed by Buddha and me, however, the basics were anything but easy, fluid or graceful. A neutral observer would have thought that I was experiencing rigor mortis as I stiffly lumbered through the moves. I regularly toppled over, bumping into my nearest neighbors in line, with each movement that required any level of balance. And whereas the kicks of the upper belts went high in the air where they would strike an opponent in the head, my kicks would be hard pressed to do damage to a knee cap.

As bad as I was, Buddha was much worse. Oh, he was more flexible than I was, but his girth threw his balance way off. It also slowed him down considerably. He was huffing and puffing on the second basic.

And then the sweat began. It started as a few beads on his forehead, and a slight darkening of his T shirt at his arm pits. But before long the floodgates opened up and the sweat began pouring out of him in buckets. Within minutes Buddha's T shirt was soaked through. Considering the fact that Buddha was better stacked than a lot of women I know, he looked like a contestant in a wet T shirt contest.

Every time Buddha swung his arm in a knife hand strike (a karate chop in the common vernacular), the sweat would fly off the end of his fingertips, spattering those around him. And the smell that started wafting my way was indescribable. Between the sweat flying and the malodorous smells emanating from him I had to move further and further away from Buddha, as did everyone else. But Buddha loved what he was doing. He had a big shit-eating grin plastered on his face the whole time we were doing basics.

We took a break. Ray ordered all the windows opened even though it was pretty chilly outside and told everyone to get drinks of water. Buddha was ebullient.

"Isn't this smashing? I can't believe I waited so long to do this. My body is built for Tae Kwon Do. This is much easier than I expected, don't you think?"

"I don't know. It looks easy when they do it but my body sure isn't built for this stuff. I can't bend the way they do and I can already tell that I'm gonna be really sore tonight," I said, eyeing the female purple belt as she walked over to the water fountain. "I've gotta get a drink," I added and quickly moved away from Buddha and headed for the fountain. I didn't know what I would do when I got there. I had always been kind of shy with girls in high school, but I was gonna try to be more outgoing with them now that I was in college. She would be my first test.

I stood behind the female purple belt waiting my turn. I looked admiringly at her posterior as she leaned over to get her drink. Then I looked over toward her head and saw that she was watching me watch her as she was drinking. She finished and continued looking at me with a severe expression on her face. Embarrassed, I smiled stupidly again and tried to cover.

"I was admiring your, uh, uniform. Do you know where I can get one?"

"Ray can order them – for anyone who lasts long enough to need one. I don't think you need to worry about it," she said, looking at me as though she were talking to a cat that had just entered the room with a rat in its mouth. With that she turned on her barefoot heels and walked away, leaving me to muse on our little conversation. I had the distinct impression that she didn't like me too much. But I was determined to win her over with my charm and wit, at least if I could muster up any.

Ray called everyone back so we could do the forms, which turned out to be a lot like choreographed dance routines. They were just a series of basic moves in different combinations which he said were designed to get us used to connecting the moves together. Each belt level had to learn its own forms to be promoted to the next belt level. Ray began assigning different upper belts to work with each belt level group.

When he got to white belts, which included Buddha and me, he looked around for someone to teach us. Everyone else was busy so he called over to the purple belts.

"Kim, come over and teach these new people the white belt forms." My heart leaped. My female purple belt had turned around when he called. She was going to be our teacher. And now I knew her name! This was my chance to get to know her better and impress her.

She came over, surveying us, and then began her instruction.

"All right, this is the first form."

She demonstrated a series of arm movements and leg movements that covered the floor in the pattern of the letter "H".

"Now let's do it again – everyone, with me."

She began to repeat the moves, this time with each of us following her. After doing it with her a few times she asked us to do it without her so that she could watch us and help position our legs and arms properly while we were moving.

I called over to her. "Kim, is my arm in the right position?" I was standing in a semi-squatting position, with my feet apart, holding my right arm in line with and along the right side of my body, forming a 90-degree angle from my elbow. I had my hand in a fist and held so that my fingers were facing toward my face. My arm was being held just low enough so that I could look to my right over the top of my fist with my head turned to the side. It was a pretty awkward position because my arm had to be twisted to get into that position and it hurt.

Glaring, she came over to me and said through clenched teeth, "Kim is my last name." Now that I thought about it, Ray did seem to refer to everybody by their last names. Considering that we hadn't been introduced I could see that it might be considered a little rude to have called her by her last name.

"Sorry," I said. "I heard Ray call you that. I'm Jerry."

I expected her to tell me her first name but she didn't. Instead she continued glaring at me and then said, "Your hand isn't far enough back."

She put her hand on my fist and twisted my hand, moving it further toward my back. But because I wasn't sufficiently stretched my arm couldn't move back that far. As she twisted my hand I tipped over backward and ended up flat on my back on the mat. I think she had a little streak of sadism in her because the sight of me splayed out across the mat seemed to improve her disposition considerably. She even smiled a little.

I affected my most pathetic look and groaned a bit, hoping for some sympathy, then said in a weak voice, "Now that you've crippled me will you tell me your first name?"

She studied me for a moment and then said, "Get up."

"That's an odd first name," I said as I picked myself up off the mat and dusted myself off. I was thinking of sulking but at that moment Ray announced that we were going to begin sparring.

The class formed a large circle and sat down. Ray stood in the middle and gave us the ground rules.

"Everyone will spar. I want no contact. If you have the control to stop your punches and kicks just short of your opponent, then you'll be able to strike an opponent when you need to do it. Use good combinations of basics."

He looked over toward me and the other white belts.

"I want you new people to pay attention. You'll go last."

He finished his instructions and then called one of the brown belts to spar with him. They were fantastic. They squared off against one another and began throwing a flurry of punches and kicks – side kicks, front kicks, roundhouse kicks, spinning back kicks – and all delivered at head level. The punches and kicks came close but always stopped just short of striking. That was a good thing because if they had connected I expect their heads would have been knocked off and splattered against the wall.

They went on like that for about two minutes and then Ray selected the next couple to spar. This continued as he went through the upper belts. The beautiful Ms. Kim sparred with another purple belt and I have to admit, she was good. As with her form patterns she was very graceful, but tough. I could see the determination in her eyes. She outfought her opponent with great control, never making contact with him through the entire battle.

After the upper belts finished sparring it was our turn. Ray pointed to Buddha.

"What's your name?"

Buddha gulped and said, "Um, Chan, sir. Brad Chan."

"Allright, Chan. Get in the middle." Then Ray looked around and selected a brown belt to spar with him. "Remember, no contact," Ray said.

They bowed and then squared off against each other. Ray told them to begin and they began. At least the brown belt began. Buddha had a unique style. It consisted mostly of standing there and getting pummeled (figuratively because there was no contact) by the brown belt.

It reminded me a lot of the old Three Stooges episodes where Moe or someone else is fighting with Curley. Curley's hands are covering his stomach so Moe punches him in the face. Then Curley raises his hands to protect his face and Moe punches him in the stomach. He then lowers his hands to his stomach again and gets hit in the face, and it goes on and on that way. Well, that's how Buddha fought – not much skill, but as the movie reviewers might say, he was hugely entertaining. And the best part was that Buddha moved so little he didn't sweat much, and the atmosphere in the room stayed relatively pure.

The other white belts finished sparring. They had gone up against various upper belts. None of the white belts was very good, but they were all much better than Buddha.

I wasn't selected until last. By that time I was pretty whipped up to do better than the other white belts and show Ms. Kim that I wasn't the loser she apparently thought I was. Being dead last I had watched everybody else in the class spar, so I figured I had to have learned something.

I was standing in the middle of the mat, nervously looking at all those eyes staring at me. Ray scanned the room for my opponent and then said, "Kim, spar with Taylor." She got up and stood across from me. We bowed to each other and Ray repeated his mantra, "Remember, no touch. Begin."

I assumed the fighting stance, which involved turning my body so that it was about three quarters facing Ms. Kim with my fists up in a fighting position as a boxer would hold his fists. She did the same and we looked at each other waiting to see who would make the first move. I did. I lunged toward her, throwing a tenuous front kick, the only kick I could execute without losing my balance. She easily blocked the kick and countered with a series of rapid fire punches to my unprotected head. If contact had been allowed I would have been out for the count at that point but we continued.

I spun around and jumped back out of her range, thinking about what to do next. While I was thinking she attacked, throwing a series of side kicks at me. Being too clumsy to block them I just jumped back out of the way in response to each kick. It was crude but effective. None of the kicks came close to me.

Now I was starting to feel pretty confident. That hadn't been too bad, I thought. I was getting the hang of this stuff. It was time for me to take charge. I changed my stance somewhat, turning my body so that it was sideways to her in what was called a horse riding stance. This was the stance we used in the basics when we were doing a series of side kicks. She immediately saw that I was getting ready to do side kicks and she adjusted her stance.

My plan was to do a couple of side kicks and then, when she lowered her guard to block my last knee-high side kick I would instead fake the last side kick and throw a punch to her head. I began my side kicks, which weren't very good to begin with. Nonetheless, I exaggerated the preparation for each move so that she could easily see them coming and block them as I proceeded. On what was supposed to be the third poor sidekick in the series I exaggerated it even more. She reacted just as I had planned. She looked down, lowering her fists to make a very lazy block of my feeble kick. As she committed to blocking the kick I suddenly slid sideways throwing a back-handed punch to her head. Her guard was down and the punch was right on target. My knuckles stopped a few inches from her face.

From the side I heard Ray say, "Nice move, Taylor." I glanced over at him quickly and saw that he was smiling. Then I looked at Ms. Kim and saw that she wasn't smiling. In fact, she was pissed – really pissed. I guess I embarrassed her. She gritted her teeth and attacked, throwing a flurry of kicks and punches toward my head. They were coming pretty close, too. And they weren't little love taps. I had my fists up to block and she was whacking my arms hard enough to make them sting.

I kept backing up, trying to get away from these shots, keeping my fists up when she pulled the same thing on me that I had pulled on her – almost. While my fists were up she changed her attack and came in with a low front kick that was below my guard. The only difference was that whereas I had stopped my punch a few inches from her head she didn't pull her kick. She gave me a good solid whack with the bridge of her foot right between my legs.

I felt a numbing pain and went down like I had been hit with a stun gun. Through the haze of intense pain I heard Ray yell, "Kim, I said no contact."

"Sorry, I slipped," she replied.

I looked up and saw the two of them standing over me asking if I was O.K.? I just lay there, curled up in a ball, writhing around on the mat, unable to talk and hardly able to breathe. I kept thinking to myself, I should have worn a cup. I should have worn a cup. I had thought about wearing a cup before I left but decided I didn't need it because beginners couldn't do enough to get hurt, right? Big mistake there!

After a few minutes of looking at me and waiting for me to say something I heard Ray say, "We better call security." That roused me from my reverie.

"No, I'm all right," I said weakly. Again I used my most pathetic voice but this time I wasn't faking.

With Ray's and Buddha's help slowly I got up. Ray lined us up again and lectured everybody on the need to be in control when we spar. He looked over at Ms. Kim.

"When I say control, I mean two kinds of control – physical and mental. People who can't control their emotions will be asked to leave the class." He obviously wasn't convinced that she had "slipped."

I looked over at her and her head was down, a look of remorse on her face. I actually felt a little sorry for her, getting chewed out in front of everybody.

We finished the class and bowed to Ray, who dismissed us for the night. I started limping toward the door with Buddha at my side. But before I got to the door Ms. Kim walked up to me, her eyes downcast, and said, "I'm sorry." That was it. Then she turned and continued out the door.

I stared after her. Was that little "I'm sorry" all I got after she tried to play her rendition of Tchaikovsky's Christmas classic on my body?

I was about to make a comment to Brad when she poked her head back through the doorway, looked at me and said, "Karen."

I stood there gaping at her, my mouth wide open like a dead fish. I don't know whether that was because I was so shocked that she had come back and was now speaking to me, or if it was because I had no idea what she was talking about. She apparently interpreted it as the latter because she added,

"My first name – it's Karen."

She gave me another look and I thought I saw the corners of her mouth curve upward ever so slightly into a semi-smile. Then she vanished through the doorway like an apparition.

# FIVE

The next day, after attending my morning classes, I made my way to the dining hall, arriving a little before noon. I looked all around but didn't see Karen Kim in the dining hall. The night before, after I returned to my room following Tae Kwon Do class, I had looked her up in the university phone directory. It said that she was living in Room 211 of Crosby Hall, which was just around the corner from the dining center. I expected that she usually ate at this dining center rather than one of the more distant ones spread around campus.

Failing to see Karen, I headed over to the fraternity table. It was still a little early but most of my pledge brothers were there, including Buddha. As I got closer I noticed that they were all smirking and glancing at me. I dropped my books on the table and Mad Dog said, "Yo, Percy."

"Yo, Mad Dog," I responded flatly, imitating him. Before he could say anything else I turned and went to get my lunch. A few minutes later I returned with a nutritious plate of tuna casserole, a ham sandwich and two glasses of soda. I set my tray on the table and sat down.

I was taking my first mouthful of casserole when Mad Dog opened the conversation.

"I hear a girl in your karate class rang your chimes last night."

Chortling all around. I grunted noncommittally. He continued.

"When I was in the Army protecting the family jewels was the first thing they taught us in self defense. The opponent always will try to score a hit below the belt if you let him. You have to either cover up or toughen up."

Arnie Rosen, a/k/a Yaz snorted.

"Waddayah mean, toughen up? How're you gonna toughen up your gonads?"

Unfazed, Mad Dog responded, "Conditioning, Yaz. It's like anything else – conditioning. Back when I was in self defense class my buddy and I practiced taking shots to the nuts on a daily basis. We'd stand there facing each other with our legs apart and first I'd kick him and then he'd kick me. We'd do it about ten times each. And I can tell you, with Army boots on, you gotta be conditioned to take that."

We all looked at each other in disbelief.

"You're a crazy bastard, Mad Dog," Yaz said, shaking his head. A big grin just lit up Mad Dog's face.

I decided to change the subject before it caused me to lose my appetite.

"How are you guys coming with your notebooks?"

"Not bad," Buddha said, leafing through his book. "I've got 12 names so far."

"How many brothers are there in total?" I asked.

"About 45," Yaz replied. "I know most of them from hangin' around over the last three years. About 40 live on campus; they should be pretty easy to get. The last five live off campus. They'll be a bitch to get."

"Any of you guys figure out what Burdick's nickname means?" I asked.

"Nope," Buddha replied.

"Hey, Yaz," Mad Dog interjected. "You've been around here for three years. You must know why they call him C.P."

"Yeah, I do. But he told me not to tell any of yous or he'd blackball me. So as Waldo would tell you, can't say."

"Well, has anyone gotten any more clues?" I asked.

"One of the brothers told me to think about what it would be like if you were on a camping trip in Canada in the middle of the winter," Buddha replied.

"What the hell does that mean, Buddha?" Mad Dog asked.

Yaz chuckled to himself and said, "Good clue." We all stared at him.

"How is it good?" I asked.

He only laughed again. "Can't say."

We all sighed in exasperation.

It was now a little after noon and a lot of the brothers started filtering in and coming to the table. Randy had also arrived. As he walked up to the table a group of the brothers said in unison in their dumbest sounding voices – "Duuuub." Randy nodded to them and us and waited for Cheever to arrive with his lunch.

My pledge brothers and I were trying to finish up our lunches fast so that we could concentrate on scoring some more interviews. As soon as Randy got his lunch he wolfed it down so he could do the same.

I finished my lunch and looked around the dining hall again quickly to see if Karen Kim had come in. She was nowhere in sight so I joined my pledge brothers on notebook patrol.

Pickings were pretty good. A number of the bros I hadn't yet interviewed were at the lunch table that day and I was able to complete four more.

My first interviews were with Steve Elton and Allessandro Soave. I had heard that these two, in addition to being the closest of friends, were also the undisputed studs of the fraternity. They were "chick magnets." Women were said to be irresistibly attracted to both of them, and they rarely went back to their rooms alone after a party.

The funny thing was that their styles were so different. Steve Elton, whose nickname was Elrod, was kind of crude and a bit of a hick. He liked to tell rude jokes and he wasn't known for having great manners. He told me that he was from a small town in rural Florida where his parents owned a citrus farm.

Looking at him and talking to him for a while, it seemed to me that what he lacked in sophistication he made up for in charm and good looks. Elrod was about six feet tall with short blond hair and very blue eyes. He was on the varsity swim team and obviously he was in great shape. In fact, he'd done some modeling and had appeared in some of the photos decorating the walls in Abercrombie & Fitch stores. Friendly and funny, he's the kind of guy that you can't help liking.

Allessandro Soave had two nicknames. One was Sandro, a short version of his name. The other was Suave, which was both a take-off on his last name and a description of his personality. In contrast to Elrod, Sandro exuded sophistication from every pore. He was from Milan, Italy. His father was some kind of business tycoon who also owned vineyards and made wine for export. Sandro had grown up traveling throughout Europe. He was very smooth and well mannered.

Like Elrod, Sandro also was a good-looking guy. He had longish black hair, brown eyes and was about five-ten or eleven. A striker on the varsity soccer team, he was also in prime condition.

Both Elrod and Sandro were juniors. Elrod was a marine biology major and Sandro a pre-med microbiology major.

I asked each of them the secret of their success with women. Their responses, though expressed differently, were similar.

Elrod replied, almost immediately with his Southern twang, "You have to make these gals know what it's like to feel properly loved. When I meet a gal I like, I ignore every other gal. I make her feel like she's the only one in the world for me. And when we go to bed I treat her like it's our first time together – which it usually is," and he laughed.

When I asked Sandro the question, he was thoughtful for a moment, and then he responded with his refined Italian accent, "I treat a woman as a creature to be cherished and worshipped. She becomes the center of my universe and all my attention is directed toward her and her pleasure."

I thought about what the two of them told me. I was going to have to try that approach with Karen Kim when I saw her again.

My next interview was with a very tall and wide, neckless football player named Joe Rock. He was a sophomore history major from Goshen, New York. I learned that his nickname was Felix.

I asked him how he came by that nickname.

"Well, it drives me crazy how the house gets so messy all the time. So whenever I'm over there I'm constantly cleaning up after those slobs who leave their shit around everywhere. And the dishes – sometimes I find dishes in the sink that have been there for a week and they smell disgusting. So I wig out and rag on these guys to clean them up, and of course they never do it, so I have to do it myself.

"Oh, and I like to cook. I usually cook the special house dinners and bake things once in a while. And I can't stand wrinkled clothes so I iron my clothes after I wash them. Even my underwear. So that's why they call me Felix."

I was nodding my head in agreement but I realized that I didn't know what that had to do with the name Felix.

"I don't think I follow you. Why do they call you Felix?"

"Because I do those things," he replied.

"But why Felix as opposed to Mr. Clean or something else?" I inquired.

"Oh, you know – Felix Unger? The Odd Couple?"

It clicked. I had seen the T.V. show in re-runs once.

"Got it," I smiled. "Do you like that nickname?" I asked.

"It's better than the alternative nickname some of them call me."

"What's that?"

"Martha – for Martha Stewart."

I started to laugh and he grabbed me by the shirt, lifted me off the seat like I was weightless and pulled me roughly over toward him like he was going to bite my head off. Now I could see why he was a starting offensive lineman on the football team.

"Don't ever call me that if you want to join this fraternity. Understand?"

I gulped and nodded. He looked satisfied and set me down.

I started straightening out my shirt when he frowned at me again. I closed my eyes and braced to get pulverized by him but no punch came. I opened one eye and saw he was rummaging around in his backpack. Then he pulled something out. It was a sewing kit.

"I'm sorry. I loosened one of your buttons when I grabbed your shirt. Let me just put in a few stitches so it doesn't come off," Felix said.

After sewing the button on my shirt he signed my notebook, gave me a friendly pat on the back that almost knocked me out of my seat and admonished me to do my house chores well and keep the place clean.

My last interview was with brother Ali Hassaan a/k/a Sheik, who lived off campus in Somerville, a town next to Cambridge. I heard that Sheik didn't get to campus too often. I didn't have a car and I was told that Somerville was a pain in the ass to get to by public transportation. So everyone said that we should try to get Sheik as soon as he was spotted on campus.

Sheik, a senior majoring in political science, turned out to be quite an interesting guy and an entrepreneur. He was old compared to us – in his late twenties. He was Saudi Arabian but said he didn't come from a wealthy family; he was putting himself through college. As a child, during the Gulf War, he'd made a lot of money smuggling goods into Kuwait under the noses of the Iraqi military. After the war ended, he used his skills to smuggle "decadent Western luxury items" into Iran.

"It was dangerous work because if they catch you you're camel dung. But I made good money – a lot of money," he said with a heavy accent.

Sheik bought a triple-decker house with some of the money he made during his smuggling adventures. He lived in one unit with two other brothers and rented out the other two units.

Sheik seemed to be a really nice person but I could easily picture him as a smuggler. He was a little shorter than me, but he had terrible posture which made him appear somewhat hunched over. He had thick black hair, with thick, bushy eyebrows and a mustache to match. The eyelid on his right eye appeared not to open up all the way. It was half closed over his eye, which contributed toward making him look like a pirate. He also had a scar on his left cheek that completed the image.

I asked him how he had come to join the fraternity.

"When I was a freshman I lived in Anthony Hall, one of the men's dormitories across campus. As you might imagine, I was not a very popular guy. I guess people looked at me and thought I was the type to slit their throats and rob them while they slept. But one person in my dormitory was friendly to me – a fellow named Steve Smith. He is a brother in the fraternity who graduated last year. He asked me to come over to the house and meet the other brothers. I did that and like him, they welcomed me. I guess one more oddball like me fit right in with all the rest. They invited me to pledge and it was the best decision I ever made."

I'd been reading through the SEX Manual and I had noticed that one of the fraternity's mottos was "Strength Through Diversity." They sure had taken that one to heart in this fraternity and I liked that. I was feeling pretty good again about pledging after getting these interviews.

My first chemistry lab was scheduled to begin in half an hour. I started to collect my books and get ready to go when Toddler, my Pledge Trainer, came sauntering up to the table for a late lunch. He greeted everyone at the table and then sat down next to me.

"Hey, Percy. How's your notebook coming?"

"Pretty well," I said. "Just got four more interviews done today."

"Did you get Sheik?" he asked.

"Yep, just got him." Sheik smiled and nodded.

"Good," said Toddler. "He's tough to find sometimes."

"That's what kept me alive," Sheik said, winking his good eye.

Toddler asked to see my notebook and flipped through the pages.

"Hmmm. You're making pretty good progress. Keep it up. That shows the fraternity how committed you are to joining." He returned my notebook to me.

"I thought the brothers were assigning us a special project to see how committed we are?" I commented.

"Oh, we are. But that's just one of the things that shows commitment. All the brothers are watching you guys and evaluating everything you do. We only initiate men who really want to be part of this organization, as demonstrated by accomplishing all of the requirements of the pledge program. So don't slack off in any of your responsibilities or you may not make it."

"When are we getting our assignments for the special projects?" I asked.

"We're working on them now. Hopefully we'll be able to assign them by the next pledge meeting."

"So what types of projects will they be?"

Toddler looked at me for a second or two, and then gave a laugh that could only be described as sinister.

"You'll just have to wait and see. But I'm sure that you'll all enjoy doing them almost as much as we enjoy thinking them up," he replied. I didn't like the sound of that either.

# SIX

I arrived at the Chemistry Building about 1:20 pm for my 1:30 lab, and went hunting for the room. It was supposed to be in Room 202b, which I assumed was on the second floor. But after searching awhile on that floor I couldn't find it. All the rooms ended with odd numbers.

I found Room 201a and Room 203a, but no 202. I was wondering if there was an invisible, hidden room like the train platform in "Harry Potter." I poked my head into 201a and I saw Randy and Cheever standing there speaking with a female Graduate T.A. I walked over to them.

"Hi, Randy, Cheever. Do you know where Room 202b is?"

Randy said, "Hell, I don't know where THIS room is – and I'm standing in it. If Cheever hadn't found it for me I'd still be wanderin' around like a tourist at Neiman Marcus."

The T.A., a pretty blond woman with the name L. Wellman on her lab coat, looked at me and said, "What room did you say you're looking for?"

"202b."

"Oh, that's Mr. Congeniality's room. This building is separated into two different wings – the "a" wing and the "b" wing. You have to go down the hall and through the glass doors at the end of the hall. It looks like you're going out of the building but once you go through the doors you'll see the other wing. All the even numbered rooms are over there. We all say the architect who designed this place must have been on drugs at the time," and she laughed.

"Thanks," I said, then added, "Who's Mr. Congeniality?"

"Your T.A., Percy Jordan."

At that moment she started staring at me as if I looked familiar to her, but she didn't say anything. She just had a puzzled, quizzical look on her face as if she was trying to recall something.

"Why do you call him Mr. Congeniality?" I asked.

"You'll see soon enough."

I thanked her for the information and left. I followed her directions and found my room. I looked at my watch – 1:33 pm. Despite getting lost I was pretty much on time. I walked into the room. I was greeted by the sound of a nasal voice with a British accent, screaming at me.

"You're late."

I looked up and there was Percy Jordan, in his white lab coat, glaring at me. All of the other students in the room were staring at Percy with their mouths wide open.

I looked at Percy, then I looked at my watch again. It still said 1:33 pm.

"Is my watch slow? It says 1:33," I said.

"Exactly," Percy shouted. "You're late. This lab doesn't begin at 1:33. It begins at 1:30. You've wasted three minutes of my valuable time, and I won't have it. I expect everyone in this lab to arrive on time or your tardiness will be reflected in the grade you receive from me. Understand?"

I was stunned by his overreaction. So were all the other students. We all just stood there looking at him in silence. He marched over to me, put his face close to mine, and through clenched teeth growled, "I said, do you understand?"

"Yes," I replied.

"Good, now get over to that table," and he pointed to a black lab table that had no one in front of it. I walked over to the table, sulking.

Percy began to speak in his nasal British accent.

"As I was saying when I was so rudely interrupted, this lab class meets once a week for three and one half hours. Each week you will have an assigned lab project to complete. That project will require you, not only to conduct the experiment, but to prepare the lab report. The project is not done until the report is completed to my satisfaction. And I will expect perfection," he growled.

"I will be in the lab to supervise your work each week, and to observe you. I will be grading you on your work in the laboratory, as well as on your report. Each grade will count for 50% of your lab grade. Your lab grade will be 35% of your overall grade in the class, so don't screw up."

While he lectured us he goose-stepped around the lab like the director of a Hitler Youth camp. After finishing his opening monologue he went into a pedantic lecture on how we were to conduct ourselves in "his" laboratory, how we were to approach the lab work and how much we would be charged for broken lab equipment.

"Any questions?" he asked, glaring around the room in a way that told me he wanted none.

"Aren't you supposed to be going over Prof. Harnash's lectures, and helping us understand the other course material," one of the female students asked.

Percy approached and after giving her the once over, like a farmer appraising a piece of livestock, he put his arm around her.

"I'll answer whatever questions you have at my private office hours, my dear." He gave her a leering grin and she responded with a shiver and then pulled away from him as if he were a rabid dog.

Percy then assigned our lab project and we began work, with Percy circulating around the room so that he could be sure to interfere with our work.

The lab project was interesting. It involved each of us being given a complex solution of unknown chemicals. We had to use various means of breaking down the complex solution into simpler components and then analyzing them to discover what those components were. It was a mystery to be solved through deductive reasoning and once we actually got started on the lab project itself I began to enjoy the project and feel better. For one thing, I realized that Percy didn't have anything against me personally. He was an equal opportunity asshole, giving everyone a hard time – except the good-looking girls in the class. As with the girl who asked the initial question, Percy would put his arm around them and give them extra instruction in his kindest and gentlest voice. He was unbelievably oily.

The lab itself was a moderate-sized room containing a dozen black lab tables with built-in sinks, spigots giving us access to various gasses, and covered with various pieces of lab equipment, including beakers, test tubes, burners, tubing, etc. A large chemical locker was situated in the back of the room as well as an emergency shower in case someone was covered with dangerous chemicals or in the event of fire. The facilities all were brand new and state of the art. If it weren't for having to deal with Percy for three and a half hours the lab class would have been an enjoyable experience.

A little before five we were cleaning up and Percy was giving us our final harangue of the day.

"With a few exceptions," he smiled at the attractive girls in the class, "the work I observed today was pitiful. You people are all supposed to have had advanced placement training in your secondary schools before you arrived at university, but it was certainly not evident today. Unless there is a dramatic turnaround in this class, I expect that a great many of you will receive failing grades." He glanced around the room. "I'll expect to see you next week – on time." He glared at me as he said that. Then he turned and strode out of the lab.

We all looked around at each other and then laughed – nervously. Talking through my nose with my imitation of a British accent, I said to the girl next to me, "You people are the biggest disappointment of my academic career. You can't even arrive on time. You are all going to fail, fail, fail."

"God, you sound just like him," she laughed. "You kind of look like him, too," she said staring at me with a look of wonder on her face.

"Isn't he the worst?" a male student said.

"I was getting so weirded out," a girl across the room said. "Ooh, when he put his arm around me I wanted to jump under the emergency shower and wash off. He's so slimey. And his hands grope like a thousand-fingers massage machine," she laughed anxiously.

Another male student said, "I don't know about you all, but I don't think I can take that guy for a whole semester. And it sounds like he intends to flunk us all, with a few exceptions. Somebody should do something about that guy."

We all nodded in agreement although at the time no one had any bright ideas concerning what could be done about him, if anything. We all left, deep in thought, about how to get rid of Percy Jordan.

# SEVEN

A few nights later I had the great pleasure of seeing Percy Jordan again, outside of the lab. It was in the P.R.C. Pub, a local dive in Cambridge. Several of the brothers had invited me and Randy out to dinner at this venerable hole-in-the-wall. They had chosen the P.R.C. Pub primarily because it had cheap drinks and half price appetizers until 7:00 pm.

The P.R.C. was a dark, narrow pub, crowded with small tables scattered around the room. It had a tin ceiling badly in need of a paint job. Lighting was provided by old-fashioned wall sconces, their light bulbs covered with rust colored lamp shades that cast an orange glow along the walls of the pub. On one side of the room was a long, carved wooden bar, a row of worn out chrome and vinyl bar stools lined up in front of it. The walls were decorated with an attractive assortment of paintings on black velvet – a bullfighter, Elvis and a fruit bowl. At the front of the P.R.C. was the entry door and next to that a large picture window looking out on beautiful Massachusetts Avenue a/k/a Mass. Ave.

The lure of half price appetizers was strong. The P.R.C. was already starting to crowd up at 5:00 when we arrived, but we found one open table surrounded by three open chairs at the front of the room near the picture window. There were five of us, so the three brothers grabbed the chairs and left Randy and me to fend for ourselves. We were both able to wrest loose chairs from other tables and we brought those chairs up front and crowded around our little table.

Anxiously we eyed two girls sitting at a table next to us. They must have been concerned that we had designs on them, because they kept glancing over at us nervously and then hurriedly finished up their drinks and left.

In reality, it was their table that interested us. When they stood up to leave we quickly grabbed their table and slid it over next to ours, so we could spread out a little. This made us a nice little island in what had become a sea of customers by that time.

We ordered some drinks and an assortment of appetizers for our dinner and then kicked back to enjoy the ambiance.

I had never been to the P.R.C. before, but it seemed like a nice, cozy pub.

"What does P.R.C. stand for?" I asked.

"The People's Republic of Cambridge," replied Red Neck. "This town is full of pinko, liberal, commies."

Ted Kim, a Korean-American brother from Flushing, New York, whose nickname was Kim Chee, laughed.

"Geez, Red Neck. To you John Ashcroft is a liberal. I don't think Cambridge is any more liberal than a lot of places in the Northeast. There sure seem to be more than enough conservatives around to cancel out the liberals as far as I can see."

Waldo agreed with each of them.

"You're both right. I think probably there are more liberals around here than there are conservatives. But the conservatives, like Red Neck, have such big mouths that it seems like there are more of them around than there really are." He looked at Randy and me. "That's why we have to pledge about two or three moderates or liberals for every one conservative." He winked at us.

Our waitress arrived with the drinks. Although not terribly pretty, she was friendly. She appeared to be about 30 years old and spoke with a heavy Irish brogue.

"Well, lads. You picked the busiest night this week to come here. One of our cooks didn't show up tonight and our kitchen is all backed up. So it'll be awhile before I can bring you your appetizers."

"Why don't you go back into the kitchen and help out the cooks?" Red Neck said jokingly.

"Me?" she laughed. "God, no. You obviously haven't sampled me cooking before. If I was to go back there and cook we'd have this place cleared out lickety split. I'll get you your food as soon as I can."

"No problem," Waldo said as she walked away. We sipped our drinks.

"So Jer, why don't you tell these guys about the girl who busted your stones the other day in your karate class?" Randy suggested.

"Tae Kwon Do class," I corrected.

"Tae Kwon Do? You're talking about my people," Kim Chee remarked.

"So what happened?" Red Neck asked.

I told the story. They all laughed.

Then Kim Chee said, "Wait a minute. I know Karen Kim. A friend of a friend of my parents tried to fix me up with her once when I first came to school. I went on a date with her."

"What happened?" I asked.

"Oh, nothing. We didn't really hit it off."

"Why not?" I inquired.

"Jerry's in love with her," Randy taunted.

"I am not... I'm just curious. She is beautiful."

"Oh, she's beautiful, all right. But very tough, Percy. Korean women can be very tough," Kim Chee remarked.

"What do you mean?" I asked.

"It's cultural. Maybe it's bred into them through their parents, who had to live through rough times under the Japanese Occupation and during the war. But a lot of Korean women can be very strong-willed, resilient and tough. They're like carnivorous plants. Very beautiful and attractive, but once you get smitten you're caught in their vice-like grip and under their control," he explained.

"So why didn't you get along with her?" I pressed on.

"We just weren't compatible. No special reason. But it sounds like you aren't too compatible with her either," he added, snickering.

"You never know," I countered.

I was about to take a sip of my drink when I heard a familiar nasal voice with a British accent. As usual, it was screaming. We all turned to look in the direction of the commotion, as did everyone else in the pub. When we looked we saw Percy Jordan sitting across the room, yelling at the nice Irish waitress who had served us. Also seated at the table with Percy was a very attractive blond woman wearing a slinky, low cut dress. She was smoking a cigarette and seemed oblivious to his outburst.

Everyone in the pub could hear everything he was saying. He was angry because his food order hadn't yet arrived and he was taking it out on the waitress, swearing and calling her every name in the book. She just stood there, her mouth open in shock, tears welling up in her eyes at the abuse he was directing at her.

We looked at each other and then Waldo, Red Neck and Kim Chee, angry looks on their faces, got up as one and began moving toward Percy's table to come to the waitress' aid. But the bartender and bouncer got to Percy first, pulling him up roughly and dragging him out of the pub. Percy was literally kicking and screaming like a spoiled kid having a tantrum as they dragged his ass out of there.

In the meantime Waldo and the others had reached the waitress and Waldo had his arm around her, comforting her. The woman who had been sitting with Percy continued sitting at the table, calmly smoking her cigarette as if nothing had happened. Then, a minute or two later she snubbed it out nonchalantly, stood up and without looking at anyone slowly walked out of the pub like some character from a film noir detective movie.

After a time everything settled down and returned to normal. Waldo, Kim Chee and Red Neck returned to the table, commenting on what had happened.

"What an asshole that guy was," muttered Red Neck. "I'd like to kick his ass."

"Yeah, I can't believe that guy. Who do you think he is?" added Waldo.

"Actually, I can help you there. That's my chemistry T.A., Percy Jordan," I said.

The light of recognition clicked on in Randy's face.

"That jerk is the T.A. that you look like? Percy? I didn't recognize him in the short time he was here," Randy said.

Waldo, Red Neck and Kim Chee all looked surprised.

"That was Percy?" they said.

"Jer, if I were you, I'd have plastered surgery done so you don't look so much like that prick," Randy suggested.

"I'd rather give Jordan a little plastic surgery – with my fist," Red Neck said, still incensed.

I told them the story of what had happened in my lab and did my imitation of his voice. They all laughed.

Waldo said, "Now that I think about it, you really do look like the guy. And you sound like him too." There was general agreement with that. "This presents some interesting possibilities," he added.

"What do you mean by that?" I asked.

"Oh, nothing," he said non-committally, looking at the other two brothers.

"Who was that woman with him?" Kim Chee asked.

"Yeah, she was a fox. But the coldest fish I've ever seen," Waldo added.

"I don't know. I've never seen her before. I suppose she was his girlfriend," I said.

"Who in their right mind would go out with that creep?" Kim Chee exclaimed.

"Especially if he hits on everything that moves, like you said he did in your lab," Red Neck added.

"Well, if she is his girlfriend, she must be used to the way he acts. She didn't bat an eye when he was hollerin' at the waitress, or when he got his ass thrown out of here," Randy said.

"Yeah, she must be used to it," I suggested.


On the way back to my dorm room I thought about Percy and the hot, cold blond with him. She was obviously gorgeous and could probably go out with anyone. Why did she hang around with a miserable bastard like Percy? I couldn't come up with a reason. Then I speculated that anyone as obviously cold-hearted as she was would be no prize either. She might be good to get in the sack for a night, but she sure wasn't the kind of girl you'd want to bring home to meet Mom. I guess they were birds of a feather.

I arrived back at my dorm room and found my roommate Jeff in, staring at his computer screen. That struck me as odd, considering the fact that he had a blank, white screen in front of him.

"Wassup?" I asked.

"Look at this," he said, pointing to the screen. I looked but didn't see anything.

"What am I supposed to see?"

He pointed again and as I looked closely I could see little spots of moisture on the screen.

"I sneezed, and the little spots of snot look like rainbows."

I looked again and he was right. The light refracting through the spots did have rainbow colors in them. It was the kind of thing an addled mind like Jeff's would notice.

"Interesting. Are you stoned?" I asked.

"Not yet. Why?"

"Just wondering."

"Where were you?" Jeff asked.

"In a bar in Central Square, the PRC Pub. Have you been there yet?" I asked.

"No. I was never there. But I've heard of it. How was it?"

"The bar itself is a pretty good place, but not tonight," I replied.

"Why not?"

I told him what had happened at the pub that night, including the part about Percy and his girlfriend and my musings on why she was his girlfriend. As I was telling him about it Jeff actually looked thoughtful. He was quiet for a few seconds.

"I know him."

"Who?"

"Percy Jordan."

"How do you know him?" I asked.

"He made me flunk chemistry last semester."

"What do you mean?" I asked. "I thought you were a freshman?"

"I am, because I flunked half my classes last year and didn't get enough credits. So I'm still technically a freshman, but this is actually my second year. Chemistry was one of the classes I took last year, second semester, and I had Jordan for my T.A. He was just the way you described him. And he caused a bunch of us to flunk chemistry by screwing us on our lab grades.

"It wasn't a big deal for me because I flunked so many other classes that I had to repeat a semester anyway. But there were a lot of people whose G.P.A.s were really screwed up by him. They wanted to kill the guy. A lot of people complained to Professor Harnash about him, too. I'm surprised Harnash didn't throw Jordan out of his program."

"Wow, I didn't know that. Learn something new every night. That is weird that Harnash let him come back. Percy sure hasn't turned over a new leaf. So that can't be the reason they let him stay."

"Doesn't sound that way," Jeff agreed.

"Do you know who his girlfriend is or why she's even with that jerk?" I asked, still curious.

"Nope. I don't know who she is but I can tell you why she's with him."

"Why?" I asked, expecting to hear him make a comment about Percy's anatomy.

"Because the guy's rolling in cash. He always used to show off, flashing wads of bills around in the lab and talking about where he was going out to dinner, or what concert he was going to, things like that. He's such an asshole. He just did it to make us jealous. Maybe he's a drug dealer or something. But if she's hanging around with him you can be sure he must be paying her to do it."

I hadn't thought of that. I guess that was as good a reason as any.

I grabbed my toothbrush at about the same time that Jeff got up and started putting on his shoes.

"Where are you going?" I asked.

He grinned and said, "The night is young!"

# EIGHT

The next day, after classes and an early dinner, I went over to the gym for my second Tae Kwon Do class. I had kept my eyes open for Karen Kim and had even hung around her dorm a while hoping to run into her. But I hadn't seen her anywhere. I was looking forward to class where I expected to see her.

I got into the locker room and was assaulted by a sight no human should ever have to see. All five feet five inches and 250 pounds of Buddha standing buck naked in front of me. He was just pulling on his jock and when he got it on I was struck by how much he looked like a sumo wrestler about to do battle. All he needed was the topknot.

Buddha saw me approach and greeted me with a big smile.

"What do you think?" he said, flexing his flabby biceps and assuming a muscle-man pose as though he was showing off his physique.

"Uhh, err," I sputtered, not knowing what he wanted me to say.

"Do you think I look like Buddha?"

I had to admit that he did. In fact, I wouldn't have been surprised to see someone walk up to him, rub his belly and make a wish.

"I guess you do, a little," I replied.

"Buddha was a cool dude. He also spent his life searching for Divine enlightenment. That's why I like the nickname," he said.

I started to change clothes.

Buddha said, "Do you think that purple belt, Karen, will be at class tonight?

"I hope so. I kind of like her," I said.

"You like her?" he exclaimed, incredulous. "After what she did to you?"

"Well, she won't do that again," I said.

"How do you know?"

I had just put on my jock and I pulled the hard plastic cup that went with it out of my gym bag. I inserted the cup in place and rapped on it with my knuckles.

"Let her try!" I laughed. "Besides, she likes me," I added.

"She doesn't like you in the least," he countered.

"Then why did she smile at me when she left the class last time?" I asked.

He thought a moment then said, "I don't remember her smiling at you. She looked like she might have had gas, but that wasn't a smile."

"Well I disagree. I think she likes me a lot. She just might not know it yet."

Buddha just shook his head in disbelief.

We finished dressing and went up to the wrestling room. Pretty much the same folks were there as had been at the last class, except Karen. I was crestfallen. After all, she was the main reason why I was continuing with the class. And the funny thing was that I didn't know why I liked her. That's why I had dodged Buddha's question. She was certainly beautiful, graceful and athletic. But to date her personality hadn't been anything to write home about – at least when it came to her reaction to me. I guess that I just found her kind of exotic, mysterious and alluring for that reason. Or maybe it was just the challenge? I don't know. But I wasn't going to find out tonight because she wasn't here.

Ray saw us as we came in, nodded, and said, "Stretch out." We stretched.

After a few minutes he called the class to order and we lined up. We stretched some more and he was just about to start the basics when Karen Kim came rushing into the room looking flustered. She bowed, looked at Ray, apologized for being late, and began to stretch hurriedly. We started the basics and she joined the rest of the class in basics when we were about halfway through them.

After we had finished the basics Ray announced that he wanted to do more stretching exercises. He began pairing up upper belts with the new people. I was hoping that he would pair me up with Karen and I maneuvered my way over to her so that he would see me near her when he selected my partner.

"Taylor and Kim," he said, pointing to the two of us. I looked at Karen and a dark look passed over her face. Or maybe it was an embarrassed look. I couldn't tell. Then I started to feel a little embarrassed myself and I felt my face flushing. But at the same time I was exhilarated at the prospect of being able to talk to her.

Ray directed the upper belts to teach us how to do a split stretch. This involved both of us sitting on the floor facing each other. Karen was to spread out her legs as far apart as she could and I was supposed to place my feet along the insides of her calves. Then I was to grab her wrists and pull backwards so that her upper body came forward while at the same time I was to push on her calves with my legs to stretch her legs further apart.

It was a wasted effort with her. Her limbs were as limber as a rubber band. Before I even had my feet on her calves she was able spread her legs into a full split and touch her face to the floor. In fact, I couldn't stretch my legs far enough apart to push on her calves and when I grabbed her wrists I went all the way backwards until I was lying on my back on the floor, putting no tension on her upper body at all.

When we began the stretching she said nothing other than to direct me in what to do with terse commands. Seeing that she wasn't going to break the ice, I dove in.

"So…," I said.

She looked at me.

"So what?" she replied.

I thought a moment. "So, uh, er, how did you get so flexible?"

"From stretching," she replied.

"How long does it take to loosen up? I'm pretty stiff."

She gave me a look at that remark as though she was trying to figure out whether I was being suggestive or just making an innocent remark. After a few moments she replied, curtly, "Some people never loosen up no matter how much they try. They recognize their limitations and quit."

Now it was my turn to try to figure out what she was telling me. Were we still talking about stretching or something else?

Karen finished doing the split stretch and it was my turn. I spread my legs as far apart as I could under my own steam, which was about one quarter as far as Karen had been able to stretch her legs. She put her feet on each of my calves, grabbed my wrists with her hands and yanked on them while pushing with her feet.

I understand that in medieval England they sometimes ripped apart prisoners by having horses pull them apart by their limbs. I never really appreciated what that might feel like before Karen gave me the old wishbone routine just then. I thought she had a bit of the sadist in her, and clearly she was in her sadistic element when she began splitting me up the middle.

I emitted a howl like a coyote caught in a bear trap.

"Is that too much?" she said, innocently.

"Too much," I gasped through clenched teeth, beating the floor with my hand. She backed off marginally and I felt the ligaments and tendons in my thighs twang back into place like bow strings that have suddenly been released. After a few more minutes of torture, we finished the split stretch and moved on to the next one.

Between stretches I decided to continue the small talk.

"So how long have you been doing Tae Kwon Do?" I said, placing special emphasis on Tae Kwon Do so that she would know that I remembered how she had reproached me at the last class for calling it Karate.

"Three years."

"Are you a junior, then?" I inquired.

"I'm a sophomore. I started at another school before I started college."

At least she seemed to be loosening up a little. I guess ripping me in half took some of the aggression out of her.

"A private Tae Kwon Do school, or a club at a college like this?" I asked.

"A private school run by a 4th Degree Black Belt, in the town where I live. His style of Tae Kwon Do is a little different from what we do here, so I had to start over and learn new form patterns, but it gave me a good foundation for the fighting."

"I've seen your fighting style," I said with a grin. She blushed and looked away.

We started the next stretch, which was similar to the prior stretch in that its goal was also a split that inflicted as much pain as possible.

"This stretch will help you when you're doing side kicks and roundhouse kicks," Ray said.

The stretch consisted of sitting on the floor with your legs as far apart as possible and then having your partner stand behind you to push down on your back. With that extra pressure applied to your back you were supposed to spread your legs further apart and try to touch your nose to the floor.

Karen went first, and as before, she spread her legs out to about 180 degrees and dropped her head right down to the mat. She looked as though she was resting there. She seemed completely relaxed and comfortable. Of course, this left me with nothing to do since I couldn't push her through the floor. So I continued our conversation.

"What town are you from?" I asked.

"A suburb of Detroit – Bloomfield Hills."

"Is your family originally from Korea?" I inquired, trying to confirm what Kim Chee had told me the night before.

"Yes. My parents came here for their training and stayed. So I was born in Michigan and I've lived there my whole life," she replied as she finished her stretch.

"What kind of training did your parents do here?" I asked.

"My mother's a cardiologist and my father has a Ph.D. in Engineering. She did her internship here after med school and my father got his Ph.D. at Michigan. Now he works for G.M."

"Oh really? My Dad's an engineer, too. He works for Boeing. And my Mom's a social worker," I added.

I assumed the torture position and leaned as far forward as I could. I felt Karen's hands on my shoulders and then the pressure began as I focused on the mat. It was only about a foot from my nose but it seemed a hundred miles away when I had to touch my nose to it.

"Relax, don't tense up, and you'll stretch further," Ray called over encouragingly. That was easy for him to say. But the thought of someone pushing down on my back made me want to resist and push back. So of course I was tense.

Karen continued pushing on my back and increasing the downward pressure as I continued moving closer to the mat with my face. Of course, I was in agony. If people were made to stretch that far they would have been born with more elastic joints and connective tissues.

Karen was now putting her knee on my back and pressing on me with all her weight. She wasn't particularly heavy, but it was plenty to make me feel like a wishbone again.

"So where are you from?" she asked me.

"Se – aa – l," I groaned.

"Where?"

She let up on the pressure, mercifully, and I started to straighten up.

"Seattle," I said.

"Oh, I've heard it's beautiful there."

"It is. I love living there with the mountains and the ocean both nearby," I replied, taking a tentative step or two to see whether I had pulled anything.

At that point Ray called everybody back and we started with the forms. Ray took the white belts through our forms and when it came time to spar he gave me a green belt for a partner. I did pretty well against him, too – probably because I was now able to kick about three times higher than I had been able at the start of the practice.

At the break Ray was going over something with Karen so I didn't get to speak with her again at that time. But Buddha came up to me at the break to check in.

"Did she clobber you again?"

"No, we're getting along famously. I told you, she likes me. In fact I'm going to ask her to come to the party at the house this weekend."

Buddha had an apprehensive look on his face as he walked away.

As the class ended, I scooted over to Karen before she could leave so I could ask her to the party. We had gotten along so well that I was confident she would accept.

"Uh, Karen. I'm pledging a fraternity and there's a party at the house on Saturday night. I was wondering if you'd like to come?"

She looked at me for a few moments and the look on her face showed that she was doing some mental wrestling. Then she said, "I don't think so."

I was dumbfounded. "Why not?"

"Because I don't like frats," she said simply.

"You sound like my mother," I replied.

"Your mother sounds like a smart woman," she responded.

"My mother married a fraternity man, so I guess she is pretty smart," I countered. Touché. She didn't have a retort for that. I continued. "Well, will you at least think about coming to the party? It's at the Sigma Epsilon Chi house, starting about ten o'clock. There'll be a lot of other girls there." She cringed.

"I don't think so," she said again. "See you at the next class." Then she left.

I couldn't believe it. How close-minded could someone be? I started to drag myself out of the wrestling room when Buddha caught up to me.

"Is she coming to the party?" he asked.

"Nope. She doesn't like fraternities," I said in a depressed tone.

"Well, it's probably better that way. It looks like she's kind of high strung and if she got mad at you during the party she'd probably beat you up again." Buddha was quite the philosopher.

"Maybe you're right," I whispered to myself. "Maybe you're right."

# NINE

When rushing I had attended some small closed parties at the house, but only the brothers, their friends and rushees had been invited to those parties. The first really big party of the year was Saturday night. It was open to anyone and everyone who cared to attend.

A lot of planning and preparation went into throwing a big open party, not the least of which was some urban renewal on the house. We pledges spent a good part of the day at the house on Saturday before the party, helping to get it cleaned up so that our guests wouldn't be scared away when they stepped foot in the door. There was a festive mood throughout the fraternity, with everyone anticipating the fun that we were going to have later that night.

The fraternity Social Chairman, Doug Flintlock, nicknamed Beeker because he was chemistry major, had been planning the party for weeks. As I overheard him telling Waldo about the preparations, it sounded like he had everything under control.

"Let's see. I've got three half kegs of beer in the refrigerator in the kitchen, and another ten cases of beer on ice in tubs. I bought enough juices and vodka to make about ten gallons of punch, and I have plenty of munchies. I hired a great dance band to play tonight. I've sent invitations out to all the sororities on campus, posted notices at all the womens' colleges, sent email invitations to my friends at the womens' colleges and sororities, and I even posted it on the fraternity web page. This is gonna be great!" Beeker said this enthusiastically, throwing his arms up in the air for emphasis and accidentally striking a lamp, sending it flying to the floor where it broke with a loud crash.

"Ooops, sorry!" he murmured self-consciously. But nobody paid much attention. Beeker was always breaking things. When he walked into a room he invariably left a path of carnage and devastation in his wake. It was no wonder he held the record for the highest lab breakage expenses of anyone in the Chemistry Dept.

When Beeker walked into someone's bedroom you'd see the room's occupant begin to scurry around, trying to remove anything breakable or fragile. To a certain extent the whole house had been Beeker-proofed, but there was still the occasional casualty like the lamp.

In addition to the normal clean-up we rolled up the rugs and put away the fraternity charter, plaques, composite photographs of the brothers and anything else that was easily damaged or carried away by drunken revelers. We finished up in the late afternoon and the house looked pretty good, if I say so myself. Maybe good enough to get it off the condemned list.

I took the rest of the afternoon off to study, do a few errands and rest up for the party. Around 10:00 pm I took a shower and got gussied up. Then I headed over to the house with my notebook in my pocket. After all, this might be the perfect opportunity to get some of those hard-to-find brothers for interviews.

I arrived at the house about 11:00 pm. Pretty crowded even though it was still early. Beeker had done a great job getting the word out to the girls. It looked like they had arrived by the busload. Most of them were huddled together in small groups scattered throughout the house, talking among themselves, covertly eying the guys. Likewise, most of the guys were lounging around, not so subtly checking out the girls. The band was playing top forty cover tunes, but no one was dancing yet. Tuney stood next to the band, singing along with the musicians in the group.

Other than Sandro and Elrod, who were both already paired off with two of the best looking girls there and well on their way to hooking up, everyone else seemed to be biding their time like boxers measuring up their opponents in the early rounds. Once the alcohol started to kick in, no doubt there would be more mingling among the sexes.

I was debating with myself whether to try to hook up with one of the girls there or just hang out and bond with the guys. I was still a little annoyed that Karen Kim had turned down my invitation to attend the party and I didn't know if I was up to being rejected again so soon. Hanging out with the guys was also less work. I didn't have to be careful of what I said or did when I was with the guys. I could be myself. Much less stressful.

On the other hand, if I was successful with a girl the rewards would be far greater. I was no Casanova and though I could talk the talk with the best of them, the truth is that I had never actually scored with a girl. But parties at the SEX house were infamous. When my pledge brothers and I were cleaning the house that afternoon the brothers assured us that our chances of scoring at the party were very high. Well, not for Buddha – they gave him only a fair chance at best – but Buddha took that as a major improvement over his usual odds. So we all had high expectations.

I weighed my choices and decided that the night was young and I had plenty of time to do both. I'd have a few cups of courage to loosen myself up, hang out with the bros awhile, and then start cruising for babes.

I went up to the bar and got a cup of beer, fresh from the tap. Buddha and Mad Dog were sitting there with one of the brothers, Alex Linsky. Felix was behind the bar, a great hulking figure with a mop, muttering to himself about how sloppy someone had been, allowing the tap to leak beer onto the floor.

I took a sip of beer and smacked my lips.

"Hey, this is great beer. Anyone know what kind it is?"

"I think it's Harpoon – it might be their I.P.A. or a lager," Alex replied.

"It's really good. Where is Harpoon from? I never heard of it?"

"It's a local Boston beer. Sometimes we go down to the brewery for tours and tastings. You should go sometime. The tour's great.

You stand in the bar drinking and when it's time for the tour they just point through the window to the different parts of the brewery," Alex informed us. "Saves a lot of time away from drinking the beer!"

Buddha sampled his beer, his eyes closed while he tasted. He opened his eyes looking thoughtful.

"You know, this has an aftertaste of lychee nuts."

Not having tasted lychee nuts myself, I couldn't comment. Alex just laughed.

Felix finished mopping behind the bar and said to Alex, "Keep an eye on that tap. If it starts to leak again let me know?"

"Will do."

"Thanks, Sigmund." Felix picked up the mop and left with it, heading for the kitchen. No doubt there were other battles with dirt and grime to be won there.

I hadn't interviewed Alex yet and thought this would be a good time to get him in my notebook.

"Why do they call you Sigmund?" I asked.

"I'm a social psychology major and I've done a few graduate level courses with some of my professors – a lot of psych experiments. So they started calling me Sigmund Freud, even though Freud never did any social psychology, and the name stuck. It's a lot better than the original nickname I got when I first pledged," he added.

"What's that?"

"Ass wipe. I had diarrhea for about the first month of school from the rotten dining center food."

"Gee, I didn't know you could ever change your nickname once you got it," Buddha said.

"It doesn't happen too often but nicknames are a fluid thing. They only work when they match the person they're attached to. And they say as much about the people who give them to you as they do about you. That's why you can have different nicknames in different social groups. In fact, I've done some social psych experiments looking at how different people react to different nicknames. Pretty interesting stuff."

"What exactly is social psychology?" I asked.

"Well, think of it as the study of what people do in groups and how they react in certain situations," he replied.

"Is it sort of like what happens on the old Candid Camera T.V. show?" I asked.

"Yeah, that would fit within the category of social psychology."

Buddha and I got the rest of Sigmund's information. Among other things we learned that he was a senior from San Diego, California. He had been president of the fraternity in his junior year. He hoped to go to graduate school in psychology when he finished college. He had a girl friend who was a knock out and had been selected as the SEX Goddess, which is an annual award recognizing a girl who is friendly with everyone in the fraternity and who does a lot to help the fraternity each year. Her name was Tina, short for Christine, and she was expected over at the house later that evening.

We were also interested to learn that Sigmund was the chairman of the committee that was to decide on our special pledge projects. We tried to worm out of him what we would have to do for our projects but it was like trying to get a word out of Marcel Marceau.

"You'll find out soon enough. In fact, I think we're supposed to have them for your next pledge meeting on Monday night. Don't worry. You'll enjoy them," he said with a wink.

Sigmund was equally tight-lipped when we asked him what C.P.'s nickname meant. He just repeated the same clues we had been given before – that it was some kind of take-off on C.P.'s last name, Burdick, and the fact that C.P. was from Canada. But he did add one additional clue.

"Were either of you ever boy scouts?" he asked.

"I was," I replied.

"Did you ever go overnight camping in the woods in the winter?"

"Yeah, lots of times."

"Think about what you did first thing in the morning after you got up and how it felt. That's a clue." Then Sigmund left to go find Tina.

"What's he talking about?" Buddha said with a quizzical look on his face. "What do you do first thing in the morning on a winter camping trip?"

"Beats me. Make a fire? Melt snow in a pot for water? I don't know. That clue's more cryptic than the others." I continued drinking my beer and musing on the subject but after awhile put it to the back of my mind to think about another time.


By 1:00 am the party was in full swing. The house was jam packed with people. The band was humming. The dance floor was writhing with contorting bodies. The decibel level was high, the temperature in the house higher, and the feeling of excitement the highest.

I saw brother Tino Sanchez walk by, a beautiful girl draped on his arm, heading to the dance floor and knew it was time to start thinking about hooking up. I knew this because Tino Sanchez was only about 5 ft. tall. His nickname was not Tiny, as you might have guessed. It was Pygmy.

The girl he was with had a good 5 inches on him. Maybe she fell for a line he used about being a professional jockey before attending college. Or maybe she just had a "thing" for very short guys. But I figured it was more likely that the booze and atmosphere had just gotten to Pygmy's companion.

The tune, "Is she really going out with him?" started running through my mind as I wandered around looking for the girl of my dreams.

I had had my share of the beer and I was feeling pretty loose now. My confidence level was much improved and I was getting ready to make my move. I figured I'd start out on the dance floor to break the ice and then who knows where it would lead? Now all I needed was the girl. Unfortunately, I still hadn't found the right one. So I decided to grab just one more beer and circulate upstairs for awhile.

I went upstairs, beer in hand, and worked my way over to the living room, a.k.a. the Thunder Dome. True to form the WWF matches had begun. When I arrived it appeared that Mad Dog was the champion, having just defeated Red Neck in a wrestling match, and he was looking for another challenger. In the meantime, Red Neck was protesting his defeat, claiming that Mad Dog had used some illegal military move to subdue him and win the match. Waldo and Sigmund were shaking their heads, saying that the match had been fairly won and Red Neck was vanquished. Red Neck skulked away toward the basement, muttering to himself that the Yankee had cheated.

The next challenger was Sheik. This was going to be worth watching!

Sheik and Mad Dog eyed each other, circling with arms out and legs in crouching position, thigh muscles ready to spring. They circled that way a few times measuring each other.

I was getting bored with this little dance when Mad Dog made a lunge at Sheik's legs, trying for the take down. But as Mad Dog got down to where Sheik's legs had been they were no longer there. Like a cat Sheik had nimbly jumped up and to the side, leaving Mad Dog clutching at nothing but air. A surprised look flashed across his face. He became even more surprised when he realized that the Sheik had spun around behind him and had him by the waist.

Mad Dog tried to spin around and break free of the Sheik's grip but the Sheik held on and began picking Mad Dog up off the floor. Now Mad Dog is no lightweight. He works out regularly, plus he has the military self defense training. The Sheik, in contrast, appeared much smaller and much less muscular than Mad Dog. But he was a mysterious and wily competitor. Maybe his experiences smuggling had toughened him up for the rigors of wrestling in the SEX house Thunderdome.

The Sheik got Mad Dog off his feet, then he gave Mad Dog a quick twist over his waist and dropped Mad Dog on his head. Mad Dog crumpled on the floor, dazed, and Sheik flopped on top of him, pinning Mad Dog's shoulders for the requisite three-second count. Upon being declared the winner the Sheik sprang into the air, arms upraised in a pose like Rocky after he made it to the top of the steps at the Philadelphia Museum of Art.

Mad Dog moaned and wriggled on the floor for about 30 seconds, then slowly got up rubbing his head. Between the rug burns, the bump on his head and the hangover he would have, he was going to be a hurting buckaroo the next morning.

I was going over to console Mad Dog on his loss when I felt a tap on my shoulder. I turned around and saw Sigmund with his arm around an attractive girl with short blond hair and a disarming smile. I liked her immediately.

"Jerry, this is my girlfriend, Tina. She's also the SEX Goddess of the house. Tina, this is Jerry."

"Hi," I said.

She looked at me with a quizzical expression and said, "Jerry? That's a strange nickname." Then she looked at Sigmund and said, "You guys must be slipping in your old age. Surely you could have come up with something better than that?"

There are some girls who have the kind of voice that perks you up and makes you feel good. Tina had one of those voices. It sounded like sunshine when she spoke. I liked her even more.

"Actually, Jerry's my real name. Well, you know, short for Gerald. The nickname the fraternity gave me is – Percy."

"Percy? How did they come up with that?" she asked with a laugh.

I explained the sordid history of how my nickname had come about, finishing with a firm statement that I really didn't look like the guy.

With a twinkle in her eye she smiled at me and said, "I'm sure you're much better looking than he is, no matter what."

I blushed.

"I hadn't heard the whole story about how you got that nickname. This has definite possibilities," Sigmund interjected, nodding to himself. I wondered what that meant.

Just then Beeker sauntered over to us, a smug look on his face.

"Hey, Beeks. Pretty nice party," Sigmund said.

"Yes, you've outdone yourself, Beeker," Tina added with an admiring smile.

Beeker beamed. He looked like the cat that had swallowed the canary.

"Thanks. It definitely meets the Pygmy test," he boasted.

Surprised looks flashed across Tina's and Sigmund's faces.

"No!" Tina gasped.

"You're kidding," Sigmund howled with laughter.

"What?" I said looking at the three of them. It was obviously an inside joke. "What's the Pygmy test?"

"Have you met Tino Sanchez – Pygmy?" Sigmund said. I nodded. "When Beeker was running for Social Chairman the cornerstone of his election platform was that his parties would be so good that even Pygmy would get laid."

"I saw him with a real fox on the dance floor a little while ago. You don't mean...?" I asked.

"Yep," Beeker almost shouted. "I saw him take her into the library, turn out the light and shut the door. I think he's doing the dirty deed in the library as we speak." Beeker was speaking to us, but he said it so loudly that half the people in the living room overheard him and they were now looking at us. Among them was Waldo, who came hurriedly over to us, a look of concern on his face.

"Beeker," he said excitedly. "What did you say about the library?"

"That Pygmy just took a woman in there and I think he's gonna get lucky. My party passes the Pygmy test!" Beeker replied with a look of pride.

But Waldo didn't look too pleased to hear this. In fact, he looked like the person on Survivor II who has just learned that he's gotta eat the pale, beady-eyed grub wiggling around on the dish in front of him to not be banished from the competition. Waldo's face contorted, then turned a couple shades of magenta, before he erupted.

"That idiot. What does he think this is? Does he want to ruin our reputation?" Waldo stormed over to the library, slid back the door, and shouted, "What's going on here?"

As we looked into the library we could see Pygmy, bare-assed, with his back to us, climbing up onto the desk and wriggling under some coats which were obviously covering his companion. Before climbing up onto the desk Pygmy had given Waldo a quick glance, but then completely ignored Waldo and gone about his business. Waldo yelled at him several times but Pygmy refused to come out or to respond. Waldo, at a loss for what else to do, closed the door to the library and stormed away muttering. The crowd in the living room just applauded outside the door.

I went back downstairs and ran into Kim Chee.

"Hey, Percy, where's your girlfriend, Karen?" he asked.

"She didn't want to come to the party. Said she doesn't like fraternities."

"Too bad. But there are lots of other women here. Any luck?"

"No, but I haven't really been looking yet."

Kim Chee looked at me like he felt sorry for me. Then he said, "Come on over here with me. I'll introduce you to some women I know from Wellesley."

He led me over to a couple girls that were hanging out at the end of the bar and introduced me. Both of them were sophomores at Wellesley College. One, named Lisa, was pretty. She was slim and had a nice figure, with lots of curves in all the right places. She had light brown hair, and was just a little shorter than me. When she smiled at me little dimples surfaced on her cheeks.

Her friend, Ronnie, was not so blessed in the appearance department. She was short and also had plenty of curves, but they were in all the wrong places. Her hair was black, cut into sort of a Napolean look. She had a swarthy complexion with a single thick, dark eyebrow that extended above both her eyes, kind of like Bert from Sesame Street. She also could have used a shave.

I don't know why it is, but it seems to me that along with taxes and death one thing in life that you can count on is that any attractive girl will always have an unattractive friend. They seem to go hand in hand. Maybe it's some type of chemical reaction that brings them together. Perhaps subconsciously the attractive ones gravitate to friends who are unattractive because it makes the attractive ones look even better in contrast. Likewise, subconsciously the unattractive ones gravitate to the graceful and good-looking girls and use them as bait to attract lots of guys so that they can try to trap one of the overflow guys who appear.

Whatever the reason, that's what you're faced with when you meet one of these lovely and lithesome ladies. If you hit it off with her you have the inevitable dilemma of how to ditch the clinging, clumsy and unattractive friend.

So I found myself that evening. Lisa was very nice but apparently quite devoted to her old chum Ronnie. Ronnie was like Lisa's shadow. If I led Lisa over to the tap to get another beer, Ronnie came along, too, even if her cup was still full. If Lisa went to the restroom her shadow was with her. If I asked Lisa to dance, Ronnie would join the two of us on the dance floor as well.

Finally, my opening arrived. Ronnie announced that she had to go to the restroom. Lisa said that she didn't have to use the facilities but she was about to go along for company when I held her back.

"We'll be right here," I said to Ronnie, who had a distressed look on her face at the thought of being parted from Lisa. Ronnie paused, conflicted. Like a child who senses when her parents are about to go out on the town, leaving her in the hands of the dreaded babysitter, perhaps Ronnie sensed that she would be given the slip when her back was turned. But the pressure of a full bladder was too much and soon she walked out of the room and began to climb the stairs up to the second floor where the ladies' restroom was located.

The moment Ronnie was safely up the stairs I was going to make my move. But before I could even think of how to broach the subject Lisa made her own move.

"So, it's getting pretty late. Waddaya say we get out of here and go back to your dorm room?" she said.

I was startled, but I avoided gasping, closed my open mouth and did my best to maintain my cool.

"Gee, I was just going to suggest that," I said with all the charm and sophistication I could muster.

"Great," she said beaming. "We'll pick up Ronnie on our way out." My second shock of the night.

"Ronnie?" I gasped.

"Sure, silly. We can't leave Ronnie behind. I have the car and she'll have no way to get back to Wellesley."

"Can't you let her take the car and I'll get you a ride back later?" I pleaded.

"No, she doesn't have her license. And besides, she and I like to do it together." She gave me a slightly wicked smile. "Have you ever done it with two women at the same time?"

My heart started beating wildly. I hadn't done it with one yet. Now I had the chance to do two at one time, although with that mustache I had my doubts about Ronnie's gender. My imagination ran wild trying to picture what it would be like. I looked at Lisa and saw that she was staring at me, apparently waiting for an answer.

I gulped. "Uh, no, I've never done it … with two girls, I mean."

"Well, then you're in for a treat, aren't you?"

"Yeah," I said blankly, still not believing my good luck.

Thoughts continued to race through my mind. Should I do this or try to make a graceful exit and get out of it? I was intrigued with the idea of having sex with two girls at the same time but I was also a little scared and intimidated. Would I embarrass myself? How do you go about doing it with two girls at the same time? What's the procedure?

Lisa must have seen the concern in my face because she put her arms around me.

"Don't worry about a thing, Jerry. Ronnie and I have done it together with guys plenty of times. We'll show you what to do."

Was that supposed to make me feel better, I thought to myself? How many guys had they done it with? Wasn't I special?

Just then Ronnie came back.

"Jerry's going to take us back to his dorm room, Ronnie. He's never done it with two before."

Ronnie tilted her head sideways, like a bird, and she gave me a syrupy smile. It was the type of smile that my mother and all her social worker friends used when they were looking at something cute and helpless, like an injured puppy. It made me cringe.

"Don't worry, Jerry. We'll be gentle with you," she said. I cringed some more.

Lisa took one of my hands in hers. Ronnie took my other hand and the two of them began leading me up the steps and out of the house. Tuney was standing on the back steps of the house speaking with three of his friends. As he saw us leaving, he and his friends stopped talking and all four of them burst into song with perfect barbershop quartet harmony.

"Goodnight ladies, goodnight ladies, goodnight ladies, we're sorry you have to go…"

I saw Kim Chee and a couple of the brothers step out onto the steps. Kim Chee saw me and then grinning, pointed toward my companions and me. He said something to the other brothers. They all leered at us as we walked away. Well, if nothing else, maybe this would improve my image in the house.

# TEN

My dorm was located all the way across campus from the fraternity house. The three of us meandered through the campus. It was a beautiful evening, with a clear sky, the moon and stars shining brightly. Lisa and Ronnie seemed to be enjoying the cool night air, chatting about the party and gossiping about their other friends as we walked along. I didn't join in the conversation. I was too nervous thinking about what was to come.

It had also finally dawned on me that I had forgotten about my roommate, Jeff. Although it was a little after 3:00 am, I didn't really expect him to be in the room. But what would happen if he came in while we were in the act? I guess it would be another learning experience for me. College sure was turning out to be full of new experiences.

We finally arrived at my dorm. I opened the exterior door with my key and we walked through the lobby area. Thankfully it was empty. We climbed the stairs up to the third floor. My room was located on the far side of the dorm at the end of the corridor. As was usually the case there were a number of rooms with doors open and lights on between the entryway to the third floor and my room.

Music was coming from the open doors. To get to my room we were going to have to run the gauntlet of my hall mates' rooms.

The three of us were still hand-in-hand-in-hand. I don't know why but I was a little embarrassed about being seen going to my room with two girls. No doubt the clowns in my dorm would make all kinds of jokes and give me endless grief about it. The only thing to be done was to walk quickly, look straight ahead and hope they didn't notice us as we walked by the open doors.

I started to do that as we came to the first open door but my plan was thwarted by Lisa who stopped in front of the door, looked in and asked the group of people in the room whether they had anything to drink. In the room were three of my hall mates, David Chin, Pat Martino and Bill Stern. They looked up at the two girls and me with looks of surprise on their faces.

Pat Martino broke the silence. "Sure, we've got a few beers around." He went to the small refrigerator in the corner of the room and brought out a six pack of beer. "So, Jerry, are you going to introduce us to your friends?" he said, passing out beers to all.

"Yeah," I stammered. "Lisa and Ronnie, this is Pat, David and Bill, my hall mates. Lisa and Ronnie both go to Wellesley."

There were greetings all around and we exchanged small talk for the next few minutes. I was anxious to get out of there. I looked at my watch – 3:20 am.

"We'd better get going if you're going to get back to Wellesley soon," I said in an attempt to throw my hall mates off the mark. But Ronnie thwarted that effort.

"We're not going back tonight. We're sleeping with you," she said matter-of-factly.

At that remark the mouths of Bill, David and Pat all dropped wide open. The three of them looked like those carnival characters with the open mouths that you try to shoot water in and blow up the balloons. They looked pretty comical and in spite of myself I laughed nervously.

"Well, I guess we'll be going. Thanks for the beer," I croaked.

"Nice meeting you guys. Thanks," Lisa and Ronnie chimed together. We all left and proceeded quickly past the other open doors to my room. I looked backwards and saw David, Pat and Bill all peeking out the door looking at us.

The door to my room was closed and locked with the light out. A good sign. I unlocked it and peered in. Jeff's bed was empty. I breathed a sigh of relief then opened the door wide, turned on the lights, ushered the girls in and shut the door.

"This is it," I said, pointing around the room. "Typical double."
They looked around.

"It's nice," Lisa said.

"Yes, bigger than a double at Wellesley," added Ronnie.

"Whose AC/DC poster is that?" Lisa asked.

"My roommate's."

"How can he listen to that stuff?"

"It suits his personality."

"What do you mean? Does he go both ways?" Ronnie asked with a laugh.

"No, I didn't mean that. You know, he's just a heavy metal kind of guy – lots of booze, drugs, that kind of thing." We all laughed.

"Is this your poster?" Lisa inquired. She was pointing to a poster showing all of the different model jets manufactured by Boeing.

"Yeah, my Dad's an engineer at Boeing. He gave me that poster."

"Did your father work on any of those jets?" Ronnie asked.

"A few of them. He worked on the two biggest ones here."

"Oh, I like the big ones," Ronnie said.

"So do I. Do you have a big one?" Lisa asked, putting her arms around my neck and kissing me. I returned the kiss, oblivious to Ronnie's presence until I felt her reach around from behind me and start to undo my belt.

"This is so weird," I thought to myself, as she got the belt unbuckled and started unbuttoning my jeans. But I continued kissing Lisa and tried to ignore Ronnie's ministrations.

It wasn't easy to ignore Ronnie because soon she had my jeans unbuttoned, my fly unzipped and she was pulling my jeans down around my ankles. Once she had my jeans down she yanked down my boxers, leaving me standing there bare-assed, still embracing Lisa.

What Ronnie hoped to accomplish by doing that I didn't know. I still had my sneakers on and she couldn't get the jeans or my boxers off me without removing my shoes.

Now I'd had a fair amount to drink that night, and I wasn't the surest on my feet to begin with. But once my jeans and boxers were around my ankles I couldn't move my feet and this made my balance even more precarious. Lisa and I had our upper bodies locked in a clench and as our kissing became more intense our bodies began swaying. The combination of that movement, my inability to move my feet and the drinks I had was a recipe for disaster.

Still, I might have stayed on my feet, if Ronnie hadn't decided to bite me on the ass at that moment. When I felt her teeth clutch a mouthful my right gluteus maximus I was so startled that I lost my balance. And being unable to save myself by moving my feet, I went down hard, right on top of Ronnie, taking Lisa with me. Ronnie had removed her shirt before starting her vampire routine, and there we were, as though playing Twister, a heap of writhing bodies on the floor with a topless and rather grotesque Ronnie, a bottomless me with my boxers and jeans down around my ankles, and the attractive Lisa, her arms intertwined in mine. A tangle of body parts and partially clad bodies, I imagine we resembled a particularly kinky Picasso painting.

So of course at that moment the door to my room opened and in walked my roommate Jeff with half a dozen friends. Jeff and his friends had obviously been partying hearty that night, but they were still astute enough to observe this unusual spectacle on the floor of our dorm room. They didn't say a thing. They just stood there staring.

Neither Lisa nor Ronnie is shy, but this group of a half dozen wasted guys staring at them in our present predicament seemed to unnerve them. They both yelped and then Ronnie quickly untwisted herself from the wreckage, scampered for her shirt and put it on. Lisa scrambled to her feet and straightened her clothes a bit as I slowly got up and pulled up my boxers.

Once Ronnie had her shirt back on Lisa said, "It's getting kind of late. I think we better be heading back to our school, don't you Ronnie?" Ronnie voiced her agreement. With assurances that we should all get together again some time soon, the two of them made a quick getaway, leaving me, Jeff and Jeff's friends standing there gazing after them.

After a minute or two the shock seemed to wear off.

"Hey, Jer, sorry if we interrupted your party. You should have left a note on the door or something," Jeff said apologetically.

"That's all right," I said. "Things weren't going all that well anyway." I started to pull my jeans back up.

Jeff stood looking at me, shaking his head and grinning.

"You, stud. I never knew you had it in you."

I grinned back at him, thinking to myself, "Neither did I."

# ELEVEN

Brrring, Brrring, Brrring. The telephone in my dorm room rang. It was 7:00 am on a Sunday morning. I'd been sleeping approximately three hours. Who could be calling so early on a Sunday morning?

I picked up the phone. "What is it?" I said groggily.

"Jerry, sweetie, it's Mom. Are you up yet? I wanted to catch you before you went to breakfast."

"Huh?" I replied.

"Jerry, is that you? It's Mom."

I guess my lecture about calling early hadn't sunk in. I tried to concentrate.

"Mom, why are you calling me so early on a Sunday morning?"

"Well, I didn't want to miss you. I thought you might go to breakfast early today so you could get started on your homework. I know how it is in college. I expect you didn't do any homework yesterday."

"Mom, I'm tired. I got to bed late last night. What's up?"

"Well, I thought you might be calling us today, and I wanted to let you know that your father and I are going out of town. He's got a conference in San Francisco for a few days and I'm going along. I didn't want you to worry if you tried to call us at home and we didn't answer."

"Thanks, Mom," I said wearily. "Have a good trip."

"Jerry, you sound awful. I hope you're taking care of yourself. You know you'll get sick if you don't get enough rest."

"Thanks, Mom."

"All right. I can tell that you don't want to talk now. Get some sleep. Good bye."

"Good bye, Mom. Say 'Hi' to Dad for me."

"I will."

She hung up. I looked over at Jeff's bed to see if the phone had woken him up. He was staring at me through half-closed eyes. I waved at him. No reaction. He was still asleep. I sighed to myself and rolled over. My alarm would be going off in another two and a half hours. I had to be at the fraternity house at 10:00 am for the Sunday morning cleanup.

I got to the house about 10:20 am, unkempt and out of breath. I had overslept! When the alarm went off I thought I was hitting the snooze button to give myself another seven minutes of sleep but instead I had shut off the alarm. Randy called me at 10:10 trying to find out why I wasn't at the house. I explained.

"Well, Felix is madder'n a wet hen that yer late. You better get your butt over here fast," he said. I jumped out of bed, threw on my clothes and ran all the way to the house.

When I first walked into the house I didn't see or hear anyone. I looked around on the first floor, but the place was empty. I decided to check the basement. As I walked down the stairs I still didn't hear anyone, which was odd considering that a house clean-up was supposed to be in progress.

I went through the threshold into the bar area and there were all of my pledge brothers and a bunch of the brothers standing in a double line, looking at me. I stopped and looked at them, preparing to get chewed out for being late. Tuney stepped out in front of the line, took out a pitch pipe and blew a note. Then raising his hands as though he was conducting a chorus, he and the others began singing the theme song from the movie, "Beauty and the Beast."

I stood watching this, not understanding. When they finished singing, Kim Chee stepped forward.

"Three cheers for Percy, who spent the night with Beauty and the Beast." They all hip, hip, hoorayed.

"Huh?" I said.

"Lisa and Ronnie. Didn't you spend the night with them after I fixed you up?" Kim Chee said grinning broadly.

I debated whether to lie and say that I did, but if Kim Chee knew them that well he'd probably find out the truth.

"No, my roommate came in with a bunch of friends so they left," I said dejectedly.

Everyone groaned.

"All right, all right," Felix broke in. "Not only is he late for the clean-up but he didn't even get laid. So let's get back to work. This house still stinks. Let's keep cleaning. On three, hut."

Felix, who had volunteered to be the House Manager and in charge of clean-ups three semesters in a row, directed us to our various assignments. Because I was late he assigned me to clean out the window wells of the basement windows. This was a particularly loathsome task because when people got sick they would often just throw up into the basement window wells rather than making a run for the bathroom upstairs, which was usually occupied anyway.

I began cleaning out the window wells with a mop. Randy was mopping up the spilled beer on the floor near where I was working.

"So gimme the whole story. How far did you get before your roommate came in?" Randy inquired.

I told him my sad history. He whistled appreciatively.

"Wow. Sounds like you missed out on a great time. These guys tell me the two of them are like a tag team from World Wrestling Federation. The pretty one starts working you over and just when you're hot and getting' ready to finish it with her she tags off and the ugly one takes over. I guess that's like getting a cold shower. She works you over and then tags back to the pretty one who gets you heated up again. That can go on back and forth with the two of 'em for hours."

"Who told you that?" I asked.

"Well, let's see. Kim Chee, C.P., Red Neck, Sheik, Pygmy..."

"They've spent the night with Pygmy?" I asked, incredulous.

"From what I've heard, they've spent the night with a good half of the male population on campus. They're intimous."

I thought about that. I'd have to be a little more discriminating in the future.

It took us a few hours to get the house back up to its usual state of semi-clean dilapidation. As we were finishing up, Toddler, dressed in a bathrobe, looked in on us as he was heading to the bathroom to take a shower.

"Pledge meeting tonight at 7:00 sharp. Tonight you get your special project assignments. So don't miss it," he said with a grin, as he continued on to the bathroom.

After the clean-up all of the pledges went to lunch together, speculating about what the brothers were going to make us do.

"You guys don't think they're going to haze us – you know, make us do push ups, eat nasty things, blow smoke in our faces, stuff like that?" Buddha asked.

"I don't care what they make us do. The tougher the better. Did I ever tell you guys about what they made us do when we started boot camp?" Mad Dog began.

"Yes, yes, yes," we all protested, begging him not to tell us again.

"Yaz, you've been around the house for a couple years. You must have some idea what they're going to do to us?" I asked.

"I do, but I'm sworn to secrecy on that, too. All I can tell you is they don't haze. And the projects will be different for each one of us – and they change from year to year. They don't have any set projects as far as I can tell. It seems to be whatever their devious minds think up at the time."

"Well, I'm not gonna worry about it. Whatever it is, I'm sure Cheever will help me out with it," Randy stated confidently.

"Don't count on it," Yaz said ominously.

# TWELVE

We all arrived at the house early, not wanting to be late for the pledge meeting. A lot of the brothers were milling around in the living room and T.V. room, like spectators at the Coliseum, just waiting for the lions to be released. Apparently giving us our special projects was a spectator sport.

Toddler sauntered into the room humming "I Still Haven't Found What I'm Looking For" and called us to the library for the start of our meeting. We began moving the desk out of the middle of the room so we could arrange the chairs in a circle when Yaz bent over and picked up something pink and lacey.

"What's this?" he asked.

We all crowded around to look. It was a pair of panties.

"Hey, how'd that get here?" Mad Dog said with a laugh, taking them from Yaz. "I'd like to see what they were filled with before they got left here." He held the panties up to his face and sniffed. We all cringed, disgusted.

"You're a sick puppy," Yaz told him.

"I'm just seeing if they have a scent," Mad Dog replied.

Toddler came over and inspected the panties.

"I bet those belong to the woman that Pygmy had in here last night. Dub, run up to his room and put them on his bed. He can give 'em back to her if he wants to," Toddler said.

Randy took the panties from Toddler and ran out of the room. He came back in a few minutes, beaming.

"What's so funny?" Toddler asked.

"Pygmy was in his bed sleepin' like a babe, so I draped the panties over his face," he said laughing. We all laughed at that, especially Toddler who ran out to have someone take a picture of Pygmy with the panties on his face.

After that, things settled down and we began the pledge meeting. We started out with the usual business. Toddler gave us a written quiz on the material in the SEX Manual covering the founding and ideals of the fraternity. Most of us did well. I got all the answers right, but poor Randy missed half of them.

"You know, Dub, we fool around and try to have fun here, but we're not all fun and games," Toddler said, irritated. "The material in the Manual is important – especially the material on this week's test. If you don't care about our ideals then maybe you don't belong here," he scolded.

"I care, I care," Randy said nervously. "I just didn't have much time to study. Cheever was off for the weekend and I had to do my own homework this weekend. So I ran out of time."

"Well, you're gonna have to make up this quiz." Toddler looked at me. "Percy, can you study with him and make sure he learns the material by the end of the week?"

"Sure," I replied.

After the quiz we talked about a community service project we were going to do as a pledge class, we did some planning for a scavenger hunt that we had coming up, and Toddler gave us some additional reading assignments. Then he checked on how our grades at school were looking and he suggested some academic resources that were available to us. Finally, he checked our notebooks to see how many names we were missing and the regular part of the meeting was over.

"Now we're going to assign you your special projects. For that let's move to the living room. Sigmund is in charge of the committee that devises these projects and he'll be announcing them," Toddler informed us.

We moved to the living room where a large number of brothers had assembled, with Sigmund standing in the center of the room. He signaled us to come over to him and sat us down in the middle of the room.

"Pledge brothers," he began, using his best stentorian voice. "As you know, pledgeship is a probationary period. It's a time when pledges evaluate the fraternity and the brothers evaluate the pledges to see if they want to make a long-term commitment to each other. One of the ways the fraternity evaluates the pledges is by assigning each pledge a special project. These projects are designed to challenge the pledge brother and to allow the fraternity to evaluate the pledge's creativity, his enthusiasm and drive to join the fraternity and to accomplish a useful purpose.

"Each of the brothers before you has successfully completed a special pledge project and you are now going to be called upon to do the same." The brothers snapped their fingers in agreement.

"A committee composed of a number of brothers including myself has given your projects a great deal of thought. Each of these projects has been devised specifically for each individual pledge. And now, without further ado, it is my great pleasure to announce the special projects for this pledge class." He flipped through his notes, then settled on a page.

"Pledge Brother Yaz, please stand up."

Yaz rose.

"Yaz, as you know I've been doing original research in social psychology with the Psych Department. Not long ago the professors I'm working with suggested a social psych experiment to assist them in learning how people react in a particular situation. But they need someone to work with them to conduct the experiment. Now I knew you'd be interested in helping to advance science so I volunteered you to work with them on this experiment for your special project." More snaps from the brothers. Yaz looked apprehensive.

"Yaz, you are going to participate by standing in Harvard Square, Downtown Crossing, Quincy Market and other heavily traveled locations around Boston and while you're standing there you're going to shout 'There are Cyborgs among us.' You'll also have some literature to pass out informing the public of this deadly cyborg peril. People from the Psych Department will be monitoring how the public reacts to you."

Yaz sat down with an unhappy look on his face. The last thing he wanted to do was walk around in public giving the impression that he was psychotic. But that's what made it a challenge. If they had assigned it to Mad Dog there would have been no challenge to him as far as I could tell because he was half way to being psychotic already.

From the cheers that went up around the room it sounded like the brothers liked Yaz's project. It didn't sound too bad to me. I was hoping that my project would be no worse.

"Pledge Brother Dub, your turn," Sigmund said, signaling with his index finger for Randy to stand.

Randy stood.

"I always like to explore how people react in different situations, and I've been responsible for conducting my own psychology research. One particular area that fascinates me is how people react in role reversal situations.

"Pledge Brother Dub, it has not escaped the notice of the brothers that you have a valet who takes care of you here at school. Believe it or not we are more astute than we look. Now what better way to explore the impact of role reversals than by having you switch places with your valet. Your special project will be to exchange roles with Mr. Cheever for a period of a month. Other than going to school and fulfilling your other pledge responsibilities, which you will continue to do, you will do all the other things that Mr. Cheever currently does for you, except you'll do them for Mr. Cheever. So if he washes and irons your clothes, now you'll wash and iron your clothes and his clothes. If he cooked for you then you'll cook for him. You and he will keep a journal and I'll observe and interview both of you periodically as part of the research project. Got it? Any questions?"

Randy had sort of a vacant, confused look on his face. He scratched his head.

"Now let me get this straight," he began. "You want me to wash Cheever's clothes?"

"Among other things," Sigmund replied.

"But what if I don't know how to wash clothes?"

"I'm sure Mr. Cheever will give you some tips."

"What if Cheever doesn't want to cooperate?" Randy asked.

"Oh, he does. We've already talked to him. He told us whatever will help 'Master Randall' to be initiated into the fraternity, he's happy to assist."

"Oh. I guess that's all right, then," Randy replied doubtfully, and sat down. After the earlier tongue-lashing I guess he didn't want to push his luck with any more questions.

Sigmund looked through his notes and then turned to Mad Dog.

"Pledge Brother Mad Dog, you're next."

Mad Dog jumped to his feet, smiling eagerly.

"Mad Dog. I'm sure you've met my girlfriend and the fraternity SEX Goddess, Tina? Well, Tina informed me that the Early Childhood Development section of the Psychology Department, where she does a lot of work, is in desperate need of assistance. I volunteered you to work in that department for the next month to help them out. Essentially you are going to be helping to take care of babies and toddlers in the Day Care Center while they're short-handed."

The smile on Mad Dog's face quickly faded and a frown replaced it.

"I don't know how to take care of babies. That's women's work," he protested.

"Mad Dog, if you want to join the fraternity then you better get in touch with your feminine side fast. Because that's your project," Sigmund said sternly. Everyone chuckled at that as Mad Dog sat down grumbling. I hoped that the Day Care Center was well insured if Mad Dog was going to be taking care of babies. That was like giving an idiot a gun. It was something I had to see.

"Next, Pledge Brother Buddha."

Buddha stood up, his legs shaking a bit, which caused sympathetic jiggling of the rolls of fat on his belly. He looked really nervous.

"Pledge Brother Buddha, you and your pledge brothers are attempting to join our brotherhood," Sigmund began. Buddha continued quaking. At least his belly continued jiggling.

"Membership in our fraternity carries many obligations which remain with you for the rest of your life. These obligations go hand-in-hand with the privileges. We think that before you can join us you need to have a better understanding of who we are and how we came into being." He stopped and gave Buddha a severe look which resulted in Buddha's face turning a shade paler than it had been.

"Pledge Brother Buddha, your special project will be," he paused for dramatic effect, "to research the history of our fraternity chapter and write a ten page essay that you will deliver to your pledge brothers."

Buddha looked surprised. Then after a few moments he said in a quiet voice, "Is that all?" He sounded disappointed. I was a little disappointed myself after the big buildup, although it did make me feel better about what they might make me do. Maybe it would be something easy like Buddha's assignment.

Sigmund nodded his head. I looked around the room. I would have expected the brothers to be in an uproar over something as tame as this assignment, but they all seemed to be smiling and nodding approvingly. Go figure.

"And to research the history of our chapter of the fraternity, of course you will have to spend a day meeting with and interviewing our oldest living alumnus, Brother Tookie Caraway."

At this finger snaps and shouts of encouragement began all around the room, as well as some rather sinister laughter. That didn't bode well.

Buddha sat down and I was next.

Sigmund walked over to the fireplace mantle, rested his hand on it and looked around the room. His eyes found and rested on me. He gave me a friendly smile. I smiled back, feeling pretty confident that they had run out of ideas and were going to give me something easy like they did with Buddha.

"Last, but not least, Pledge Brother Percy," he said still smiling benignly at me.

"Pledge Brother Percy, I must confess that I and the other committee members had been wracking our brains trying to come up with just the right special project to give you – without success I might add." He paused, a concerned look on his face.

Hah, I was right! They had run out of ideas. This was going to be a piece of cake.

"We were really at a loss about what to do with you, and we were thinking about another essay writing assignment – until the party last night." Some of the brothers started whistling and hooting. Tuney started humming the Beauty and the Beast theme again.

"Oh, no," I thought to myself, "this must have something to do with Lisa and Ronnie. Why did I ever get involved with them?" Sigmund continued.

"When I learned the history behind your nickname I thought that it had some possibilities for another social psychology project. I've given it some additional thought and discussed it with the other committee members and we've come up with the perfect project for you. You'll also have the opportunity to help further scientific research."

There was now complete silence in the room. Everyone was giving Sigmund his full attention.

"First, let me give you a little background. One area that my professor has been studying is the way in which people process information. We all have preconceived frames of reference in our minds, developed over the years from our experiences. We process information by comparing it with these frames of reference in our minds and try to fit it into the appropriate box, so to speak.

"For example, if I told you that my great grandfather was a pirate, without telling you anything else you would probably form certain impressions in your mind about my great grandfather." He pointed to Red Neck.

"Where did my great grandfather do his pirating?"

"What?"

"If I tell you my great grandfather was a pirate, where do you think he did his pirating?"

"Uh, on a ship?" Red Neck replied.

"O.K. And where did he sail his ship?" Sigmund asked Waldo.

"In the Caribbean?" Waldo responded.

"What was the weather like where he did his pirating?" he asked Tuney.

"It's too darn hot, it makes my sweat depart," Tuney sang.

"And sunny," Toddler added.

"What did he wear when he did his pirating?" Sigmund asked.

"Baggy pants, a tri-cornered hat, and an eye patch," C.P. shouted.

"And an earring," Felix added.

"And he had a parrot on his shoulder," Toddler yelled, "and a peg leg."

"All right. All right. You all get the picture," Sigmund continued. "We all have these pre-conceived ideas in our heads and we try to make the information we receive conform to those ideas. But what happens when that information doesn't fit neatly into the little boxes that we have in our heads? What if it's contrary to impressions that we've already formed? What happens then?"

There was complete silence throughout the room, puzzled looks on everyone's face. Even though they were talking about me I have to admit I was finding this discussion pretty interesting.

"Chaos," Sigmund relied. "Well, maybe not chaos. The bottom line is that we don't really know what happens and that's what my professor is studying.

"Now what does all of this have to do with Pledge Brother Percy?"

I was wondering that myself.

"Well, we know that Percy bears a remarkable resemblance to his namesake, a graduate student in the Chemistry Department, here at school. We also know that that grad student is a son of a bitch who everyone hates. Now how would people react if, all of a sudden, that grad student became a nice guy?"

I was beginning to get the picture and I didn't like it one bit.

"Pledge Brother Percy, your special project is to impersonate your chemistry graduate assistant and be nice to people. We'll monitor their reactions and record the observations."

Once again, shouts of approval rose up from the brothers, many of whom were slapping Sigmund heartily on the back.

"But I don't even look much like the guy. No one will believe I'm him. And what if the real Percy sees me? I'll get expelled, or at the least he'll flunk me in lab and report me to Professor Harnash who will flunk me," I pleaded.

"You won't have any trouble and you won't get expelled or flunk out. From what Red Neck and Kim Chee have told me you're a dead ringer for the guy. And you can check out his movements for a while, figure out his schedule and then just impersonate him when he's not around. He'll never see you," Sigmund responded.

Toddler came over to me.

"That's your assignment. If it looks like you're going to have any problems we'll change it. But right now it seems like it'll be fine. No more discussion," he said with finality.


After the meeting ended all of the pledges got together for a private pow-wow in one of the lounges of a dorm. All of us had grim looks on our faces except for Buddha. Mad Dog began the discussion.

"Geez, I can't believe they're making me take care of babies. I don't know how to take care of babies. I'll probably kill one of 'em by mistake. And think of the raft of shit I'll get from the other guys in ROTC."

"Well, how would you like to have to act like a nut case in public?" Yaz said. "What if someone I know sees me? They'll think I'm a god-damned loon. And what the hell is a cyborg anyway?"

"An alien," I said.

"There, see? I'm gonna be a nut who thinks the aliens have landed," he said disgustedly.

"I dunno what you're so steamed about," Randy piped in. "How'd you like to be paying a guy to be your valet and you have to wait on him? I don't even know how to do half the things I'm s'posed to do fer him. That's why I have a valet."

"I feel sooo sorry for you," Mad Dog said mockingly. "You're not paying him anyway, your old man is. And everyone should know how to iron, cook, clean and do those other kinds of things you've had done for you all your life. In the Army we had to do those things every day. I would get up at the crack of dawn…"

"Well, I'm not in the Army," Randy interrupted angrily, "and I don't wanna be. I can't believe how unloyal Cheever is. Imagine him agreein' to make me wait on him. Wait till this is over. He'll be up to 'is eyeballs in alligators when this is through!"

"Well, its been nice knowing you guys," I said. "But I figure I'll be expelled before long and that'll be the end of my college career. Short but eventful." I sighed.

"Don't worry, Jer. I'm sure you'll do fine. It'll probably be fun," Buddha said optimistically.

"How the hell did you get off so easy?" Mad Dog barked at Buddha menacingly. Buddha cringed and took a step back involuntarily.

"I don't know? Maybe they just ran out of other ideas when they got to me?" he suggested sheepishly.

"Don't think you're off the hook," Yaz said. "Did you hear them laughing? You're gonna have to spend the day with old Tookie Caraway."

"So?" all of us said in unison.

"I never met the guy but from what I hear he's a genuine psycho. I've seen pictures of him. He looks like that professor from the movie 'Back To The Future.' And apparently he was a real inventor but he had a few loose screws and he was put away for awhile."

A worried look came over Buddha's face.

"It sounded too good to be true," he said shaking his head.

We continued to discuss our projects and what we were going to have to do to get through them. In the end we agreed that whatever happened we would all try to help each other out as much as we could to complete our projects. They were going to be challenges. But it was nice to know that each one of us was not alone. We could fall back on each other to get through them together. Maybe that's what the brothers were hoping we'd learn from the experience.

# THIRTEEN

When I woke up the next morning I felt terrible. It seemed like I hadn't slept a wink the night before. I kept tossing and turning, worrying about how I was going to do this project. I had decided to follow Sigmund's advice. I was going to have to check out Percy's mannerisms more closely and also get more information about his schedule so I could impersonate him when he wasn't around. I'd start today, seeing what I could find out about him. Then I'd study his mannerisms and voice tomorrow when I had lab.

I attended my morning classes, including my large chemistry class lecture. I received an unexpected bonus. Although the graduate assistants normally didn't attend Professor Harnash's lectures, Percy was there today for some reason.

I decided to sit down in the front of the lecture hall rather than in my customary spot in the last row. From up front I could keep an eye on Percy and maybe pick up some tips on how best to impersonate him.

As I was moving down toward the front of the room I saw Randy walk in, carrying his own books with no Cheever in tow. I nodded to him, signaling him to follow me down to the front of the room. He nodded agreement and caught me as I parked myself in the second row.

"Why we sittin' down here? It's gonna be mighty hard to do the crossword puzzle up front under Harnash's nose."

I shushed him and said, "Keep it down. Look who's here." I pointed over to Percy, who was a short distance away, sneering at some undergraduate who had the poor judgment to ask him a question.

Randy looked at Percy and then back at me. "What's he doin' here?"

"Dunno. But I'm gonna take advantage and try to study him a little since he's here."

"Oh, good idear."

We sat down and watched Percy. He looked about the same as always. He wore a flannel shirt in a plaid tartan of some type and a worn pair of jeans with a braided leather belt. On his feet he wore a pair of Reebok sneakers. I mentally surveyed his wardrobe, thinking about similar clothes that I owned. I was pretty sure that I had most everything that I needed. I would just have to get a pair of tortoise-shell glasses like Percy's, cut my hair a little shorter and dye it a slightly darker shade.

Percy was just finishing chewing out the student who had asked him a question. His accent was definitely British. I'm certainly no expert, but it didn't sound refined like Cheever's accent. There was a twinge of cockney in it, as though Percy had grown up on the wrong side of the tracks. But at the same time there was a tone of superiority and contempt in his voice when he spoke. No matter what he said his voice sounded condescending and he seemed to be sneering. No doubt about it. He was a most unpleasant bloke.

Percy leveled a final insult at the undergraduate and then slumped down in a chair in the front row. I watched him sitting there. He just closed his eyes and appeared to be napping. A few minutes later Professor Harnash strode into the lecture hall, descended the steps to the front of the room and dropped a pile of books onto the desk in front with a loud bang. He fussed with some papers for a few moments and then seemed to notice Percy. An irritated look came over his face and he walked determinedly over to where Percy was slumped.

"Jordan," he said sternly.

Percy opened his eyes and fixed them on Professor Harnash, but he didn't sit up. He remained in his slumped position.

"Yes?" he replied, lackadaisically.

"I just received another complaint about you – this time from an undergraduate who said you refused to answer his questions about last week's lab a few minutes ago. What's the matter with you? Haven't I warned you about this?"

Percy just stared at him with a bored expression on his face. Then he shrugged his shoulders, still slumped in the chair in a disrespectful way. "Is that why you wanted me here?"

Professor Harnash glared at him, but then looked around and noticed Randy and me watching from the next row. He looked back at Percy and said, "Now is not a good time to talk. I want to see you in my office as soon as the class is over. Understand?"

Percy shrugged again, then got up and slithered out of the lecture hall. Professor Harnash, shaking his head, just watched him go, then returned to his desk to prepare his lecture.

"Wow, did you see that? There's a grad student who's not long for this world," I said.

"Yaah! Harnash is gonna kick his ass outta here faster'n shit through a goose. You better impersonate ole Percy fast before he's expelled," Randy agreed.


After class I decided to go up to the Chemistry Dept. offices to see what I could learn about Percy's schedule. I checked my notes and found the room number of Percy's office. It took me about ten minutes to find his office. Fortunately, no one was there. But on his door his schedule was listed. In addition to my lab he had two other labs as well as some brief office hours.

I copied down the information, then looked at the Chemistry Dept. bulletin board. There was nothing of interest there, other than an invitation to all graduate students, postdoctoral fellows and faculty to attend the Chemistry Dept. bimonthly buffet dinner on Friday evening. I wondered if Percy ever attended that dinner? I doubted that he was the social butterfly-type who mixed with the other grad students, but perhaps he attended to brown nose the professors.

I noted the time and location of the dinner. Maybe I could make use of the information down the line.

The next day I was almost looking forward to attending lab. I had spoken with Beeker, who told me that from what he heard Percy was hated by his fellow grad students almost as much as he was hated by his undergraduate students. And he had never attended the buffet dinners sponsored by the Chemistry Dept.

The dinners had been started a few years ago in response to a grad student committing suicide. The thought had apparently been to make the department more "warm and fuzzy" by creating these artificial social events to get the faculty and graduate students to interact. As it turned out, a lot of the grad students attended to get the free meal and booze. The faculty members rarely came to the dinner, although a few were always assigned to be there to give the impression that the faculty supported the concept.

Beeker thought that the upcoming dinner would be the perfect occasion for me to impersonate Percy.

"First, there's little chance Percy will show up, which is key. Second, there should be a lot of people around – other grad students – who know the guy and can't stand him. So you'll have the opportunity to mess with their heads and get some good data for the experiment. There shouldn't be a lot of faculty there, so even if they figure out that you're not the real Percy there's less likelihood that you'll get in trouble. Finally, I think that I can get an invite to attend from some of my profs and my teaching assistants. So I can help watch your back," he informed me.

I agreed. It was a good opportunity to get it over with, hopefully without getting myself expelled in the process. Now I just needed to study Percy a little more in lab in anticipation of my impersonation and I'd be ready.

I arrived early at the lab, eager to eye-ball Percy some more. Gradually the other undergraduate students filtered into the lab, quietly expounding on what a jerk Percy was and how they were dreading having to deal with him again today. This was the usual topic of conversation while we waited for Percy, who after the first lab was perpetually late. We began setting up for our labs, the conversation about Percy continuing. Still he hadn't arrived.

We started doing our lab work. Percy was nowhere to be seen, a fact that disappointed no one except me. I liked the guy no better than anyone else but I did want to get one more good session with him to help me prepare for my part. Besides, I was getting a little anxious. What if he'd been fired? If he was fired then I couldn't very well show up as Percy at the department dinner.

By now the mood in the lab was positively jovial. The discussion was no longer quiet. People were boisterously celebrating the fact that Percy wasn't there and speculating on where he might be.

"I bet they finally fired him. They figured out what a jerk he is and got rid of him," one student speculated.

"No way," another one said. "They've always known what an asshole he is. Why fire him now?"

"Yeah, plus, if they fired him they would have sent another teaching assistant to be here today. At least they would have told us. I think he's just playing hooky."

"I'll bet he's getting some afternoon delight with one of his bimbo girlfriends and forgot all about us."

"What do you mean 'one' of them. How many does he have?" another student asked.

"I don't know. But I saw him hot 'n heavy with at least two last week. He was making out with a redhead in his car behind the Chemistry Building as I was leaving last Tuesday, and then I saw him in a bar in Brighton a couple days later. He was making out with a blond at the bar. It definitely was a different woman. Then I saw him with the redhead again here at school yesterday. I don't see what any of them see in the prick."

The speculation continued throughout the afternoon and Percy never showed up. We finished our labs and left late in the afternoon. When Harnash found out about Percy blowing off the lab he was sure to be fired. I just hoped it wouldn't be until after the department dinner coming up on Friday.

# FOURTEEN

That evening I went to my first Tae Kwon Do class since the party. I saw Buddha in the locker room, sneezing.

"Hey, Buddha, have you started your research project yet?" I asked.

"Well, sort of. I began going through the chapter archives in the library and I went up to the attic today to dig through some old scrap books and photos they stashed up there." He sneezed again.

"Have you got a cold?" I asked.

"No. It's all that dust on the books and papers I've been reading. I felt like Lawrence of Arabia fighting my way through the desert sands when I went up in the attic. The dust is making my allergies act up." He sneezed again. "How's your project coming?"

"I dunno," I replied. "I was gonna check Percy out at lab today to try to learn his mannerisms, but the creep never showed up at lab. Right now I'm planning to impersonate him at a Chemistry Department dinner on Friday. I just hope they don't fire the guy before then. Hey, when do you meet that crazy alumnus?"

"They haven't told me yet." He laughed nervously.

"I'm sure it'll go fine whenever it is," I said encouragingly. Buddha just shrugged his shoulders and shook his head. "Hey, maybe we can all go along. You know – 'all for one, one for all'?" I added, smiling.

"Maybe."

We went up to the wrestling room. I immediately scanned the room looking for Karen Kim. She was over in the corner, stretching. She was as beautiful as ever. I walked over to her and began stretching. She looked up and nodded to me.

"Hi," I said. "How was your weekend."

"Not bad. How was your big party."

I blushed, but recovered quickly and said, "Umm, O.K."

"You don't sound too enthusiastic."

"Well, it was crowded and noisy, you know, a typical big party." She continued stretching without looking at me.

"It would have been a lot nicer if you had stopped by," I added. "You would have been the best looking girl there." She looked up at that and I gave her my warmest smile.

"In college we're called women. And from your description I'm glad that I missed it. Here, stretch my leg." Karen leaned against the wall, lifted her right leg sideways into a straddle and put her right foot in my hands. "Lift my leg until I tell you to stop."

I began lifting her leg slowly. I stopped when I got it as high as my chest.

"Higher," she said. I lifted it to the level of my chin.

"Higher." I lifted it up so that it was just above my head. Her legs were almost 180 degrees from one another.

"That's good. Hold it there," she grunted. I held it there.

"So, maybe the party was a bad idea. Maybe we should just go out for a pizza or maybe catch a movie instead? Much less noisy and crowded. What do you think?" I asked.

"Lower my leg," she replied. I complied. "Now do the other one." She gave me her left leg and I hoisted it quickly above my head.

"Easy," she groaned. "This leg isn't as well stretched." I lowered it slightly.

"That's good," she said.

"So what do you say? Do you want to go out for dinner or a movie?" I asked again.

"Lower it," she responded, pointing to her leg. I let it down. She gave her legs a quick shaking to loosen them up after the stretch, looked at me and said, "Now I'll stretch your legs."

I leaned against the wall and slowly raised my right leg sideways to about the level of Karen's knee. She bent down and grabbed my ankle and began to lift my leg slowly. When she got it to about the height of her waist my hamstrings felt as taut as a bent bowstring.

"Ouch! Hold it there," I croaked. She stopped and let me adjust to the stretch. The pain slowly eased. I tried to return the conversation to the subject of our going out on a date.

"I'm still waiting for an answer to my question. Will you go out with me?"

Karen yanked my leg up higher and I yelped with pain. "Enough, enough. Let it down," I gasped. She lowered my leg and I massaged my aching hamstrings.

"Let's do the other leg so they're evenly stretched," she instructed.

"You mean evenly crippled. Jeez, you're trying to kill me, just because I asked you out on a date."

Karen looked at me and grinned.

"I told you, I don't date frat boys." She put special emphasis on the word 'boys.' "Now give me your other leg," she ordered.

"O.K., O.K. But take it easy this time. I'm not Gumby, you know!" With some apprehension I leaned against the wall again and gave her my left leg. She began stretching it, but this time very slowly, allowing me time to adjust to the stretch at each level as she raised my leg higher and higher. She got it up to about the level of her elbow and I told her to stop. She held it there.

"If you don't date fraternity men then how do you know what it's like to date one? I think it's pretty closed-minded of you to lump all fraternity members together into a single stereotype," I argued. "You should at least go out with me once before condemning me! Besides," I added, "I'm not even a brother yet. I'm just a pledge."

Karen looked thoughtful and lowered my leg.

"Tell you what. I'll think about it and let you know by the end of class."

"Fair enough," I replied smiling.

The rest of the class flew by in a whirl. I couldn't concentrate on anything. I kept wondering what Karen's answer was going to be, hoping that she would agree to go out with me. It was a wonder

I didn't get killed during the sparring considering how distracted I was. Fortunately I was teamed up with Buddha as my sparring partner. Sparring with Buddha, I felt like David Carradine in the old 'Kung Fu' television show. The entire match felt like it was in slow motion because Buddha threw moves at a snail's pace. It was more like T'ai Chi Ch'uan than Tae Kwon Do. So I didn't have to be too on the ball to avoid getting hit inadvertently.

At last the class ended and I maneuvered my way over toward Karen as we were leaving the room.

"So what's the verdict?" I asked, not wanting to mince words.

An indecisive look came over her face and she stood there for a few seconds without answering. Then she responded, "Oh, what the hell. You're only pledging so I guess I can make an exception. But just one date," she added sternly.

"Great," I said, trying to be nonchalant. "How about Friday night – late? I have to do something earlier in the evening."

"Fine. Give me a call. I'm in the school phone directory."

"Good. I'll do that. See you."

"Yep. See you Friday," she replied, and she was gone.

Buddha and I walked together to the locker room.

"Jeepers, Jer. What's gotten into you?" he asked.

"What do you mean?"

"You're bouncing down these stairs like your dancing or something."

I looked at him with a big, shit-eating grin and said, "We're going on a date!"

# FIFTEEN

I finished my classes early on Thursday and went over to the Theatre Department to meet Tuney, who had offered to help me get ready for my big impersonation. Tuney had told me to meet him in the Little Theatre auditorium. When I arrived no one was there. The room was empty.

I walked down the aisle, looking toward the stage. On stage was an elaborate Japanese set with a red Pagoda-like building and a simple rock garden. There were colorful banners streaming across the set as though a festival had been taking place. I called out.

"Hello, Tuney?" There was no response. "Hello? Is anyone here?" I continued walking down the aisle toward the front of the auditorium. As I reached the front I heard a noise. I looked up and there on the stage was someone dressed in a full kimono with shaved head, top knot and samurai swords. He wore heavy make-up and I couldn't tell if he was really Asian or just made to look Asian. I stared up at him as he walked down stage toward me. He got to the edge of the stage and stared at me.

"Who are you?" I asked.

"Do you want to know who I am? I am a brother of Japan," he sang to me.

"Hi, Tuney," I said, immediately recognizing his voice.

"Whaddoya think?" he said enthusiastically, holding his arms out to his sides so I could get the full effect. "Isn't this great? We're doing a production of the Mikado and we just got in these costumes."

"You look… interesting," I commented.

Tuney got down off the stage, reached into his kimono and pulled out a pair of tortoise shell glasses. He handed them to me.

"Voila! Are these the right kind? I had to look all over through the costume department to find them. I remembered them being used when we produced 'The Importance of Being Ernest,' about a year ago. What a great production that was." He burst into song again. "Those were the days my friend, we hoped the show would never end…"

"Hey, those look great. Just like the ones Jordan wears. Thanks a lot," I said gratefully. Tuney beamed.

"Now, we have to do your hair. I saw Jordan and I think we have to take off about an inch all around to get your hair the right length. Sit down in that chair on stage and I'll cut it," Tuney instructed.

"Wait a minute. Do you know how to cut hair?" I asked suspiciously.

"Of course. I've played Sweeny Todd, the demon barber of Fleet Street. I did more shaving and throat slitting than hair cutting in that show, but I figured I better learn how to cut hair at the time just in case I needed it."

I sat in the chair and Tuney put a towel around my neck. He pulled a pair of scissors out of his kimono sleeve and began snipping at my hair. As he snipped he hummed, clipping in time to the music. He cut away for about ten minutes, then reached into his kimono once again and removed a mirror. He held it out in front of me.

"Well, how does it look? Put on the glasses."

I put on the glasses he gave me and looked at myself in the mirror.

"Not bad," I admitted. "If my hair was just a little darker I'd look a lot like Percy Jordan."

"Not to worry," said Tuney, reaching into his kimono and pulling out a bottle. "Hair dye," he explained. "Close your eyes."

Tuney applied the dye and combed it through my hair. He fussed with my hair for a while and then pronounced me finished. I looked in the mirror again and had to admit that I looked just like Jordan.

"Now for your voice lessons."

"My what?"

"Voice lessons. You can't expect to fool anyone if you don't sound like him."

"But Tuney, you don't know what he sounds like. How are you going to give me voice lessons?"

"That's easy. I just need help from someone who knows how he speaks."

"Who's that?" I asked. Just then I heard a loud crash from the back of the stage and then the canvas set behind us ripped and through the gash fell Beeker.

"Jesus, don't you have any lights back there. Someone could get killed," Beeker growled, picking himself up off the floor.

"It hasn't been a problem for anyone else," Tuney said coldly. "Do you know how long it took to create that set you just destroyed?"

"No, and I don't really care. You're lucky I wasn't injured." Beeker said, dusting himself off when he first noticed me. "Yikes," he said recoiling backwards in surprise.

"Hi Beeker," I said sheepishly.

Beeker walked over and stared at me intently.

"Is that you, Jerry? My God, the resemblance is... frightening!"

"Thanks. I'll take that as a compliment, I guess."

"Wow," exclaimed Beeker, walking around me and looking from all sides. "You are definitely going to fool people."

"I hope so," I said, not feeling quite so confident.

Tuney walked over, pushing Beeker aside and straightened out my collar where it had been tucked in for the hair dying.

"All right, Beeker. We have him looking the part. Now we need him to speak like our pernicious graduate student. Jerry, or Percy rather, say something and try to sound like Jordan."

"What do you want me to say?" I asked.

Tuney grinned and sang, "The rain in Spain goes mainly down the drain." Then, speaking, he said, "Sorry. I couldn't resist. Say anything you want."

In my best imitation of Jordan's nasal voice, I said: "You students are idiots. You disgust me."

"Not bad, not bad," said Beeker, nodding his head. "But I think you need to make your voice a little deeper. And I'm not sure if the accent is quite right. His accent isn't quite so proper, it's more... um..."

"Cockney?" Tuney suggested.

"Yeah, Cockney."

"Try it again, a little deeper and more Cockney," instructed Tuney. I said it again.

"The voice is deep enough now but you're too heavy on the accent," Beeker advised. I tried it again, this time cutting back on the Cockney a little.

"Yes, yes, that's it," shouted Beeker ecstatically, jumping up and down. As he did so he hit the chair on which I'd been sitting, tripping over it and falling off the end of the stage into the pit. He reappeared almost instantly.

"I'm up, I'm up," he yelled, rubbing his head. Tuney just shook his head.

I got my Percy Jordan wardrobe together and then headed over to the house for our weekly pledge meeting. Toddler was waiting for us in the library. Randy was missing.

"Where's Dub? Has anyone seen him?" Toddler asked. Nobody had. Just then the door of the library opened and in walked Randy, wearing a black suit with a starched white shirt, a dark tie and a derby on his head – the perfect butler. His hands were both covered in white bandages and on his face he wore a look of pure misery.

"Sorry I'm late. Cheever was giving me a lesson in ironing so I could iron his clothes and I ended up burning myself. It ain't as easy as it looks!" Randy said in an apologetic tone.

"No problem. We were just getting started. Sit down," said Toddler. Randy plopped down in the armchair next to me, winced and then jumped up. As he did so we heard a ripping sound. We all looked down at the seat of the arm chair and saw a particularly nasty-looking spring sticking out. Randy twisted his head around trying to see his back side. As he turned I could see a large rent in the back of his pants.

"Oh, great. Now I'm gonna have to git me a sewing lesson, too. Let's see how many times I can stick myself," Randy said dejectedly.

"Sit over there," Toddler said, pointing to another arm chair. Randy dragged himself over, examined the chair for any errant springs, and after satisfying himself that no danger was lurking he settled into the chair.

"O.K., gentlemen. I want to check your notebooks for signatures of brothers. You're all supposed to have them completed by Sunday. I'll go through them while you take your pledge quiz this week. Pass them in."

We all reached into our pockets and passed our notebooks over to Toddler. Then he passed out our quizzes and began thumbing through the notebooks while we were taking the quiz.

I was a little anxious about Toddler going through my notebook. In the excitement of everything else that was going on I hadn't been too conscientious about getting the rest of the signatures I needed. I kept glancing over at Toddler, who was shaking his head disgustedly as he was going through the notebooks.

We finished our quizzes and passed them in to Toddler.

"Well, I've gone through your notebooks. Buddha, you're missing twelve signatures." He stared accusingly at Buddha, then stared at the rest of us. "And Buddha's got the most signatures of any of you. You guys are going to be in trouble if you don't get on the stick with your notebooks. What's the problem?" Toddler asked.

There was no response from any of us.

"I'm only gonna say it one more time. You guys have certain responsibilities. None of this stuff is too hard and the brothers are going to be watching you, so you'd better get your acts together.

"Now I want to talk about the scavenger hunt coming up this Saturday night and give you the ground rules again. Every year we do this scavenger hunt, giving the pledge class a chance to use its powers of deduction to find the brothers. The brothers will be hiding somewhere on campus with some cases of beer and you'll have three hours to find us. You'll be given clues that will lead you to other clues. Eventually the clues will lead you to where the brothers are hiding. You'll get your first clue on Saturday night at 7:00 sharp and you'll have until 10:00 to find us. You should all be at the house a little before 7:00 to get that clue. Do any of you have any questions about the scavenger hunt?"

"Are there any places on campus that are off limits for the brothers to be hiding that we can eliminate from consideration?" I asked.

"No. The entire campus is fair game for the brothers."

"Do we have to follow the clues, or can we just search around the campus without looking at them?" Buddha inquired. Toddler thought about that a moment, then replied.

"You aren't obligated to look for and follow the clues, if you don't want to. But the campus is pretty big and the chance of you finding the bros without the clues is pretty remote."

Yaz spoke up. "Are the brothers allowed to repeat any hiding place they used in the past?"

"Good question, Yaz. You would think of that. But yes, they are allowed to repeat locations. As I said before, the entire campus is fair game," Toddler responded. "Any other questions?" He looked over at Randy. "Do you have any questions, Dub?"

Randy looked at Toddler, then he looked around at the rest of us, a searching look in his eyes.

"Uh, uh,... how much beer will the brothers have?" he finally said. We all laughed.

"At least half a dozen cases," Toddler responded. "Anything else? Good. I'll see you all Saturday night – after 10:00 pm, I expect," he said facetiously.

We got our things together and went over to Mad Dog's dorm room to make plans for the hunt. It was the first time I had been there. One side of the room (the side Mad Dog's roommate used) looked like a normal dorm room. It had the requisite messy desk, unmade bed, dirty underwear on the floor, a few Playboy Magazines scattered around, a poster of Aerosmith and a movie poster of Russell Crowe in Gladiator on the wall.

The other side of the room looked like it had been transported in its entirety from a barracks in the Quantico Marine base. Everything on Mad Dog's side of the room was immaculately clean and orderly. Every object was in its place. The bed was made with the sheets and covers perfectly positioned and pulled so tightly that I expect you could have bounced a coin off it. On the walls were military posters of various sizes and descriptions. There was one of a Marine in full camouflage uniform and the caption, 'The more you sweat in peace, the less you bleed in war.' There was another one of troops running in camouflage uniforms, bearing the caption, 'Nobody ever drowned in sweat.' On the door of his closet there was a poster of Oliver North, with the caption, 'Patriot.'

We walked into the room and Mad Dog pulled over some chairs for us to sit on.

"Nice decorations, Mad Dog," Yaz said sarcastically. Mad Dog apparently didn't catch the sarcasm.

"Thanks. If only I could get rid of my dirt bag roommate and get someone normal in here, I could get the other side fixed up as nice as my side of the room. Hey, any of you guys want to see me bounce a coin off my bed?"

We declined, then sat down and began discussing the scavenger hunt.

"Yaz," I asked, "why did you ask if the brothers could repeat hiding places? Do you know where they've hidden in the past?"

"Sure. Last year they were in one of the women's bathrooms on the third floor of Lovejoy Hall. The year before that they were in the observatory of the astronomy building. And I think they were in the office of one of the English professors the year before. I heard that one year they even hid out in the Chancellor's office. I guess somebody had gotten a hold of a master key and they slipped in there."

"Wow, no wonder Toddler said to follow the clues," Buddha said.

"What kind of clues do they give?" I asked.

"Could be anything? They might give us a map, sort of like a treasure map, that will take us someplace to find another clue. We might get a poem to read or a riddle to solve. It could be anything. We just have to wait and see," Yaz replied.

"Maybe some of us should just search around campus instead of followin' clues," Randy piped in.

Mad Dog laughed. "Another good idea from the guy whose only question was how much beer the brothers would have with them."

We all laughed again. Then Buddha said, "Why did you ask that question, Dub?"

Randy looked around at us, shrugged his shoulders a little and said, "I dunno. I guess I jist figured that if they're drinkin' a lot they'll have to stay close to a pisser and maybe we can catch 'em running out to take a leak?"

We all looked at each other and smiles began to break out around the room.

"Hey, not bad. Who says there's nothing going on between those ears," Yaz exclaimed.

"Yeah, good one Randy," I said.

"It must be the suit and hat he's wearing. Something must have rubbed off from Cheever," Buddha suggested.

"Well, if there's one thing I know a lot about it's drinkin' beer and pissin' it out again," Randy added proudly.

"Randy, how goes it with the butler routine?" I asked.

"Not too good. I ruined a couple sets of clothes usin' that danged washin' machine. Mixed all the different colors together and used the real hot water. Well that turned everthin' pink and shrunk all my stuff. I'm thinkin' of sendin' the clothes to the Early Childhood Development Department. They can use 'em as doll clothes. I can just see 'em puttin' little pink boxer shorts on some of them dolls."

"Well, at least you're keeping your sense of humor about it," I said. Randy responded with one of those mirthless laughs you read about in classic novels.

"Speaking of Early Childhood Development, have you started yet, Mad Dog?" Buddha asked.

"No, next week. And I don't want to talk about it," he said gruffly. End of subject.

"How about you, Percy. When's the big day?"

"Tomorrow," I said. I told them about Tuney and Beeker helping me get ready and the plan to show up at the department dinner. They were suitably impressed, each offering to hang around and help out if I got into trouble.

"How about you, Yaz?" Mad Dog inquired. "When do you get to make your public debut?"

A worried look came over Yaz' face. "Next week they're taking me over to Quincy Market and Downtown Crossing in Boston at lunchtime to do it. I don't know if I can go through with it. I never mentioned this to anyone but...," he paused, "I have a public speaking phobia. I can't speak in front of crowds. I get paralyzed." His voice cracked.

We all started saying words of encouragement to him and patting him on the back. In a way it made me feel a little better knowing that I wasn't the only one who was having a hard time making a fool of myself.

As I walked back to my dorm room after our meeting I thought about all of our special projects and the thing I had to do tomorrow. I had to hand it to Sigmund and the other brothers. They sure knew how to make our pledge class come together fast. And I had the sneaking suspicion that they also knew how to make us find out what we had buried deep down inside ourselves. Pledging was certainly turning out to be a learning experience. I just hoped that I would still be around to appreciate it after tomorrow.

# SIXTEEN

Friday morning at last! Five minutes before my alarm clock was set to ring I shut it off. I'd slept fitfully the night before, waking up every hour or so. I'd look at the clock and note the time, then look over at Jeff, staring at me in his sleep across the dark room, before rolling over to try to fall asleep again.

But how was I to sleep? I had too much on my mind. It wasn't enough that I was going to try to impersonate Percy Jordan today and maybe get my ass thrown out of school. I also had my first (and maybe my last) date with Karen tonight.

That thought was almost driven from my mind because I was so anxious about Percy. I would think about my Percy impersonation and fret for a while over that. Then I'd begin to calm down. Just as I had calmed myself down enough to begin dozing off to sleep again, the thought of my date with Karen would pop into my head, and jerk me instantly awake again. It was a vicious cycle.

Assuming that I got through the Chemistry Department dinner all right, what was I going to do with Karen? Should we go to a movie in Harvard Square? Should we just go out to one of the bars in Central Square and have a few drinks? Maybe we could crash a party on campus? Or would she like to go to one of the nightclubs over by Fenway Park?

I weighed these and other options in my head, finally deciding on a movie and then drinks. *Kung Fu Hustle* was still playing in the Square. Karen was interested in martial arts. Maybe she hadn't seen it yet? Buddha didn't like it much but Karen would probably like it. That would put her in a good mood. Then after the movie we could go to a quiet bar, have a few drinks and get to know each other better.

Having settled that in my mind I started to drift off again, only to start awake as I thought about contingency plans if she had already seen the film and didn't want to see it again. Images of disasters with my date and with the Chemistry Department dinner kept penetrating my thoughts, preventing me from sleeping soundly.

I was actually relieved that it was now time to get up. I dragged myself out of bed, grabbed my towel and toiletries kit, and made my way down the hall to the bathroom, deep in thought about the events of the day to come. I planned to attend my morning classes, then hide out in the library for a few hours right after lunch to do some homework and study. I'd call Karen to see if she wanted to see a movie and make arrangements to meet up with her later. Then around 4:00 pm I'd head back to my room to change into my Percy Jordan wardrobe and practice speaking like him. The dinner would begin about 6:00 pm, so I should have plenty of time to get everything done and try to relax my nerves a little before the dinner.

The day was going as planned until just after I finished lunch. As I was walking over to the library I remembered that I hadn't called Karen yet. I ducked into the nearest building to find a pay phone. I was so preoccupied that I hadn't noticed it was the Chemistry Building.

I found a pay phone in the lobby area and dialed the phone number for Karen Kim that I had looked up in the student phone directory. Busy. Oh, great! I hung up and decided to wait a few minutes to dial again. As I started to dial, I heard a woman's voice coming from behind me.

"I s'pose you're calling one of them bimbos you've been hittin' on when you thought I wasn't looking?" The voice was infected with an almost overpowering Boston accent.

I turned around. Confronting me was a girl (I mean woman), probably about twenty years old, with big, black hair. In fact, her hair was teased up so high that it looked something like the hair on one of those Wishnik troll dolls. She was wearing too much make-up and long dangly earrings that made her look like a gypsy.

She was staring at me with venom in her eyes. Each of her hands was balled up into a tight fist, and her fists were resting against her hips in an attitude of expectation and defiance. She had on a tight stretchy pink T shirt that was about two sizes too small for her. Across her enormous breasts were the words "Italian Stallion." Maybe she was a Rocky fan?

She wore very tight designer jeans which molded to her curves and high spike heels. I had never seen her before but my first guess was that she might be a hooker. Why was she so angry with me? I stood there silent, gaping at her.

"Don't give me that innocent routine," she almost spat at me. "D'you think I'm stupid? D'you think I don't know what's been going on?"

I started doing an involuntary imitation of Porky Pig as I stuttered, trying to get out a response. But before I could say anything, she lit into me again, the index finger of her right hand now pointing accusingly at me. Amazingly, I didn't hear the letter "r" pronounced once in her diatribe.

"You listen to me, Percy Jordan. You think you're wicked clever but you're not as smart as you think. I'm on to you! You told me that you loved me. You promised me that I was the only one for you and you wouldn't go out with anyone else ever again. Well, I'm holdin' you to it. You think about it, Percy. You think about it. I'll be at the Daily Catch tonight at 7pm. That's the restaurant on Hanover Street in the North End, just below my apartment. You be there at 7pm tonight and you be ready to apologize to me and keep your promise or I swear…," she paused, her eyes darting wildly around. "I swear, I'll leave you and I'll turn you in to the cops and that'll be the end of your play money!"

She continued to look at me with those wild, angry eyes, and then turned on her spike heels and stormed out of the building. I stood there dumbstruck, feeling like a trailer park that was just grazed by a tornado – happy that it had missed me but feeling a new sense of vulnerability.

"Jeeees-zus!" I said aloud, shocked and amazed by what had just taken place. That was surreal! And what kind of kinky shit was Percy Jordan doing? I was just glad that I was going to do my impersonation later that day and not have anything further to do with Percy Jordan's seamy personal life again!

Then it dawned on me. She thought I was Percy. I wasn't even wearing my glasses or the type of clothes he normally wears and I fooled his girlfriend. I must really look like him, and if I can fool his girlfriend I should be able to fool anyone. All right, so I didn't say anything – a minor issue. I was going to work on that this afternoon. I'd get the voice down, no problem.

I was still pondering this, but feeling pretty confident nonetheless, as I started to leave the building. Suddenly I remembered why I was there. I moved back to the pay phone and dialed Karen's phone number again. This time it rang!

"Hello?"

"Uh, hello. Is Karen there?"

"This is she."

"Oh, hi, Karen. Uh, this is a Jerry... You know, from Tae Kwon Do class?" I added.

"Hello."

"Um, I was calling you about getting together tonight? Remember, we had a – we we're going to do something together?"

"Yes?"

"I, uh, have to do something earlier tonight. But I was thinking, maybe we could go to a movie in Harvard Square, and then get a drink?" I paused to get a reaction. There was none. "Is that O.K. with you?"

"I guess so. What time do you want to meet?"

"8:30? At the Out-Of-Town Newsstand in the Square?"

"O.K. I'll see you there. Bye."

She hung up and I let out a sigh of relief. That was a load off my mind. Now I could focus on the other load on my mind – impersonating Percy Jordan at the dinner!

I turned to leave when I was stopped by another female voice calling to me from behind. This time it was an elderly female voice, made rough and shaky, no doubt, by too many cigarettes over the years.

"Mr. Jordan, there you are. May I have a word with you?"

The sound of the voice shot through me like a lightning bolt. I hadn't had a chance to warm up my Percy Jordan vocal chords yet today. I didn't want to have to perform without at least a little rehearsal. I turned around slowly, with trepidation, desperately trying to think of what I should do to extricate myself from this potential disaster standing a few feet in front of me.

The potential disaster was a short, plump, elderly woman, with a healthy dose of foundation make-up, a little touch of rouge at the cheeks, and a light-colored lipstick covering her wrinkled lips. She had short, bristly gray hair that had been professionally cut and styled fairly recently. She wore a white knit blouse, gray slacks that matched her hair and on her ears, large, red clip-on earrings – the only source of color anywhere on her body other than on her face where she had applied the make up. I recognized her. I had seen her working up in the Chemistry Department office the last time I had been up there.

I didn't say a word, still too terrified that if I opened my mouth I'd spoil everything. I just stared at her with a supercilious sneer the way I expected that the real Percy Jordan would react to her. I waited. She walked up to me, a little out of breath, owing no doubt to the fact that she had been waddling over to me as fast as her short little legs could carry her.

"Mr. Jordan, Professor Harnash has been looking everywhere for you. He told me that if I saw you I should send you right over to his office immediately." She looked around as if making sure that no one else was around who might be listening. "He says it has something to do with you missing some labs and office hours," she whispered in a tone that suggested she was giving me a warning.

I continued looking at her with my sneer glued to my face. She stared at me, a puzzled look coming over her face. But still I said nothing.

"Well, are you going up to the professor's office?" she inquired.

My mind raced. What should I do and say? Should I say anything? Won't she get suspicious if I just stare at her like Harpo Marx? I decided that I had better say something. In my best Percy Jordan voice, which I masked somewhat with my hand, I cleared my throat and said, "Some other time." Then turning, I quickly walked out of the door to the Chemistry Building and proceeded on to my dormitory at as fast a clip as I could muster without raising suspicion. I suspect that I looked a little like one of those Olympic race walkers as I traversed the campus but no one stopped me and I returned to my dormitory room safely.

I had planned to spend the next few hours in the library, but these last two chance encounters with members of the Percy Jordan fan club had convinced me that the better course was to lay low until the dinner. I didn't want to be confused with Percy again until I was good and ready.

I returned to the Chem Building about 6:15 pm, wearing my glasses and dressed in the usual Percy Jordan uniform of jeans and a plaid shirt. When I looked in the mirror I had to admit that my resemblance to Percy was uncanny. Cutting and darkening my hair made all the difference in the world, and the glasses were the icing on the cake. Percy's own mother wouldn't have been able to tell us apart from appearance alone – at least, not unless he had some hidden tattoos or birth marks in places I wouldn't care to think about.

My voice was something altogether different. I had spent the afternoon in my dorm room practicing my Percy Jordan voice and accent. Unfortunately, I didn't have a recording of his voice for comparison. So my efforts really involved trying to make my voice sound as much like my memory of how his voice sounded when I heard him last. Who knew how good my memory was on that point? I'd done my best and I had to hope it was good enough, unless I could spot Beeker quickly and let him hear me speak before I spoke with anyone else.

I made my way warily into the lobby of the building, keeping my eyes peeled for Jordan. He was number one on my list of people I didn't want to run into tonight. Professor Harash was probably a close second, given the fact that he apparently was planning to chew Jordan out for missing his labs and office hours. Don't get me wrong. I had nothing against Jordan getting his ass chewed out. In fact, I was all in favor of it happening, as often as possible. But I preferred that it happen with him present rather than with me standing in for him. After all, I wanted him to enjoy the experience, too.

The dinner was supposed to take place in the Faculty Lounge. I looked at the building directory and saw that the Lounge was on the second floor. I decided to walk up the stairs rather than taking the elevator where I might run into someone I didn't want to see. I climbed the stairs slowly, listening for any sound of someone coming. There were no sounds except my footsteps and my heart beats, which were almost drowning out the sound of my footsteps.

I arrived at the second floor landing and crept slowly over to the door. I cracked the door slightly and peered out. I gave a short sigh of relief. There was no one in the hallway but Beeker, looking at his watch, then at the elevator, while pacing nervously back and forth. I called out to him in a hushed tone.

"Beeker!"

There are some insects that can jump straight up into the air, many times their height, from a standing still position. A grasshopper is one that comes to mind. Well, when I called out his name, Beeker came as close as is humanly possible to resembling a grasshopper. Who said white men can't jump? With a startled yell Beeker leaped straight up into the air. I don't know how high he actually got, but it was high enough for his head to bang against the plastic "Exit" sign, which came crashing down on top of him as he fell against the wall and crumpled to the floor.

"Beeker! Beeker! Are you all right?" I yelled, rushing to his side. He moaned, rubbing his head, and looked up at me from where he lay in a heap on the floor.

"Don't sneak up on me like that. With all the coffee I drink it might be fatal!" He started to get up and I noticed that he was shaking. That was a good sign. He always shook from the massive doses of caffeine he ingested. If he wasn't shaking I would have been worried.

"Sorry," I apologized. "I was just trying to get your attention so we could talk before I went in there. Can we go somewhere to talk where no one will see me?"

Beeker and I looked around fast and then ducked into the Men's Room. We checked under the stalls to make sure no one was in there and then Beeker said, "O.K. We've gotta relax. There's nothing to worry about. I already checked out the room and Jordan's not there."

"How about Harnash? Is he there?" I asked.

"No. He never comes to these dinners. Why?"

I explained how Percy had missed his labs and some office hours this week and how Harnash was apparently on the warpath about it.

"Jeez!" exclaimed Beeker. "What a stupid thing to do – pissing off Harnash! Harnash brings in more government research money than most of the rest of the professors combined. He's got the most clout in the department. Jordan's ass is grass. Just wait and see."

"That's fine with me just as long as it isn't my ass impersonating his when it happens!"

"The Faculty Lounge is just down the hall. Lemme go in first so I can tell Sigmund, Pygmy and Dub that you're here. Then…"

"They're here?" I asked, surprised.

"Sure. A lot of guys wanted to come and watch but they can see it on the videotape."

"Videotape? What videotape?" I asked.

"This is for the Social Psych Department. It's got to be videotaped."

"But how are you gonna videotape it?"

"Don't worry about that. You just give me a couple of minutes and then walk in like you own the place. And remember, you're supposed to be 'Good Percy'. That's what Sigmund said will really mess people up. So no matter how they react to you, you be the nicest guy in the world. O.K.?"

I nodded. "Hey, Beeker. Listen to the way I speak and let me know if it sounds like Jordan."

"Go ahead."

I said a few sentences and Beeker grinned.

"Sounds perfect to me!" I beamed back at him, feeling a little more confident than I had before.

Beeker went to the door, peeked out quickly, looking from side to side, and then gave me a thumbs-up sign as he left. I looked at my watch. It was 6:25 pm. I gave him two minutes, then peeked out the door. The corridor was empty.

I walked up to a dark wooden door containing a large pane of opaque textured glass. Stenciled across the glass in gold letters were the words "Faculty Lounge." I could hear voices coming from the other side of the door. This was it. I took a deep breath, and then swung the door open so hard that it crashed against the doorstop with a very loud bang. I strode into the room.


Cinderella couldn't have asked for a grander entrance than I was making. Thanks to the adrenaline rush that made me swing the door too hard and the corresponding crash that followed, all eyes were on me as I entered the room. From the looks of surprise plastered on the faces of the persons assembled, I gathered that Percy Jordan was not a frequent visitor at the department dinners. And from the frowns on many other faces, I gathered that most of the people in the room shared my dislike for Mr. Jordan.

Reflexively, I responded by screwing my face up into the sneer that I had seen so often on Percy Jordan's face. But then remembering that I was not supposed to be the heavy, I relaxed my face into a more benign expression and moved on into the room.


The Faculty Lounge was an Art Deco affair, with dark brown woodwork and white walls. The light fixtures were cream-colored globes circled with metal rings – they looked something like little Saturn planets floating on chains that dropped from the ceiling. There were matching wall sconces made up of half-globes with rings around them dotting the walls at intervals. A sickly yellow glow filtered out into the room from the light fixtures, giving everyone in the room a jaundiced look. Light also came into the room through several large picture windows.

The floor was covered with an industrial-grade, olive colored carpet. At the back of the room the wall was concealed behind a set of bookshelves overcrowded with chemistry books, newspapers, magazines and assorted papers. In front of the bookshelves was a large green plastic trash can labeled, "Recycling."

Scattered throughout the room were over-sized brown leather chairs with small brown leather hassocks and a sofa. On several large, dark tables near the front of the room were assorted foods in chafing dishes with sterno flames beneath, a coffee urn, soft drinks and an ice tub filled with cans of beer and a few bottles of wine. There were also several newspaper and magazine-covered coffee tables located throughout the room.

I sauntered up to the food and drinks tables, nodding to people as I went. I recognized a number of the graduate students but no one else. I selected a Budweiser beer, popped open the can and took a long swig.

"Care for an hors d'oeuvre?" someone asked from behind me. I turned around. Standing in front of me, dressed in black pants, a white shirt and a black clip-on bow tie, was Sigmund. He was holding a tray of crackers covered with something that resembled animal droppings.

"What's on those crackers?" I asked, intrigued.

"Looks like guano," Sigmund replied. "I wouldn't eat them if I were you."

"What are you doing here?" I asked.

"Just watching your back, my friend. If you get into any trouble we'll cover you. Just relax and have fun."

"I heard Pygmy and Randy are here, too. Where are they?" I asked, looking around.

"Oh, they're around. Don't worry about them. Just stick to business. Here, someone's coming," Sigmund said quickly, handing me one of the crackers. I took it just as one of the Teaching Assistants for my chemistry class, Laura Wellman, came up to me.

"Well Percy, I'm surprised to see you here," she said coldly.

"I had to come. I missed seeing your lovely face," I said in my best Percy accent without any trace of sarcasm in my voice. "Here, have an hors d'oeuvre." I handed her the guano delight cracker, smiling pleasantly.

She stared at me with a perplexed look on her face. But she accepted the cracker and took a bite. "Umm, that's good. What is it?"

"Don't ask," Sigmund replied, walking away.

"So Percy, where have you been over the past few days? I heard you missed your lab. Harnash was livid. Has he found you yet?"

I waved my hand in a way that suggested that I was unconcerned.

"Had a spot of domestic trouble with my significant other," I said nonchalantly.

"Which one?" she asked mockingly.

I wondered whether she knew any of Percy's girlfriends. I sure didn't know any of their names. Was she playing with me or did she really expect an answer? I decided I had better answer.

"Which one do you think?" I said playfully, smiling at her. That threw her off again. She stared at me quizzically. Then she nodded as though she was ready to play the game and answered.

"Well, let's see. I guess I have three choices... or are there more?"

"No, no. Just three," I said pleasantly, bluffing.

"All right. I'd say the most likely candidate is the blond bombshell, hard-hearted Svetlana Olaf. She's the meanest of your three girlfriends, so I'd vote her most likely to give you domestic troubles." She looked at me inquiringly. I tried to look back as non-committal as possible, saying nothing. Laura was not mincing words in describing Percy's girlfriend. Svetlana must be the blond I had seen with Percy in the bar when he started abusing the waitress.

"No? Then my second guess is your red-headed friend, Bridget. When I saw her at the park with Professor Byerson's kids the other day she didn't seem too happy with you. Is she the one?"

Again, I tried not to give anything away. I just looked at her, smiling slightly.

"Not her either? Then it must be your friend with the big hair from Revere or the North End. What's her name?"

Panic hit me. Now I was in trouble. That must be the woman who had accosted me earlier in the day. I knew where she lived but she never told me her name. I stalled.

"She lives in the North End," I said.

"O.K. But what's her name again? Josey, isn't it?"

"Uh... yeah," I replied.

"Is she your domestic problem?" Laura asked, a knowing look on her face.

"This week," I replied, grinning. Just then another graduate student, Nikesh Rastinjani, sauntered up to us.

"Hey, Nicky. Percy says he's been a.w.o.l. because of domestic problems," Laura said to him. "Nicky and I had been speculating on what might have happened to you," she explained to me.

"You're going to have a lot more than domestic troubles when Harnash gets his hands on you. He'll have you deported back to the U.K. when he sees you," Nicky said, the glee in his voice undisguised. "I'm surprised you had the nerve to show up here. But then again, I suppose you knew that Harnash never comes to these dinners."

"Well, he's missing out on a smashing good time then," I replied in my sincerest voice.

Nicky looked at me strangely, his brow wrinkled.

"Have you got a cold or something? You sound different," he said.

"I think I am coming down with something. You better stay back. I wouldn't want you to catch something from me."

"You've become quite the altruist lately," he remarked coldly. "What's the matter. Are you looking for people to speak up for you with Harnash when he throws you out of the department? ... If you are you're wasting your time on me."

"Not at all," I replied. "Whatever Professor Harnash does to me is no more than I deserve. I know I haven't been the kindest bloke around in the past and I regret it, that's all."

I smiled at both of them. They looked at me, then at each other, then back at me again with questioning looks on their faces. I took another gulp of my beer, trying to think of something else to say to keep the conversation going.

"So why doesn't the good professor attend these soirees?" I asked jovially. Nicky and Laura looked at each other and laughed.

"Probably because they wouldn't let his girlfriends attend," Nicky replied. "You'd know something about that," he added nastily. I pretended I didn't understand him.

"No, I didn't know he had a girlfriend. I thought he was married," I said.

"Girlfriends – plural! And of course he's married. But the women I've seen him with coming out of the Charles Hotel sure weren't his wife," Laura whispered in a conspiratorial tone, looking around to make sure no one heard her.

133

That old fox Harnash. Who'd have thunk it? He sure didn't look like the kind of guy that would attract women.

I went to take another sip of my beer when I realized I had finished it.

"I'm going to get another beer. Would either of you like something? I'll be happy to get it for you." They just stared at me again. I guess Percy offering to do anything for them was unexpected.

"Well, then. Cheerio," I said, walking over to the beer table. I got another can of Budweiser and began walking over toward the bookshelves. I glanced casually in the direction of Nicky and Laura. They were still together, staring at me and talking animatedly. I guess that Percy's personality transformation was having some effect on people. I only hoped that I could keep it up without anyone catching on that I was an imposter.

I was musing on this when I heard a "Pssst." I looked around but no one was standing anywhere near me. I began looking at the bookshelves when I heard it again.

"Pssst. Pssst."

I looked all around the room again but no one was there.

"Down here," a voice whispered.

I looked down. All I saw was the green rubber trash can with the "Recycling" sign on it. Then I noticed the lid of the trash can move slightly. I blinked. Was it really moving? It moved again and I saw it crack open a tiny amount. There was an eye staring at me from the crack. I looked around the room to make sure no one was looking. Then I leaned over, lifted the trash can lid slightly while I pretended to throw something in it. As I lifted the lid I saw Pygmy in the trash can holding a camcorder.

"Pyg... I mean Tino. What are you doing in here?"

"I'm videotaping, obviously. And you're not giving me much to videotape. Put my lid down and keep mingling with people," he said in an irritated voice. I quickly dropped the lid and heard a thump.

"Ouch. Be careful!" came up out of the trash can.

"Sorry," I whispered. I looked carefully at the front of the trash can and noticed, for the first time, that one of the "C"s in "Recycling" was cutout and there was a hole behind it. I could just make out the camera lens in the hole. So that's how he was doing it! Pretty clever.

I looked around again. No one seemed to have noticed me talking to the trash can. That would shake them up a little, too, I thought. Now where should I go? I saw a group of three older professor-types, clustered together, talking. I decided that I had to mingle with them sooner or later, so I might as well get it over with now. I took another sip of my beer for liquid courage, then walked over and joined their little cluster.

"Good evening," I opened. They all looked at me like I was a cancerous growth. I tried again.

"These department dinners are a smashing idea, don't you think? I wish I had attended them more often. I'm certainly not going to miss another one," I commented in what I hoped came across as a jovial voice, but which sounded more nervous than jovial to me.

One of the professors, a tall severe-looking man with gray-flecked hair, glasses and a goatee, dressed in a tweed jacket and woven tie, looked at me over the top of his glasses. After regarding me for what seemed like minutes he spoke in a deep baritone voice.

"Mr. Jordan. Based on what I've heard from Professor Harnash, I have a suspicion that you will not have many more opportunities to enjoy these dinners. I suggest that you make the most of this one."

I gulped, but tried my best not to be intimidated.

"You're probably right. I have been remiss lately and I intend to apologize to Professor Harnash when I see him and try to make it up to him. I've really been so lucky having the opportunity to work with someone so talented," I said, sincerity dripping from my tongue.

The three professors all had surprised expressions on their faces, and they looked at each other, saying nothing. But after a very uncomfortable period of silence, one of them, an Asian-American woman who appeared to be in her early 50s, with short black hair, wire-rimmed glasses and a conservative-looking navy business suit, broke the silence.

"Well, that's what I want to hear. Professor Harnash said that you had been very disrespectful toward him. You should be ashamed of yourself acting like that! And from what I've seen, your behavior toward the other graduate students is no better. I hope you apologize to all of them."

"Oh, I intend to," I said. "I have behaved terribly. I've had some domest... uh, personal problems. But I've seen the error of my ways," I said regretfully. The three professors seemed to soften a little at that. I excused myself to get something to eat.

I was walking toward the food table again, just passing another group of graduate students who were speaking with another professor-type, when someone called out, "Mr. Jordan, I'd like a word with you."

I glanced in that direction and saw that it had come from the professor-type, a rotund man in his 40s with brilliant red hair and a brilliant red face. I walked over to him and he eyed me coolly. The other graduate assistants standing around likewise didn't appear to be members of the Percy Fan Club.

"Yes, sir. I'm always happy to oblige. And isn't it a splendid evening?" I said, greeting all of them pleasantly. The now familiar surprised looks came over their faces.

"Uh, yes, I suppose it is," the professor said, warily. "Are you all right, Mr. Jordan? You haven't sustained any closed head injuries lately, have you?"

"Couldn't be better, professor," I replied, ebulliently.

The professor and graduate students looked at each other, then at me, perplexed looks on their faces.

"So how may I help you?" I asked.

"Excuse me?" the professor replied.

"You called me over." He stared blankly at me.

"Oh, so I did... Are you sure you're all right? You sound different."

"I'm jolly good. Fit as a fiddle. Couldn't be better. What did you want to ask me?"

Neither he nor the graduate students knew what to make of me, but the professor regained his composure.

"Aren't you helping Professor Harnash with that research project he's been doing for the government – the one involving permeable membrane fuel cell technology?"

Panic seized me again. I had no idea if Jordan was helping Prof. Harnash with that project and I had no idea what permeable membrane fuel cell technology was. I had to think fast!

"Ah, bi, duh, ah, bi, duh," I replied. So much for fast thinking.

"Excuse me?" the professor stared, clearly not comprehending my very lucid reply. I had to do better than "Ah, bi, duh, ah, bi, duh." I decided to gamble again.

"I meant, yes. I'm working with him on that project."

"Splendid. I thought you were. Could you explain your research to us?"

"Excuse me?" I gulped.

"Your research. You know, describe the complex chemical reactions that permit the fuel cells to release energy."

I guess I lost that gamble, I thought to myself. How was I going to get out of this one? At this point I could barely explain how to get to the Chemistry Building, let alone how some cutting edge chemical technology worked. The minute I opened my mouth on this one they'd figure out that I was an imposter.

"I'm glad you asked me about that. It really is a fascinating new technology," I said, glancing around the room quickly as I stalled for time. I saw Beeker and caught his eye. He must have recognized that "deer in the headlights" look in my eye because he hustled over to our little group immediately after I looked at him, spilling his drink as he arrived.

"Oops, sorry," Beeker said, trying to mop up some of his drink from the professor's shoe.

"Oh, look," I said. "It's Beck... I mean, Douglas Flintlock. Douglas do you know everyone here?" He did. There were greetings all around.

"So," Beeker said. "What is everyone discussing?" Bad opening, I thought. I had hoped that he would change the subject but the fool was taking us right back to it.

"Mr. Jordan was just about to explain to us the research project he is doing with Professor Harnash," the professor replied.

"Oh," Beeker croaked. I wondered if my face looked as panic-stricken at that moment as Beeker's. I was glad that he recognized the gravity of the situation. Now all he had to do was find a solution.

"Uh, isn't that top secret government information? I thought you couldn't reveal information about government research," Beeker said, giving me a knowing look and trying to read whether I had caught his drift. I had. I gave him a subtle wink to let him know all was well with the world again. I was about to say that I couldn't talk about the research – top secret, hush-hush, can't say and all that rot, when the professor chimed in.

"No, this research will be used by the defense department, no doubt. But Professor Harnash told me it's being funded by the Dept. of Energy, ostensibly for non-defense applications. So it's not top secret. Otherwise Mr. Jordan here, who is not a U.S. citizen, couldn't work on it because he doesn't have a security clearance. Isn't that right, Mr. Jordan?"

My hopes were dashed. I felt as crestfallen as Beeker looked.

"So tell us about the research," the professor asked again.

I looked at Beeker. He looked at me. It was clear that neither of us had another plan. I was getting ready to confess that I was an imposter when fate intervened. Well, it wasn't really fate. It was Randy Bradford, which is almost as good.

Just as I was about to respond I heard Randy's voice. I turned to look and there was Randy, dressed in Cheever's butler uniform, complete with white gloves and derby, barreling toward us carrying a tray containing a chafing dish of mini egg rolls. Beneath the chafing dish was a lit can of sterno, keeping the food warm. Randy was asking people if they wanted an egg roll, but he was not stopping to give them any egg rolls.

I figured he had seen my distress signal and he was coming over to lend a hand. But Randy was not the most graceful butler that ever buttled. Clearly he was out of his element. The chafing dish was precariously balanced on the tray and rocking from side to side as he moved, and the sterno sliding back and forth as Randy pitched and rolled with each step.

Randy was a study in grim determination. With tongue sticking out the corner of his mouth and his eyes glued to the chafing dish, he wobbled toward us, trying to keep the chafing dish and sterno on the tray. But he was concentrating so hard on the chafing dish and sterno that he didn't notice a small brown leather hassock in front of one of the armchairs. As he came to the hassock, he tripped, causing the chafing dish, egg rolls and sterno to go flying. We were all pelted with mini egg rolls that felt like mini-bricks as they hit us.

The chafing dish landed on Beeker's foot, causing him to clutch his foot in his hand and begin jumping around while yelling that his foot had been broken. In the meantime, the lit can of sterno landed on a nearby coffee table, immediately igniting some newspapers that had been placed on the table.

Pandemonium broke out. People were running around the room, yelling and trying to find a fire extinguisher. While hopping around Beeker collided with the professor and one of the grad students, leaving them lying in a heap on the floor. Beeker continued his whirling dervish act and struck one of the bookcases, causing half the books to fall, mostly on his head.

The fire spread to the coffee table itself and I tried to beat it out with some large journals. Sigmund came over with a towel and also began beating on the flames, trying to douse the fire. By this time Randy was back on his feet and yelling.

"What are you guys tryin' to do?"

"We're trying to smother the flames," Sigmund yelled back.

"I can smother them," Randy replied. He ran to the table where the food and drinks had been, picked up the tub of ice, and ran back toward us, throwing the contents of the ice tub toward the burning coffee table and us. Sigmund and I were both struck by ice cubes and ice water, causing us to fall back away from the coffee table and hit the floor. But that partially doused the fire. Randy then removed his jacket and used it to beat out the remaining flames.

The room was now quite peaceful. Most of the people who had been at the dinner had run out of the room when the fire began and the few remaining people were standing around the room with shocked looks on their faces. Randy was standing next to what was left of the coffee table and the debris of the burnt newspapers, grinning. Sigmund and I sat on the floor, our clothes wet from the water. Pink welts were rising on our faces where we had been pelted with the ice cubes. Beeker, lying in a heap of books in front of a tipped bookcase, was just beginning to stir.

"Well, that was exciteratin', wasn't it?" Randy exclaimed while beginning to dust off his jacket. He began collecting some of the debris scattered about the floor.

"Sure was," I agreed, not really knowing what exciteratin' meant.

Sigmund got up, feeling the welts on his face. He winced as he touched them.

"Dub, what possessed you to bring the chafing dish and the lit sterno over on the tray, as opposed to just putting the food on a plate and carrying it around?" Sigmund inquired.

"I didn't want it to git cold," Randy said, defensively. Sigmund just shook his head with a look of disbelief on his face. Randy cowered, figuring he was in big trouble now. But then Sigmund brightened.

"Well, it's over now. And fortunately no one got hurt," Sigmund exclaimed. Then he winced again. "Or at least, no one got hurt too much." Randy looked relieved.

I got up and walked over to Beeker to help him up. He had a nice shiner around his left eye but otherwise seemed unscathed. He groaned a few times and then dusted himself off.

"Wow, talk about being saved by the bell!" he chirped, and winked at me with his undamaged eye. I winked back.

"Well, blokes. It appears that this dinner is over. I've had a corker of a time," I said in a voice loud enough for the remaining Chemistry Dept. personnel to hear me. "Best be shoving off."

"Wait, I'll go with you," Randy said, forgetting that he was supposed to be working at the event. He looked down and noticed that he was now holding a huge mound of soggy, filthy, burnt newspapers and magazines in his arms. "Just have to get rid of these."

Sigmund, Beeker and I yelled, "No," all at the same time but it was too late. Randy had crossed the room, pulled the lid up off of the trash can with the "Recycling" sign on it, dumped the mound of dirty, wet debris in the trash can and replaced the lid. He started walking away from the trash can, then stopped and a surprised look came over his face. He stood there for a few seconds, looked back at the trashcan and then looked at us in a questioning way, as if to say, "Did I just do what I think I did?" We all nodded, "Yes."

A pained expression came back over Randy's face and he croaked, "Oops!"

# SEVENTEEN

I looked at my watch again – 8:15 pm. I'd been standing in front of the Out-of-Town Newsstand at Harvard Square since 8:00 pm. Now that my impersonation of Percy Jordan was completed, and I was still a student in good standing, I felt as though half the weight of the world was off me. Now I just had to get through this date with Karen Kim and I could relax.

All right. I know I shouldn't be comparing my impersonation of Percy to a date with Karen. Impersonating Percy was something I had to do. My date with Karen was something I wanted to do, wasn't it?

As I stood there thinking about it I realized that there were similarities between both. No one really forced me to impersonate Percy. I could have decided not to do it. But I wanted to test myself, to see if I could do it. And I'd succeeded – more or less with a little help. My date with Karen was also going to be a challenge. I liked her – at least I think I did. Or maybe it was curiosity that attracted me to her. Whatever it was, I wanted to get to know her better but she also intimidated the hell out of me. I was looking forward to this date. But I was also scared to death.

Now I knew what Dickens meant when he wrote, "They were the best of times. They were the worst of times." That's what it was like for me. There was conflict and contradiction in just about every aspect of my life now. I guess that's part of the growing process. "So get used to it, buddy-boy," I told myself.

8:20 pm. – only ten minutes to go. I hoped that she wouldn't be late. I didn't think I could take the anxiety. I could hear my heart beating above the din of the crowd – students, tourists and the Young Republicans, which is what I called the punk rocker local kids who hung out in Harvard Square with their skateboards, pierced body parts and purple hair. They were all there, eating, talking, listening to street performers playing music. And my heart was thumping right in time with the music.

I had begun to muse on where we'd go after the movie when I felt a tap on my shoulder. I turned around and there was Karen, wearing jeans, a red cotton print shirt, a navy sweater vest and most importantly, a friendly smile. She looked great!

I smiled back. Then a frown came to her face.

"What happened to you?" she asked.

"Excuse me?"

"What happened to you – your face?"

"Oh, that," I said. "I got hit by some ice cubes."

"Ice cubes? How did that happen?"

"It's a long story. I'll tell you about it later. We should check out the movie schedule."

We walked over to the movie theatre. I suggested that we see *Kung Fu Hustle*. But Karen had already seen it. So instead we saw *Shall We Dance*, which Karen wanted to see to compare with the Japanese original. I would have selected something else if I was on my own, but that night I was going to be as agreeable as I possibly could to keep her in a good mood. Anyway, the movie turned out to be pretty entertaining, for a chick-flick.

We arrived just as the movie previews were beginning so we didn't have time to talk until after the movie ended. After the film we decided to go to the Hong Kong to have a drink. The Hong Kong is a local Chinese restaurant that had become a real icon in Harvard Square.

We entered the restaurant, and fought our way up the stairs to the bar. It was packed, but thanks to Karen's quick eyes we were able to snag a table just as another couple was getting up to go.

Firmly settled at our little table, we ordered drinks. All around us people were reveling, drinking the contents of scorpion bowls

– large ceramic bowls filled with a high-octane concoction that the customers drank through multiple long, spindly straws. We watched the other customers and talked about the movie while we waited for our drinks. But once our drinks arrived I tried to shift the conversation away from the movie and onto more substantive matters.

"Hey, on that preview we saw for the Korean movie, were you reading the subtitles or do you speak Korean?"

"A little of both. We speak Korean occasionally around the house so I understood a lot of what was being said." She sipped her drink and appeared to be thinking. Then she looked at me.

"So, you were going to tell me how you got hit in the face with ice cubes." Her face darkened. "I'll bet it was stupid frat hazing, wasn't it?"

I laughed and told her the story of Percy Jordan and my project to impersonate him. I included the parts about his various girlfriends, what he was like as a Teaching Assistant, his recent hooky playing and the trouble he was in with Professor Harnash, and I gave her a blow-by-blow description of the earlier events of the day. She was clicking her tongue throughout, trying to look very severe and disgusted with everything, but I could tell that she was holding back laughs at least part of the time.

"And that's the end of my woeful tale."

"So what happened to the little guy, the one you call Pygmy?" she asked.

"Well, he couldn't come out of the trash can until all the other Chemistry Dept. folks left the room. So I guess he was in there, covered with wet, dirty newspapers for about half an hour.

"When he finally came out he was madder than a wet hen – I think he looked a little like a wet hen, too. Sigmund had expected that. He sent Randy away before Pygmy came out. I guess Sigmund talked to him and calmed him down. The video apparently came out fine. I haven't seen it yet. I still have to look at it before I write up my report for the Social Psych Department."

Karen clicked her tongue again.

"You know, that was a really stupid thing you did. You could have been expelled. Those guys were real jerks to make you do that."

"They didn't make me. Yaz – he's another one of the pledges – he told us that a few years ago two of the pledges refused to do the projects they were assigned. Nothing happened to them. They were just given other boring projects to do. So I could have gotten out of this if I'd really wanted to. I did it for the challenge." She shook her head.

"Well, then maybe you're a little crazy, too."

"Life would be pretty boring if we weren't all a little crazy," I replied. She sat there thinking about that for awhile and then grinned at me.

"Maybe you're right," she said. "But I'm still not a fan of frats and I never will be."

"I can live with that... if you'll go out with me again sometime."

"I'll think about it," she responded, but in a serious tone, indicating that she really was going to have to think about it.

"Are you ready to get outta here?" I said, looking at my watch and seeing that it was almost 1:00 am.

"Sure."

I went with her back to her dorm.

"Thanks for the evening. I had a good time. I'll see you at Tae Kwon Do," she said while opening the outside door to her dorm.

"Yeah, I had fun, too. That was a great movie suggestion." There was no offer for me to go inside and no signal to me that I should give her a goodnight kiss. We stood there uncomfortably looking at each other for a while longer, then she broke the silence.

"Good night."

"Uh, yeah. Good night," I replied, and she was gone.

I was mentally kicking myself as I walked back to my dorm room. What a wimp I was. I should have made a move to kiss her. No, if I had done that I would have scared her off. But by not kissing her she'll think I'm a nerd. But if I had tried to kiss her she might have walloped me.

Eventually I gave up the debate. There was no use in second guessing myself. Only time would tell.

I arrived back at my dorm room to find my roommate, Jeff, hosting a game of Texas Hold'em in our room with three of his friends. After the round of greetings I plopped down on my bed, exhausted.

Jeff continued playing cards for a few minutes and then glanced over at me.

"You look tired. Rough day?"

"Long day. But it's been great," I replied.

"Oh, so your date with the woman warrior went well?"

"Perfectly."

"I wouldn't say that, if you're back here and she's not," Jeff responded. He was being facetious.

"It's not that kind of relationship," I said.

"I guess not." He flopped the cards and examined the cards closely. Then he said to me, matter-of-factly, "I wish you had told me that before I spoke with your Mom."

"You spoke with my mother?" I said, sitting up with some alarm. "When?"

"Tonight. About midnight."

"My mother called here about midnight? Was it some kind of emergency? Should I call home?" I said nervously, starting to get up so I could go to the phone. But Jeff waved a hand at me nonchalantly, gesturing for me to sit back down.

"No emergency. She said that you had gotten bent out of shape because she called you so early in the morning so instead she was calling you late at night so you wouldn't complain."

I relaxed and slouched back down onto my bed. Good old Mom. That was considerate of her. And it goes to show you that you can teach an old dog new tricks, not that I'm equating my mother with an old dog but… well, you know what I mean.

"So did you tell her I'd call her in the morning?"

"Probably."

"What does that mean – probably?" I asked, a little annoyed. He and the others folded on that hand and Jeff picked up the cards and began shuffling them. Then he looked back over toward me.

"She said she could stay up for a little while longer if I thought you would be back soon. But I told her you were out on a date and I didn't expect you back until sometime tomorrow." I sat up sharply.

"You told my mother that? You idiot, why did you tell her that?"

"Because I thought you were more of a ladies' man than you apparently are," he replied.

"What did my mother say when you told her that?"

"She asked if you were practicing safe sex."

"Oh, God." I placed my hand on my forehead, shaking my head from side to side. "What did you tell her," I said apprehensively, sitting on the edge of the bed and leaning forward. Jeff, dealing out the cards, replied without looking at me.

"I told her you weren't the last time I saw you with those two women from the party."

I jumped up off the bed and ran over to him grabbing him by the shoulders.

"You told my mother about them?" I asked incredulously.

"She pried it out of me. Initially I told her I didn't know, but then she started grilling me about your dates and before I knew it I'd spilled the beans. I mean, what was I supposed to do? She's very good at getting information. She could tell when I was lying," he said nervously.

I had to admit that my mother was good at that kind of thing. I could never get away with anything when she was around. It must have been her social worker training. I let go of Jeff.

"You didn't tell her what happened in the room with the two of them and me, did you?" I asked, not really wanting to hear the answer. Jeff looked at me sheepishly.

"Not at first." I shook my head in disbelief.

"Thanks a lot," I groaned.

"But she didn't seem to be mad or anything," Jeff said encouragingly. "She just thanked me for the info and said she'd be calling you soon."

That I could believe. So much for my perfect day.

# EIGHTEEN

I got up around 9:30 the next morning, still tired because Jeff's card game lasted until about 3:00 am. I would have liked to have slept in but I had to be at the fraternity house at 10:00 for the house clean-up with the other pledges and new brothers. After the clean-up my pledge brothers and I were going to try to complete getting names in our notebooks. We were also going to hunt for clues as to where the brothers were going to be hiding for the scavenger hunt later that night.

The clean-up took about an hour and a half. Felix was in charge, but he was nursing a hangover. So he directed us from a couch in the living room, where he lay like a wounded general.

Actually the house wasn't in too bad shape. There hadn't been a party the night before because of the scavenger hunt tonight, so the usual party debris was absent. But there was still a scattering of brothers crashed on couches here and there. We had to work around them as we cleaned up the house.

When we finished, my pledge brothers and I met in the library. I told them about my successful impersonation of Percy Jordan and how Randy had saved me with his pyromaniac routine. We were all laughing.

"So, Dub. What did Pygmy do to you when he saw you afterward?" Buddha asked.

"Nothin' yet. He hasn't seen me. I got outta there faster'n a hunting dog that cornered a skunk." Yaz changed the subject.

"Hey, did any of you guys get any good clues as to where the brothers will be hiding tonight?"

We all shook our heads.

"The closest I got was a comment from one of them that their decision where to hide it was 'academic'," Mad Dog said. "Do you think that means anything?"

"Maybe it means that they'll be hiding in one of the academic buildings," I speculated.

"Did anyone get anything else?" Yaz asked again. No response.

"Well, we better keep our ears open today."

"Has anyone figured out Burdick's nickname?" Buddha asked. No response again.

"Maybe someone will tip you off when you try to get more interviews today. Let's meet back here early – about 6:00 – to compare notes before the scavenger hunt," Yaz suggested. We all agreed and scattered to work on our interviews.

I spent much of the rest of the day chasing around the campus trying to interview brothers whose names I was missing from my notebook. I made pretty good progress, adding another dozen signatures to my book. They were all tight-lipped about where they'd be hiding for the scavenger hunt, but I did get another clue about CP. One of the brothers, a junior whose name was Howard Billings but whose nickname was "Homer" because he looked a little like Homer Simpson, gave me the clue.

"The 'C' stands for one word and the 'P' stands for another word." That's all he would say. I thought about that and the earlier clues we'd received but it didn't help. I figured that the first letter must stand for Canadian. I had no idea about the second clue. Canadian Prince? Canadian Polarbear? Maybe some of the other guys would have more information.

I put in a few hours of homework and did some web surfing, had a quick dinner at which I got one more signature, and then headed over to the house a little before 6:00 pm. It was eerily quiet. There were almost no brothers there. No doubt they were making last minute arrangements for the scavenger hunt.

My pledge brothers wandered in over the next few minutes. Everyone had been successful in getting more signatures although none of us had them all. No one had any further clues about CP. I told them my new clue but we couldn't come up with anything definitive. No one had learned any other clues about the scavenger hunt. So we sat and waited.

A few minutes before 7:00 pm, Toddler came into the library where we were sitting and placed an envelope on the desk.

"All right, boys. Here's your first clue. You can open it at 7:00 sharp. You'll have three hours to find the brothers and the beer. Do you have any questions?" Toddler asked.

"Are you going to join the brothers," I asked. If he was, maybe we could just follow him and forego following the clues.

"Nice try, Percy," he said smiling. "No, I'll be here in the house waiting for the brothers to come back here after 10:00 pm when you haven't found 'em." I smiled back.

"It was worth a try," I said. Toddler nodded.

"O.K. It's time. Go to it and have a grand and glorious time. Good luck." After saying that Toddler left the room.

Mad Dog snatched up the envelope and tore it open.

"Be careful, you don't want to tear the clue," Buddha cautioned. Mad Dog read it and then passed it to me. It was some type of poem. It read:

> *Budweiser is kept*
> *Cold, fresh and properly chilled*
> *For Waldo to drink*

I passed it on to the others who also read it. Randy scratched his head.

"What the hell is this?"

"It's haiku – a Japanese poem comprised of 17 syllables and three lines, with five syllables in the first line, seven in the second and five in the last," Buddha replied.

"But what's it supposed to mean?" Mad Dog asked.

"That's what we've gotta figure out," said Yaz.

"Is this clue supposed to tell us where they are?" I asked.

"I don't think so," replied Yaz. "I think it's just supposed to take us to another clue, which will take us to another and another. At least that's what Toddler said they do on this hunt."

"O.K. then. Let's figure it out," Mad Dog ordered as though he were speaking to a bunch of privates.

We all looked at the haiku and screwed up our faces thinking about what it meant.

"It's talking about beer. Do you think it could mean the pub at the student center or maybe the Faculty Club. They both sell beer," I suggested hopefully.

"But Waldo doesn't go to the Faculty Club. It says 'for Waldo to drink.' That can't be right," Buddha observed.

"Well the student center then. Waldo goes there," I replied, defensive.

"I don't think so. A lot of guys go there. Why single out Waldo? Besides, it's too large an area to cover. Where would we look for another clue?" Yaz said critically.

We all sat thinking again.

"I wish Cheever was here. He'd have it figgered out in no time," Randy predicted.

"Well he's not here. And you're supposed to be taking his place, Dub. So what do you think it means?" Yaz asked grouchily. Randy sat there with a blank expression on his face for a while, but then his face lit up.

"Doesn't Waldo have a little refrigerator in his room? Why don't we look there?" Randy suggested.

"Good idea," we all said, clapping him on the back.

We went up to Waldo's room. The door was shut. I was hoping that it wouldn't be locked. Mad Dog tried the door. It opened. We went into Waldo's room. It was a medium-sized single with a loft bed. The walls of the room had no posters or art work on them. Instead they were covered with certificates commemorating Waldo's accomplishments – National Honor Society, Debate Club, President of the Chess Club, Student Senate President, Dean's Lists, and various Certificates of Appreciation from the fraternity as well as a Citation from the President of the SEX international fraternity. All of the certificates were neatly framed and grouped on several walls. The third wall was covered with an enormous bulletin board containing what looked like thousands of yellow post-it sheets with notes scrawled across them.

The loft bed was against the last wall. Underneath the bed was a built-in chest of drawers and cabinets that Waldo must have used for a closet. Next to the built-ins was a small refrigerator.

We went immediately to the refrigerator and found it empty except for a solitary Budweiser beer can with a note taped to it. Yaz grabbed the note and opened the folded sheet of paper. We all clustered around to read what it said.

> *Congratulations, pledges! You have successfully found the first clue, which is that we are not in a dormitory. Your next clue is in an envelope that has been deposited in the campus post office in P.O. Box 8134. To open the P.O. Box you must know the three-number combination. To obtain that three-number combination you must answer the following questions:*
>
> *1... How many birthdays has an 18 year old experienced if he was born in a leap year?*
> *2... How many times have the Boston Red Sox won the World Series since 1918?*
> *3... What is the sum of the numbers in Sherlock Holmes' address?*

We immediately took off for the campus post office, discussing the clues as we went.

"The second question is a gift. It's one," I said as we loped along, looking at the note.

"Don't remind me," Yaz groaned, no doubt having post traumatic stress flashbacks to the Red Sox beating the Yankees after being down three games to none, and then going on to win the Series.

"Well, the first question is a gift, too! It's 18," Mad Dog said.

"I don't know," Randy said doubtfully. "If someone's born in a leap year their birthday comes up only every other year. It leaps every other year."

"I think it's every four years, not every other year. But I'm not sure that's what they want," I said. I looked at the note again.

"Hmmm. It does say 'experienced.' I guess that technically you experience the birthday only every four years. Maybe you're right, Randy."

"I think we experience a birthday only once," Buddha opined.

"This is a trick question. We'll have to try each number and see which one works," Yaz suggested. "What about the last question? Any Sherlock Holmes fans?"

"The address is two twenty-something B," Mad Dog said.

"I think it's 221 or 223," Buddha added.

"I vote for 221 – I think that's right," I said.

"O.K. Then the sum would be five, right?" Yaz asked.

"Should be, if that's what they're asking," Mad Dog replied.

We hurried along and reached the post office. It was housed in an old, one story brick building that had once contained the student union. The P.O. boxes were still used by some student organizations but not by individual students. So none of us had seen them before. They were ancient and had three dials that looked like little sundials. To open a box you had to move each dial to the proper number of the combination. There was a metal tab in the middle of the box that apparently had to be turned to unlatch the door. Each door had a little glass window in it. We could see a white envelope through the window of P.O. Box 8134 enticing us as we arrived.

We moved the second dial to one and the third dial to the number five. We saw that the numbers on the dials only went up to nine, so that eliminated 18 as a choice on the first dial. We moved the first dial to the number four and tried the latch. The door didn't open. Then we moved the first dial to the number one and tried it again. We heard a click, the metal tab turned and the door opened. We shouted triumphantly and Yaz grabbed the envelope and opened it carefully. Two sheets of paper came out. He opened the first one – another message. It read:

> *We knew you could do it. Congratulations on getting this clue. We are located in the top floor of a building. We hope you have time left to follow the attached directions and find the next clue. Keep up the good work.*

I looked at my watch. It was 7:35 pm. There was plenty of time. But who knew how many clues we were going to have to find?

We opened up the other piece of paper. It was full of directions – sort of like a treasure map.

> *Your search begins on the front steps of the university's repository of knowledge. Proceed west approximately 235 feet where you will come to a father figure. From there proceed north approximately 300 feet. You will be at the source of wide ends. Climb up seven stairs and turn right. Walk as far as you can on that step. When you can go no further in that direction turn left, go up the stairs and enter the building you see. Once in that building find the room of bells and whistles. Go to the person in charge and say 'Show us the money.' You will be given the next clue.*

"Wow. This could be tricky. What's a repository of knowledge?" Buddha asked.

"Computer Center?" I guessed.

"Could be any of the academic buildings," Yaz suggested.

"How about the library?" Mad Dog asked.

"It might be one of the bathrooms," Randy suggested. We all turned to look at him like he was from Mars.

"A bathroom? Dub, how is a bathroom a repository of knowledge?" Yaz asked incredulously.

"Well, I do my best reading in the can. I learn a lot there."

"I like the library," I said, changing the subject.

"Yeah, let's start off with the library. If we don't come to the next item on the list – something that might be a father figure, then we can go back and start over from the Computer Center. Everyone agree?" Yaz asked. Nods all around.

"What about skipping that and going to the 'source of wide ends?" Buddha interjected. "That sounds like the football stadium, doesn't it?"

"No. In football it's wide receivers or tight ends – not wide ends," Mad Dog replied.

"Yeah. I don't know what that means. Plus, if it is the football stadium it's too big a place to be in the right position. Better stick with Plan A," I suggested.

We ran to the library and circled around to the front steps. We looked at the directions again.

"O.K. We've gotta go west approximately 235 feet. West is that way. How are we gonna measure?" Mad Dog said.

"My feet are size eleven," Randy said. "I can pace it off."

"Good, but make sure you don't put more than an inch between steps," Yaz instructed.

Randy led the way, waddling along by placing one foot after the other. The rest of us followed closely behind, counting out each step in unison. "One, two, three, four..." I guess we looked pretty strange because a number of people walking by stopped to stare at us. But one, an elderly Indian man with long unkempt gray hair, thick glasses and an over-sized cardigan sweater, who looked a little like an Indian Professor Irwin Corey, started following us and counting along.

"One hundred seventy eight, one hundred seventy nine, one hundred eighty..."

We got to 235 and stopped. There was nothing immediately in front of us.

"Oh great, we should have started from the Computer Center," I said.

"Not necessarily," Buddha cautioned. "Let's look around a little. Maybe we weren't traveling exactly west, or maybe our pacing was off a little."

We began looking around. Irwin Corey was still with us and he began looking around, too, although I'm sure he had no idea what we were looking for. We were in the middle of one of the campus quadrangles. There were two dormitories about 40 feet to our left. There were a number of trees nearby. There were also several statues 30 to 40 feet to our right.

"Do you think any of those dormitories could be our target?" Mad Dog asked.

"I don't know. What would they have to do with a father figure?" Yaz asked.

"Father figure? Father figure? Is that what you are seeking," Irwin Corey asked with a heavy accent.

"Yes, do you know where we can find one?" Buddha asked.

"I am a father figure," he replied. We looked at each other. Mad Dog rolled his eyes.

"Do you know anything about where the Sigma Epsilon Chi fraternity is hiding?" I asked, thinking that maybe he was planted by the chapter.

"In its fraternity house?" he guessed. I sighed.

"We're supposed to be looking for an object that is a father figure. Do you know what that might be?" Yaz asked, exasperation sounding in his voice.

"It might be the father of the university. That statue over there is his figure," Irwin Corey said, pointing toward a statue.

"Yes," we all said. "Thanks, thanks a lot!" We ran over to the statue and looked at the directions. Irwin Corey waved and walked off in the opposite direction.

"We need to go 300 feet north. Which way is north?" Randy asked.

"That way," Mad Dog pointed. "Let's go."

We repeated our 'Make Way for Ducklings' act, with Randy waddling along at the lead and the rest of us following behind, counting. When we got to 250 steps I could see where we were going – the dining center. I knew we were on the right track now. It had stairs in front of it and now the description in the directions – source of the wide ends – made sense. Just about everyone gained weight in their freshman year from eating all the high starch foods there.

We got to the dining center at about the 290th step.

"Close enough. This is it. Let's go," Mad Dog said. We quickly climbed the seven steps, turned right and walked along the step. It turned a corner and came to an end in front of the Student Union. We charged up the stairs and entered the Student Union. I looked at my watch. It was now 8:15 pm.

"Room of bells and whistles. Room of bells and whistles. What is that?" Yaz asked quickly.

"The bar," Randy replied.

"Huh?" we all said.

"You know. You drink a lot and you hear bells and whistles," he replied, completely serious.

"I think they mean the game room," Buddha said excitedly.

"Why don't we try the game room first and if that's no good we try the bar?" I suggested. There was general agreement and we galloped up the stairs to the game room.

The game room was on the third floor of the Student Union. Along one side of the room it was filled with video games and pinball machines. The remainder of the room contained a couple of ping pong tables, an air hockey table and a pool table. Near the entrance was a counter where the game room manager sat, making change, supplying ping pong balls and paddles, pool balls, etc.

The Student Union was crowded that night and the game room had attracted its fair share of the crowd. All of the games and machines were in use when we tramped into the room, and the bells, whistles, beeps and bonks from the machines combined with the shouts, cheers and moans of the patrons, created a cacophony of sounds.

We went immediately to the manager's counter. The manager was a short and very rotund woman with shocking red hair, blue eyes and a thick spray of freckles across her cherubic face. Despite the noise, which was already giving me a headache, she had a jovial smile on her face. She seemed to be having a great time. She wore a name tag – Becky.

We all stood at the counter and Yaz introduced us.

"We're the pledges from Sigma Epsilon Chi. You're supposed to have something for us," he said in a loud voice.

"I can't hear you," Becky replied smiling broadly. "What did you say?"

"I said we're from Sigma Epsilon Chi. Do you have something for us?" He screamed this time.

"I might," she said, looking us over and winking at Buddha who smiled and winked back.

"Can we have it?" Yaz yelled in reply.

"You're supposed to use a certain phrase," Becky countered. Yaz looked at the directions.

"Oh, show us the money," he said.

"What did you say?" Becky yelled.

There were now other people waiting in line behind us and we were already wasting too much time. I stepped forward and yelled.

"Show us the money." As I did so a nerdy-looking guy standing behind me yelped and ran out of the room. I must have scared him by yelling. But fortunately, Becky heard me. She nodded and smiled at us, and produced an envelope which she handed to Yaz.

"That's what I was waiting for. I hope you find what you're looking for," she said.

Just then the nerd who had run out of the room when I yelled returned with a campus cop. The cop had his gun drawn and the nerd was pointing at us.

"Freeze," yelled the cop, pointing his gun at us. We froze, and just about everyone else in the room hit the deck.

Now it may not have been a big deal to Mad Dog to have a gun pointed at him. I imagine that that sort of thing happens to you all the time in the military. But I wasn't used to it. And I was not filled with confidence in having a campus cop – not even a real cop – standing there pointing what was probably a loaded gun at me.

"Put your hands up into the air – slowly," the campus cop ordered in a Dirty Harry voice. We complied – very slowly. None of us wanted to startle this guy. The dweeb who had run out of the room and brought the cop kept pointing at us.

"They're the ones. They're the ones. I saw them robbing the place with my own eyes," he squeaked nervously.

"Rob the place? Are you nuts?" Mad Dog said. "We weren't robbing anyone?" He started to move toward the campus cop, who shook his gun menacingly at Mad Dog.

"Get back, you. Don't move or I'll shoot." Now the cop sounded more nervous than the little dweeb who brought him. Mad Dog stiffened and didn't move, no doubt not wanting to be an inadvertent casualty at the hands of this pseudo-cop.

We were standing there, nervously, wondering what to do when we heard Becky's voice shouting across the counter.

"Officer Simpson, you big boob. Put that gun down. These boys weren't robbing me. They were picking up a package that was left for them. Show him boys."

Very slowly Yaz raised his arm showing Officer Simpson the envelope he held gingerly on the corner, between his thumb and index finger. Simpson edged forward slowly, and as he got close to Yaz he snatched the envelope out of Yaz's fingers. Still keeping his eye on us, he passed the envelope to the little dweeb and asked the dweeb to open it. The dweeb followed his instructions and extracted a yellow $500 bill.

"Uh, it's Monopoly money," the dweeb said and gulped.

"Monopoly money?" Simpson replied. He glanced quickly over at the bill that was being held by the dweeb. One look at the yellow bill was all it took. He lowered his gun and holstered it, then looked at us nervously. One of his eyebrows began to twitch.

"I'm, uh, sorry. This guy told me you were robbing the place," he said, jerking his thumb toward the dweeb and giving him a dirty look.

"Well it looked like they were," the dweeb said defensively.

"I should charge you for making a false report of a crime," Simpson said angrily to the dweeb.

"Don't bother," Yaz said. "We don't have time to get involved in this. Besides, no one got hurt." We all nodded in agreement, although I could see that Mad Dog could have eaten the nerd alive if he had had the chance. Yaz snatched the yellow bill back and replaced it in the envelope.

"Go on, get out, Officer Simpson. And make sure you've got a real crime before you come in with guns blazing again," Becky scolded.

"We don't have to tell anyone about this ..." Officer Simpson began in a placating voice but Becky gave him such a glowering look that he stopped speaking. With a sheepish look on his face, he quickly backed out of the room and was gone. The nerd started to head over to one of the video games but he was stopped by a yell from Becky.

"Where do you think you're going," she barked.

"To play a video game?" he relied, his voice a whisper.

"Get out, you little runt," she yelled, pointing toward the door. He yelped again, and ran out. Everyone else started to get back on their feet and return to what they were doing. Buddha gave Becky an admiring look.

"You were magnificent!" he said.

Becky looked at him shyly.

"Oh, it was nothing. That's the third time that dimwit, Officer Simpson, has come into the game room with his gun drawn. And the first two times were just like this one. The man's a menace. He might have hurt someone." She looked at Buddha when she said that.

"Well, thanks a lot for your help, but we're on a tight schedule and that cop just made us lose more time," Yaz said curtly. We all said our goodbyes – Buddha said an extra long one – and we left the game room to examine our Monopoly money.

I checked my watch again. It was 8:45 pm. We had an hour and fifteen minutes left to find the brothers.

Yaz opened the envelope and removed the yellow bill. It was indeed a $500 Monopoly bill. He turned it over. There was writing on the back.

> *Congratulations on finding this clue. We are in an academic building. There is one more clue to go. To get to the final clue, see below.*
>
> *782.81*
> *G92B*
> *1966*

"An academic building. We already knew that. This clue was a waste of time," Mad Dog said unhappily.

"Well, we didn't know for sure. Now we're certain. So that doesn't hurt," I said, trying to sound optimistic even though I didn't feel that way.

"Hey, we've only got one more clue to go. We can still do it," Buddha said enthusiastically, trying to rally the troops.

"What do you think those letters and numbers mean below the clue?" Yaz asked. We all looked.

"That's the call number for a book. Let's see, it must be a book about drama or the theatre from the look of the number," Randy said nonchalantly.

We all looked at him in amazement. He was like an idiot savant or something.

"How in the world would you know that's the call number of a book, let alone what kind of a book it is?" I asked.

"Easy. My Mom's a librarian. She's got all the books in our house organerized using the Dewey Decimal System. I haven't read too many of 'em, but I know how they're organerized."

We ran back to the library and up to the circulation desk. We showed the call number to the librarian and asked where to find the book. She directed us to the fifth floor stacks. As we got to that section of the stacks we could see that we were in the theatre arts section. Randy was apparently right on the money.

We found the correct section of the bookshelves and searched until we found the correct call number. Yaz pulled out the book and laughed. It was the script to a musical play entitled *Baker Street* based on the Sherlock Holmes stories.

"Quite the sense of humor the brothers have, don't you think?"

"Yeah, I'm sure Tuney had something to do with this selection," Buddha remarked.

Yaz opened the book and began flipping through the pages. As he did so, a sheet of paper fell out and floated lazily to the floor. Mad Dog snatched it up.

"It's a note from the brothers," he exclaimed excitedly. "It says: 'Congratulations on finding the final clue. You can find us in the academic building that would be most closely associated with Sherlock Holmes' mortal enemy.' Geez, what do you think that means?"

"Professor Moriarity," I yelled jumping up and down. "It's Professor Moriarity. That's Holmes' mortal enemy." I had been a Sherlock Holmes fan since I was a little kid and had read all of the Sherlock Holmes stories.

"I knew that. But what does it mean?" Mad Dog repeated, frustration evident in his voice.

"Is there a Moriarity Building on campus?" Buddha asked.

"I'm a junior and I've never heard of it if there is one," Yaz replied shaking his head.

"Hey, maybe there's a real Professor Moriarity teaching here," I suggested. "Has anyone ever heard of someone with that name?" They all shook their heads.

"I know! Let's check a faculty directory. I bet they've got one at the Circulation Desk," Yaz yelled, and we all went thundering down the stairs toward the Circulation Desk like a herd of pachyderms. I checked my watch again. 9:20 pm. Only 40 minutes left.

We were in luck. There was a faculty directory at the Circulation Desk. We riffled through it but there was no Moriarity listed in it.

"Damn!" we all said simultaneously.

"What do we do now?" Randy said, disappointed. We looked at each other with blank expressions on our faces. "Let's look at the clue again. Maybe that will help," I suggested, trying to sound positive. I looked at my watch. Five more minutes had passed and we were down to 35 minutes to find the brothers. We all crowded around, looking at the final clue.

"Hmmm… Academic building that would be most closely associated with Sherlock Holmes' mortal enemy. Academic building that would be most closely associated with Sherlock Holmes' mortal enemy," I repeated again. Then I had an idea. "Do you think they might mean the building where Professor Moriarity would teach if he were a professor here?" I mused.

"Yes! That must be it," Yaz said excitedly. "So, what kind of professor was he?" This last question was directed at me.

"Jeez, I have no idea," I replied.

"I thought you said you read all the Sherlock Holmes books?" he said.

"I did. But about ten years ago. I can't remember what kind of professor he was."

"All right. Anyone know? Academic building that would be most closely associated with Sherlock Holmes' mortal enemy?" Yaz inquired. Silence.

"We could go back up to the stacks and look in that book again?" Mad Dog said. "Maybe it's in there?"

"Naw, we don't have time to read through that whole book," Yaz replied. "We've just got to make a good guess and go for it."

"Well, I remember reading Sherlock Holmes stories, too. Professor Moriarity was always creating diabolical inventions to kill Holmes – you know, like special weapons and bullets. I bet he was a physics professor, or maybe chemistry," Buddha volunteered.

"Hey, you're right!" Randy agreed. "I didn't read the book, but I think I saw the show on T.V. Professor Moriarity was that little dwarf guy who ran around tryin' to trap Sherlock Holmes and his partner when they rode around in their private train car. He was always workin' with chemicals. And Holmes would get out of the traps by using little gizmos he had up his sleeve like that little gun, right?"

"Huh?" I said.

"Dub, you're thinking of 'The Wild Wild West', not Sherlock Holmes," Mad Dog scolded.

"I loved that show," Yaz said.

"Me too," I added. Mad Dog looked at us. His face was growing crimson.

"If you guys have finished reminiscing, we only have about a half hour to find the brothers. I say we go to the Physics Building or the Chemistry Building now and look for them," Mad Dog ordered.

"You're right," Yaz agreed. "Which one first?" I suggested Physics. I had seen enough of the Chemistry Building lately. But I was out-voted, and we were off.

"The game's afoot," I yelled to the others as we ran across campus in the direction of the Chemistry Building.

"I thought it was a scavenger hunt," Randy yelled back, not understanding my expression. I let it pass.

We arrived at the Chemistry Building, which was unlocked but very dark. There were lights on in the lobby and a few offices on the lower floors, but none toward the top of the building where the brothers were supposed to be hiding.

"This place looks awful dark for the brothers to be partying here," Randy said anxiously. I was a bit anxious myself. It didn't look like anyone could be hiding in the building, let alone a whole fraternity.

"Of course it's dark. They don't want to make it obvious," Mad Dog lectured. "It's like what we learned in the Army. You have

162

to blend in with your surroundings. Make yourself inconspicuous while you wait for the enemy to blunder into range. Then you crush them." When he said the word 'crush' he smacked his hand down against a door so that it made a really loud noise. That in turn made all the rest of us jump.

"Jeezus, you scared the hell outta me," I said.

"Yeah, me too," Buddha agreed. "Cut it out." Mad Dog snickered a little.

"All right. All right. But you guys are being a bunch of wooses. I know they're in this building. I can feel them hiding up there. Let's go!" With that he charged up the stairs, the rest of us following close behind.

We got to the second floor and ran down the hall to a door that had a light on. We listened at the door and heard nothing. We tried the door and it opened into a classroom which was empty. We ran along the corridor to another room that was lit. Again, an empty classroom.

"Why are we wasting our time down here?" Yaz exclaimed, his voice sounding anguished. "The clue said they're on the top floor."

"I'm just trying to be thorough, in case they gave us a bum steer," Mad Dog said haughtily.

"Well, I don't think they're giving us a bum steer. Let's check out the top floor so that if we've got the wrong building we have time to try the Physics Building," Yaz said, irritation in his voice.

We climbed up four more floors until we reached the top floor. There were no lights on and it was kind of spooky roaming around on the top floor of an academic building in the middle of a weekend night.

"You know, it's kind of spooky roaming around on the top floor of an academic building in the middle of a weekend night," I said.

"En-how," Randy agreed.

"Where do you think the light switches are?" Yaz asked in a whisper.

"Why are you whispering?" Buddha asked. Yaz stared at him a few seconds.

"I don't know. Seems like the thing to do," he finally replied, again in a whisper. We all nodded. Then suddenly, a beam of light burned through the darkness, causing all of us to gasp in surprise.

"Shit!" Randy said. "Who is it?"

"Me," we heard Mad Dog's voice. He was holding a flashlight, sweeping the walls as he looked for a light switch.

"Hey, where'd you get that?" Buddha asked.

"Ever since I was an Eagle Scout my motto has been to be prepared," Mad Dog replied. "I brought it with me. Thought we might need it." We were duly impressed. We followed Mad Dog as he moved along the dark corridor, searching for the light switch. He found it in the middle of the corridor and flipped on the lights.

As the corridor became flooded with light, it looked much less foreboding. It was just an old corridor in an old academic building and it appeared to be empty. We listened at the doors, which looked as though they hadn't been opened in years.

"What's up here?" I asked, surprised by the abandoned look of the place.

Yaz replied. "I think these used to be offices, but they probably don't use 'em anymore. Looks like they mothballed this floor."

We didn't hear anything at any of the doors. We tried them but they were all locked.

"Well, I think we struck out here." Yaz looked at his watch. "We've got ten minutes before 10:00. Think we have time to try the Physics Building?"

"Let's give it a shot," Buddha said. "Let's take these stairs." He pointed to a door labeled 'Exit' at the opposite end of the building from which we had come. We opened the door and to our surprise saw that there was another staircase leading upwards. We all stopped dead in our tracks when we saw the staircase. We looked at the staircase, then looked at each other, and big excited grins crept over our faces. There was another floor – an attic – that we had not known existed. The brothers must be up there. We had them!

Silently, we began to tread up the stairs. As we ascended, I began to notice an awful odor.

"God, that's nasty," I whispered to Randy, wrinkling up my nose.

"They should have taken my advice and parked themselves next to a bathroom," Randy replied softly.

"That's the familiar fragrance of farts, coming from thirty guys drinking beer together in a small room," Mad Dog added. "Don't anyone light a match when we break in on 'em or it'll feel like we're in the middle of a napalm attack!" he whispered, chuckling.

"I hope it doesn't smell that bad when I break wind," Buddha said softly.

We continued up to the top of the stairs and stopped. Immediately in front of us was a smallish metal door. We listened but heard nothing.

"They're in there," Mad Dog said positively. "You can smell it." At this point we could certainly smell something. And if it was that strong outside the door I was not really interested in getting a full whiff of it once we opened the door.

"God damn," Yaz said softly. "What have they been eating? I hope they have gas masks in there or they'll all be asphyxiated."

Mad Dog turned on his flashlight, put his left hand on the doorknob and flashed one last eager grin before turning the knob and shoving his shoulder against the door.

"Got you!" we all shouted as we stormed into the room, falling over each other and landing in a heap on the floor of the dark room. Our noses were assaulted by the most horrible smell I have ever experienced, outside of my high school gym locker. If we had found the brothers they sure were quiet. The only sound in the room was coming from us, puffing and groaning as we tried to get up off the floor.

After a brief struggle we had righted ourselves and Mad Dog started to slowly move the torch light around the room. It looked like an old storage room. It was full of old desks, file cabinets, and lab equipment, all covered in dust and cobwebs. But no brothers.

"Damn, struck out!" Yaz said.

"What is this place?" Buddha asked.

"What stinks?" Mad Dog asked, also wrinkling his nose.

"Is there a light switch?" Randy asked.

"Here," I said, flipping the switch. The room was immediately bathed in a yellow glow, cast by an old dusty light fixture. We looked around and saw that the room definitely was empty. Or was it? Mad Dog tapped me on the shoulder, grinning again, and pointed toward a file cabinet at the back of the room. I looked and saw shoes and legs just visible at the side of the cabinet. Someone was sitting behind the cabinet, hiding.

We all looked at each other. Yaz put his finger to his lips, signaling us to keep quiet. We began tiptoeing toward the file cabinet, getting ready to spring on the brother or brothers hiding back there. We stopped a foot away, and Yaz held up one finger, then two and then three fingers while mouthing the words, one, two, three.

On 'three' we all jumped forward where we could see him. And there, slumped in a chair next to the file cabinet, was the dead body of Percy Jordan, looking a lot like a stuffed frog waiting to be dissected in biology class.

# NINETEEN

I got to the dining center a little after noon. I had stayed in bed until about 11:00 am and I was still beat. We had all been answering questions for campus security and the police until about 4:00 am. It was about 4:30 am when I got back to my dorm room; for once, my roommate Jeff was in bed before me.

I was exhausted. But when my head hit the pillow I was just too wound up with the evening's events to sleep. No wonder nobody had seen Percy for days. He was obviously dead as a doornail up in the attic of the Chemistry Building. But if he had been dead for days they would figure that out at the autopsy, wouldn't they? When they did, what were they going to make of the fact that Percy, or at least someone they thought was Percy, had been at the Chemistry Dept. dinner on Friday night?

Campus security and the police hadn't asked anything about that, but when they figured it out they were going to start asking a lot of questions. And the answers were all going to lead back to me. My stellar college career was about to crash and burn again – for the second time in two days! I had tossed and turned all night thinking about everything that had happened and everything that was still to come.

I got my lunch and then walked over to the table where we usually ate. None of my pledge brothers were there but a lot of the brothers and a few of their girlfriends were at the table when I arrived. Everyone seemed to be absorbed in the school newspaper.

167

As I sat down, everyone looked up. Then, as though a starter pistol had shot off, they began peppering me with rapid fire questions, all at the same time.

"Hey, Percy, the article said you pledges found the body, what did it look like?"

"It says there was a suicide note. What did it say?"

"Could you tell what killed him?"

"What was it like finding him? It must have been creepy!"

"How did you guys end up in the Chemistry Building? We were in the Math Building."

The questions went on and on. I tried to answer them as best I could. In a perverse sort of way I was actually starting to enjoy being the center of attention as I described how we had followed the clues that led us to the Chemistry Building attic, where we found the body.

I described the body, which had turned a shade of green, and told them about the suicide note we had found next to it. He had obviously planned to do this ahead of time because the note had been typed out rather than hand written. I told everyone what it said:

> *This University, this department and Harnash all suck. Graduate students are treated like slaves. Advising professors have too much power over our lives. I can't take the pressure anymore. The World sucks. They are sucking the blood from us, so I might as well save them the trouble.*

"My, God," Elrod said, shaking his head. "He must have been really bitter."

"Yeah, I think they really do grind the grad students down though," Felix added. "And they're all competing for just a few academic jobs when they graduate."

"The Chemistry Department is supposed to be the worst for that. The article says that there have been a bunch of suicides in the Chemistry Department. In fact, I think I remember one just a few years ago. That's when Beeker said they started those department dinners – supposed to improve morale," Waldo informed us.

"I don't think they succeeded," I said morosely.

"How did he do it? Could you tell? The article didn't say," one of the girlfriends giggled nervously.

"I think he poisoned himself. There was an empty bottle of sleeping pills there and some other chemical containers near where we found him," I replied.

"Sure is funny that he did it up in the attic," Red Neck suggested.

"What do you mean?" I asked.

"Why go up into the attic of the Chemistry Department to kill himself when he could do it more comfortably in the privacy of his own home?"

"Maybe he thought it would make a bigger impact on the University if he did it there?" Waldo suggested. "And he might have needed to go to the department to get some of those poisons he took. Since he was there he decided to kill himself where he was."

"But why did he go up to the attic?" I asked, following Red Neck's line of thought.

"I know. He was afraid someone would find him before the poison could work, so he went someplace in the building that nobody ever goes," Elrod interjected enthusiastically.

"I don't know," I replied, somewhat doubtfully. "Now that I think about it, it does seem strange. He didn't strike me as someone who felt the pressure of authority. In fact, he seemed not to care a lick about authority. And you know, I just remembered – he never signed the suicide note. Isn't that weird? Don't they always sign the suicide note?"

I saw nods of agreement around the table.

"You don't think that someone murdered him, do you?" one of the girlfriends asked, sheepishly.

"I don't know," I replied. "But it just seems kind of strange. And I know there are lots of people who hated the guy. So I could see someone killing him."

Everyone chewed on that silently for a while.

"Well, the newspaper says it was a suicide. The police will investigate it and if it's not they'll figure it out. It's none of our business," Waldo said with a tone of finality in his voice. But while it might not be any of his business, I was concerned that my little impersonation of Percy Jordan might lead the police back to me. If it turns out that it wasn't suicide, then I might be thought of as a suspect for impersonating him. Maybe they'd think that I did that to cover up the murder and keep it from being discovered longer?

As I thought about these new possibilities, my heart started racing and I got a sick feeling in my stomach. The latter might have been caused by my lunch, but not the racing heart.

The more I thought about it the more resolved I became. I was not going down without a fight. I was going to conduct my own investigation, and if it turned out that Percy Jordan was murdered, then I was going to have to find the murderer before it got pinned on me!

It was about 1:00 pm and everyone at the lunch table had drifted off in various directions. I remained at the table, deep in thought about how I might begin investigating whether Percy had been murdered, or whether it was just suicide. I was just thinking about getting up to go when someone called my name. I looked up. It was Karen Kim, walking toward me at a quick pace, a copy of the campus newspaper tucked under her arm.

"Jerry," she said excitedly as she pulled up a chair and sat down next to me. "Is this true? Did you find the body? Tell me what happened."

This was the most animated I had ever seen Karen – other than when she was kicking my butt at Tae Kwon Do class. It was great to see her this way without me being in pain. I got equally excited as I began telling her the whole story. She listened with rapt attention, particularly when I told her about my suspicion that Percy might have had some help killing himself and that I might be accused of being his helper.

"My god, that's amazing," Karen exclaimed, obviously with a newfound appreciation for my powers of deduction. "What an incredibly stupid thing to do. You could be in deep trouble." All right, so she wasn't impressed.

"Hey, I didn't know the creep was gonna get killed," I said defensively.

"So what are you going to do?"

"I don't know. Just try to find out what happened to him, I guess."

"How?"

I shrugged.

"I guess the first thing I have to do is find out if they did an autopsy and see how he died. See if it looks like a suicide or not. Then, if it looks like it's not suicide, I have to figure out who would have a motive to kill him. Or maybe I just try to figure out who doesn't have a motive. That might be easier." I grinned at her. She smiled back.

"I'll help you," she said. My heart leaped at that.

"You will? Great," I replied, beaming.

"Where do you want to start?" she asked.

"How about with you and me going out to a movie tonight," I said eagerly. The smile faded from her face.

"Jerry, I told you I don't date frat guys."

"But we went on a date Friday night and ..." I protested. She held up her hand to cut me off.

"That was an experiment, but I've decided to stick to my policy."

"But we had a great time. At least I had a great time. Didn't you?" I asked.

"Yes, I had a good time," she replied, humoring me.

"Then why did the experiment fail?"

She stood silently looking at me, then replied, "Jerry, I like you. I think you're a really nice guy and I like being friends with you. But look at the trouble you're in because of that stupid fraternity." She paused as though waiting for a response. I didn't say anything. She continued.

"Maybe you'll come to your senses at some point. In the meantime, I'm not going to date you again as long as you stay involved with that fraternity. I'll be your friend, and I'll help you look into this thing, but I will not be your girlfriend."

I looked at her. So that was it. The old bribe me to stop pledging the fraternity by hinting that you might date me if I do routine. Hmmm. It was a tempting offer, but I couldn't stop pledging now.

After all, it wasn't the fraternity's fault that Percy Jordan killed himself or got killed. More importantly, I realized that I really liked the guys in the fraternity. It was almost like having a family at school – a rather crazy family, but a family nonetheless. Somehow they made me feel safe.

"I can't stop pledging the fraternity," I said firmly. "But I'm glad to have your friendship and your help. I think you're wrong about the fraternity. Someday maybe I'll convince you." I smiled at her.

"Don't hold your breath on that one," she replied, also smiling. She got up to go, saying she had errands to run and studying to do. I got up too and walked her out.

"Tell you what. I sort of met that campus cop last night. You know, the one I was telling you about who tried to arrest us at the student union game room?" She nodded. "Maybe tomorrow I'll speak to him and see if he can tell me what the autopsy findings are. I don't suppose that they'll have done the autopsy before tomorrow anyway, this being Sunday. If I find out anything I'll let you know at Tae Kwon Do."

"Don't you think he might get suspicious if you speak with him?"

"I don't think anyone would believe him if he did say he was suspicious," I replied confidently as I waved goodbye.

# TWENTY

I had mucho studying and other schoolwork to do for the rest of the afternoon. I went back to my dorm room to pick up some books before going to the library. When I got to my room, my roommate, Jeff, was finally awake. I had left him conked out asleep, when I left the room for lunch.

"Jeff Van Winkle," I greeted him cheerily. "Glad you regained consciousness today."

Jeff was at his desk, apparently doing some schoolwork himself. Must be a special occasion, I thought. He just grunted in reply when I spoke to him, not really paying much attention to me.

"You missed the big news from last night, apparently," I continued. Another grunt was all I got in response to that comment.

"Percy Jordan's no longer among the living." I said it matter-of-factly, but made sure it was loud enough so that he couldn't miss it. But he didn't respond, so I said it again. "Percy Jordan's dead."

This time Jeff did react. He stopped writing and turned toward me.

"How do you know?"

"When I saw him last night he was being fitted for a new suit – a body bag."

Jeff stared at me silently for a few seconds. Then he said, "Who killed him?"

It was my turn to stare at him.

"What makes you think someone killed him?" I asked, suspicious.

"He was a no good son-of-a-bitch. People like that are too rotten to die of natural causes. They just live on forever until someone has the good sense to take them out of everyone else's misery."

I'd never seen this cynical side of Jeff before. Then I remembered that Jeff and a lot of other people had been forced to repeat a year of college. Percy was at least partly responsible for torpedoing them in chemistry lab the year before. So there was no love lost there.

I started to ruminate: did Jeff hate the guy enough to kill him? Jeff didn't seem like the kind of guy who could muster up enough ambition to even think about killing Percy Jordan let alone do it.

"Actually, they think it was suicide," I responded to Jeff's comment.

"I don't believe that," he said quickly.

"Why not?"

"That jerk was so self-centered and narcissistic that he couldn't have killed himself. If he even so much as thought of killing himself, he'd just have to take one look in the mirror and he'd change his mind. No, it had to be someone else."

"Well, he was a pretty good looking guy after all," I smirked. Jeff looked at me like I was on one of his recreational drugs. "So who do you think would want to kill him?" I asked. He looked thoughtful.

"He had so many enemies that it could be anyone."

"Even you?" I said smiling.

"Like I said, could be anyone. Even you," he replied, smiling back.

That was interesting. He didn't deny that it could have been him. I went to my desk and began collecting my books and other accoutrements of academia to take with me to the library. As I was doing this I thought to myself, "Jeff didn't ask me how he died." That was strange, too. Why didn't he want to know how Percy died? Did he already know?

I got everything together and started to head for the door.

"I'm going to the libe," I said. "Should be back after dinner if anyone's looking for me."

As I said that Jeff snapped his fingers as though he was just remembering something.

"Oh, I forgot to tell you. Your Mom called again." I looked at him suspiciously.

"What did she want?"

"Just to talk with her sweet baby boy."

"She didn't say that," I said. "Did she?"

He laughed. "No, but I'm sure she was thinking it, from the tone of her voice."

"How long did you speak with her?" I asked.

"Not long, ten, fifteen minutes tops."

"Ten or fifteen minutes? What were you talking about for that long?"

"Mostly your love life." I slapped the palm of my hand against my forehead. I couldn't believe this.

"All right. What did you tell her this time?"

"Nothing."

"For ten or fifteen minutes?" I said, incredulous.

"She did most of the talking," he replied defensively.

"Well, what did she say to you?"

"Let's see. She talked about how shy you were growing up – she thought it had something to do with your delayed toilet training as a toddler – and how awkward you were with girls in high school."

I held my hand up, signaling that I had had enough.

"Did you tell her anything about me?" I asked, anxiously.

"Well, she asked if you were getting any action and I told her you were still hot on the karate chick, but I didn't know if you were getting anything."

"Do me a favor. Don't tell my Mom anything else. O.K.? I'll do my own reporting, if you don't mind." He shrugged his shoulders and I left. I was going to have to speak to my mother soon.


After studying and dinner I went over to the house for our pledge meeting. I arrived early and went into the living room. Sheik, Tuney, C.P. and Randy were sitting around a card table, playing Scrabble. I walked up just as Randy was laying down tiles to make a very long word.

"Umbragatious," he said approvingly. Everyone stared at the word on the tiles.

"That's not a word," Sheik said, shaking his head.

"Sure it's a word," Randy replied confidently.

"What does it mean?" C.P. asked.

"Well, it's one who takes umbrage at things."

"That's not a word, I'm positive, and I don't even speak English," Sheik said. "You want us to look it up in the dictionary like we did your last one?"

Randy shook his head and began removing the tiles from the board. He pored over them, contemplating an alternative word.

"What was the other word you tried?" I asked.

"Advantigeous," he replied matter-of-factly. "And I'm sure that's a real word too. 'I come from an advantigeous background.' We just don't have an unbridged dictionary here."

Just then Toddler came into the room and asked us to move to the library for the pledge meeting. We started to get up and Tuney burst into song.

"The party's over. It's time to end all our play."

We went to the library. Mad Dog, Yaz and Buddha were already there. After the requisite quiz and reading assignments for the week, Toddler started talking about upcoming events.

"Yaz told me that for your community service project you guys are going to help out with the reading program at some of the Charlestown elementary schools, is that right?"

We nodded.

"When do you start?"

"Thursday or Friday of this week. The schools will call me tomorrow and let me know," Yaz replied.

"Good. Community service is really important to the fraternity," Toddler stated. "Now, what about your special projects? Percy, er, Jerry has done his. In light of the... you know, what happened, we decided not to have him write it up and present it to the Psych Department. Better to just let it lie. And Dub is working on his buttling now. Mad Dog, when do you start at the Early Childhood Development Center?"

We looked at Mad Dog. "Next week," he said glumly.

"O.K. And Yaz, how about you? When are the Cyborg's going to be among us?"

"I start at Downtown Crossing tomorrow at lunch time," he said unhappily.

"Great. That just leaves Buddha," he said looking at his notes. "And I guess that we haven't lined up Tookie yet. How are you doing with the other research?"

"O.K.," Buddha said brightly.

"Excellent. That's it for my part of the meeting," Toddler said. "Pledge brothers, have a grand and glorious rest of the evening." He left the room whistling "Stuck In A Moment."

After the meeting Randy and I went out to the Hong Kong for some Chinese food.

"So how's it going playing butler?" I asked.

"It sucks. I'm not cut out for this."

"What kinds of things have you been doing?"

"Well, Cheever has actually been pretty good. He takes a lot of time off so I don't have to wait on him very much. But I'm doing my own laundry, cleaning my own dorm room, making my own bed, ironing. Doin' homework on my own. It's brutal."

I smiled inwardly.

"I thought you were supposed to do Cheever's laundry and things, too?" I said.

"He won't let me. I burned holes in a couple of his shirts trying to use the iron. And I turned all his white clothes pink in the laundry. I'm just not domestical." He sighed.

I looked at his clothes. He was wearing his butler suit. I noticed that the shirt was perfectly white and burn-free.

"Why haven't you burned holes in your shirts and turned them pink?"

He leaned over and whispered to me in a conspiratorial tone.

"Actually, I have. I keep buying new shirts as I wreck 'em. And my other white clothes are pink." He pulled his shirt-tail out and up, revealing the pink waistband of his boxer shorts peeking out from just above his pants.

"I have to buy new boxers every time I want to go to the gym so no one will see me in pink shorts in the locker room," he said with an embarrassed tone in his voice. "And most of my shorts have shrunk so I get wedgies ever' time I bend over to tie my shoes." I laughed.

"I don't know. I kinda like the pink look. Makes you fit right in here." The Hong Kong's walls were painted pink. "Maybe you should just drop trou and become a doorman here?"

He gave me one of those looks that most people reserve for road kill. We sipped our drinks in silence for a few minutes, allowing the refreshing liquid to restore our tissues.

"Hey, Randy. I've been thinking about Percy Jordan. I have a funny feeling about him. I think maybe he didn't kill himself. I think that maybe he was murdered."

"Why d'you think that?" he asked, interested.

I explained my discussion with Jeff about all the people who hated the guy, as well as my concerns about the unsigned suicide note. Randy whistled appreciatively.

"I didn't really think about it, but you might be right. Who are the prime suspects?"

I thought for a moment.

"Well, I know he was seeing three different women. I met two of them. One seemed like she was the jealous type. The other was just mean. I could see either of them doing it. Then there's the possibility that he was selling drugs. At least he always had a lot of money, I heard. Maybe he was killed over drugs? Then there are the usual assortment of colleagues – you know, other grad students that hate him, although probably not enough to kill him. There are a bunch of students he flunked in chemistry lab last year who hate him. Some of them may want to kill him. So I don't know. There's a lot."

We both mulled it over for a while.

"Do you think the police will figure it out?" Randy asked.

"Don't know that either. Maybe they'll just stick with the suicide theory. But I'm gonna try to find out the autopsy results and look into it myself."

By the time I got back to my dorm room it was late at night again. As usual, Jeff was out somewhere. I turned on my computer to check my email before I went to sleep. There was a note from my folks, or more precisely, from my Mom. It was short but to the point.

> *Where have you been? Call me. Love, Mom.*
> *P.S. I hope you're practicing safe sex.*

I was definitely going to have to call her, I thought to myself, as I drifted off to sleep that night.

# TWENTY-ONE

Monday morning I woke to a cool and crisp October day in New England. The sunshine sparkled as it streamed through the windows of my room. I continued to lay in bed, cataloguing all the things I had to do today – classes in the morning, a trip to Downtown Crossing at noon to watch Yaz do his cyborg routine, and then a visit to the Campus Police to see good old Officer Simpson. It was going to be a busy day.

I completed my last morning class at 11:00 and hooked up with my pledge brothers. We hiked to the Red Line of the MBTA, also known as the "T", and hopped on the subway train. We were taking it to Park Street, a short walk from Downtown Crossing where we would see Yaz.

As the subway train emerged from the tunnel on the Cambridge side and began crossing the Charles River, we were all treated to a glorious view. The sky above the brick townhouses on Beacon Hill was a rich blue. The sun glinted off the rippling waters of the Charles and off the gold dome of the State House.

Leaves were just starting to change, with red, yellow and orange hues sprinkled among the leaves of the trees that lined the Esplanade along the riverbank. People jogged and rode their bikes on paths that outlined the riverbank. I felt an almost overpowering urge to jump out of the train and join them as we passed by.

The train re-entered the tunnel on the Boston side of the river, and minutes later we were deposited at Park Street station. We climbed the stairs and emerged from the subway station onto Boston Common.

Crossing Tremont Street was a bit of an ordeal. We barely survived the crossing because of the maniacal drivers. But once safely across we quickly walked the short block to Downtown Crossing.

Downtown Crossing at lunchtime on a weekday is one of the most crowded places to be found in Boston. In addition to the many small retailers and restaurants in the area catering to the lunch-time traffic, Macy's and Filene's Department Stores are located there. The downtown Financial District is also nearby, generating large crowds of people catching up on their shopping, eating lunch, or just hanging out and people watching.

And there were plenty of interesting people to watch.

"Why do you think the brothers chose this place for Yaz to do his project?" Buddha asked.

"Probably just so that there'd be a big audience for him acting like a weirdo," Mad Dog suggested.

"I dunno," Randy said. "There are already enough weirdos around here. Shit. Some of 'em look like they just escaped from a penal colony on Star Trek. I hope the crowd notices Yaz."

Randy, dressed in his butler suit and derby, might fit the description himself, I thought. But as I looked around I saw that he was right. There were lots of people around, many of them acting very strangely.

I noticed several people standing near a hot dog vendor, pointing excitedly and chattering incomprehensibly at anyone purchasing a hot dog. I saw others standing on benches and inspecting the tops of peoples' heads as they passed by. I even saw one man, dressed in ragged clothes, sneaking up behind people and picking at the backs of their heads as though he were trying to remove nits. Bizarro!

"Where do you think Yaz is?" Buddha asked.

"Let's look around," Mad Dog ordered, leading the way.

We found Yaz in a little park area on the other side of Filene's. He was standing on a plastic milk crate wearing a NY Yankees hat, Groucho Marx glasses – the thick black kind with the big plastic nose and mustache attached. But his most prominent feature was the large sandwich board sign he was wearing. It said, in bold letters printed on front and back:

*ALIENS HAVE LANDED.   THEY ARE EVERYWHERE. BEWARE!*

He was passing out green sheets of paper and yelling.

"There are cyborgs among us, there are cyborgs among us!"

Most people walking through gave him a nervous look before speeding up as they passed him by.

"Jeez, looks like he's doing a good job making people think he's off his rocker," Mad Dog commented, impressed.

Just then we saw Sigmund. He'd been standing with a couple people holding notebooks – probably social psych folks observing the crowd – when he noticed us and came over. He began shaking hands with each of us.

"Hi guys. Here to check out Yaz in all his glory?"

At that moment an old woman wearing a thick gray wool overcoat, red fuzzy ear muffs, zebra striped mittens and black army boots came over and began clicking her tongue at us.

"You should be ashamed of yourselves, doing that kind of thing in public," she said in a disapproving tone.

"Excuse me?" Buddha said.

"You heard me. It's bad enough you're here but do you have to do that stuff where everybody can see you? Have you no shame?"

We looked around at each other but we didn't know what to say. What was she talking about?

"Don't worry about it, boys," Sigmund said to us in a whisper out of the corner of his mouth. "I'll explain later." Then turning to the old woman he said in a loud voice, "Darn it. You caught us. Just do me a favor and please don't report us."

At that the woman's eyes glinted and she backed away. Then she shuffled over to Yaz where she began chattering to him while periodically looking back at us and pointing.

"What was that all about?" I asked.

"Oh, nothing. Just one of Yaz's new cyborg hunters hot on the trail," Sigmund replied.

"On the trail of what?" Mad Dog asked.

"Cyborgs – us," Sigmund replied matter-of-factly as though it was all perfectly obvious.

"I'm confused," Randy said.   For once I thought he was justified.

"Maybe this will help clear things up," Sygmund said, handing us a green sheet of paper that looked like the ones Yaz was passing out. "A little something I wrote up for Yaz," Sigmund said, chuckling, as he handed it to Randy.  We all looked at it.

There were little flying saucers, stars and moons decorating the margins of the paper.  In the middle was the text:

> *Are you aware that we have been invaded by aliens?  There are cyborgs among us, living in our neighborhoods, teaching in our schools, on our police forces, running our government.*
>
> *What can we do about this plague?  We must expose them.  How?  By finding them and telling the world that they are among us.*
>
> *How can you identify cyborgs?  They can appear as men or women, with long or short hair, but they have one trait in common: a bald spot in the upper back part of their heads.  Sometimes they try to disguise it with shoe polish or wigs.  Don't be fooled.  Beware!  They also like to eat hot dogs because hot dogs remind them of the worms that are eaten on their planet.  Anyone eating a hot dog might be a cyborg.  Cyborgs eliminate waste from their bodies through their noses.  Anyone blowing his or her nose could be a cyborg taking a crap.  Cyborgs' sex organs are hidden in their hands. They have sex by shaking hands.  Whenever you see two people shaking hands vigorously it is probably cyborgs having sex so they can reproduce and take over the Earth.  Beware!*

> *What should you do when you identify a cyborg? Do not let them know that you are on to them. Inform me so that I can have them put under special surveillance by the World Cyborg Squad.*
>
> *Beware!*

I stared at the paper in disbelief.

"Do you mean when we were shaking hands she thought we were..." I asked, disgusted.

"Yeah, she thought we were giving each other a hand job, so to speak," Sigmund laughed.

"I can't believe people really believe this stuff," Mad Dog said.

"Just look around," Sygmund replied.

We walked over to Yaz, who was standing on his milk crate, exhorting the crowd to beware of this new peril.

"How's it going, Yaz?" Buddha asked.

"Not bad, not bad." He got down off his perch, glanced casually at a ragged looking man who was standing nearby muttering to himself, and said, "I'm taking a break, Luigi. Back in five."

We walked off to the side and sat down on a bench.

"Is that guy one of the Social Psych grad students watching you?" I asked.

"Hell, no. He's one of my acolytes. Thinks I'm the balls, that I'm gonna save the world from the cyborgs. He's nuts. But he's not such a bad guy."

"You like these loonies?" Mad Dog said, incredulously.

"I like you and you're half-way there yourself."

Mad Dog didn't know whether that was an insult or a compliment.

"Yaz, I thought you were nervous about speaking in public. What happened?" Buddha asked.

"I was. When I started out I wasn't into it at all. But then Sygmund came up to me and said that if I didn't put my heart in it he'd make me do it on campus. That was a motivator. And he gave me these glasses, which helped since no one could really tell who I am. So I started laying it on, and next thing I know these whackos start coming out of the woodwork to be my followers. I'm a born leader and I didn't even know it."

We got back to campus in time for me to attend my afternoon class. When I finished I made my way to the Campus Police Headquarters.

"Is Officer Simpson in?" I inquired at the front desk. A man in the uniform of a sergeant told me to walk down the hallway and look in the last office on the left. I walked down the corridor past several offices on the right, but there was only a rest room on the left. I decided that the sergeant must have meant the last office on the right so I popped my head in the open door. There was an officer there but it wasn't Simpson.

"Is Officer Simpson here?"

"Last door on the left," he replied.

"But that's a rest room, isn't it?" He nodded.

"Last door on the left," he repeated.

I walked to the last door on the left again. It said "MEN" on the door. I slowly opened the door and peaked in. There was a stall, a urinal, a sink, a small desk, and an unhappy-looking Simpson all crammed together in the room.

"Uh, Officer Simpson?" I asked.

"Yes."

"I'm a student here. My name's Jerry Taylor. Do you have a few minutes to talk with me?"

"Sure, kid. I'm not doin' much of anything right now. Come on in. Take a seat," he said gesturing toward the toilet, which contained the only other seat in the room.

"Thanks. I'll stand."

He squinted at me. "You look familiar. Where have I seen you before?"

"I was one of the guys you tried to arrest in the Game Room at the union the other night."

"Oh." He stared at me. "That's what got me moved into here," he said, spreading his arms to take in the restroom.

"What do you mean?"

"Well, it wasn't my first, uh, mistake. A few weeks ago I had the Chancellor's car towed from the Faculty Club parking lot. It wasn't really my fault. I was wearing my sun glasses and the color looked different, so I thought it was someone else's car parked in his reserved parking place.

"Then a few weeks before that I accidentally arrested the new football coach. That wasn't my fault either. I saw him slinking around the stadium early in the morning before a football game and I thought he was some hacker trying to disrupt the game with some prank. No one told me there was a new coach.

"Then let's see, before that I accidentally locked the curator of one of the school museums into his office. I found the door unlocked and I didn't notice the light on in his bathroom, so I locked the door. I didn't know he was in there and didn't have a key.

"And then there was the accidental discharge of my firearm, but that's another story..."

"Sorry to hear you've been having so many problems," I interrupted.

"Well, as I say, they're not really my fault, but when the Chief heard about what happened in the union he went ballistic and said he was moving my office in here until I did something positive."

"Maybe I can help you out, then," I said.

"How?"

"You know about the Chemistry Dept. grad student whose body was found over the weekend?"

"The suicide? Yeah, I heard about it."

"Well, I'm not so sure it was a suicide. I was in one of his classes and I know a little about him. He's not the type who would commit suicide. I was wondering if you could let me see the autopsy report so I could see what it said?"

He eyed me suspiciously.

"Why are you so interested in this guy?"

"Just because I knew him, and... I knew there were a lot of people who didn't like him. I just want to make sure that all the possibilities are considered. And if I'm right and it isn't suicide maybe you can solve the case and get back in your Chief's good graces," I suggested, hoping he'd take the bribe. He did.

"Well, it is kind of damp in here. I sure would like to get back into my old office. And I guess there's no harm in just looking at the report. What did you say this guy's name was?"

"Percy Jordan."

"O.K. Hang on a few minutes while I try to find the file."

He left the room and I stood there waiting. While I was there another campus cop came in to use the restroom. He gave me a look like I was some pervert loitering in the restroom at Grand Central Station. I decided to wait outside the restroom for Simpson's return and quickly exited. As the other cop left he eyed me again.

"Just waiting for Officer Simpson," I said as he walked by.

A few minutes later Simpson returned. He started to lead me back into the restroom.

"Is there someplace else we can talk? I feel a little funny hanging out in there," I said.

"Sure. I understand. I guess I'm getting used to the place."

We went to an empty office and he handed me the autopsy report. The death was listed as a suicide with the exact 'cause of death' being an overdose of barbiturates and ingestion of hydrochloric acid. There were no other injuries or anything else that would suggest a struggle.

I sat there shaking my head.

"Why are you shaking your head? It says it was a suicide. It says there was a suicide note, too."

"It just doesn't make sense," I said. "Why the acid? That's caustic. It burns. Why would he want to kill himself with something that painful? It almost sounds like something the mob would do to punish someone. And the suicide note could be a fake, too. Is it in the file? I can show you what I mean." He started thumbing through the file.

"How would someone like Jordan have any connection with the mob? Besides, the mob would be more likely to just shoot someone. And why aren't there signs of struggle. If he was murdered there would be some sign of struggle, maybe a knock on the head or something like that," Officer Simpson suggested, still looking through the file. "There's no suicide note in here. There's a memo that says it was impounded. There's not even a copy," he added, shutting the file.

What he said about the mob made sense. Maybe he was right.

"I guess you're right," I said reluctantly. "But I still have a funny feeling about it. Maybe I'll just poke around a little and see if I can learn anything else."

"Well, if you want the advice of a professional, you're wasting your time, kid. Take it from me – it's a suicide."

"Thanks. You're probably right."

As I left, I asked myself if I should take the advice of a guy who has a restroom for an office? Not!

# TWENTY-TWO

I met my pledge brothers for lunch in the dining center the next day. We hashed out further plans for our upcoming community service project in Charlestown, then I filled everyone in on what I learned from the autopsy report on Percy Jordan. I wanted to get their advice. There was plenty of interest but no consensus of opinion.

"Jordan was a bully, and bullies are cowards," Mad Dog lectured us. "He wouldn't have the stones to drink acid. I vote it was murder."

"I'd leave well enough alone. The Medical Examiner says it was a suicide. Why rock the boat? Besides, I don't know that anyone really cares one way or the other with that guy," Yaz suggested.

"I read in the school newspaper that there's going to be a memorial service for him on Friday afternoon. Maybe you should go – you might get more information," Buddha said.

"That's a good idea. It can't hurt just to go to that and see if I learn anything," I replied.

Just then Randy arrived. He'd gone to the post office to pick up his and Cheever's mail, and he'd offered to get mine as well. As he got to the table he placed a box in front of me.

"Care package from home," he said.

"Hey, thanks for picking it up for me, Randy."

"No problem. Git anything good?"

I began opening the box. There was a note from my Mom on top. It read:

*Dear Jerry: Your father found some CDs you forgot to pack so we have enclosed them. I just made a batch of cookies – chocolate chip, your favorite – so I thought I would send some for you to enjoy. Share them with your nice roommate, Jeff. He's a very interesting person.*

*It's quiet at home without you here. Your father and I can't wait to have you back home for Thanksgiving. Call me.*

*Love, Mom*

*P.S. A patient of mine told me a catchy phrase – 'Don't try to love unless you wear the glove.' Isn't that catchy? So I'm also sending you some 'gloves.' Be careful.*

My Mom was getting weirder and weirder since I left for school, I thought. Why would she be sending me gloves when it was only October? Oh, well, her heart's in the right place. I began removing items from the box.

Randy asked again, "What d'ya git?"

"Oh, just some goodies from my Mom to help make college life more bearable. Let's see. I got some CDs that I'd left home – Rolling Stones, U 2 and Springsteen," I said pulling out the CDs.

"And this bag of cookies." I removed a large bag of chocolate chip cookies and began passing it around.

"And I'm supposed to have a pair of gloves," I said looking back into the box. There was a paper bag in the bottom of the box. I pulled it out and reached inside. There was a small box inside it. I pulled it out and in my hand was a box of Trojan ribbed condoms.

We all stared at the box of Trojans.

"Gee, all my Mom sends me are vitamins. Your Mom's all right," Yaz said, laughing.

When I got back to my dorm room after my afternoon classes I called home.

"Hello," I heard my mother's voice.

"Mom, it's me."

"Jerry, sweetie, how are you? Where have you been? Why haven't you called?"

"Mom, I've been really busy lately and it's been too late to call you when I got back to my room."

"Did you get my package? I sent it last week."

"Yes, Mom. About the package..."

"Jerry," she interrupted me. "I've heard from your roommate Jeff that you've been – experimenting – and that's fine, that's what college is for – experimentation – but you have to be careful. Experiments are O.K. so long as they're done safely."

"Mom..."

"Your father and I know that you got off to a slow start – it was probably that delayed toilet training – and you're probably trying to make up for lost time now, but ..."

"Mom ..."

"Yes, dear?"

"Mom, I don't know what Jeff told you but whatever it was it wasn't true."

"He told me he found you in a ménage à trios on the floor in your dorm room, and he said that the young ladies with you had their hands on your 'crown jewels'."

"No, Mom. It must have been one of Jeff's hallucinations. He's a heavy drug user, you know – very unstable. He's always making up incredible stories."

"Well, he sounded very convincing to me." She paused. "But I suppose that is a trait of the disturbed mind. They're convinced that the hallucinations are real," she added somewhat doubtfully.

"Exactly," I replied. She gave what sounded like a sigh of relief.

"Well, that makes me feel better. But are you dating at all?"

"There is someone that I've dated once. She's in the same martial arts class with me. But it's nothing serious."

"Martial arts? That's dangerous. Why are you in martial arts?"

"It's not dangerous. It's good exercise and I've always wanted to try it, Mom."

"It most certainly is dangerous, young man – moving around over a dirty gym floor with bare feet. It causes blisters!"

"Blisters?" I asked. "How are blisters dangerous?"

"If they get infected they can be very dangerous. Abraham Lincoln's son died of a blister, you know."

"Mom, I think I have to get going."

"All right, dear. I'm glad that you're having fun at college. And I'm happy to hear that you're dating. If things do get more serious, just remember one thing – be sure to wear a cover if you're gonna be a lover."

"Mom, where are you getting these expressions?"

"Catchy, isn't it? I have this new patient. He's uses all sorts of interesting expressions like that. He's a hip hopper."

"Well, Mom, gotta run. Tell Dad I said hello."

"I will dear. Be sure to take care of yourself, and call again soon."

"Yep, I will. And thanks for the care package."

"You're welcome, dear. We love you."

I hung up, feeling confident that Jeff Bliss' credibility was now shot and I wouldn't have to worry about him spilling the beans to my parents anymore.

I thought about whether I should tell my parents about this Percy Jordan thing. Probably not, at least for the time being. I mean, if my Mom is worried about blisters, what would she do if I told her I'm involved in a possible murder investigation? Besides, I had no doubt that whatever turned up, I could handle it by myself.


That evening I met Karen at Tae Kwon do class and immediately after class I briefed her on everything I'd learned so far about Percy from the autopsy report – which wasn't much.

"Why don't you let it rest? I agree with – was it Yaz?" she said.

"Yeah. But I can't let it rest. It just doesn't feel right, and it's bothering me. It's probably nothing – probably was a suicide. But if I can get a little more information maybe I can satisfy myself ..."

"If you stopped pledging that stupid fraternity and we started dating maybe you wouldn't have to satisfy yourself anymore."

My eyebrow went up. Her eyebrow went up in reply.

"I don't know. I'm not easily satisfied," I replied, smiling.

"Neither am I," she said, challenging me. I was about to respond to the challenge when I remembered that I had already been through this and I wasn't prepared to stop pledging or to drop this Percy Jordan thing – at least not yet.

"Well, it's a tempting offer, but I think for the time-being we just can't get no satisfaction." I sang the last few words and smiled at her. "I mean, I've gotta try to figure out whether Percy Jordan was murdered and I need to keep going forward pledging the fraternity."

"O.K., Mick. But I have a bad feeling about this."

"That makes two of us."

"So what are your plans," Karen asked.

"Well, my pledge class is going to Charlestown on Thursday to help out with the reading programs at some of the elementary schools, and ..."

"Why are you doing that?" she interrupted.

"Oh, it's a community service project. The fraternity does a lot of projects to help out people in the community – and they require the pledge class to do it too. So we picked this project – helping little kids that are dyslexic or have other reading problems. We're gonna help out once a week for the rest of the semester."

"Oh, I hadn't heard that." She looked surprised.

"Anyway, when I finish up there I'm gonna be pretty close to the North End, where one of Percy's girlfriends lives. So I'll see if I can find her and ask her some questions. And then on Friday I'm gonna attend the Memorial Service for Percy to see if I can find out anything there."

"Hmmm. I'm busy all day Thursday, but I don't have any classes on Fridays. Tell you what – I'll go to the Memorial Service with you."

"Really? That'll be great," I said, meaning it. "I think it's supposed to be at 3:00 – at the Chemistry Building in the large lecture hall on the first floor. Let's meet in the lobby – about 2:45?"

"Sure. See you then."

# TWENTY-THREE

On Thursday, my pledge class made the trek to the elementary school in Charlestown to help out with the reading program. We all took the T to the Fleet Center where the Boston Celtics and Bruins play, then we walked along Causeway Street and over the bridge to Charlestown.

We passed by Old Ironsides – the U.S.S. Constitution, then we trudged up Bunker Hill past the monument and another few blocks until we came to the school. We met the reading specialist, who set us up with a bunch of great little kids who, unfortunately, couldn't read worth a damn.

We spent a few hours at the school working with the kids. We didn't make a lot of progress but there was some improvement. And the kids and reading specialist really seemed to appreciate our having come to help. It made us all feel good about what we were doing, and made us want to come back the following week.

After leaving the school we walked back through Charlestown toward the bridge and Causeway Street.

"Jeez, those kids were cute, even if they were dissing me about my Yankees hat," Yaz said.

"Yeah, they were cute," Buddha agreed. "They loved my nickname."

"They did. And that was great when they all started rubbing your belly and making wishes," Mad Dog said. We all laughed.

"I thought those kids were pretty smart, even if they were dislexus," Randy said. "A few of them had to tell <u>me</u> what some of the words meant, if you can believe it." More than a few eyes rolled at that remark.

When we had crossed the bridge and arrived at Causeway Street I left my pledge brothers to walk over to the North End, which someone had pointed out was just to my left.

"O.K. guys, this is where we part. Wish me luck."

"Hey, be careful. I've heard that there are still a lot of mafia living in the North End, and if Percy was involved with drugs or something, there might be a connection," Yaz said.

I nodded.

"You want company, just to help out in case you get into a scrape? I can come with you if you want," Mad Dog offered.

"No, thanks. I'll be all right. If I'm with anyone she might wig out. I'll get more info if I'm by myself," I replied.

"O.K., bud. But be careful." He sounded like my mother. But I appreciated the fact that he offered.

I walked past Phillippo's Restaurant and followed the road along the waterfront. On my right a patchwork of old brick buildings rose up from the street like battlements on an old castle. On my left I could see Boston Harbor. As I strolled along I admired the view of the ships and boats as they bobbed in the harbor.

A few minutes later I arrived at Hanover Street. I turned right and walked down the street, passing one Italian restaurant after another until at last I came to The Daily Catch, a restaurant that specializes in calamari dishes. I could see the chefs tossing frying pans full of food over open flames right next to the ogling customers. The food must be really good I thought, looking at the long line of people waiting outside for a table.

I looked up and scanned the windows above the restaurant. Those must be the apartments, but how could I get up to them? I looked down at the street level and saw a door in the building near the restaurant entrance. I went over to it and saw a series of mailboxes and buzzers with names next to them.

It looked like there were two apartments on the second floor and one on the third. The names next to the buzzers were Fellini and

Spamito on the second floor, and Chin on the third floor. Chin? What kind of an Italian name was that?

Josey didn't look like a Chin, so I decided to try buzzing the second floor apartments. I tried Fellini. A gruff voice that could have been male or female, I couldn't tell which, answered over the intercom with a heavy Italian accent.

"Who dare?"

"Uh, I'm looking for... Josey?"

"Huh? Josey?" It didn't sound like he or she knew Josey. Bad sign!

"Yes, I'm looking for Josey," I repeated.

I heard some muttering and then the person said something in Italian. I heard in reply from someone else, the word – Josephina. Then the person I was speaking with said, "Si, si, Josephina."

"Right, Josephina," I said. "Is she there?"

"Next door, Josephina."

"Oh, O.K. Thank you."

As I rang the buzzer for Spamito, I hoped that they spoke English. I buzzed once and got no answer, so I buzzed again. After about 30 seconds I heard the voice of an old man come over the intercom. He also had an Italian accent, but thankfully he was speaking in English.

"What is it?"

"Uh, is Josephina there?"

"Josephina? You mean Josey?"

"Yes, Josey. Is she there?" I asked.

"Never heard of her," he replied.

"But you just said you knew her name was Josey."

"Maybe I did and maybe I didn't."

"Well, is she there?" I asked again.

"Who wants to know?"

"My name's Jerry Taylor. I knew a friend of hers who died recently – Percy Jordan. I wanted to speak with her about him."

There was silence for about a minute after that. Then the intercom came back to life and I heard him say, "You can come in."

The lock buzzed and I opened the door. There was a dark narrow hallway with a set of rickety old wooden stairs. I went up the stairs and as I got to the second floor I could smell the aromas of cooking tomato sauce, garlic and spices. It smelled great and reminded me of how hungry I was. My mouth started watering and my stomach starting growling softly.

I walked down the second floor hallway and saw two doors. I went up to the door with "Spamito" on the nameplate and knocked. The door opened and I was face-to-face with a fat old Italian man. He had a nose that looked like it had been broken a few times in the past, multiple dark puffy bags under his watery eyes, and a full head of gray hair. He was wearing a sport shirt with an open collar and a sport coat.

"Come in. Josey's not here right now. She went to Mike's Pastry for some cannolis for dessert. She'll be back in a few minutes. Come sit down."

As I walked in the smell of cooking aromas hit me even harder. They were coming from this apartment. I was licking my lips with hunger as he led me down a hallway and into a living room that was occupied by another old man, an old woman and two men who appeared to be in their twenties. The second old man was tall and thin, but bald with wispy gray hair and heavy eyelids that made him look sleepy. He apparently had the same tailor; he was dressed in a similar sport shirt and sport coat.

The old woman was a heavy weight contender but no taller than five feet three inches. She was dressed in a plain black dress and on her feet she wore sensible black shoes. She had thick ankles, the kind that flowed down over the tops of her shoes. Her hair was short and gray, and she had a large dark mole on her cheek.

But her most remarkable features were her eyes. They were a deep brown, but incredibly intense. They looked like gypsy eyes.

The two younger men had similar features and looked like they were brothers. They were both lean and looked strong. They had black hair, cut short, and Mediterranean complexions. Both wore jeans and collarless shirts. One wore a Boston Red Sox baseball jacket and the other had an expensive-looking sport coat. Both had vacant looks, suggesting that there wasn't too much working upstairs.

It was strange that all of the men were wearing jackets inside the apartment. The heat was pumping out of clanking radiators, and it must have been close to 80 degrees in there.

"My brother, Rocco. My sister, Madonna. My nephews, Salvatore and Pasquale. And I'm Vito. We're Josey's aunt and uncles. Sal and Pasquale here are her brothers," the first man explained.

"Hi," I said as I walked into the room. "I'm Jerry."

"Sit down, sit down," Vito said gesturing toward an armchair. I sat in the armchair and noticed a bowl of peanuts on the table next to me. The five of them stared at me. I stared back at them uncomfortably. I was nervous and hungry. I took a couple peanuts and popped them in my mouth.

"Do you all live here with Josey," I asked to make conversation and end the silence.

"Off and on, when we're not, uh, staying somewhere else," Vito replied.

"Oh, do you travel for work?" I asked.

"You might say that. Occasionally we're unavoidably detained."

"What kind of work do you do?"

"Rocco, the boys and me have a family business. We're in the trash removal business. People who have trash they need removed, they call us and we get rid of it for 'em. We been doing it for years. And my sister, there, she's a seer."

"A seer?" I asked, looking from Vito to Madonna.

"Madonna has the gift. She can see into the future." Madonna continued staring at me as though trying to burn a hole through me with her intense gypsy eyes, but said nothing. I squirmed in my chair and ate some more peanuts.

"Oh," I said doubtfully. "That must be useful being able to see the future."

"It is a curse!" Madonna growled at me in a thick accent. She did it so abruptly, so unexpectedly, that she caught me by surprise and I jumped backward, falling out of the chair.

"Show me your palms," she demanded. I quickly scrambled to my feet and held out my hands, palms up.

"Bring them to me, here." I scampered over to her immediately and she grasped my hands in an iron grip. She stared intently at my palms, tracing the lines in my hand with her index finger. She released my hands, then looked at me with her intense gaze. She closed her eyes and then began to gently rock back and forth, muttering to herself. This went on for two or three minutes and it was giving me the creeps. I sat back in my chair, nervously nibbling more peanuts.

As suddenly as it began the muttering stopped. Then she stared straight at me again and said, "You will find what you are looking for. But you will also be in great danger." She shook her head, a look of concern on her face.

I didn't know what to make of that. I didn't believe in fortunetellers. On the other hand, if she really could see into the future this might be a useful opportunity to learn whether I was going to have success with Karen Kim.

"What about my love life?" I asked. "Do you see anything about that in my palms?"

"I see that at present your love life is in your palms," she said. I blushed. "But that will change," she added. "That will be five dollars, please."

"Five dollars?" I asked.

"She usually gets ten," Vito said. "She's giving you a discount because she likes you."

As I got out my wallet and paid Madonna, the door opened and Josey walked in, her arms full of bags labeled with 'Mike's Pastry' on them. It was the same woman who had accosted me in the Chemistry Building the week before.

"We have a visitor," Vito said, pointing to me. Josey stopped and stared at me. Vito stood up and smacked Salvatore and Pasquale hard across the backs of their heads with the back of his hand. "Get up and help your sister."

"Sure Uncle Vito," they said mechanically as though they were used to getting whacked by their uncle. They got up and took the bags from Josey who stood staring at me. They looked inside the bags.

"Ummm, cannolis," one of them said.

"Yumm, tiramisu," the other said. My stomach made a loud gurgle that everyone could hear. I ate a few more peanuts to try to appease it.

"Josey, come over here. This is Jerry, he's come to see you," Vito said.

She walked forward slowly, still staring at me, a shocked look on her face.

"You look like …," she broke off.

"Percy Jordan?" I said.

"Yes …" She gulped, then burst into tears and ran out of the room.

"She's a little sensitive right now on account of that guy's a stiff now, if you know what I mean," Vito explained.

"Sure, I understand," I said. My stomach moaned again.

"Are you O.K.?" Rocco asked. He had a high tenor voice.

"Oh, yeah. Just my stomach rumbling a little bit."

"Come have dinner with us. Josey'll be fine in a little while. You can talk to her later," Vito said.

Not one to turn down a free dinner, I readily agreed. As I got up I looked down at the bowl of peanuts. They were all gone.

"Sorry for eating all your peanuts," I said.

"Don't worry about it," Madonna said in her thick accent. "Once I suck all the chocolate off I don't like them nomore anyways."

That comment temporarily took my appetite away, but I had committed to dinner and I couldn't back out now. And once I saw the chow my appetite came right back. It turned out to be delicious.

We had Chicken Marsala, penne pasta with "gravy," big homemade meatballs, fresh Italian bread, all with homemade wine made by Vito and Rocco. They said that Josey actually crushed the grapes using her feet – in the bathtub, no less. Silently I prayed that she washed her feet first. But I didn't want to ask.

About halfway through the dinner, Vito got up and took off his coat. He was wearing a shoulder holster and gun. Once he did it, Rocco, Sal and Pasquale, whom they called Pat, also got up and took off their coats. They were also wearing shoulder holsters and guns. I stared at them, looking at the guns. Vito looked over at me and shrugged his shoulders.

"Sometimes there are rats in the landfills. The guns are for protection from the rats. Right Rocco?" he said.

"Yeah, sometimes we have to shoot a few rats," Rocco responded, laughing. "Especially when da poison don't work." At that Vito, Sal and Pat started laughing, too.

I nodded. All right, so maybe these guys were all mafia killers. And maybe they killed Percy Jordan. But they seemed like nice mafia killers. And what could I do about it now? Nothing. So I drank some more wine and took another bite of my pasta.

Josey came out again and joined us for dessert. While we ate dessert Rocco sang opera arias. He had a nice high singing voice. If I didn't know better I would think that he was a soprano.

After finishing our cannolis, tiramisu and strong coffee which almost made me gag, everyone else left the room, leaving me and Josey alone to talk.

"Josey," I said, "I'm sorry to surprise you like this. I was in one of Percy's chemistry classes over at the college. People told us that we looked like each other so we got to be a little friendly. And I learned that he was dating you. So when he, uh, passed away, I thought I'd see if there was anything I could do for you."

O.K. I lied. I'd prefer to call it a pretext. After all, for all I know Josey or her family might have bumped off Percy. I couldn't go up to them and say I was investigating his death to see if he was murdered, and by the way, did you do it?

Josey looked at me.

"You don't look old enough to be in Percy's classes," she said, somewhat suspiciously.

I laughed.

"Not in a class he was taking – in a class he was teaching. I'm in the freshman chemistry class. Percy was one of the grad students helping Prof. Harnash teach the class. Percy was my lab instructor."

A look of understanding came over her face and then her expression softened.

"Oh, yeah, he told me he was teaching a class. He never mentioned you – unless you're one of them 'stuck up, rich, dumb ass, shit-head jerks' he said was in the class he was teaching," she said with her heavy Boston accent.

"Can't be me. I'm not rich." She laughed, so I figure she got the joke.

"Gee, you're nice." Then as an afterthought she added, "I'm surprised you got along with Percy."

"Maybe I'm his not-so-evil twin," I said. She stared blankly at me. Didn't get that one. I decided to change the subject.

"So, I was really surprised when I learned that Percy committed suicide," I said, trying to move the discussion to the business at hand. "Any idea why he might have done that?"

"Well …," she hesitated. "It's possible that he killed himself because I was gonna leave him."

"Really?" I said.

"He was a louse. I found out he was playing around with other women when he was supposedly in love with me. He was just a dirty liar. I'm glad he's dead." She sniffled.

"When did you find this out? You know, about him playing around?" I asked, feigning surprise.

"A few weeks ago. I went over to the college to surprise him for lunch, and as I was just getting near the parking lot I saw his car pull out. He had some blond with him. So I says to myself, relax, it's probably just someone he works with. It's nothing to worry about. So I don't mention it to him.

"A week later I'm talking to him and I say, let's go out to a movie. An' he says, no, he's too busy. An' I says, but it's Friday night, you can't be working on Friday night. An' he says he is and he'll call me. So I leave him alone, but then I decide he's working too hard and he should take some time off. So I go over to his apartment Saturday morning to see him and cook breakfast for him, and just as I'm pulling up I see that blond witch again. She's coming out of Percy's apartment door, carrying an overnight bag.

"So I'm bullshit now, but I don't wanna confront him, if ya know what I mean, because, like, I'm so bullshit that I don't trust myself. So I go shopping to cool down, figuring I'll talk to him later that night.

"Well, I go back to his apartment that night about 11:00 and I knock on the door cause I forgot my key, and there's no one there. So I decides to wait. So I get back in my car and I wait. An' I fall asleep in my car, waitin' for him cause at 1:00 he's still not there. And about 2:00 I wake up when a car drives by and I look and it's Percy's car pulling into the driveway.

"So I'm about to get out when I see both doors open and another bimbo – this one with red hair – gets out of the car. An' she goes into his apartment with him and an overnight bag.

"So now I'm really ripshit an' I wait to see if she leaves, but she don't. The lights go on for a few minutes then they go off, and that's it. If I'd had a gun with me I'd have blown then both away, but I didn't so I went home."

"Wow," I said, understanding why she was so upset with him. "So what happened next."

"Well, I thought about what to do and I decided to give him a choice. Either he gives up them other bimbos, or I was finished with him. So last week I went over to the school and I found him and told him it was them or me. If he didn't give up them bimbos I was finished with him."

"I guess he didn't give them up?" I asked.

"No. I told him to meet me at the restaurant downstairs, but he never showed. Maybe that's when he... killed himself." She sniffled again, then grabbed a tissue and blew her nose with a loud honk.

"Did you tell anyone about what Percy was doing?" I asked.

"Just Uncle Vito. I told him all about it after I caught Percy with the redhead. I came home and he saw I was upset. So he asked me what was the matter and I told him."

"What did he say about it," I asked.

"He said not to worry about it. He said Percy was a rat and there were lots of good men around and I'd find someone better."

Jesus, I thought. Vito called Percy a rat! Didn't he say he used his gun to kill rats, when the poison didn't work? I was pretty sure that Josey had nothing to do with Percy's death, and she seemed to think it was a suicide. But maybe Vito, Rocco and the boys had killed Percy?

On the other hand, calling Percy a rat could be just a coincidence, couldn't it? And I remembered Josey saying something to me about turning Percy in to the police when I was impersonating him. Maybe that could have caused him to kill himself. Clearly I needed more information.

"You mentioned that you had a key to Percy's apartment. Do you still have it?" I asked.

"Sure, it's right here," she said, producing a key ring and showing me a key.

"This might sound a little funny, but would you mind lending it to me? I want to take a look around his apartment and see if there's anything in there that might help me figure out if he did commit suicide or whether someone might have killed him."

"Do you think someone might have killed him?" she asked, surprised.

"I don't know. But maybe looking around his apartment will help me figure it out."

She nodded, took the key off the ring and handed it to me.

"His apartment was the first floor of a house in Inman Square over in Cambridge." She wrote down the address and handed it to me.

"Josey, was Percy involved in anything, uh, illegal?"

"Whaddoya mean, illegal?" she asked.

"You know, something that could get him in trouble with the police? I'm just wondering if he was about to get in trouble with the police whether that would also make him depressed and maybe want to kill himself. Or maybe someone that he was involved with might have had a reason to want him killed. It might help me to figure out what happened to him."

Josey looked around to make sure no one else was listening, then she leaned closer to me.

"Well, now that he's dead, I guess there's no harm in telling," she said. I leaned closer.

"I don't know exactly what he was doing, but he was getting a lot of money from somewhere. He said he came from a poor family in England and he'd gone through college on scholarships cause he was wicked smart, and he said he couldn't have gone to college if he didn't get them scholarships. But then he started buying lots of things – you know, a nice stereo system, a computer, a new giant screen T.V. and then a car.

"So I asks him where he was getting all the money all of a sudden. An' he said he had his sources an' he winked at me." She paused. "In my family you learn not to ask too many questions, so I didn't ask him anything else. But I figured he was doing something he shouldn't have been doing. Maybe selling drugs or something."

As she was talking she had started speaking more and more softly, causing me to lean closer and closer to hear what she was saying. As soon as she finished speaking she grabbed me around the neck, pulled me to her and kissed me.

"You look like Percy, but you're a lot nicer. I think I like you better."

Her lips were soft and the kiss made me tingle all over. But the last thing in the world I needed was to get caught up in a sawed off shot gun wedding with the niece of some Mafioso hit men. I was happy with my family. I didn't want to join The Family.

Nervously, I looked at my watch and got up.

"Oh, wow, I didn't realize it was so late. I really have to be getting back to campus. Thanks a lot for talking to me. And thank your uncles and aunt for dinner. It was great. Don't bother getting up. I know my way out," I said.

"Call me sometime," Josey said.

"I will. Don't you worry."

# TWENTY-FOUR

The next day, after my classes and a few hours of study in the library, I went to the Chemistry Building for Percy Jordan's Memorial Service. I didn't really know what to expect, but I was hoping to get more clues.

I met Karen in the lobby at 2:45 on the dot. She was looking good, wearing a conservative but very attractive dress. I, on the other hand, was dressed in a pair of jeans and a regular shirt – no tie and no jacket.

"Glad to see you dressed for the occasion," she said, eyeing me dubiously.

"Yeah, I guess I didn't think about the dress code for this. But at least I'm wearing a collared shirt," I said brightly.

"Yeah, you meet the dress code for a Boston cab driver. But you're never gonna make it as a funeral director."

I told Karen about my close encounter with Josey, leaving out her aunt's comments and the kiss at the end. Karen agreed that Vito and Rocco sounded suspicious.

We walked to the door of the large lecture hall where my chemistry class was usually held, which was where the signs said the service would take place. I laughed.

"I guess they want a room big enough to hold the standing room only crowd they expect to get for Percy's memorial service," I said sarcastically. "They might be better off holding it in the janitor's closet, for all the people they're gonna get."

I opened the door to the hall and let out a gasp. The room was pretty full.

"Jesus, why are all these people here? Everyone hated Jordan," I exclaimed. I heard a series of crashes and turned to look, along with half the room. It was Beeker, who had just tripped over a bunch of folding chairs that came crashing down in a domino effect.

Karen and I went over to him and I helped him pick up the chairs.

"Thanks. Someone must have moved 'em in my way while I wasn't looking," he said, dusting himself off.

"Beeker, this is my friend, Karen Kim. Karen, this is Beeker."

"Hi," Beeker said, holding out his hand to shake.

Karen said, "Hello," and reluctantly held out her hand.

"Don't worry. I'm not holding any sharp objects right now. It's safe to shake," Beeker said jovially.

"Beeker, what are you doing here, and why are all these people here?" I asked.

"Well, it's a big deal when a student kills himself, and this is the third one in the past six years for the Chem Department. So the department and the administration put out the word that they wanted a big turnout for the service to make it look like the school really cares. The professors put the squeeze on everyone majoring in chemistry to come. I guess they were afraid that no one would show up for Jordan."

"They were probably right," I said.

"Why are you here?" Beeker asked me.

"Oh, just curiosity. I'm still trying to figure out if it really was suicide or whether someone killed him."

"Yeah, right," Beeker said. "Why are you here, Karen?"

"I'm with him," she said smiling, jerking her thumb toward me.

Just then the microphone crackled into life. We looked down and there was Professor Harnash, addressing the crowd.

"My friends, colleagues and other members of the university community. This is a very sad day for all of us, but particularly for the Chemistry Department, because we have failed one of our own. Percy Jordan was a talented and well-lik ... er, respected member of our department family, and he will be sorely missed. As many of you know, he was my research assistant and like a son to me." He paused and looked down, seeming to need a few seconds to compose himself.

I leaned over to Karen and Beeker and said in a whisper, "What bullshit. From the way they were fighting one day in class they looked more like enemies." Harnash got himself together and continued.

"And like a father and son, Percy and I had our arguments from time to time – our personality conflicts, but underlying all that I think we both admired and respected each other."

"I think he's just trying not to speak ill of the dead – because he knows what a prick Percy was," Beeker whispered back.

"As I mentioned before, Percy's death represents a failure by our department to create the type of supportive environment that our graduate students need and deserve. His suicide comes on the heels of the suicides of other talented graduate students in our department. We had made changes – changes that were intended to make our department more nurturing and to give advising professors less power over graduate students' lives.

"We've tried to reduce the pressure on our graduate students and to make them feel more autonomous and less like slaves of their advising professors. But Percy's death teaches us that we need to try harder – and I can promise you that we will."

At that there was applause from the crowd, most of it coming from the grad students. No doubt they were anticipating a department makeover by Disney.

Prof. Harnash finished his remarks and gave the microphone to other professors and grad students, who also pretended to like Percy Jordan. The compliments they lavished on him now that he was dead were a complete crock – and everyone knew it. I quickly grew bored and began looking around at the crowd in the room.

I'd say that most of the people sitting in the room were as bored as I was. Oh, there were the professor-types scattered around, stoically trying to appear engaged in what was being said, but I could see them wriggling in their seats. Other people were looking around. Some seemed to be reading or doing homework. I noticed several with Palm Pilots or Blackberrys out, checking their emails. They were obviously passing messages back and forth and sniggering.

No doubt they were trying to figure out who the speakers were discussing. It sure wasn't the Percy Jordan that I knew.

I continued scanning the room. Suddenly I felt a tap on my shoulder. It was Beeker. He leaned over and pointed through the crowd to a seat across the room and a few rows up where a woman with rusty orangish-red hair was sitting.

"I think she's one of Percy's girlfriends," Beeker whispered. Karen and I looked. She was pretty, with pale skin which set off her blue eye shadow and lip stick that matched her hair color. She was wearing a black dress. Halloween was coming up in about a week and between her hair and the dress she was ready for it.

"I've seen her before," Beeker explained. "I think she's Professor Byerson's nanny. You know, she takes care of his kids. Oh, and rumor has it, she's also a witch!"

"A witch? She's dressed for it," Karen said.

"And I guess that helps explain why she was dating Percy," I added, smiling. "Someone told me about her at the Chem Department dinner, but they didn't mention the part about the witch. I think they said her name was Gidget," I said.

"Gidget? You've got to be kidding. What self-respecting witch would have a name like Gidget?" Karen asked.

"Gidget, Midget, Bridget? It was something like that," I said.

"I think it's Bridget," Beeker said.

"Well, I'm gonna try to speak with her and see if I can find out anything when this thing ends," I replied.

"I'm coming with you," Karen said.

We waited for the service to end. The speakers droned on. All of a sudden, on the other side of the room someone stood up and began to leave. It was a tall blond woman. I looked casually then I did a double take. It was Percy's other girl friend, Svetlana the Ice Queen. She had been there the whole time and I hadn't noticed her. Now she was leaving.

I nudged Karen, pointed out Svetlana, and asked her what we should do. I was panic-stricken. I didn't want to lose Svetlana or Bridget, but we couldn't chase after both of them at the same time. Karen was decisive.

"I'll follow Blondie. You stay here and go after the red head. I'll call you later to let you know what I find out," she said. With that she got up and left discreetly to follow Svetlana.


The memorial service ended about fifteen minutes later. My eyes had glazed over in boredom. I shook myself awake, said goodbye to Beeker and maneuvered through the crowd with my eye on Bridget as I tried to get alongside her. She flowed along ahead of me.

I was thinking about how to start the conversation. I could put my arm around her, give her a kiss and in my best British accent tell her that I was really Percy and my death had been faked because I was on a secret mission for the C.I.A. Or maybe I could tell her that I was Percy's long lost twin brother, just in from the U.K. to attend the memorial service. Or I could just not mention Percy at all and try some other line, like, "Wanna join me for a little eye of newt?"

She left the building and I caught up to her just as she was opening the door of a little red Hyundai. It had several bumper stickers on the back bumper and rear window. One said, "Salem, MA – Witch City, U.S.A." Another one said, "Witches Do It With Broomsticks." There was also a bumper sticker containing a circle with a star inside it and the phrase, "Witch Power."

"Uh, excuse me," I said. She turned to look at me, then her eyes grew wide and her mouth opened. "Can I speak with you for a few minutes?"

Her eyes appeared to roll up in her head and she put her arms out to her side and began swaying and moaning as though she was going into some kind of a trance.

"Oooooh! Ooooh! AAAhhhh!" she wailed, her voice going up in pitch on each successive ooh and aah.

I looked around self-consciously to see if anyone was watching me standing there with her. Fortunately no one appeared to have noticed us. She continued swaying and moaning.

"Excuse me?" I said impatiently. "I need to talk with you."

She opened one eye and peaked at me. I held my arms out, palms up, to signal that I was waiting for her. Finally she knocked off the trance routine and spoke to me in a wispy, spooky voice with a touch of a British accent.

"Percy, you're back. My incantations have been successful."

"I'm not Percy," I said. "I was one of the students he taught. I just look a little like him."

"I feel the spirit of Percy Jordan in you. His spirit has returned in your body. You may not realize it but you are Percy." With that she wrapped her arms around my neck and planted a long deep kiss on me just as Josey had. Her lipstick tasted like pumpkin pie, a personal favorite of mine. I tried to eat it off her lips as I returned her kiss and her embrace.

We were both starting to heat up, but then my conscience sent me a little brain email.

"Have you lost your mind?" it said. "You're not Percy Jordan, you're Jerry Taylor. You've never seen this woman before in your life. She's a witch. You're standing in a parking lot just outside the Chemistry Building in the middle of campus. And you're dating Karen Kim. You can't hook up with this woman."

"I'm not dating Karen Kim," I thought, defensively. "We're just friends." I didn't have a response to the other comments made by my conscience.

"You're not likely to become more than just friends if she finds out you've been doing the nasty with the witch," my conscience warned.

"O.K., O.K., stop it. I give up," I thought. I'd better stop kissing the witch or before long we'll be in the back seat of the car playing hide the magic wand. I stopped kissing her and pushed away from her.

"We can't do this. I'm not Percy. I need to talk to you about his death," I said.

"You are Percy. I feel his spirit in you."

"O.K. If you think I'm Percy, then I'm Percy," I said, trying to humor her. "Let's say I've come back to find out if someone killed me."

"Oooooh! Ooooh! AAAhhhh!" she started up again.

"Excuse me," I said again, breaking her out of her reverie.

"I sensed that you were a troubled spirit," she replied in what must have been her most mystical voice.

"I'm troubled, all right. Can you answer some questions for me?"

She looked at me without speaking. I took that as an invitation to ask my questions.

"Did Percy ever say that there was anyone who didn't like him, who might want to see him harmed?"

"Everyone," she replied.

"Everyone?" I asked.

"You told me that everyone hated you, Percy."

"What about you?" I asked. "You liked him, or, um, me, didn't you?"

"No."

"But I heard that you were dating Percy? I mean, you were dating me." She smiled slyly.

"Not because I liked your personality ..." She let her words drift off, suggesting she liked Percy for something else and I could imagine what that was. "You have a unique ... aura. My congress with you was purely to advance my spiritual development as an apprentice witch."

"You're not a real witch?" I asked, surprised.

"I'm training," she said defensively.

"Is there a school for that?" I asked, curious about how one becomes a real witch.

"There's no Hogwarts, if that's what you mean. I'm sort of self-studying. I go to a lot of movies about witches and the supernatural – you know, the Exorcist, Rosemary's Baby, The Witches of Eastwick – and I read books. And I visit Salem a lot."

"So why did you think having, uh, congress with Percy would make you a better witch?"

"You're so evil. I figured you must be an emissary of the Dark Lord, Percy."

She's not the only one who thought that. Now we were getting somewhere. Maybe I could find out what evil things he had been up to.

"So what evil things has Percy ... I mean, have I been up to?" I asked. She laughed.

"Well, let's see. What have you told me about? You said you've been giving your students low and failing grades because you like to see the 'stuck up little overachieving shits get a taste of failure for a change.' You've been pretending to be in love with a woman in a mafia family so that you can make connections for dealing drugs. You've been having sex with a lesbian to try to break up her relationship with her girlfriend. You've been blackmailing someone. You've been poking your finger in the bottom of chocolates to see what's inside them, and then putting the ones you don't like back into the box. Oh, and you don't lift the seat when you pee."

I figured Percy was unlikely to get killed over the chocolates or for dribbling on the seat. I was intrigued by the business about the lesbian, but I figured that that probably wouldn't get Percy murdered either. Intentionally failing students was a closer call. I suspect more than one of the obsessive-compulsive nerds in school would kill over something like that. Drugs came up again. And blackmail was something new I hadn't heard about before.

"Was I already dealing drugs or just thinking about it?" I asked. "And who have I been blackmailing?"

"You didn't tell me, Percy. Don't you know?"

"No, like I said, I'm not Percy, even if his spirit is in me. I don't know what he knows," I said in frustration.

"Well, then, there's only one thing to do. We should have a séance to release Percy's spirit from your body. Then the spirit will tell us whether Percy killed himself or if he was killed by someone else, and if so, who did it. Some friends of mine and I will be holding a séance on Halloween night just before midnight. You should come."

I was skeptical about the séance idea, but I took down her address in Watertown where the séance was supposed to take place, and her phone number. I told her I'd think about it.


I received a call from Karen Kim much later that night.

"I followed the blond – Svetlana. I had to borrow my roommate's car to stay after her. You'll never guess where she went," Karen said excitedly.

"Where?"

"I followed her to the South End, over past the Back Bay. She went to a bar called 'Girl's Night Out.' It's a lesbian bar. I went in and I saw her sitting and looking pretty cozy with another woman there. Are you sure she's the woman you saw with Percy? I don't think he or any other man is her type."

I told Karen what I had learned from Bridget. Svetlana must be the lesbian Percy was boffing, although why a lesbian would start up a relationship with him in the first place was beyond me.

"We'll have to talk with her to see if we can find out anything else," I said to Karen. "But how can we find her? We don't know where she lives."

"Not a problem," Karen said smugly. "I know where she works."

"Where?"

"At 'Girls Night Out.' When I was in there I saw a sign that had her picture on it. Apparently she's a singer and she's performing there this weekend."

"You're kidding? Great work. So how do we speak to her?" I said.

"That's easy. This weekend we go to the bar and watch her show."

"Oh, right. We go to the bar and ..." My voice trailed off. "Wait a minute. I'm a guy. I can't go to a lesbian bar."

"Sure you can."

"But, they won't let me in."

"There's no sign that says guys can't come in."

"But I'll probably be the only guy in there. It'll be weird," I insisted.

"It'll be weird for me, too. But if you feel insecure get some of your frat boys to come along." She said this with a little laugh, so I assumed she was being facetious.

"Well, maybe I will," I replied. "When do you want to go?"

"Tomorrow night."

# TWENTY-FIVE

Saturday was a busy day for me. We had the clean-up at the house in the morning and then my pledge brothers and I all went to lunch together to try to get a few more brothers' interviews. We were successful in getting two more brothers in our notebooks, including Sam Formicola and Tom Phibbs. We were especially happy to get these two brothers in our notebooks because they lived in an apartment off campus and weren't around too often.

Sam's nickname is Chewy, which is short for Chewbacca. Sam is tall, has a scruffy beard and a hairdo sort of like Andrea Bocelli, the Italian opera singer. In fact he looks a lot like Andrea Bocelli, but to the brothers he looked a lot like a wookie. I guess maybe there's not a great difference between Bocelli and a wookie.

Tom is known as Zen. He started out as a pre-med major, but took a religion course as an elective to fulfill a school requirement to take some classes outside of the sciences. (The university wants everyone to be well-rounded). Zen liked the class so much that he started taking more of them and eventually changed his major to Eastern Religions. He began spending more and more time meditating and less time exercising, which made him especially well-rounded. Now he was pretty reclusive, usually showing up around the house or the dining center only once or twice a month.

We tried getting them to spill the beans on CP's nickname, but without success. Chewy responded by asking us who CP was. Zen's response, though completely Zen-like, was no more enlightening.

"What is in a name? What is Burr? What is Dick? What is C? What is P?"

At lunch I also tried recruiting people to come to the bar with me and Karen so I wouldn't be the only guy there. I decided not to tell them what kind of bar it was for fear that no one would come if they knew in advance.

I got two takers – Randy and Buddha. Randy was going stag but Buddha said he would bring a date when I told him Karen was coming. I was a little concerned about Buddha getting in trouble with a date if he and his date didn't know what he was getting into. So as we were leaving the dining center I pulled him aside and told him about "Girl's Night Out."

"Oh, how fun!" he said. "I've never been to a lesbian bar before. That'll be smashing."

"What about your date. Will she be freaked out?" I asked.

"No, I think she'll want to come. But I'll warn her in advance. I'll still go even if she doesn't."


I spent the rest of the day in the library. I had a paper to finish up, some other homework and I had to study for a test. I worked straight through until dinner, where I saw Buddha. He confirmed that his date was happy to come along to the lesbian bar. I called Karen to confirm and let her know that I and three others would be coming.

"Did you tell them what kind of a bar it is?" she asked suspiciously.

"Sure, most of them."

"Most?"

"Well, I forgot to mention it to Randy, but I'm sure he won't mind."

We decided to meet outside Karen's dorm at 10:00. Karen would drive us to the bar using her roommate's car.

I decided to drop by Randy's dorm rooms to confirm with him. Although Randy lived in a dorm, he actually had two rooms – one for him and one for Cheever. Apparently his Dad had agreed to make a very large donation to the university on the condition that the school let Randy use two rooms so he would have a place for Cheever to stay.

I had been in Randy's rooms when Cheever was taking care of things and they had been amazing. They looked like something you might see at Oxford. The school-issue furnishings had been removed and replaced with brand new furniture and handsome bookshelves. The walls had been repainted and decorated with beautiful artwork from Randy's family's collection. Thick plush carpeting had been installed. A large screen T.V. and state of the art sound system completed the effect.

The extra room, where Cheever stayed, had been outfitted with small kitchen appliances enabling him to prepare meals, drinks and snacks for Randy and his guests. Of course, the whole place was impeccably clean and neat.

As I approached the rooms I was wondering how things would look now that Randy was in charge of taking care of the place. I knocked on the door. After a few seconds it opened and Randy stood there, in his butler suit, looking disheveled.

"Oh, hi, c'mon in."

I walked into the room. It looked like a bomb had hit it. There were clothes lying around everywhere, many with burn holes in them. The ironing board was out. There were books and papers scattered around. Trash and dirty dishes decorated shelves, the table and the bed. In the middle of it all Cheever was sitting on the sofa, dressed in jeans and an Aloha shirt, reading the newspaper. He rose when he saw me.

"Master Taylor, it's most gratifying to see you again."

"It's good to see you, too, Cheever," I said looking around. He noticed the dubious expression on my face as I glanced around the room.

"Circumstances are indeed desperate, sir. I have endeavored to provide assistance to Master Randall. Unfortunately, he has declined to accept my assistance."

"Has he been trying to take care of everything on his own?" I asked.

"Indeed, sir."

"And he won't let you help him at all?"

217

"Indeed, sir. Initially he accepted some limited advice, but of late he has become rather obstreperous in his refusal to receive constructive criticism."

"I don't have strep. My throat feels fine," Randy said.

"Randy, why don't you let Cheever help you out? You could at least follow his advice," I said.

"Because I'm mad. This project they gave me is stupid and I'm tired of having to cook 'n clean 'n wash 'n do ever'thing else. I'm not cut out for this. I can't do it."

"I have endeavored to explain to Master Randall that the skills which he lacks are acquired rather than innate. By assiduous study he could acquire the requisite skills necessary to accomplishing his tasks, making the fraternal organization's requirements much more benign."

"What does that mean?" Randy asked.

"You can learn to wash and clean and cook and do everything else you have to do if you'd stop being a fat head and let Cheever teach you how to do it."

After some more discussion Randy finally agreed to let Cheever teach him how to buttle. I confirmed the time that we were to leave for the bar later that evening and then left Randy, sulking, but listening to Cheever as he expounded on the fine art of washing clothes.

In the excitement of the moment I forgot to mention that the bar we were going to visit was a lesbian bar. Oh, shucks. But I could let Randy know when I saw him later outside of Karen's dorm, just before we left.


I had a few hours before we had to go so I decided to head back to my room and take a little nap. I got back there and found my roommate Jeff hanging out, listening to music. So much for the nap idea.

"Wussup?" I said.

"Not much. What are you up to tonight?"

"I'm going to a lesbian bar," I said.

"A lesbian bar? From seeing you walk to the shower it looks like they did a pretty good job with your sex change operation. I never would have guessed that you're really a lesbian," he said, grinning.

"It's one of my best kept secrets."

"O.K. So why are you going to a lesbian bar."

"A woman that Percy Jordan used to 'date' is performing there and I want to talk to her."

"Is she a lesbian? If she is, why was she dating him?"

"I understand she's a lesbian. Why she was dating him I have no idea. Maybe I'll find out tonight."

"Why do you even care?" Jeff asked.

"I'm still trying to figure out whether he committed suicide or if he was murdered. She might have some answers."

I went over to Karen's dorm a little before 10:00. Karen was waiting out on the steps of the dorm. I sat down to wait for Randy, Buddha and Buddha's date.

"Ready for a night out, girl?" I said cheerfully as I sat down.

"You bet, boy."

"Have you ever been in one of these bars before," I asked.

"Just yesterday when I followed Svetlana. Why? Are you trying to find out if I'm a lesbian?" she said, laughing.

"No, no," I said quickly. "I was just gonna ask if you knew what they were like, you know, what should I expect?"

"Well, there weren't a lot of people there when I followed Svetlana in. So I don't know what it'll be like. It just looked like a regular bar when I looked in."

Just then Randy walked up. Randy was out of the butler clothes now. He was dressed in jeans, a collared shirt and a v-neck sweater.

"Howdy," he said. I introduced him to Karen and vice versa.

"Can I wear jeans to this bar where we're going?" he asked. I shrugged my shoulders, not having thought of that, and looked at Karen.

"It looked like the kind of bar where you can wear anything you want," she said.

"Except a dick," I thought to myself.

Just then Buddha came sauntering up with his date. It was none other than the woman who was managing the game room at the student union the night we were there looking for clues.

"Hi," he said. "Sorry we're a little late. Randy, Jerry do you remember Becky, from the game room at the student union? This is Randy, Jerry and Karen."

Becky slapped me on the back in greeting, almost knocking me over.

"How are you," she said in a boisterous voice.

"Well, I was good before you collapsed my lung," I said. She laughed.

"Just toughening you up," she said. Then she shook hands with Karen.

"Brad tells me you're in Tae Kwon Do class with him. He said you're very good."

Karen smiled bashfully. Randy asked, "Who's Brad."

"Buddha," I answered.

After the introductions we piled into Karen's roommate's car, a VW beetle. Karen drove and I got to ride shotgun in the front, next to her. Becky and Buddha, the BBs, got in the back, sitting behind Karen and in the middle. The shocks of the car compressed and we tilted down to the left. Randy wedged himself in the small amount of space that was left in the back behind me and we were off.

I learned that Becky lived off campus in Somerville, the next town over from Cambridge. She was an electrical engineering major and she worked part-time at the Student Center in the game room as a manager. But she also repaired the pinball machines when they went on the blink, using those electrical engineering skills.

Karen crossed over the Charles River on the Mass. Ave. bridge and continued down Mass. Ave. past Symphony Hall until we got over to the South End. I had never been in that part of town before, but I heard that it had been a very fashionable part of Boston at one time. Then it had fallen into decay and stayed that way until the 1970s when a lot of gay professional types began moving in and fixing up the old buildings. Restaurants, stores and theatres followed them and now the area, although still in transition, had become a very funky and fun part of town, catering to a real mix of people – students, professionals, working class, gay and straight, all races.

We all looked at the neat store fronts, the stately old architecture, the many restaurants and the variety of people walking around as we drove down Tremont Street and then off a side street where Karen found a parking place.

"The bar's just down the street, around the corner," she said as we got out of the car and locked up. Five minutes later we were outside an old wooden building with a large dark picture window at the front. Above the large wooden door was a sign that appeared to be hand-painted in brightly colored letters – "Girl's Night Out." Around the lettering in the same bright colors were little circles with plus-signs attached underneath them, the ancient Roman symbol for females.

I looked around for signs with pictures of men with red circles around them and diagonal red lines running through the circles, but I didn't see any. I guess that was a good sign.

We stood outside for a few seconds and then Karen charged ahead, opening the door and walking through. I took a deep breath, then followed her with Buddha, Becky and Randy right behind me.

It was very dark and about half full of people inside. Lining the wall near the door was a long bar at which several female bartenders were scurrying about, trying to fill drink orders for the patrons clustered around the bar, all of whom appeared to be female.

Just beyond the bar there were tables spread out around the room, some empty and some full, and beyond that a small stage. There was no one on the stage when we arrived.

I scanned the crowd seeing if there were any other men in the room beside Randy, Buddha and myself. I saw none. I looked at the women scattered around the room. They were a mix of women, some who had short hair and were dressed in a masculine manner and others who had longer hair and whose wardrobes appeared to be feminine.

We found a table about halfway to the stage and staked it out. Randy and I took drink orders and bellied up to the bar to buy the first round. I felt a little self-conscious about being there, imagining in my own paranoid way that everyone was staring at me and loathing me for being male. Randy, on the other hand, was looking around everywhere like he had a rubber neck. He was gawking and smiling.

He looked at me.

"Hey, this place is great, look at all the chicks here. And not many guys. Easy pickin's."

"Yeah, look at 'em," I said less than enthusiastically.

"Maybe I'll hook up!" he said.

"You never know," I replied.

We placed our drink order. The bartender didn't try to bite our heads off – another good sign, I thought. Randy tried flirting with the bartender, who was quite attractive. She was pleasant enough to him, and didn't punch him out. Of course, she didn't give him her phone number either.

We got back to the table with the drinks. There was another woman there, talking to Karen. As I set Karen's drink in front of her the other woman said goodbye and walked off.

"Who was that?" I whispered.

"Just someone asking me for a date."

At that moment the lights went up on the stage and Svetlana stepped out with a guitar.

"She's a hotty," Randy commented, admiring Svetlana.

"That's ironic," I said. "The Ice Queen is a hotty."

Svetlana began tuning her guitar while starting what for her was supposed to be stage banter with the audience. She had a definite Eastern European accent and a definite lack of talent at stage banter.

"My first song is about a love affair that terminated. It is called, 'You Bitch'."

Then she strummed her guitar and lit into the song, which described a relationship with a woman that had gone sour as a result of the other woman cheating on her with a man. The audience moaned when they heard the sad tale. No doubt many of them had had their hearts broken by men who stole away their girlfriends.

When she finished she got a stirring round of applause from the crowd.

"That was a funny song," Randy said. "I think she got her lyrics mixed up a little. But the tune was nice."

Svetlana's next song was a ballad called, "Bobitt Can You Spare A Knife?" After that she sang a light comic piece entitled, "Look At Me I'm Ellen G."

A waitress came by our table to take drink orders. Randy inquired about the Men's Room and the waitress directed him upstairs to the "unisex" restroom. He came back about half an hour later.

"What happened to you?" Buddha asked.

"There's a pool room upstairs. And it's all girls playin'. So I decided to play a game."

"How did you do?" Becky asked.

"I got my ass kicked by a tough looking chick," he replied. Then he leaned over to me and whispered, confidentially, "I think that chick might have been a dike. Her voice was deeper than mine." He chuckled.

"You might be right," I replied. "Hey, where's the restroom?"

"Oh, right at the top of the stairs. You can't miss it," Randy said.

I excused myself and went up the stairs. When I got to the top I saw the pool room. There were two pool tables and about a dozen women standing around, several with pool cues in their hand. As with the crowd downstairs they ranged from masculine-looking women to very feminine women. There were some sleeveless shirts being worn and I saw a fair number of tattoos adorning the shoulders of some of the women. As one of the pool players leaned over the table to take a shot her shirt rose up a little and I saw a couple tattoos on her lower back just above her butt.

I watched the pool players for a few minutes then went into the restroom. Along one side of the room were stalls. On the other side there were a couple of sinks and to my surprise a couple urinals. I inspected them closely. There were no little guillotines attached to the urinals, so I figured it was safe to use them.

I unzipped and began relieving myself. Just as I started I heard the restroom door open. I was expecting to hear the footsteps stop and the stall door open but the steps continued and out of the corner of my eye I saw someone pull up to the urinal next to me. I breathed a sigh of relief. It had to be Buddha; he was the only other guy in the joint.

"Is Svetlana still singing?" I said, glancing over to make eye contact with Buddha. But as I did that I realized that I wasn't looking at Buddha. I was looking at a woman with a crew cut and a stern expression on her face. I glanced down to see what she was doing. She wore a plaid flannel shirt and jeans. She cranked down her jeans, straddled the urinal and let it rip.

"She's still singing," the woman said in a deep, gravelly voice that sounded like she'd smoked too many cigarettes in the past. Then she added, "You're missing the urinal."

I looked down and saw that she was right. My aim had gone wide when I twisted to look at her.

"Sorry," I said, correcting my aim. "You've got very good aim," I said, trying to make conversation.

"Thanks. It took a lot of practice. But now I prefer a urinal to sitting on a seat. Especially in a public toilet. The seats can be so dirty. If I could take a crap in a urinal I would." She chuckled.

We both finished up and washed our hands. Then she turned to me.

"Hi, I'm Molly McGuire. That's my real name, by the way." She held out her hand to shake. I took it and I thought she was going to crush my hand.

"Jerry Taylor. Pleased to meet you."

We left the restroom together. Molly went over to the pool tables and picked up a beer. I waved to her and went back downstairs.

Svetlana was just finishing up her first set when I returned to our table. She took a quick bow and then went out back. The bar put on a radio (thank goodness it was normal music) and some of the women started dancing together.

"Shoot. I was hoping she'd stay out in the bar so I could talk to her," I said.

"I think someone else is going to play next, so she'll probably be out here," Karen said. "So how was the restroom?"

"Interesting," I replied.

"Is everyone enjoying the bar?" Karen asked.

"Interesting," Buddha said.

"Different," Becky replied, laughing.

"I'd agree with both of them," I added.

"I like this place. There's almost no guys here. I feel like a kid in a candy store," Randy replied exuberantly. "Look at that." He pointed to some women dancing. "These gals are so starved fer men they're even dancin' with each other."

"They are dancing with each other," Karen agreed, smiling. Then she looked at me and mouthed, "Didn't you tell him?"

I mouthed back, "I forgot," and shrugged my shoulders. We both laughed.

Randy nudged me. "Hey, see that table over there? Those gals are checking us out. I bet they come over here to ask me to dance – they want a real man."

I looked over at the table and there were a couple women there, looking our way and giggling bashfully. Then, one of them got up and started walking toward us. Randy nudged me in the ribs.

"What did I tell you." As the woman got to our table he stood up, bowed and said, "Welcome young lady. I bet you're looking for a dance partner."

"How did you know?" she said, smiling with surprise.

"I'm clairbuoyant," Randy said, his head swelling before our eyes. He held out his hand waiting for her to accept it. She walked right past him, leaned down toward Karen and asked Karen to dance. Karen accepted and went out onto the dance floor with the woman. Randy stood there, his mouth agape.

"I can't believe it," he said finally. "I wonder if that woman's a lesbian. I think there might be a couple of them lesbians at this bar tonight."

We all laughed. The song ended and Karen came running up.

"Lisa – the woman I was dancing with – is Svetlana's manager. She said we can talk to Svetlana in her dressing room. She's going down to tell Svetlana now," she said excitedly.

"Great work," I said patting her lightly on the back. I would have preferred to give her a kiss but I was afraid to do it since we weren't supposed to be romantically involved.

Lisa the manager came up to the table.

"O.K. You're all set. Lana's dressing room is the first door on the right, down the stairs."

We thanked her and Karen and I went down the stairs. We found the first door on the right and knocked.

"Come in."

We entered the dressing room. Lana a/k/a Svetlana was dressed in a bathrobe, sitting in front of a dressing table loaded with make-up, combs, flowers and all sorts of other detritus. She waved her hand weakly gesturing us toward a sofa in her room. We sat down.

"Lisa said you wanted to speak about Percy Jordan," she said. "What about him?"

"We're trying to find out if he really committed suicide or if someone might have killed him," Karen asked.

"I know nothing about such things, and I care less."

"Then why were you at the Memorial Service for Percy?" I asked. She looked at me and appeared to be somewhat shaken that we knew she had been at the service.

"I was just curious to see who might be there," she replied.

"Do you know of anyone who might have wanted to kill Percy?" Karen asked.

"No. There are many people who disliked him, but I know of no one in particular."

"We heard that he was, uh, dating you to try to make you break up with someone else you were dating. Is that true?" I asked. I was kind of enjoying the alternating interrogation that was going on. It made me feel like I was Elliot Ness giving the third degree to some hood.

"He spoke of wanting me to break up with my partner many times. I never listened to him."

"Did he threaten to tell your partner about your relationship with him? Did you pay him money to keep him from telling her?" Karen asked.

"No. I have no money. He knew that."

"Was he blackmailing someone else to get money?" I asked. She hesitated.

"Why are you asking these questions? Why do you care about these things?" she asked.

"I was one of Percy's students. I was one of the people who found his body. I want to know what happened to him," I replied.

"Well, he did say that he was blackmailing someone."

"Did he say who it was?" Karen asked.

"He just said a 'fat cat.' He didn't tell me any names."

"Did he say why he was blackmailing that person?" I asked.

"To get money, of course. That is a silly question."

"No, I mean, what kind of information he had to use in his blackmailing. What dirt did he have on his victim?" I explained.

"Stealing. He said the 'fat cat' was stealing money, so Percy was just getting 'his percentage.' That was all he said."

"Do you know how he knew this person who was stealing? Was it from the university? Was it from someone he knew somewhere else? Did it have anything to do with drugs or the mafia?" Karen asked.

"He used drugs. I don't know where he knew this person who was stealing."

"Did Percy sell drugs? Did he get money from that?" I asked.

"I don't know if he sold drugs. Like I said, he used them. He might have sold them." She looked at her watch. "I have to go. I cannot answer anymore questions."

"Oh, can I ask just one more?" I asked.

"You just did," she replied.

"All right. Can I ask just two more?"

"O.K. Make it fast."

"Do you know if any students ever threatened Percy?" I asked. She thought a moment.

"I think that a student from last year did say he wanted to kill Percy. And no, I don't remember who he was. Percy thought it was funny. He was happy he made a student that mad."

"Did he report the threat to the regular police or the Campus Police?" Karen asked.

"For you I answer another question or two," she said, smiling at Karen. "No, he did not report. He thought it was funny."

"If you think of the name of the student who threatened him could you call me?" Karen asked. Lana nodded and Karen gave Lana her phone number.


We went back upstairs and found Becky, Buddha and Randy all up dancing. Becky and Buddha were dancing, not so much cheek-to-cheek as belly-to-belly. The big surprise was Randy. He had insinuated himself into a group of a half dozen women who were all dancing together. They didn't seem to be paying any attention to him, but he seemed to be having a great time surrounded by all these women.

After the dance ended, they all came back to the table, laughing.

"Are you dancing machines about ready to take off?" I asked.

"Sure," Buddha and Becky said.

"How about you, Romeo?" I asked Randy.

"Yep. But let me just get the phone number of this gal I was dancing with," he said pointing to a woman walking past our table.

"Excuse me, darlin'. I'd be mighty pleased if you'd give me your phone number," Randy said, smiling at her. She stopped and looked at him.

"Do you know this is a lesbian bar and everyone in here is a lesbian?" she asked.

Randy stared at her, a blank look on his face, then said, "I knew that."

# TWENTY-SIX

I slept in late Sunday morning to fortify myself for Tae Kwon Do class.

On Sundays Ray held class in the Women's Dance Studio. The name was a throwback to the days when it was built. It was attached to a dorm that had been for women only; at that time only women used the studio. Now the dorm and the studio both were co-ed. But having survived my evening sojourn to the lesbian bar, I would have been game to use it even if it wasn't co-ed.

The Women's Dance Studio was a beautiful facility. It was a very large rectangular room with high ceilings giving it an even more spacious look. Along one side of the room were oversized windows looking out onto the Charles River. Sunlight streamed in on the shiny blond wooden dance floor. All of the other walls were covered with full-length mirrors so that the dancers (or martial artists in our case) could see themselves in action. It was a Narcissist's paradise.

So why would I need to fortify myself for a practice at the dance studio, you might ask? It was the size of the room. We had fourteen basic moves that we practiced at the beginning of every class. We would line up on one side of the room and do a series of front kicks, one after the other, across the entire room until we reached the far wall. Then we'd turn around and do another series of moves – maybe side kicks, upper blocks, single arm blocks or round house kicks – all the way back to the other end of the room. In our usual practice area we could fit in maybe five or six kicks or blocks in a row before coming to the opposite wall and having to stop. But in this huge dance studio we could fit a good twenty or thirty moves in each direction without stopping.

From Ray's perspective it was an opportunity to work on our endurance. From the students' perspective it was an opportunity to appreciate what it must be like to be bulimic because we all felt like tossing our breakfast after only a few basics. It was a brutal workout. I needed to muster all the energy I could on Sunday mornings, especially when there was no clean-up at the house. And there was no clean-up that morning.

After getting up, doing my morning ablutions and studying my pledge book for our quiz at the pledge meeting that night, I went to the Dining Center for brunch. The big topics of discussion were Halloween, which was coming up soon, and Mad Dog beginning his special project in the Early Childhood Development Center, which was scheduled to start on Monday.

Some people were taking odds on whether he'd make it through the first day. Others were speculating that he'd be putting the toddlers through close order drill and teaching them the finer points of using a bayonet. I had no morning classes the next day so I figured I'd drop by the Early Childhood Development Center to see Mad Dog in action.

After brunch I stole off to the library for some school work and then I headed over to Tae Kwon Do class. In a way I was eager to get to class because I wanted to see Karen and talk about Percy with her.

When I entered the dance studio the first thing I noticed were stacks of wood, cut into squares, neatly piled up on one side of the room. Ray was leaning over the piles.

"What's up with the wood?" I asked. A devious grin came over Ray's face.

"We're gonna do a little board breaking today."

"How are we gonna do that?" I asked.

"Use your head," he replied.

I thought about that. Did he mean that my question was stupid and I should be able to figure it out for myself? Or did he mean I should literally hit the boards with my head? I wasn't sure, but in case he meant the former, I decided not to ask him which he meant. I just grunted as though I understood and walked away to start stretching out with Buddha, who had just waddled into the room.

"Yo, Buddha," I greeted him. "We're breaking boards today."

"Cool," he replied.

"Have you ever heard of people breaking boards with their heads?" I asked nonchalantly.

"Sure. Your head's the hardest part of your body. I've heard that's the easiest way to break a board," he replied. I tucked that away in the old noggin for future reference and continued stretching.

Karen arrived a few minutes later and came over to where we were stretching.

"Hi guys, recovered from getting in touch with your feminine side last night?" she asked, smiling.

"Yeah. That was wild. I'm a lot more feminine than some of those women," Buddha said, shaking his head.

"All right. Line up for basics," Ray shouted. We got up as instructed and went through basics. Ray must have been eager to get to the board breaking because he only made us do about twenty of each basic move. So when the basics were over I was only 80% dead rather than completely dead.

After the basics ended Ray called us over to where he had the boards lined up so we could try board breaking. First he gave us a demonstration. He handed four boards to Buddha and me and had us hold them straight out towards him. I held one side of the boards and Buddha held the other. We held the boards straight out and locked our elbows as he instructed so the boards wouldn't move when he hit them. Then he had a couple other students support our elbows and our shoulders for some reason.

Ray took a few steps back focusing intently on the boards. Then a scowl spread over his face. It was the nastiest scowl I had ever seen and it was directed at the boards. You'd think the boards would break just from the look he was giving them.

He stepped forward determinedly, pulled back his fist and let it explode forward. I almost dropped the boards from the crushing impact as his fist slammed into the wood. Now I understood why he had other people supporting our elbows and shoulders.

Immediately after the impact there was a release of all tension on the wood as the four boards snapped cleanly in half and sailed away.

He did another demonstration breaking four boards using his foot in a side kick. Then he did a combination break of three boards with a high front kick and three boards with a knife-hand chop. Each time all the boards broke and I was thinking to myself that it looked pretty easy. I could do that, I thought smugly to myself. Just let me at 'em.

After Ray finished his demonstrations he had the rest of the class do some breaks. He started with the upper belts. When it was Karen's turn she used a front kick to break three boards just as easy as pie. Then she broke three boards using an elbow smash.

"Great breaking," I said, complementing her on her breaks. She beamed back at me.

The other upper belts completed their board breaking and then it was time for the white belts. Ray looked around and then pointed at me.

"Taylor, come up here and give it a try."

"Sure," I said. I got up eagerly and walked over to the wood piles. I selected four boards. Then I heard Ray laughing.

"Taylor, put down three of those. Try it with one," he instructed. One? Did he think I was a wimp or something? If I only broke one board I'd be a laughing stock.

"I can do 'em," I said.

"Taylor, you can't break four boards. Try one," Ray said again.

"I've been watching. It doesn't look hard. I can do it," I said stubbornly.

"Taylor, it's harder than it looks. Use one board."

Who was he kidding? I knew there must be a trick to it and I had seen how they did it. I knew I could break four boards.

But then again, there was an edge of irritation creeping into Ray's voice. I didn't want his scowl directed at me. I decided to compromise.

"Well how about three then?" I said, dropping one board. Ray gave an exasperated sigh.

"All right, Taylor. You can try it with two. But don't say I didn't warn you."

"Two?" I said.

"Two."

Grudgingly, I dropped another board and handed the remaining two boards to two of the other students to hold. They asked how I wanted the boards held. That was a good question. How was I going to break them? I was going to show Ray and everyone else that I was no woose. I'd punch through the boards just as he did on his first demonstration.

I directed the guys holding the boards to hold them straight out as Buddha and I had for Ray. Then I took a few steps back and looked at the boards. I focused on them, telling myself I was going to put my fist through them like a hot knife through butter. I scowled at the boards the way Ray had. O.K., maybe not as nasty a scowl as Ray had come up with, but it was nasty enough.

I pulled my fist back, stepped forward and my fist shot out at the boards. Right through, right through, right through I thought as I tried to visualize the boards exploding. I contacted the boards and there was an explosion. Unfortunately, it wasn't the boards. It felt more like my fist.

As I contacted the boards I felt the impact begin at the knuckles of my fingers, then spread through my hand, over my wrist, up my arm and all the way into my shoulder before my fist rebounded off the boards.

I heard groans coming from everyone watching me. They must have had some inkling of how much that hurt my hand, but I knew that they could not even begin to imagine the pain I was feeling at that moment.

I felt like screaming bloody murder, but I held it in. I was going to show them how tough I was. Besides, this couldn't be so hard. I must have just done something wrong, I thought to myself. I wouldn't miss a second time.

I was in pain and embarrassed but I decided to try punching the boards again. If I got them on the second try I'd be vindicated. I stepped back a couple feet then immediately stepped forward and punched the boards again.

Have you ever heard that expression, "fool me once shame on you, fool me twice, shame on me?" Well, that expression was what passed through my mind as my now-mangled fist rebounded off the boards a second time. Despite my attempt at self-control, a moan escaped me on the second hit. Out of the corner of my eye I saw everyone else cringing as they also moaned.

I had to break the boards to save face. If it was the last thing I did I would break those boards. I thought of trying it again with my fist, but I quickly rejected that idea. My fist felt like a flamenco dancer had just stomped it on. What was I going to do?

Then I remembered what Ray had told me earlier – "Use your head." That was it! I would use my head. Didn't Buddha say that it should be easiest to break boards using my head because my skull was such a hard bone? It might be a cheap way to break the boards but at this point I didn't care. I just had to get those boards broken.

I stepped back again. I scowled again, willing those boards to break. Then I lunged forward, head first. Just before everything went black I heard Ray's voice yelling, "Not your head, Taylor!"

The next thing I remember was hearing Buddha's voice saying, "I think he's waking up." I opened my eyes and found that I was lying on the floor of the dance studio looking up toward the ceiling. Buddha and Karen were standing over me, looking concerned.

"Did I break them?" I asked weakly.

"The boards or your head?" Ray asked, coming into view. "The answer is 'yes' to both," he said looking severe, but then grinning at me. "Taylor, what possessed you to hit the boards with your head?"

"You said to use my head," I replied groggily.

"Well, don't take me so literally next time."


After the practice I asked Karen if she wanted to get some coffee with me. I had a splitting headache but I wanted to talk with her about Percy to see if we could make some sense of what we had found out so far. She accepted and we went over to Peet's Coffee. I ordered a tall latte with extra milk and two aspirin on the side. Karen got a cup of herbal tea.

"How's the head?" she asked.

"Feels like Buddha's been jumping up and down on it," I said. "But it's better than my hand feels."

"Hmm. That bad? Maybe you'd better take an extra aspirin." She handed me a third, which I accepted gratefully. I washed it down with a big gulp of latte and sighed.

"Maybe you should go to the infirmary? You definitely should get your head examined," Karen said. I winced. "It must really hurt," she said, noticing my grimace.

"Not as much as your joke," I replied. "Karen, I need your advice."

"O.K. Never try to break boards with your head!"

"Not about breaking boards. About our Percy Jordan investigation," I said. "I need your advice about what our next move should be."

"Well, let's figure out what we know so far. Then we can decide where to go from here," she said very practically.

"O.K. We know Percy died from a barbiturates milkshake with a hydrochloric acid chaser. From what I can tell Percy wasn't lacking in confidence and he wasn't the depressed type so it doesn't make sense that he'd kill himself. That's one factor in favor of it being murder.

"Second, if someone was gonna kill himself I could see taking the drugs, but not drinking acid. That had to be really painful. Why not do it the easy way? The acid makes it seem like he was murdered by someone who wanted to punish him or make an example out of him."

"I agree," Karen replied. "Like a mafia hit." I nodded.

"Third, the suicide note was typed and it wasn't signed. Doesn't that seem weird? Why would he go to all the trouble to type the note but not sign it? I just don't buy it."

"And we know there are lots of people who hated the guy and might have wanted him as fertilizer," Karen added, clearly enjoying the slang.

"Right. We know that he was seeing three women at the same time. So jealousy could be a motive, and it could have been one of them. But I didn't really get the sense that any of the three of them would have been so jealous that she would have killed him," I added.

"What about the hit men relatives? They could have done it to keep him away from, was it Josey?" Karen suggested.

"Yeah."

"And you mentioned something about him being involved with drugs. That could have gotten him in trouble with the mob, too."

"Yeah, you're right. But how would the mob get hydrochloric acid from the chemistry lab, and how would they know to put his body up on the top floor of the Chem Building?" I asked.

"Well, they might have just looked around for a place to stash him and they stumbled on that room. Or, if he knew them, he could have taken them up there to speak in private and they used the opportunity to bump him off. And on the acid, how do you know it came from the lab? If they planned to kill him they could have gotten it somewhere else and brought it with them to make it look like he took it from the lab."

"You know, you're right about the acid. I just assumed it came from the lab. I better check on that with Officer Simpson," I said.

"Do you think Svetlana could have done it?" Karen asked.

"I don't know. I was thinking about that. She was at the memorial service and she was sleeping with him, apparently, even though she's a lesbian. So she must have felt something for him. But she didn't seem all that broken up when we talked to her. I was thinking that maybe her partner found out and killed him."

"That's a possibility, too. If she calls me back about the student who threatened to kill Percy I'll ask her about her partner," Karen said. I snapped my fingers.

"That's right! The student. I forgot about that. A student who threatened to kill him is a pretty good lead – revenge. The only problem is which student? There could be dozens who wanted to kill him. And there's also the 'fat cat' he was blackmailing. Eliminating a blackmailer is a good motive for murder. At least it is in the movies," I said.

"Anyone else?" Karen asked. I thought a moment.

"Well, he didn't get along very well with the other grad students, or Prof. Harnash for that matter. I suppose one of them might have had it in for him, although I don't think that's likely. Do you think I should speak with them?"

"Couldn't hurt," she replied.

"O.K. Well, then I'll try to speak with Harnash, the two grad students, and the campus cop again this week to see if I can get anything else out of them."

Karen said, "Great. If I don't hear from her I'll call Svetlana in a few days to see if she remembered the name of the student who threatened Percy and I'll find out about her partner."

# TWENTY-SEVEN

I rose early Monday morning – about 8:15. I'd set the alarm clock for 8:00 but I must have dozed through the alarm for 15 minutes.

I dragged my butt out of bed and glanced over at Jeff, who was looking right at me as he slept. No worry about my alarm clock disturbing him. After getting myself cleaned up and dressed, I ran to the Dining Center where I was supposed to meet Mad Dog and Sigmund for breakfast. I was the only pledge who had no classes this morning and I wanted to give Mad Dog some moral support. Sigmund was going to take us over to the Early Childhood Development Center where Tina would meet us.

When I got to the Dining Center Sigmund was there as well as Beeker and Tuney. Mad Dog hadn't arrived yet. I got my tray, filled it with a couple donuts, scrambled eggs, bacon, some yogurt, two glasses of juice, a coke and a cup of black coffee, then joined them at the table.

I picked up the cup of coffee and passed it to Beeker, who had asked me to get him another cup of coffee – probably his ninth of the morning. He accepted it with shaking hands, spilling coffee as he took the cup.

Tuney launched into song, "If I can't take my coffee break, someone at Starbucks cries."

"Beeker, are you sure you want another cup of coffee? It looks like you've already got the shakes down pretty well," Sigmund said in a concerned voice.

"Just one more. Can never have too much coffee," he chuckled, jerking his hand into a salt shaker that went flying off the table.

Mad Dog came into the Dining Center and sat down. He looked terrible.

"What happened to you?" I asked.

"Couldn't sleep," he replied. "I was up all night, pacing."

"Why?" I asked.

"Because of this project. I don't know how to handle little kids," he said miserably.

"Don't worry, you'll do fine. Tina will be there the whole time. She won't let you kill any of them," Sigmund said in a soothing voice.

"Aren't you gonna eat anything?" I asked.

"I'm too nervous to eat," he replied.

"Well, at least drink something," Tuney said.

"Here, take one of my juices," I said, offering it to him. He looked at it with a pained expression, but finally nodded and reached out to take it. His hand was shaking more than Beeker's. I couldn't believe that a guy like Mad Dog, with his military background and all his bravado, was scared of a bunch of little kids.

"I told Tina we'll be there by 9:30. Mad Dog, you'll work until noon today. You're scheduled to go back Wednesday and Friday, and then three days next week as well. All the same hours," Sigmund said.

"What if I don't make it past today?" Mad Dog said nervously.

"You'll survive," Beeker said. "I mean, how bad can a bunch of kids be?"

"Kids. They won't know what's wrong with Mad Dog today. Kids, they won't understand anything he'll say..." Tuney continued singing.

"We'd better get going," Sigmund said, looking at his watch. We all got up except Tuney who waved goodbye while still singing.

"You're not coming?" Beeker asked. Tuney shook his head 'no' and continued singing, but a different song.

"Why did the kids put beans in Dog's ears? They did it cause he said don't ..."

"He must be doing a kid medley," Sigmund said as we walked away from the table.

We got to the Psychology Building where the Early Childhood Development Center was located. Tina was waiting for us outside the door.

"Hi guys. How are we doing today, Mr. Mom?" she said to Mad Dog. Mad Dog said nothing. He just looked at her like a deer caught in the headlights.

"I see," she said. "Are we a little nervous?" He nodded stiffly. Tina took him by the arm and led him into the Center. We followed and Sigmund led Beeker and me into a room off the main room. It was dark and had a large window that looked into the main room. We heard voices coming from speakers above the wall.

"Two way mirror," Sigmund explained. "This way parents can watch their kids without the kids knowing they're here. And students can make observations as well. Beeker, sit here and don't move. I don't want you breaking anything. Jerry, you can sit wherever you'd like."

I was grateful that they were no longer calling me Percy after the death incident. Maybe I would get a new nickname now.

I found a seat and looked into the main room. It was set up like a large day care center. In one corner of the room there were cribs and mats rolled up. There were tables with diapers and changing supplies near by, and a number of sinks. In another corner of the room there was a little kitchen area, complete with high chairs, little lunch tables and chairs and food pantries and cupboards. But most of the room was taken up with play pens, play areas, toys, a reading area with books, a table full of water, a table full of sand and other playthings. It looked like a great place for kids, which was good, because there were loads of them in the room.

There were kids of every description. I saw babies in playpens and being held by student teachers. There were toddlers staggering around, barely able to walk. They looked a lot like the brothers at a Saturday night party. Then there were older kids who looked like they were pre-school age – four or five years old. Some of them were running around like little terrors, tormenting other kids, throwing things and yelling. I thought – maybe Mad Dog was right to be scared.

Tina was walking around the room with Mad Dog in tow, introducing him to the other staff members. I was a little disappointed that she didn't introduce him as Mad Dog; I would have enjoyed seeing the reactions of the other staff members. But I have to admit, he didn't look anything like a mad dog at that point. He was more like a whipped dog.

He seemed to be in a daze, walking like Boris Karloff in Frankenstein. But Tina kept him moving, all the while explaining the different places in the room to him and the activities that took place in each location.

After giving him the tour, Tina led Mad Dog over to a play area where the oldest kids were playing. She told the kids that Mr. Fillippo was going to play with them, too. They eyed him suspiciously but let him sit down with them. Tina left him there.

We watched Mad Dog. He just sat there like a zombie, watching the kids play. The kids ignored Mad Dog for a while, but then they seemed to become curious about him. They started staring at him shyly, then one of the bolder boys went up to him and held out some blocks. Mad Dog just stared at the kid and the kid stared at Mad Dog. This went on for a while and I wondered who would blink first. It was the kid.

"Build something," he demanded.

"What should I build?" Mad Dog said vaguely.

"A castle," the kid said. He walked over to a bucket of blocks and dragged it over to Mad Dog, then dumped it on the floor in front of Mad Dog. Tentatively, Mad Dog picked up a block and placed it on the floor. Then he picked up another and stacked it on the first. In a few minutes Mad Dog was building and stacking blocks with relish, making a tall fortress. No doubt he was reminded of Fortresses 101 from his old days in the military. He looked like he was really enjoying himself, oblivious to the kids who were watching patiently.

At last Mad Dog finished his castle and stepped aside proudly so that everyone could admire his handiwork. The kid who asked him to build the castle walked right up to it and with a scream knocked it over. Mad Dog looked on the destruction of his castle in horror, then his face turned red and I could tell he was fuming. He stood there shaking with rage, but I could almost see his brain working as he tried to figure out what to do. He couldn't hit the kid. He couldn't order him to do push-ups. So he just stood there shaking. After about twenty seconds of glaring at the kid he finally spoke.

"Why'd you knock over my castle?" he said in a stern voice.

"Because," the kid replied.

"Because why?" Mad Dog said.

"Just because."

"Well, don't do it again. It's not nice," Mad Dog said.

The kid looked at him, then walked right up to him, drew back his foot and gave Mad Dog a nice sharp kick in the lower shin. The kid was only wearing a sneaker, but he had a kick like a football place kicker. Mad Dog howled and started hopping around grabbing his shin as his face turned purple.

When he finished hopping I thought he was going to go after the kid but fortunately Tina must have heard the howl. She showed up and intercepted Mad Dog before he could do anything. We were all dying with laughter while this was going on.

Tina must have figured out that it was time for a change of scenery for old Mad Dog, because she led him away to the area where the toddlers were being fed. Tina passed him off to another woman who directed him to help feed these kids.

There were three young toddlers sitting in high chairs, eating gloppy food – orange mush – from little bowls. The woman showed Mad Dog how to feed the kids and she left Mad Dog to feed a cute little girl with long golden curls.

Mad Dog picked up the spoon, dipped it into the bowl of mush and tried to spoon it into the girl's mouth. She held her lips tightly closed and refused to open her mouth for him. He held the spoon near her mouth, asking her to open up for him. But it was to no avail. So he took another approach.

He started making faces at her, trying to get her to laugh. She smiled then opened her mouth slightly in a laugh. As soon as her mouth opened he tried to shove the spoon in, but she was wise to him. Just before the spoon got there she closed up her mouth tightly, frustrating his attempt.

Next he tried the old airplane routine, loading up the spoon with mush and pretending it was an airplane. He made the spoon swoop and dive through the air and kept telling her that her mouth was a hangar for the airplane. He asked her to open up her mouth so the airplane could go in.

She didn't seem to understand him, so he started bringing the spoon up near his mouth and opening his mouth as it got near to show her what he meant. After a while she seemed to understand. As he had the spoon make a particularly dramatic swoop down to her mouth, she opened wide and he plopped the spoon full of goop in.

Mad Dog smiled broadly at her and nodded his head. She, on the other hand, had a surprised look on her face as though she were trying to figure out what happened. She wasn't chewing. She was just sitting there in the highchair, looking confused.

"Is it good?" Mad Dog asked, encouragingly. The little girl looked at him, then opened her mouth and spit out the mush. It splattered across Mad Dog's face.

It was hard to tell which of them looked more surprised – Mad Dog or the little girl. But then both of their faces transformed. Mad Dog's face started to turn red again, a rather unflattering hue which contrasted with the orange goop covering it. The little girl's face became a very large smile as she figured out that this was pretty hilarious. Then, to add to her already great enjoyment, she picked up the mush bowl and flung it at Mad Dog, covering his hair and more of his face with the stuff. It was hard to tell who was laughing more – the little girl or us.

Mad Dog was seething but again the little girl was saved from feeling his wrath by the timely arrival of the woman who had placed him in the situation in the first place. She cleaned Mad Dog up and Tina came back to find another position for him. Mad Dog had struck out with the pre-schoolers and the toddlers, so I guess Tina decided to go one age group lower by having Mad Dog work with the babies. She must have figured he couldn't get into too much trouble there.

She took him over to the nursery area where some other women were taking care of the babies. After the introductions one of the women went to a crib and picked up a baby that had been crying. She tried to hand the baby to Mad Dog, but he backed away, a look of terror on his face.

"Oh, come on. It's easy. Just take him," she coaxed.

"No, I can't hold a baby. I'll drop it," he said.

"You will not. Here, take him." She placed the baby in his arms and he held it under his arm like a football. "No, not that way. Snuggle it up against your chest with its head resting on your shoulder like that." She pointed to one of the other women who was holding a baby and patting its back to burp it.

Mad Dog shifted the baby's position to mimic what the other woman was doing. He got the baby's head over his shoulder and stood there looking like he had just mastered organic chemistry or something.

The woman complimented him and he grinned, then started patting the baby's back like the other woman had done. After a few minutes the baby let out a belch.

"Jesus, was that you or me?" he chuckled. "You better lay off the sauce." He walked around over toward the two-way mirror where we were standing, looking at himself admiringly in the mirror. He rocked the baby gently as he moved, smiling. All of a sudden the baby threw up over Mad Dog's shoulder, causing Beeker to explode with laughter and fall over backwards in his chair.

"Something stinks," Mad Dog said. Then he glanced in the mirror and noticed the vomit on his shoulder. "Oh, God. What's that?" One of the other women caring for the babies came up to him. She had a strong southern accent.

"That's just a little good clean baby spit up. Here, I'll clean you right up." She used a towel to wipe off Mad Dog's shoulder. "There, good as new," she said. "Now, time to change him."

Mad Dog looked at her with a perplexed expression on his face. "What's wrong with him the way he is?"

"Silly. I mean you have to change his diaper."

"I can't do that."

"You have to learn sometime. It might as well be now," she replied. She directed him over to one of the changing tables and told him to lay the baby down. He did it. Then she told him to un-tape the sides of the diaper, which he did.

"Now, very slowly pull the diaper open," she instructed.

"Why slowly?" he said as he flipped the front of the diaper open quickly. At that moment a high-powered stream of pee shot up and into Mad Dog's eye, causing him to fall back, trip over a chair and land sprawling on the floor.

"That's why," she said.

After we got Mad Dog to the infirmary to have his eye examined, I went over to the Chemistry Building to see if I could get an audience with the great man – Professor Harnash. I thought he had office hours at 1:30 that afternoon and I was right, but he was going to be a little late. Tacked to his office door was a note:

> *To my students – I think the World of you, but unfortunately I'm going to be late for office hours today because of a faculty meeting. My hours will begin at 2:30 instead of 1:30. Sorry for the inconvenience.*
>
> *R.H.*

Lovely. I had a class at 2:00. I'd hoped to catch Harnash before my class. But I could come back at 3:00 after my class and still see him. I'd try to see his grad students right after lunch instead of him.

I returned to the Chem Building about 1:00 after wolfing down a quick lunch. I went to the graduate student lounge, knocked on the door and poked my head in.

"Hello?" I said, peaking into the lounge. Seated around a table, eating lunch, were Laura Wellman, Nick Rastinjani and another graduate student whom I recognized from the Chemistry Department dinner. They looked up from their lunches when I looked in.

"Hello. Can we help you?" Laura asked.

Having not really given much thought to what I would say, I decided to try the semi-honest approach.

"Uh, I was wondering if you could help me. I'm taking Prof. Harnash's Chemistry 101 class and I was in Percy Jordan's lab," I began. I saw their faces darken when I mentioned Percy's name, then a look of curiosity came over Laura's face and she stared at me.

"Anyway, I was trying to find out what's going to happen with my lab now that Percy is, uh, gone," I said. Laura kept staring at me.

"You know, you look a little like Percy," Laura said. "Nick, Joe, don't you think he looks like Percy?"

They both stared at me. I had rinsed the dye out of my hair after the dinner so it was now lighter than Percy's, and I had ditched the glasses. So I was hoping that they wouldn't place me at the dinner.

"Not really," the one she called Joe said.

"Maybe a little," Nick said, looking at me closely.

"Yeah, some people have told me that," I replied. "That was really terrible about Percy," I added, trying to direct the conversation.

"Yeah, I can't believe it," Laura said, shaking her head. "I was just talking to him the night before at the Chem Dept. dinner." I didn't want the conversation to go in that direction.

"Percy didn't really seem like the kind of person who'd commit suicide," I said. Joe snorted.

"You can say that again," he said. Nick nodded in agreement.

"You know, not many of his students liked him," I said.

"I don't like to speak ill of the dead, but truth is, not many living creatures liked him. Dogs would snarl and cats would hiss when Percy walked by," Laura said.

"Mosquitoes wouldn't even land on Percy," Nick added.

"There's even been some talk that maybe he didn't commit suicide. Maybe someone who didn't like him killed him," I suggested, hoping it would fuel the conversation. There was silence for about ten seconds, then Nick spoke again.

"I never liked the guy. I've figured from the start it was probably murder."

"Really? Who would kill Percy?" Laura replied. She sounded genuinely shocked.

"Anybody. The guy made enemies like Bill Clinton made staffers," Joe said.

"Can you think of anyone in particular that might have a grudge against him?" I asked. They scratched their heads, thinking.

"Well, he was cheating on his girlfriends. He had three of 'em. I suppose one of them could have gotten jealous," Laura suggested.

"He screwed over a lot of students in the last couple years. I wouldn't be surprised if one of them killed him. Especially if it was a chemistry student who knew where the hydrochloric acid was kept in the labs," Nick replied.

"Did the acid that Percy drank come from one of the labs here?" I asked eagerly, wondering how he would know something like that.

"Oh, I don't really know. I just assumed ..." Nick's voice trailed off.

"How did he get along with the other grad students and the faculty?" I asked.

"He didn't. We all thought he was a prick, but we just tried to ignore him," Nick said.

"I've heard there's a lot of competition in the department. Could anyone have gotten rid of him to reduce the competition?" I asked gingerly, knowing that I might be getting into touchy territory. Joe snorted again.

"Yeah, it's competitive. But Percy was no threat. He'd pissed off enough of the faculty that most of us figured he was gonna get canned sooner or later."

"How did he get along with Prof. Harnash? I saw the two of them arguing at the start of class not too long ago," I said.

"I guess they got along all right," Laura said. "I think Harnash had his problems with Percy from time to time. You know, they'd disagree about things. And Percy wasn't the most respectful guy in the world. But Harnash was his advisor and had absolute power over Percy. If Harnash had a serious problem with Percy he could just fail Percy and ruin his career. I mean, Harnash has huge clout internationally. He's a Nobel laureate, he brings in a ton of government research money. Percy would be finished if he stepped too far out of line, and he knew it."

"We all know it," Joe said somberly. Nick and Laura nodded in agreement.

I was thinking about the "fat cat" angle and blackmail. Maybe Harnash could be the "fat cat" and Percy might be holding something over his head and blackmailing him. That could account for why Percy hadn't been thrown out of the department.

"Tell me about Prof. Harnash. Does he have any secrets that Percy might have known about? There's another rumor I've heard that Percy might have been blackmailing someone and maybe that's why he got killed," I said.

They looked at each other quizzically, shrugging their shoulders.

"Nothing that I've heard about," Joe said.

"Well…" Laura began. "Prof. Harnash does have an eye for the ladies."

I guess that was something that he and Percy had in common.

"So?" Nick replied.

"He's supposedly happily married, but he's always seen with these other women coming out of various hotels. Don't you think that might be something to blackmail him about?" Laura asked. Nick and Joe shrugged their shoulders again.

"I don't know. He's not very secretive. We all know about it. Any idiot could find out about it," Nick suggested.

"But does his wife know?" I asked, getting excited. Shrugs all around. Maybe I was on to something.

"One last question. There's also a rumor that Percy might have been selling drugs and doing business with the mob. Know anything about that?" They all responded with negative head shakes.

"Well, it was just a rumor. Thanks a lot. I better be going," I said. I started to walk out of the room.

"Hey, don't you want the information about who's gonna take over your lab now that Percy's gone?" Laura asked.

"Oh, yeah," I said, remembering the pretext I used to start the conversation.


I went to my class at 2:00 and returned to the Chemistry Building at 3:00, hoping to corner Prof. Harnash during his delayed office hours.

I needn't have bothered going to class. Instead of paying attention I was mulling over the information I'd learned about Harnash, trying to decide how or if I should use it when I spoke with him. I hadn't reached any conclusions by the time I got to his office. I would just have to see what developed while I was speaking with him and decide on the fly.

When I got to his office the door was closed but I heard noises coming from within. They were rhythmic bumping noises as if someone was bumping the wall repeatedly with a rocking chair. Tenuously I knocked on the door. No response. I knocked louder.

The bumping sound stopped suddenly and from the other side of the door I heard a muffled, "Oh, damn. Not now." I heard a rustling sound that lasted about a minute, and then the door opened a crack. Prof. Harnash looked out at me, the little hair on his head was rumpled.

"Yes. What is it?" he said in an annoyed tone.

"Professor, I'm in your Chem 101 class. I'm here for your office hours," I said quickly. He glared at me for a moment.

"I've got another student with me right now. Can you come back in about half an hour?"

"Sure," I responded.

He harrumphed and closed the door quickly. Through the closed door I heard, "It's a student. We've gotta make it fast." Then there was a female voice giggling and the bumping noise began again, this time accompanied by a grunting noise. The grad students were right. He wasn't very secretive.

I decided to go get a coke and come back. I returned in about 15 minutes. The bumping and grunting had stopped but I could hear voices coming from behind the door so I figured I hadn't missed him. About ten minutes later the door swung open and a tall middle-aged woman wearing an expensive looking suit and conservatively fashionable shoes, walked out of the room. She had a small Vuitton handbag with her, but no books or papers of any kind that I could see. Prof. Harnash followed her out and glanced at me nervously. Then he cleared his throat.

"Very good work on those problem sets, Miss, uh... Smith. Be careful when you calculate the electron transfers. I'll see you in class. And do come back next week if you need another, uh ... tutoring session." He gave me another nervous glance.

"Good bye, Professor. Thank you for your lesson," she said with a classic French accent. She waved and walked away.

The Professor and I both admired the sway of her perfectly proportioned rear end as she moved down the corridor until she turned the corner. Then he looked back at me and cleared his throat again.

"Now, what can I do for you, Mr... .?" he said, gesturing for me to enter the office. As I walked in I noticed that there was a very comfy-looking oversized sofa in the room but no rocking chair. There was also a large ornately carved wooden desk, a few leather backed chairs for visitors, a coffee table strewn with scientific journals and a few lamps on a credenza behind the desk.

One wall was covered with a large bookcase, filled to overflowing with books. The other walls were covered with diplomas, framed articles about Prof. Harnash, and awards of every description including his Nobel medal in a gilded frame.

"I'm Jerry Taylor. I'm in your Chem 101 class," I repeated in case he didn't remember from when I told him before. After all, he seemed distracted.

"Have a seat, Mr. Taylor," he said motioning me to a chair, which I took. "What did you want to discuss?"

"Well, my lab T.A. was Percy Jordan and now that he's gone I was wondering how we were going to be graded," I said. I looked at his face closely for a reaction when I mentioned Percy's name but he was poker-faced.

"You have nothing to worry about, Mr. Taylor," he said. "I've already made arrangements for a new T.A. to be at your next lab. She'll review your prior lab notebooks and that will enable her to catch up on your past work so that she can grade you. Is there anything else?" He stood up as he said this, signaling me that he wanted this interview to be over. I ignored his signal and continued sitting there.

"Uh, yes, Professor. I wanted you to know that I attended the memorial service for Percy Jordan and I heard your comments. They were very moving."

"Oh, you were there? Well, it's a nasty business when something like that happens, a promising life and career snuffed out in its prime. Our department will have to do a better job looking out for our students. Anything else?"

He had sat down when he answered me, but now he was up on his feet again like a jack-in-the-box, trying to usher me out. This called for drastic measures.

"Professor, Percy Jordan's death has really un-nerved a lot of people. There are rumors floating around that he was murdered."

"Well, that's preposterous," he blustered, his face red. "He killed himself. That's what the Medical Examiner and the campus police concluded."

"I know," I said. "But there are a lot of students who don't think that Percy was the type of person who would kill himself."

"And what type of person is it that would kill himself?" he said, sitting down again.

"Well, you know, someone depressed and overwhelmed."

"Mr. Taylor," he said calmly, his hands folded on his desk in front of him. "Percy Jordan is the fifth student in our department to commit suicide over the last ten years. None of them appeared to be the 'type' to kill himself." He emphasized the word 'type.' "If they had we would have intervened and gotten them some counseling before they committed suicide. It's a very complex problem. Persons are not always what they seem."

I thought about this for a moment. That must be true. Unless they were all bumped off and it was made to look like a suicide. But that didn't seem likely.

"But, Professor, there were a lot of people who didn't like Percy Jordan. I've been checking around and I've found lots of reasons why people would want to kill Percy Jordan."

"And what are those, Mr. Taylor," he asked, showing interest.

"Well, he's screwed over a lot of students on their grades, intentionally, and I've heard that's caused at least one student to threaten his life. He was using drugs and might have been selling them, so he might have had some ties to the mob that could have gotten him killed. He was having affairs with three different women at the same time, so maybe one of them got jealous and killed him. Those are all possibilities," I said, deciding to hold back the blackmail idea.

"Well, those are very interesting thoughts. And I suppose at a superficial level they have some appeal, but I wouldn't put much stock in them, Mr. Taylor. Virtually every student thinks he got 'screwed' on his grades. If that was a sufficient motive for murder there'd be no teachers left. As for the drugs, while I had heard that Mr. Jordan may have used drugs recreationally I heard nothing about him selling drugs. I have a close relationship with the graduate students and it's a small department. Word gets around. I'd have known if he had a drug problem or if he was selling drugs, and I would have done something about it," he said in a condescending tone.

"Well, what about the women?" I asked. A wistful look came over his face.

"Ah, yes, the women. I knew, of course, that he was having relationships with a number of different women, as was his right I might add. I wouldn't interfere in that aspect of his personal life, of course. But I think that most women understand that a man needs some variety in his physical and emotional relationships. They expect a man to be sowing his wild oats, so to speak. I really doubt that they would get jealous enough to kill Mr. Jordan. No really, Mr. Taylor, I think you should abandon this idea that Mr. Jordan was murdered. None of those motives is sufficient," he said pedantically.

I decided to shake him up a little and see if he rattled.

"Would blackmail be enough of a motive I asked?" His face darkened but then became impassive again.

"What do you mean?" he asked. I thought I caught a slight tremor in his voice.

"There's another rumor that Percy Jordan was blackmailing someone who is very prominent. Do you think that would be sufficient motive for him to be murdered?" I asked coyly.

He looked at me for a few moments and then slowly he said, "It's possible, but again, it would depend on a lot of variables including the personality and make-up of the blackmailed victim, the secret the victim was trying to hide and the ramifications if the secret were discovered … If you can provide me with some of these variables I can probably give you a better assessment," he coaxed.

"All right. Let's say the victim was a prominent faculty member at a famous university. Let's say he was married, but that he was constantly hooking up with other women. Sometimes it was at hotels and other times it was on the sofa in his office during office hours. Percy Jordan finds out about it and threatens to tell his wife, so he kills Percy Jordan to keep his wife from finding out he's been playing around. What do you think about that?"

He looked at me for a few seconds and then burst out laughing. My mouth dropped open. That was hardly the reaction I expected when I decided to confront him.

"Mr. Taylor, you slay me," he said, still chortling. "I'd like you to do me a favor. I'm going to dial my home telephone number right now and I would like you to speak with my wife and tell her about my philandering. Will you do that for me?"

I stared at him, not understanding what he meant.

"I can't ..." I said hesitantly.

"Oh, but you can, Mr. Taylor, you can. I insist," he said, still chuckling. He dialed a number and handed me the phone. I held it loosely and he gestured for me to put it up to my ear. I did. It was ringing.

Someone picked up on the other end and a female voice said, "Harnash residence." Again, he gestured encouragingly to me to say something.

"Uh, hello, is this Mrs. Harnash?" I asked.

"No, this is Hannah, the Harnash's housekeeper. I'll get her," the voice responded. There was a pause for about thirty seconds and then another voice came on the phone. It was a hale and hearty sounding female voice.

"Yellow, this is Ginny," the voice boomed.

"Mrs. Harnash?" I asked again, tentatively.

"Yah, but call me Ginny. You make me feel old if you call me Mrs. Harnash."

"O.K., uh, Hello ... Ginny, this is Jerry Taylor," I said, and paused. There was a brief silence on the other end of the phone.

"Well, hello to you Jerry Taylor. Who the Hell are you? You sound young? Are you young?"

"I'm one of Prof. Harnash's students – in his Chem. 101 class," I replied.

"101? Well that's why you sound so young. You must be a baby!" she said. I took umbrage at that.

"I'm a freshman," I said, indignantly.

"Keep your boxers on, honey. I just meant you're not any of those Nervous Nellie stiffs he supervises in the graduate school."

"Nervous Nellies?" I said, not understanding. Prof. Harnash started chuckling again. He'd obviously heard her use that expression before and knew what she was talking about.

"Oh, you know. They're always so nervous, brown nosing Ronnie, afraid to do or say anything to offend him so they don't get the axe. But you don't sound like any of them." She paused. "So why are you calling? Are you looking for Ronnie? He's not here now. Probably at some hotel getting a little nookie from one of his cookies." My mouth dropped open.

"You know about that?"

"Hell yes," she boomed. "Who doesn't?"

"And you don't mind? I mean, it doesn't bother you?" I asked, incredulous.

"Oh, it used to. But when I thought about it I decided that if I looked as bad to him with my clothes off as he looks to me with his clothes off, well, it was no wonder he wanted to have sex with someone else. God knows I do. I mean for the past ten years our most effective method of birth control was keeping the light on." She chuckled. "So we reached a compromise. He can chase after whatever he wants and whoever will have him just so long as he doesn't tell me about it and he doesn't come home with a tattoo of some floozie's name on his ass."

"Oh," I said, at a loss for words.

"And I play the field myself. I particularly like young students. I'm always on the lookout for a boy-toy," she said playfully. I couldn't tell if she was being facetious or if she was serious.

"Oh," I said again.

"You're a talkative one, you are," she said. "Oh. Said it first." She laughed. "So that's my story, honey. Now, what did you want? Was it Ronnie?"

"Uh, no. I mean yes," I replied quickly. "But I'm all set. Thanks for talking. Sorry to bother you."

"No problem. Next time drop by the house and I'll give you some milk and nookies. Get it?"

"Yeah," I replied.

"How often? Heh, heh! That was a good one." She was still laughing when she hung up the phone.


I walked over to the building where campus security was located, smacking myself on the head. I'd really put my foot in my mouth accusing Harnash of being a killer. But the blackmail angle had looked pretty good to me at the time. I just had to hope that Harnash wouldn't flunk me now.

I went into the reception area and spoke to the officer at the desk.

"Is Officer Simpson still in the ...?" I said, pointing. He nodded, smiling. I walked down to the rest room, knocked on the door and peeked in. Officer Simpson was hunched over his desk, writing. Next to him a very fat campus cop was standing at a urinal, relieving himself. How could he concentrate in this place, I wondered?

"Hi, Officer Simpson," I said. He looked up, gave me a vague wave of the hand, and then continued with his writing. El Gordo, the fat cop, flushed and waddled out of the restroom without washing his hands. I made a mental note never to shake hands with him.

"Officer Simpson, can I ask you a question? It should only take a minute or two."

He looked up and gave me a frazzled look, then glanced at his watch.

"I can give you exactly two minutes. I've got to get this report out today. It's critical," he said.

"Gee, what is it?" I asked, impressed that he was getting responsibility again.

"It's a report on the missing locker keys – you know, from the lockers in the lower floor of the Student Center. And I think I've cracked it."

"What do you think happened to the keys?"

"Keynappers. They're gonna send a ransom note any day now."

"I see. Um, can I ask you a question?"

"Yes. Make it fast."

"On that Percy Jordan suicide?"

"Yes."

"Did the acid that he drank come out of one of the labs in the Chem Building?"

"Don't know. We checked but they don't keep track of how much they have in the bottles. So there's no way to tell."

Struck out again!

# TWENTY-EIGHT

I dusted the powdered sugar off my jacket as I chewed, savoring the flavor of the sweet, creamy ricotta cheese and the crunchiness of the crust shell. I decided that whoever invented cannolis was a genius. And so was the cannoli maker at Mike's Pastry, here on Hanover Street in the North End of Boston, where I was currently enjoying my treat.

As I ate my cannoli I looked around at the glass display cases filled with every type of baked good and pastry imaginable. They all looked great. And because I had missed lunch, I thought to myself, I'd be justified getting something else to eat once I polished off the cannoli.

I'd missed lunch because I had had a short meeting with my Psychology 101 professor that turned into a long meeting. I was supposed to write a paper on social psychology (my interest in the subject had been piqued by Sigmund and my experience playing Percy Jordan) and I needed some help from my professor to narrow down the choice of topics for my paper. But she went off on so many detours that I left the meeting with more questions and more possible topics than when the meeting began.

By the time my meeting ended it was too late for me to get lunch. My pledge brothers and I were supposed to meet at the T station. We were going back to Charlestown to help the elementary school kids with their reading program again. Our session with the kids had ended about half an hour earlier and I had left my pledge brothers to go to the North End.

I wanted to see if I could speak with Vito or Rocco again about Percy Jordan, hoping to learn about any connection he might have with drug dealing. But before meeting with them I had decided to stop in at Mike's Pastry for a little snack. It was just to keep my stomach from growling and disturbing people. After all, it was the polite thing to do!

Just to be doubly polite, and to give my cannoli some company, I decided to get a second cannoli, but this time filled with custard instead of ricotta. Both were great but I decided I liked the ricotta slightly better.

Well fortified, I got up and sauntered down Hanover Street toward the Daily Catch and Josey's apartment.

It was a beautiful afternoon. The sun was low in the sky because it was late in the day, but it was shining. The leaves on the trees were displayed in brilliant shades of orange, yellow and red. The air was slightly crisp. People were walking briskly up and down the street, engaged in their daily activities. And I was content as I navigated past the many shops and restaurants lining the street.

I had only gone a short way when I saw Vito and Rocco, sitting outdoors on a bench, with several other old men. As I approached I could hear the lyrical sound of the Italian language cascading off their tongues as they chatted lazily. I noticed that Vito, Rocco and the other old men were wearing jackets with bulges under their pockets. I walked up to them.

"Hi, Vito, Rocco, do you remember me?" They stared at me as if I were a phantom, but then recognition slowly came into Vito's face and a smile crept over his lips.

"It's Jerry. Hey, boys, this is our college student friend, Jerry. You know, the one I told you about. Madonna gave him a reading," he said to them. Then he looked at me again. "So how are you doin'? Ya getting' any action? Madonna said you would. And she's got the gift!"

"Well, I'm getting a lot of offers. But I haven't taken any of 'em up yet," I replied, grinning.

"You got plenty of time. Now at my age, I don't turn down any offers. Of course, they don't come so frequent anymore as it is." He laughed.

"That's for sure," Rocco agreed.

"So, what are you doin' in our neighborhood? You come to see Josey? She ain't in. She's workin' this afternoon," Vito said.

"No, actually, I stopped by to see you and Rocco. It's about Percy Jordan. It's kind of personal," I added, looking at Vito and Rocco's friends.

"No problem. We can go into my office to talk, private. Come on, Rocco," Vito said. He got up slowly and walked over to the door of Café Primo, an Italian café that was just a few doors down the street, and motioned for Rocco and me to follow him inside. The person working behind the counter nodded to him.

"My table open, Dom?" Vito asked. Dom nodded. "Bring us three espressos and three cannolis."

I don't like espresso and I was stuffed and sweeted out from the two cannolis that I'd just devoured at Mike's. I started to protest that I didn't want anything but Rocco nudged me.

"It ain't polite to turn down espresso and a cannoli when Vito offers," he said. He gave me a look that said I didn't want to be impolite to Vito, so I said nothing else.

I followed Vito to a table in the back corner of the room. There was a large plant situated near the table, effectively shielding it from the rest of the room. No other tables were close to it. Vito and Rocco dropped into seats. I sat down and started to speak, but Vito raised his hand signaling me to stop.

"Let's get our espresso and cannoli first before we talk business."

I sat there, uncomfortably, for the next five minutes until Dom came up to our table with a tray of three small espresso cups and three cannolis. He placed an espresso and a cannoli before each of us and then discreetly left the area.

Vito and Rocco each picked up the lemon peel that adorned each cup, held the peel over the black foamy liquid and twisted. Then they looked at me. I picked up my lemon peel and did the same. Vito grinned.

Then Vito and Rocco each picked up a spoon and began shoveling sugar into their cups – one spoonful, two spoonfuls, three spoonfuls. Once again they looked at me expectantly. I followed suit.

After we all had enough sugar in our tiny cups to put a normal person into a diabetic coma Vito and Rocco picked up their cups and sipped. Contented looks came over both of their faces and Vito smacked his lips. Tentatively I took a sip of my espresso. It certainly had it all. It was overly bitter, overly sour and overly sweet. I almost gagged.

"Ummm. Good," I said.

"Try the cannoli," Vito encouraged, and then began eating his with gusto. I bit into the cannoli. It was good but too rich for me to eat after those other two earlier pastries and my little cup of coffee flavored syrup. I tried putting it down several times but Rocco gave me the "look" each time I did it. So like it or not I was forced to finish the cannoli and the espresso. By that time I wasn't feeling well.

"Well, waddaya think?" Vito said enthusiastically. I forced a smile.

"Great," I said with a grimace. Vito called out to Dom, who poked his head around a corner.

"Yeah, Vito."

"Dom, get us one more round of espresso – make 'em doubles this time – and three more cannolis. I didn't have no lunch today."

After forcing down my fourth cannoli and a double espresso, I felt seriously ill. Vito, however, seemed to be hitting his stride. He had a happy look on his face and he stretched luxuriously.

"That hit the spot. Now, let's talk … Jerry, you don't look so good. You all right? You must be comin' down with somethin'."

"I think I ate too much," I groaned.

"Well we better talk fast so you can get back home and lay down. What did you want to talk about?"

"Percy Jordan. I don't really know how to say this, but, I've been hearing a lot of things about him and I was wondering if you might be able to give me some information." I burped. "Excuse me."

"What kinda things you been hearin' about him?" Vito asked.

"Well, one thing I heard is that he was using drugs – and he may have been selling drugs, too. I know that you two wouldn't know anything about that personally, but I was wondering if you might have heard something about that?" I said. They looked at each other.

"We don't know nothin' about that," Vito replied.

"Do you know anyone who might know?" I asked.

"Nope. Why are you tryin' to find out about this?"

"There are some rumors flying around that Percy may not have killed himself. That he might have been murdered. I'm just curious, trying to see if I can find out anything about him."

"Well, we know he was seeing Josey and that he was from England. That's alls we know about the guy," Vito replied. "We don't know about no drugs."


I was at the Park Street subway station feeling kind of buzzed and sick to my stomach. After leaving Vito and Rocco I had walked to Haymarket where I got on the green line of the T, taking that as far as Park Street where I had to change to the red line to get back to Cambridge.

I sat down holding my stomach and missed a couple of trains. But it was getting late and I wanted to get back to campus, so I was starting to get up when in front of me I saw Yaz with a couple homeless people.

"Yaz," I called out. He looked over in my direction, then saw me and waved. He spoke to the homeless people, who were standing on a bench looking at the tops of people's heads, and then walked over to me. I held out my hand to shake but he shook his head, no.

"What are you doing here?" I asked.

"I stayed behind to check in with my followers," he said gesturing to the homeless people he had been with.

"What do you mean 'your followers'?" I asked.

"You know, my cyborg groupies. I've been getting mail and phone calls from so many of them asking me to come back to give 'em further guidance, that I decided to stay behind. My people need me!"

"So what are you doing with 'em here?" I asked.

"Actually, I'm trying to get these people over to a homeless shelter in Central Square where they can get a meal and some help. But to do it I had to make 'em think we were hot on the trail of cyborgs. Otherwise they wouldn't come. How was your meeting with the Sopranos?"

"Useless. Plus they made me eat and drink so much that I'm sick now," I replied.

"I was gonna say, you do look a little shaky."

"I just need to lie down, or puke, or both," I groaned.

"Well, the next train should be along soon. I'm gonna get my groupies," Yaz replied, and he went over to the bench where the homeless people were standing. I got up shakily and made my way over to the tracks where the train was expected to arrive. I felt terrible, but I stood there nonetheless, hoping that if I was one of the first ones on I might get a seat.

A few minutes later I heard the sound of a subway train approaching and I saw the glimmer of light from its headlight as it illuminated the tunnel before it. Just another minute and it would be here. I was praying that it wouldn't be too crowded so I could grab a seat when it arrived.

About ten seconds later the train came into view out of the tunnel. It was a fairly new train, with two cars connected at the middle by an accordion-type contraption that compressed and expanded as the train moved around corners. I could see the bright headlight shining at the front of the train. But from my angle I couldn't tell how crowded the train was.

Now the train was only a short distance away, moving slowly into the station. I had just begun to look around for Yaz and his retinue of homeless people when I felt a sharp push on my back and I went flying forward directly into the path of the on-coming subway train.

I fell across the tracks and looked up to see the headlight of the train almost upon me. I held up my arm in a feeble attempt to ward off the approaching train. I realized that I had only seconds before I would be crushed by the train. Then I felt hands gripping me and pulling me out of the path of the train just as it crossed the tracks at the place where I had been sprawled.

I looked up and saw that Yaz and his homeless people had me.

"Jeezus, Jerry. You gotta be more careful. You could have been killed," Yaz said excitedly.

"Someone pushed me!" I replied. "Did you see who it was?"

"No. I just saw you go down in front of the train. I thought you fainted or something. You scared the Hell outta me. My friends and I were just barely able to pull you out of the train's path."

I looked at Yaz and then at his two sidekicks.

"Hey, thanks a lot. You guys saved my life. Someone tried to kill me," I said, still shaking from the experience.

"It was a cyborg," one of the homeless persons said. "I saw its bald spot."

# TWENTY-NINE

I paid for the drinks and brought them to the table where Karen and Randy were sitting. We were in the Landing, another small bar in Central Square, Cambridge, which had half price appetizers in the evening. Before us on the table were chicken wings, nachos, crab cakes and quesadillas. Definitely a bargain at half the price!

I set the drinks down on the table. Randy was wearing his butler suit, now impeccably cleaned and pressed, and he was regaling Karen with Martha Stewart-type information.

"Now if you wanna get all the stains out of a shirt you have to soak it with a little bleach and some Spray 'n Wash. But just for a few seconds if it's a colored fabric. An' when you iron it, you gotta be real careful about the temperture so you don't scorch it. I prefer using an iron that's slightly under-heated. If you spray a small amount of starch on it you'll dewrinkify the shirt as well as if you applied greater heat." Karen just nodded.

"Gee, Randy, you sound like you've learned a lot about doing laundry. Did those tips come from Cheever?" I asked.

"Yeah. And he's taught me how to cook, clean, sew and do all the other things he used to do fer me. He says I could git a job as a gentlemen's gentleman now, if I tried," Randy said proudly.

"That's great. I'll hire you," I said, smiling.

"No way. I want an employer who's gonna still be around in a year," he said with a laugh.

"Well, with that outfit you could pass as an undertaker. I could hire you to bury me," I replied.

"I don't believe you two! Almost getting killed isn't funny!" Karen said, annoyance in her voice.

"Well there's nothing I can do about it," I said. "So I might as well keep my sense of humor." She just shook her head.

"And why did you go to Prof. Harnash's office by yourself like that and basically accuse him of killing Percy Jordan? I mean, hello, are we using our brains here? If he was the killer what was there to keep him from killing you, too?" she asked, disgusted.

"O.K., O.K. So I made a little mistake there. I haven't been in the detective business very long, you know. Next time I go to confront a potential murderer I'll tell someone before I go, just in case. But fortunately, this time, he didn't turn out to be the murderer and he didn't murder me."

"And what about going back to those mob hitmen. That was a foolhardy thing to do, too. Fortunately you've got more luck than you have brains sometime," she said, throwing her hands up in an appeal to Heaven.

"Who do ya think it was that tried to make you a pancake?" Randy asked.

"I dunno. One of Yaz's homeless people said whoever it was, he was bald. But that guy smelled like a whiskey barrel. So I'm not too confident he knew what he was talking about."

"Did he give you any more of a description other than that the bad guy was bald?" Randy asked.

"No. In fact, now that I think of it the guy didn't even say it was a 'he.' He said he saw 'its' bald spot. For all I know it could have been a woman."

"If he was right, though, and it was a man who was bald, who do you think it could be?" Karen asked. I thought about it a minute.

"Karen, there are probably more than half a million men in the greater Boston area that are bald or have a bald spot. It could be anyone."

"No. I mean, which of your suspects or people associated with Percy are bald?" she said.

"Well, let's see. There's Rocco, he's one of the mafia guys from the North End that I had been visiting. He's bald. Then there's

Professor Harnash. And that graduate student, Nick Rastinjani, he has a bald spot…." I thought some more. "Oh, and that cop, Officer Simpson. He's going bald. So that doesn't get us anywhere."

"But why did it happen at that time? Why not before? You must have shaken somebody up enough for him to try to get rid of you."

"I dunno. It might be that it took him awhile to get an opportunity to try to kill me," I said.

"I doubt it. How did that guy Rocco react when you were speaking with him earlier in the day?" Karen asked.

"Maybe a little suspicious. He and Vito sure didn't want to talk about any drugs. I suppose I might have gotten them upset a little. But they seemed nice enough – except that they tried to kill me."

"They did?" Karen gasped.

"Yeah. By feeding me to death," I said, laughing.

"Very funny." She sipped her drink.

"How about you? Have you heard anything else from Svetlana?" I asked.

"No. I've been meaning to call her. I'll try tonight and let you know what she says. Hey, didn't you say you had the key to Percy's apartment?" Karen asked.

"Damn. I forgot about that. I do have one, although what I did with it I'm not sure."

"Maybe you should search his apartment," Karen suggested.

"You're right. I should do that. I'm not gonna have time this week, but maybe on the weekend, if I can still find the damned key."

"I dunno," Randy said. "We got the Halloween party Saturday night and we're s'posed to go to Tookie's house on Sunday. Hey, did you invite Karen to the Halloween party?" Randy asked.

"Shit. Forgot about that too. Karen, do you wanna go to a Halloween party Saturday night?" I asked.

"Depends. Where's it being held?"

"At the fraternity house."

"Nope," she replied without a moment's hesitation.

"Come on, Karen. You've met Buddha and Randy. You know there are nice people involved with the fraternity, right?" I said. She smiled at Randy.

"Yes. And I'm sure there are lots of other nice people involved with the fraternity, too. But I still don't like the idea of fraternities. I'll pass, thanks."

"I think you're being closed minded," I replied, sullenly.

"Maybe I am, but for now, that's the way I am."

"Yer gonna miss out on a humdinger of a party," Randy coaxed. "Lots of fun costumes and spooky decorations. And I hear one of the brothers makes a mean 'Witches' Brew' punch. Lots of booze and fruit juices are in it, and they say it's green. S'pose to look somethin' like ectoplasmic slime."

"Sounds lovely. Like a recipe for a nice hangover. Good try, Randy, but I don't think so," she responded firmly.

"All right. Yer loss."


There was a hubbub of activity around the fraternity house on Saturday morning. As usual my pledge brothers and I were there to help the brothers set up the house and decorate for the party. Beeker, as Social Chairman, was nominally in charge but Tuney was the real brains behind this party because it involved costumes and decorations. He was sashaying around the house like he was the director of a show on Broadway and we were his stage crew and cast.

"All right you guys, I need more cobwebs in this corner. And let's add a few more plastic spiders over here. I want some bats on the ceiling over there. Let's move the skeleton to the steam closet and put a sign on the outside of the door that says 'Beware. Do Not Open This Door.' Oh, and let's make some ghosts. I need sheets. Don't take any from Pygmy's room – too many stains."

Everyone there seemed to be excited about the costumes, too. Some of the brothers were comparing notes on what they were going to wear. Elrod was going as the Incredible Hulk. He used any excuse possible to walk around without a shirt and show off his buff physique.

Sheik was going as – you guessed it, a sheik. I guess he had traditional Saudi Arabian clothing that he wore every Halloween.

Felix was going to be a Viking. Tuney had raided the costume vault of the Theatre Dept. and found a Valkyrie costume that had been used by Hildegard in Wagner's ring cycle opera. Felix was a big football player, but fortunately the female opera singer who played Hildegard was bigger. So the costume fit.

My pledge brothers were not as sure about what to wear.

"I could just wear my military fatigues," Mad Dog said. "That would be the easiest thing. But some of the kids at the preschool thought I should be a Teddy Bear."

"You a Teddy Bear?" Yaz said, incredulous.

"Yeah, why not?" Mad Dog said. He sounded a little bit offended.

"How's it going at the pre-school," I asked. Mad Dog had sure seemed out of his element when I had seen him there earlier in the week.

"Pretty well. I'm starting to get the hang of it now."

"Buddha, what are you doing for a costume?" Yaz asked.

"I don't know. I could be a sumo wrestler?"

"No, not that. You'll scare away all the women," Yaz replied. "I think you should come as Charlie Chan."

"Who?" Randy asked.

"Charlie Chan. The Chinese detective," Yaz replied.

"Never heard of him," we all said.

"Jerry should come as a detective, with all the sleuthing he's been doing," Buddha replied. I had filled them in on my activities and the clues I'd found to see if they could help me figure out who had killed Percy. They all agreed that Percy was probably murdered, but they hadn't been able to come up with any new ideas about how to solve it.

"Yeah, you should come as Sherlock Holmes," Randy agreed.

"I don't know if I'm coming to the party," I said.

"Why not?" they all asked.

"Well, Karen's not coming, and I've been thinking about going to Bridget's séance. I might learn something else about Percy that'll help me and I'm sure it'll be interesting."

"If you go, can I come along?" Randy asked.

"Sure, but don't you want to go to the party?"

"To tell you the truth, I hate costume parties. They used to have 'em every year at my prep school. I'd always go as William F.

Buckley, Jr. and everyone would think I was a Kennedy. Ya know, the teeth? So I never had much fun."

"Sure, I'll let you know if it's still on."

I called Bridget later that afternoon. The séance was still on and she was thrilled that Randy and I would attend.

"I'm so happy you called. I was feeling vibrations all morning and thinking of you," she said. I wondered what she was doing when she felt those vibrations, but I didn't ask.

"It won't be a problem to have my friend Randy attend?" I asked.

"Oh, no. It's very important to have as much intellectual power as possible at a séance. It helps to channel the spirits."

"Well, I'll bring Randy along anyway," I replied. "He said he was interested in seeing a real séance."

I got directions to her apartment in Watertown and promised to be there a little before midnight.

"I'll be trembling with anticipation," she said.

# THIRTY

It was Halloween night and the ghosts and goblins were out in force as I walked across campus to Randy's dorm room around 11:00 pm. It seemed like everyone was going to a Halloween party that night. Typically the parties on campus would just start to get going about 11:00.

I knocked on Randy's door and was greeted by a dead ringer for a member of the rock band, Kiss. He was in full makeup and costume and when he saw me he stuck out his tongue rudely.

"Randy, I thought you weren't gonna wear a costume," I said.

"Excuse me, sir. Master Randall is in the W.C. But please come in," he replied in a proper British accent.

"Cheever?" I asked.

"Indeed, sir."

"Are you going to a Halloween party?" I asked.

"Yes, sir. I was favored by an invitation to attend a gathering this evening."

"I like your costume. Very authentic."

"Thank you, sir. We do our best." Just then Randy came in. He was dressed in a pair of jeans, and a blue denim shirt.

"Ready to go?" he asked.

"I am, but don't you think you should wear black?" I said, pointing to my black pants and black shirt. "I mean, after all, this is a séance."

"How do you know they wear black at a séance?" he asked. "You said you've never been at one before." He was right about that.

"If I might interject," Cheever began. "While there are no strict protocols for séances, the process being left to the discretion of the medium who is conducting the activity, the applicable literature does support Master Taylor's recommendation."

"See?" I said.

Randy went back and changed into black jeans and a dark blue shirt. He had no black shirts. Then we were off.

We took a cab (Randy's treat). Our cab driver was African and didn't appear to have a very good command of English, nor was he too familiar with directions. I gave him the address and he stared at me blankly.

"It's in Watertown. Do you know where Watertown is?" I asked.

"Waddertown? No."

"Isn't it over by the Arsinio Mall? Do you know the Arsinio Mall?" Randy asked.

"That's Arsenal Mall," I said. But the driver perked right up.

"Arsinio Mall. Arsinio Mall. Yes." He took off at high speed, but seemed to know where he was going. So Randy and I sat back. I felt a little like Mr. Toad on his wild ride in the Wind In The Willows.

Unbelievably, we eventually arrived at the correct address. We stood before a large triple-decker house. It was identical to all the other triple-deckers on the street – wood shingled, bow windows on the front, three railed porches on the back, one on each floor, in need of a good paint job.

There was a narrow wooden staircase on the side of the house, leading to the entrances to the second and third floors, and three mailboxes to the side of the staircase. I looked for the name Bridget but there were no names posted – just the unit numbers.

"I hope this is the right place," Randy said.

"It's the right address. She's supposed to be in the top floor. Let's go."

We climbed the staircase up to the third floor and looked at the door. There was a light on above the landing, outside where we were standing, but we couldn't see any light on inside. Nevertheless, we knocked.

About a minute later the door opened and I knew we were in the right place. Standing before us was Bridget, in a low cut black gown. She was wearing dark red lipstick and blue eye shadow with glitter in it. Her hair was made up in a do that looked sort of like the Bride of Frankenstein's. But even in that get-up she was hot.

When she saw us her eyes lit up. Then she went into her trance routine and started "ooohing" and "aaahing" for a while as she swayed.

"Can we come in?" I asked. She stopped swaying, put her arms around me and gave me a kiss. Then she smiled at Randy and gestured for us to enter.

Her apartment was dark except for lit candles that were strategically placed throughout. They gave off just enough light to keep us from tripping and breaking our necks, but not enough to see much of the apartment.

We had entered through the kitchen. I could see the outlines of some early model appliances, a large sink with old-fashioned faucets, and a 50s vintage table and chairs.

Bridget led us down a long corridor with rooms leading off it. Eventually we came to the end of the corridor and entered what must be the living room of the apartment.

This room was very well lit – by hundreds of candles. It was a large room with a fireplace in one corner and a bowed shape on one side. It had several windows that undoubtedly looked out onto the street in front of the house. But heavy curtains covered the windows.

There were some old arm chairs and a sofa in the room, but they had been pushed to one side. Now located in the middle of the room was a large round table, covered in a black cloth, surrounded by half a dozen chairs. In the middle of the table someone had drawn a large circle surrounding a star. In the middle of the star was a black candle. Different objects had been placed next to each point of the star. These included a box of Altoid mints, a bottle of Bass Ale, a package of French cigarettes, some pills and a test tube.

Also in the room were three other people who rose from the table when we entered. One was a young man wearing what looked like a black choir robe. He was very fat, had greasy-looking and bushy black hair, a beard and round metal-rimmed glasses. On his head he wore a colorful, cone-shaped paper party hat emblazoned with the words 'Happy Birthday.' He had the look of someone you'd expect to find at a Dungeons and Dragons convention.

The other two were both women. They also appeared to be young, probably in their twenties. One was very thin. She was dressed in a long black velvety dress adorned with glittery suns, moons and stars. She wore little make-up except for some orange lipstick. She had matching pumpkin earrings dangling from her ears, contrasting with her long dark brown hair. On her head was a similar paper party hat.

The other woman had short, curly blond hair that framed her chubby face. She wore no make-up, but her cheeks were naturally rosy. A pair of oval glasses rested low on her nose, revealing her cheerful eyes above them. Her plump figure was covered with a robe similar to the one worn by the Dungeons and Dragons fellow. She looked like she could have just finished performing with a church choir somewhere in the Midwest.

Bridget introduced her friends to us. She used her spooky voice.

"This is Odo," she said, pointing to Mr. D&D. "He's a computer programmer and an apprentice warlock. And this is Gina," she said, pointing at the woman with the pumpkin earrings.

"I'm a gypsy," Gina said with what I imagine was a gypsy accent.

"Gina's from New Jersey. She's a massage therapist. But with her gypsy blood she knows a lot about séances," Bridget added. "And this is Pat," she said, pointing to the blond haired woman. Pat just smiled at us, nodded and gave a jolly laugh. "Pat's mother was a witch. Pat's a witch in training." Pat laughed again.

"I don't know anything about séances. I'm really a baker," Pat said, chuckling.

"Odo, Pat and Gina, the spirit of Percy Jordan is contained in this body," Bridget said, putting her arm around me. "What did you say your name was?"

"Jerry."

"Oh, that's right, Jerry. And this is his friend..."

"Randy," I said. Nods all around.

"It's almost midnight. We should start the séance," Gina said, looking at her watch.

"Everyone take a seat around the table, men and women alternating," Bridget said. "Percy, I mean Jerry, you sit next to me."

We did as she asked and then joined hands. I took Bridget's hand on one side and Pat's hand on the other side. Pat giggled when I took her hand. Bridget squeezed my hand, shut her eyes and began swaying.

"What are these things on the table?" Randy asked.

"They're things Percy liked," Bridget replied.

"They'll help to coax his spirit out of the netherworld," Gina explained.

"And why are you wearing those hats?" I asked, pointing at the party hats.

"Ever hear of pyramid power?" Bridget asked.

"Yes," I said, staring at her, wondering what it had to do with the hats.

"These were the closest we could find to pyramids," Odo explained.

"Shh. We need silence," Gina said.

Bridget rocked and swayed some more and then began her 'ooohing' and 'aaahhing' routine. Pat, Gina and Odo also closed their eyes and began rocking. I looked at Randy and we both raised our eyebrows, wondering what was going on. Then Bridget started moaning and soon the others were moaning too.

It sounded like we were in the middle of an orgy. Randy and I both rolled our eyes. Then Bridget began speaking.

"Percy, Percy. I feel your presence. I feel that you are with us. Tell us that you're here." Silence. She began again.

"Percy, tell us that you're here," she repeated. Still silence. I guess Percy was playing hard to get. Or maybe his spiritual email was turned off.

I could tell that Bridget was getting frustrated, because she called out his name again, and then replied herself, making her voice sound deeper and adding a Brit accent.

"I'm here," she said in her husky Percy voice. Gina, Odo and Pat all gasped. I looked at Randy and rolled my eyes again. He just shook his head.

"Percy, what is it like in the after world?" Bridget asked.

"It's peaceful. Wonderful. I'm communing with the spirits of the dead," she replied to herself.

"Have you met anyone interesting?"

"Yes. I met Jack the Ripper."

"Oh, what was he like?" Pat asked eagerly.

"Uh,... well, he's very ... funny. A real cut-up. Left me in stitches," Bridget replied hesitantly in her Percy voice. "Oh, and Elvis is here. Thang you very much."

"Percy, this is Jerry Taylor. Do you remember me?" I asked.

"Yes, my spirit lives in you," Bridget responded.

"I'm trying to figure out how you died. What happened. Did someone kill you?" I asked.

"Life killed me," she replied.

"Was it helped along by someone else or did you do it yourself?" I asked.

"I was killed by ..."

"Yes?"

"Myself," she guessed. "Yes, that's it, I killed myself to end the pressure."

"Why did you do it, Percy?" I asked.

"Because ... I had too much pressure on me. No one liked me. I was about to get kicked out of school. Life wasn't worth living anymore."

"Why were you about to get kicked out of school?" I asked. I hadn't heard that one before. Percy must have told her that.

"My supervisor hated me. He didn't like the way I handled my labs. He said I was disrespectful." That was old news.

"Percy, were you selling drugs?" I asked.

"I don't, I mean, I wasn't selling them, just using them."

"Percy, how can I release your spirit from my body?" I asked. Bridget was silent for about a minute.

"The only way to free my soul is for you to sleep with Bridget." This time I gasped. I looked over at Randy, who was fighting to keep from laughing.

"Hey, Percy. How are the women where you are?" Randy asked. "Are ya gettin' any action?"

"I'm having congress with all of the most famous women of the past," Bridget replied.

"Like who?" Randy asked.

"Cleopatra, Marie Antoinette, Marilyn Monroe."

"Which one was best?" I asked.

"Bridget," she replied.


After the séance ended Bridget pulled some beers and wine out of the refrigerator and her friends congratulated her on her success as a medium. Either they were great liars or dimwits if they really believed that Percy was speaking through her. I guess people really do see it when they believe it.

After our little celebration everyone got up and started leaving. Pat left first. She had to be at the bakery by 6:00 am to start her baking. Odo was the next to excuse himself. He had a big program to de-bug and had to start work about 7:30 am. Gina wasn't working the next day, but she had an early haircut appointment so she bowed out as well, leaving just Randy, Bridget and me.

"Well, this has been great, Bridget, but Randy and I have to get back to campus," I said getting up.

"What about driving Percy's spirit from yer body. Don't you think you should stay?" Randy asked, grinning.

I looked at Randy and then I looked at Bridget. It was obvious that she wanted me to stay. What should I do? She was certainly attractive, but weird. Did I really want to start a relationship with a witch?

Then I thought about Karen. Shouldn't I be loyal to her? But she and I were just friends. She wanted nothing to do with me romantically. I didn't have to be back at school until later in the day tomorrow. And Randy was urging me to stay. This might be my best opportunity to get laid for the first time.

Bridget got up and walked over to me. She put her arms around me and pressed her lips to mine, giving me a deep, slow kiss. I felt the heat of her body against mine. She trembled a little as we kissed and I felt the heat rising in me.

"I think I'll see you tomorrow," I told Randy with a wink.

# THIRTY-ONE

I trudged into the Dining Center around noontime, got my lunch and plopped down at the table. Several of the brothers and my pledge brothers were seated there.

"Hey lover boy, I heard you hooked up with a hotty last night," Red Neck said, smiling.

"Yeah," I mumbled, frowning. I pushed the food around on my plate. I wasn't hungry.

"Why the sour puss? You should have a big grin on your face," Red Neck said.

"Yeah, what's the matter?" Randy asked. "She looked sweeter 'n a Texas ribeye to a man who's been on a veggie diet fer a month. Wasn't she any good in the saddle?"

"She was fine," I said glumly.

"Then what's the problem?" I gave them all an agonized look.

"Bridget said I was lousy in the sack, and that my dick wasn't as big as Percy's," I replied dejectedly. "She said not to bother calling her again."

They all stared at me in shock. But after a few seconds Sandro got up, sat down in the seat next to me and put his arm around my shoulder.

"Was that your first time – hooking up?" he asked quietly in his suave Italian accent.

"Well, if you don't count 'Beauty and the Beast', yeah," I replied.

276

"Hey, don't worry about it. It's just a matter of experience. Everyone starts out as a bad lover," he said. "I remember my first time. First I couldn't get the girl undressed. I got my hand caught in her bra strap and couldn't get it loose without her help. Then when we finally got into bed the sex was over in about ten seconds. And the first seven or eight seconds were taken up by me trying to figure out what to do." He laughed. "Not a very auspicious beginning."

"That's about what it was like for me, too," Red Neck said. There were nods of agreement all around from the brothers.

"You should read 'Men's Health.' That magazine always has lots of tips to make you a better lover," Toddler suggested.

"Lovers. Are very horny people. They're the horniest people in the world ..." Tuney sang. Everyone ignored him.

"Hey, I've got an idea. For Christmas you can ask for one of those penile implants – the Texas variety – so the next time you hook up you can pump it up for a custom fit," Felix said. I laughed, breaking the ice, and then everybody else laughed.

For the remainder of lunch I heard dozens of "embarrassing date" war stories from the brothers, along with a bunch of jokes, advice and lots of encouragement. By the time I left the Dining Center I felt a thousand times better.


Waldo turned left off the main road and the van began climbing a steep hill. We were in a residential neighborhood, winding our way past very large, old Victorian houses.

"What town is this?" Yaz asked.

"Medford," Waldo replied.

"How long has Tookie Carraway lived out here?" Buddha asked.

"Oh, maybe a hundred years," Waldo laughed. "I don't really know. As long as I remember and as long as anyone else around the house remembers."

"When did Tookie get initiated into the fraternity?" Mad Dog asked.

"Sometime during the 1920s. He's in his late 90s now, I think. He's the oldest living brother in the entire international fraternity," Waldo replied proudly.

I had learned that Sigma Epsilon Chi was actually a very large international fraternity, with several hundred chapters located at colleges throughout the United States and Canada, and many thousands of alumni from those chapters now living all over the world. The international fraternity headquarters sponsored alumni activities and kept pretty close track of the alumni. Tookie was famous throughout the international fraternity for being the oldest living alumnus. He was famous (or maybe the word infamous would be more appropriate) within our chapter for other reasons. Soon I was going to learn what they were.

At the very top of the hill Waldo pulled into the gravel driveway of a large stone house that resembled a castle. It's gray stone walls rose up three stories, framed by several round turrets extending upward along several corners of the house. There was no drawbridge or moat, but the house did have a heavy, double-wide wooden door with a rounded top. Looking at that door I could imagine a portcullis just behind it.

"Here we are – Casa Carraway," Waldo said, turning off the van's ignition.

"What kind of work did Tookie do before he retired?" Buddha asked.

"Oh, he's not retired. He's an inventor. That's part of the fun of visiting Tookie. He's always looking for subjects to test out his latest inventions," Waldo said, grinning. "But don't worry. Most of his test subjects survive."

"What type of inventions are they?" I asked.

"We'll just have to wait and see," he said evasively.

We walked up a long flagstone pathway and got to the door. There was no doorbell there but I noticed a round knob next to the door. Waldo gestured for us to step up on the landing in front of the door. I noticed that he stayed back on the flagstone pathway.

"Should we knock?" Mad Dog asked Waldo.

"No. Just pull on the knob to the right of the door."

"Oh, I've seen these in the movies. That's an old fashioned doorbell. You pull it rather than pushing it," Buddha said. He reached out, grabbed the knob and gave it a good tug. Instantly, the floor dropped out from underneath us and with a yell we were all falling straight down.

We landed in a tangle in a large pit filled with multi-shaped chunks of foam rubber. We were in a chamber under the landing. The trap door that had opened up beneath us had now risen back into place, forming a ceiling for the chamber we were in.

"What the fuck is going on?" Yaz said.

"Where are we?" Mad Dog asked.

I looked around. The chamber we were in was small and rectangular-shaped. Two of its walls were blank. A third one contained what looked like a large flat screen T.V. There was a door in the fourth wall. We began struggling to climb out of the foam rubber pit when we heard the crackle of a loudspeaker and then an ancient voice.

"Nice of you gentlemen to drop in, heh, heh, heh," the voice said. "Just relax. I'll be with you in a moment."

We continued trying to wade through the foam rubber pieces so that we could make our way out of the pit when the room became lighter. I looked up to find the source of the light and saw that it was coming from the T.V. screen. On the screen was an image of the lower portion of two legs in polyester pants. Protruding from the bottoms of the pants were a pair of shoes with platform heels.

The loudspeaker crackled into life again, this time with music. At first it was very soft as though far away. The legs and shoes on the T.V. screen began walking toward the camera. The feet continued walking and gradually the music became louder as though the feet were getting closer and closer. The music had a driving beat. It sounded vaguely familiar.

"What's that song?" I asked of no one in particular.

"'Stayin' Alive'," Yaz said. "It was the theme to an old movie called 'Saturday Night Fever.' It starred John Travolta -- before he became fat."

The music continued to crescendo and then the door to our little chamber slid open and we could see a long corridor stretching away into the distance. There was a foggy mist blowing through the corridor, but I could see movement through the mist far down the corridor. Someone was approaching.

There was now also a foggy mist surrounding the feet on the T.V. screen. It dawned on me that the feet I was seeing on the screen were attached to the body that was approaching us from that corridor.

The music was getting louder and the body in the mist was getting closer and more visible. Suddenly the walking figure emerged from the mist. It was a very old man, with a wrinkled prune-like face, great white bushes of hair for eyebrows, and a full shock of white hair combed straight back into a blow-dry do.

He was dressed in dark polyester slacks with a wide collared polyester shirt, unbuttoned down to his solar plexus, revealing a chest full of white hair. Around his neck he wore several gold chains – one contained a cross and the other a little golden horn.

His hips swayed as he walked briskly down the corridor. He could really move for an old guy! When he got to the chamber he stopped and struck a dance pose with one hand pointing up in the air and the other pointing out to his side. Then he gave a few pelvic thrusts and held the pose as the music began to fade out.

When the music stopped he looked at us and spoke.

"Welcome. Call me Tookie."


Tookie's castle looked like a disco, straight out of the 1970s. The walls in all the rooms were covered with garish wallpaper, many of the patterns containing stripes and other designs in shiny metallic colors. The floors in many of the rooms were carpeted with thick shag carpet in a variety of colors not found in nature.

There was art work on Tookie's walls, usually in psychedelic colors, enhanced by black lights strategically located throughout the building. He was apparently fond of Andy Warhol, having a variety of Warhol prints adorning the walls in many rooms.

Tookie led us to a large room that looked like it could have been the great hall. Oversized posters of Marilyn Monroe and Campbell's Soup hung on the walls, looking down at us as we entered the room. They contrasted with high stained glass windows that allowed some of the late afternoon sun to filter into the room.

Tookie directed us to a number of large, boxy looking leather sofas placed around a large square coffee table. Waldo was already seated on one of the sofas, sipping a beer. He stood up.

"How'd you like your ride? It's sort of a tradition for pledges to get dumped the first time they arrive here," Waldo said, laughing.

"Only the first time? You mean all visitors don't have that happen to them?" Yaz asked.

"Hell no. That's part of a burglar alarm system I invented. The officers of the chapter like me to use it when the pledges arrive for the first time. But usually pulling that knob just rings a bell," Tookie replied, winking.

"Tookie, the pledges are here to learn about the history of the chapter. Buddha, here, is writing an essay on the subject," Waldo said, pointing toward Buddha.

"My, my. I see how you got your nickname. Well, I'll be happy to answer your questions about the history of the fraternity, but first I have some new inventions I'm working on that I want to show you," he said. We all looked at each other anxiously at that.

"Oh, my. Where are my manners. Does anyone else need a drink?" Tookie asked.

"I'm parched," Mad Dog said.

Tookie's already lined face crinkled up further into a broad smile and he clapped his hands three times. Almost immediately we heard a whirring sound and through the door rolled a robot about the size of Pygmy.

It looked a little like R2D2 from Star Wars, except that it had little arms with metal robotic hands on it. Tookie pointed at Mad Dog and clapped twice. The robot rolled over and stopped in front of Mad Dog. It beeped a few times and lights went on and off in the part that must have been its head. It reminded me of a little dog waiting for someone to throw a ball so it could fetch it.

"What would you like? Give Joe your order," Tookie said encouragingly.

"Joe?" I asked.

"I thought it was a good name for a bartender," Tookie replied.

"I'll have a gin and tonic," Mad Dog said. Instantly the lights on Joe started blinking furiously and his little arms began gyrating. Then a door on Joe's mid-section opened and a plastic cup dropped down like on one of those coffee and hot chocolate vending machines.

Next, a few ice cubes dropped down and then a stream of colorless liquid squirted into the cup, followed by a fizzy clear liquid.

Mad Dog reached for it, but Tookie grunted. When Mad Dog looked at him he shook his head, "No." Mad Dog withdrew his hand just as a small pair of pinchers descended holding a wedge of lime. The pinchers came together, squeezing the lime into the drink below and then withdrew.

"Much better. Now try it," Tookie said proudly. Tentatively Mad Dog reached forward and snatched the cup from the chamber in Joe's mid-section. He brought it up toward his nose and sniffed.

"Smells like a G and T." He took a sip. "Hey, this is good."

Tookie beamed. "Who's next?"

"I'll have a beer," I said. "What kind does he have?"

"Oh, he brews the beer himself. It's an Octoberfest beer right now," Tookie said. He pointed at me and clapped twice. Joe's little wheels spun and he rolled over in front of me.

"I want a beer," I said. The lights started blinking again and the arms started gyrating. The door on his mid-section had closed but now it opened again and another cup fell into place. But then a stream of beer shot out of the chamber, not into the cup but right at me. I jumped up and out of the way, the entire front of my pants were soaked as though I had wet myself.

Waldo and my pledge brothers were convulsed with laughter. Tookie and I were not amused, of course. I was standing there shaking beer off my hands and looking down at my soaked pants. Tookie was fussing around, looking equally distressed.

"Gee, Sherlock, if I'd known you weren't house broken yet I never would have brought you here," Waldo said chuckling. He and some of the other brothers were now calling me Sherlock because of my efforts to get to the bottom of what happened to Percy Jordan. I guess that was some improvement over Percy.

"I'm sorry about that," Tookie said to me in a distressed voice. "Joe appears to have a loose bladder. Something must need adjusting. I'll work on it. But first we need to dry you off. I have just the thing."

He picked up something that looked like a T.V. remote control and pressed a button. A few seconds later I heard another whirring sound and in rolled another little robot. This one also resembled Joe, but instead of arms and a door on its midsection it had a large sheet metal grill attached to something that looked like duct work in a heating system.

"This is my Nor'easter robot. I use it to blow leaves out of the yard and blow snow out of my driveway. I've recently modified it with some heating and cooling components so I can use it to quickly heat or cool a room, depending on the season. Now stand still and I'll adjust it to dry off your pants – it'll be like a blow dryer for your hair."

I straightened up and stood still. Tookie fiddled with his remote control and his robot rolled into place in front of me. Little shutters on the grill opened up and I heard a fan starting to turn.

"You're sure this will work?" I asked nervously. Tookie just smiled.

"Trust me."

I looked at myself in the mirror. I was wearing a pair of shiny black pants that were so tight I couldn't sit down in them, and a polyester shirt with some garish pattern on it. What was left of my own clothes were in the trash and these specimens from Tookie's wardrobe were the only available clothes.

I was wearing these clothes because my own had caught on fire and been incinerated with the first woosh from Tookie's Nor'easter robot. Puff the Magic Dragon would have been a more fitting name for it. Tookie apparently had the thermostat set too high. What he had described as being like a blow dryer had turned out to be more like a blow torch. My pants had caught on fire immediately.

I would have been cooked but for Yaz' quick thinking. He quickly ordered another beer from robot Joe, who instantly began spraying the room and me with Octoberfest beer. It doused the flames on my pants before they had a chance to turn our little adventure into a weenie roast.

After donning Tookie's clothes I opened the door and began to walk stiffly down the corridor that led to the staircase. As soon as I began walking, the music – "Stayin' Alive" – began to play. Must be connected with the clothes, I mused.

I went downstairs and found everyone in Tookie's study. Tookie was regaling them with stories of the old days of the fraternity and what many of the brothers did after leaving school. After being razzed about my new outfit, I attempted to take a seat and joined in the discussion for a good two hours.

I was amazed at how many prominent alumni there were from our chapter and from other chapters of the fraternity, despite some of the crazy antics they had experienced while undergraduates. I guess there was hope for the present crop of brothers.

"It all boils down to this," Tookie said. "Our brothers all know how to have a good time, but the most important parts of our fraternity experience are character development, the ideals we share and learning to get along with people very different from ourselves.

"Hell, there's no magic wand that we wave over pledges to turn them into brothers. The fraternity selects youngsters like you that it thinks already have the basic building blocks to be men of good character with high ideals. You get those from your parents.

"In your pledge program they try to teach you about the fraternity and its ideals and mold you in that direction. And that doesn't mean giving up your individuality. Otherwise, how could we have room in the same fraternity for a brilliant and free-spirited inventor like myself and a stuffed shirt like old Waldo here?" He winked at Waldo when he said that.

"We're the same in that we brothers all share common ideals. And it doesn't just end with graduation. It's a life-long commitment we make to our ideals when we join this great fraternity."

I could see his eyes glistening with tears as he spoke. He was a nutty old guy, for sure. But it was obvious that the fraternity still meant a lot to him.

Even though I had been dumped, doused, incinerated, doused again and trussed up in a disco suit, I was glad that I had come and met old Tookie Carraway. But next time, I'd know enough to avoid his inventions.

# THIRTY-TWO

I got back to my dorm room about 9:00 pm, having dined at Tookie's house. His cook had made dinner for us rather than one of his robots; that's probably the only reason why his castle hadn't burnt down. The dinner was great and I was feeling calm and relaxed when I entered my room.

My feeling of calm soon ended when my roommate, Jeff, informed me that my Mom and Karen both had called and wanted me to call them back. I wasn't concerned about Karen – just my Mom.

"You didn't, uh, have another discussion with my Mom, did you?"

"Just the usual." That's what I was afraid of.

"What did you discuss?"

"Well, I did tell her that you didn't come back to the room Halloween night, but I said you might have just crashed at your fraternity house. And she asked if you were seeing any women regularly. I told her no." Thank God for that, I thought.

"Then I told her that you'd figured out that you were really gay and now you were dating guys," he added. I looked at him, a half smile on my lips.

"You didn't really tell her that? You're kidding. Aren't you?" I looked at him but I couldn't read him. He didn't respond.

"Jeff? You didn't really say that to my Mom, did you? Jeff? You didn't ...?" I was turning red and really getting worked up now.

285

"No. Don't you know me by now?" he said, grinning. That was the problem. I didn't really know him all that well, despite the fact that we had been roommates for several months.

I decided to call my Mom first because she wasn't on college time. I dialed and heard the phone ringing. After several rings, I heard the click of the receiver and then my Dad's voice saying, "Hello."

"Hey, Dad. It's me."

"Jerry, how's it going? Jeez, I haven't spoken with you in ages."

"Things are good, Dad. It's going really well." I decided not to count my near fatal close encounter with a subway train or some of the other strange things that were happening with me.

"That's great to hear. How do you like pledging your fraternity?"

I told him about my pledge brothers and the pledge program. I described some of the brothers for him and told him about their nicknames. I even told him about Tookie (leaving out the part about me almost turning part of my body into a hot dog.)

"Wow. It sounds like a great fraternity, Jer. I'm glad to hear you're enjoying it … Oh, boy. It's getting late. I better put your Mom on. By the way, how are you doing on your school work?"

I told him that I was doing pretty well – A's and B+'s on all my quizzes and papers so far. Then he put my Mom on the phone.

"Darling, how are you. It's good to hear your voice again."

"It's good to hear yours, too. I'm looking forward to getting home for Thanksgiving in a few weeks."

"How's everything going at school. Are you getting enough sleep and eating balanced meals?"

"Well, you know how it is at college. Everyone stays up late and the food in the Dining Center isn't all that great. But I'm doing as well as anyone else."

"That's what I'm worried about, Jerry. You don't have to do what everyone else does, you know. Be your own person, darling."

"Yes, Mom. Don't worry. I'm doing fine."

"You haven't gotten any blisters, have you?"

"No, Mom, no blisters."

"I worry about that."

"I know."

"I had a nice chat with your roommate, Jeff. He seems like a nice boy."

"Mom, Jeff is a real kidder. You can't believe everything he says." I looked over at him. He crossed his hands on his chest, put on his most innocent looking face and mouthed the words, "not me." Then he smirked.

"Has he told me anything that wasn't true?" she asked.

"I don't know. What did he tell you tonight?"

"Well, he said you didn't come back to your room on Halloween night. Was that true?"

"Uh, yes."

"If you had sex I hope you used a condom. I don't want you getting a disease."

"Mom, I know about those things. Don't worry. What else did Jeff tell you?" I said, changing the subject.

"He said you've been spending a lot of time with a student named Karen. He calls her your karate chick with the ball-busting kick, whatever that means. He should get together with my new patient, the hip-hopper, don't you think?"

"Yeah, they're birds of a feather," I agreed.

"So what's this Karen like?" she asked.

I told her about meeting Karen at Tae Kwon Do class and gave her a little background on Karen, but I also assured her that we were just good friends with no romantic involvement.

"Well, she sounds very nice. Maybe you'll get more serious down the line."

"I'd like to do that, but she has this thing against fraternities."

"Well, she sounds like a very sensible young lady, if you ask me." I laughed.

"She said something like that about you when I told her where you stood on fraternities."

"I like her even more. Your father and I will have to meet her sometime."


After I got off the phone with my Mom, I called Karen.

"Hey, Karen. How are you? It's me, Jerry."

"Is your roommate there? Don't say anything." I thought about that for a few seconds. If I didn't say anything then how could I tell her if he was in the room? I guess she figured that out too because a few seconds later she said in a whisper, "If he's in the room just say 'yes' now."

"Yes now," I replied.

"Don't be a wiseass," she said. "Listen, I got a call from Svetlana tonight. She had been going through some old papers and she came across something that Percy had written down about the student who had threatened to kill him. It identified the student. It was a freshman named Jeff Bliss."

I sat there stunned. I couldn't believe it. My roommate really could be a killer. I hadn't told him much about my investigation, but he certainly knew that I was looking into Percy's death and that I thought it might be a murder even though the cops had called it a suicide.

If I were the murderer I sure wouldn't want anyone nosing around, stirring up trouble and possibly causing the authorities to look more closely at Percy Jordan's death. Could Jeff be the one who had tried to get me run over at the T station?

I stood up and looked over at Jeff who was sitting at his desk, reading a comic book. I tried to nonchalantly move to a position from which I could see the crown of his head. Then I noticed, for the first time, that his hair was thinning and he had a slight bald spot at the top back part of his head. I gasped.

"Jerry, are you all right? Did you faint or something?" Karen's voice called into the receiver, a hint of panic touching it.

"Uh, no. I'm fine. Can we get together?" My voice sounded strained to me. I hope it didn't sound that way to Jeff.

"Sure. Why don't you come over to my room."

"I'll be there in about 15 minutes," I said and hung up. I tried to appear relaxed as I got my coat and started heading for the door.

"Where ya going?" Jeff asked.

"Uh, just over to Karen's room," I replied, trying to sound relaxed even though I didn't feel relaxed. I put my hand on the handle and started to open the door.

"You forgot these," I heard Jeff say. I turned to look at him and he threw something at me. I ducked and tried to knock it away before it hit me. I succeeded and looked down on the floor. It was a box of condoms.

"Oh, yeah."

"Have fun," Jeff said. "Life's short."

"That's what you think, buddy boy," I thought to myself.

I picked up the box, removed a pack of condoms, and put them in my pocket.

"Never know if I might need them," I said nervously. "See ya." I walked out the door and breathed a sigh of relief as soon as I got out.

I high-tailed it over to Karen's room and arrived there about ten minutes later. I had never actually been there before. She had a small double room with the standard dorm furniture – two desks, beds, dressers, bookshelves and one big old armchair.

She also had a small refrigerator in one corner of the room. Sitting on top of that was a small rice-cooker, as well as some boxes of crackers and other assorted packaged foods.

Along her windowsill were some plants and photographs of people. I looked at the photographs to see if there were any potential boyfriends among them, but all I saw were an older couple that must be her parents, and a younger girl whom I assumed was a younger sister. There were other photos along the other side of the room. I assumed they belonged to her roommate.

Karen had floral pattern curtains framing her large window. They matched her bedspread. There was an oriental-style rug on her floor. She also had several framed posters on her walls – a Picasso painting of what was apparently a woman, an Asian landscape of mountains and forests in the fog, and a poster from the Broadway show Aida. Quite the eclectic mix of artwork, I thought. But somehow all of the disparate elements of her room worked, giving it a cozy, comfortable feel.

She motioned me towards the armchair and I plopped down into it. We both giggled nervously, as though we were sharing a naughty secret.

"What exactly did Svetlana tell you?" I asked.

"Just what I said."

"Did she say anything else about the threats – whether he was going to shoot Percy, stab him, poison him – you know, anything like that?"

"Nope. Just that they came from Jeff Bliss last year when he was a freshman. What are you gonna do?"

That was a good question. I didn't have an answer. After awhile I said, "I guess I've just got to find out if he's the killer."

"How are you gonna do that?"

"Don't know. Maybe I'll check with the campus cops again to see if they know anything about it."

"And you haven't searched Percy's apartment yet. Maybe you'll find something there?"

I nodded. Those were a couple leads I could follow up on.

"But what're you gonna do in the interim? I mean, you can't stay in that room with him. He could kill you in your sleep." I thought about that.

"I'll just have to sleep with one eye open. If he can do it with two I can do it with one."

"What are you blithering about? This is serious."

"O.K. O.K. I don't know what to do. But if he was gonna kill me he could have done it last night or any other time he felt like it."

"Maybe he was waiting for the right opportunity?" Karen suggested.

"I don't think they could get much better than what he's already had," I replied.

"Well I don't care. I don't think you should sleep there for the time being – just in case he's the killer."

An idea hit me like a ton of bricks. This was Karen's way of inviting me to sleep with her. She must just be too shy to ask me outright. She's trying to maneuver me into suggesting it, I thought.

Not wanting to let her down, I dropped the suggestion.

"All right. You're right. It's too dangerous for me to sleep in my dorm room with Jeff. Now where else can I sleep? Let's see …" She looked at me without speaking. She was going to play this game to the end.

"Hey, I know. Maybe I could sleep here?" I suggested, making it sound like something that just popped into my head. I waited for her to agree.

"In your dreams," she replied.

"Yep. That's what I want to do – have my dreams here."

"You can't sleep here. Where will I sleep?"

"Here too?" I asked sheepishly, looking over toward the bed that I assumed was hers.

She narrowed her eyes at me. I was starting to get the distinct impression that maybe she didn't want me to stay with her.

"All right. My roommate's away and one of my hall mates has an extra bed. Let me see if I can stay in her room tonight. If I can you can crash here."

I sighed. So much for my great idea. I just embarrassed myself again.

"Never mind," I said. "I can stay at the house."

# THIRTY-THREE

I woke up feeling groggy and not knowing where I was at first. I was stiff and sore, and I literally had a pain in my ass. I opened my eyes and looked around, before remembering that I was in the living room at the house sleeping on a broken down sofa.

I rolled off the sofa and rubbed my sore butt. Then I gazed at the sofa and saw a vicious-looking spring sticking out around the place that my butt had previously been occupying. I didn't remember it sticking out last night, but springs in the furniture at the house, like Alan Funt, had a way of showing up when you least expected them.

I sat back down on a more benign portion of the sofa and tried to rub the sleep from my eyes. I hadn't gotten much sleep because a number of the brothers had been watching a "Monty Python and the Holy Grail" DVD the night before. I tried falling asleep but with so many guys running around saying, "Neet, Neet", there was just too much commotion and noise.

When the movie ended Toddler found me a few blankets and a pillow, and I had staked out my claim to the best looking of the available sofas about 1:00 am. But people continued coming into the house, waking me up periodically, and the Little Couch of Horrors was so lumpy and uneven that it felt like I was sleeping on the rack. I tossed and turned most of the night.

Before retiring for the night I had filled in the brothers on Karen's news about Jeff Bliss. They had agreed that I should stay at the house until we knew one way or the other whether Jeff had something to do with Percy's death.

Beeker was going to check around the Chem Department to see if anyone there had heard anything about threats on Percy's life. He wasn't going to mention Jeff's name unless someone else knew about Jeff. There was no sense in getting the guy in trouble if it turned out that he had nothing to do with Percy's death.

I checked my watch. It was now about 8:30 am. I didn't have any clean clothes or my toothbrush with me so I trudged back to my dorm room. Jeff was sitting on his bed, bending down to tie his shoes when I walked in.

"Hey, congratulations, I guess you scored," Jeff said without looking up from tying his shoes. He finished and looked up. "Jesus, from the way you look, you must have been up humping all night."

I looked in the mirror. My hair stuck out like Larry's from the Three Stooges. My eyes were bloodshot and I had dark shadowy bags underneath them. I certainly looked like I had been up most of the night. I wish Jeff had been right, but I wasn't going to let him know how wrong he was.

I looked at him. Jeff seemed completely friendly and full of bonhomie, but I wasn't going to take any chances. I grunted a greeting to him, peeled off my clothes, grabbed a towel and my toiletries kit, all without taking my eyes off of him. Then I backed out of the room.

Once out of the room I turned and walked down to the bathroom looking forward to a good long shower. I hadn't been under the water for more than a couple minutes when I heard Jeff's voice, in the bathroom, yelling my name.

I froze. He had me trapped in the shower with no place to go. He could shoot me through the shower curtain, or do a Psycho act on me with a knife. Maybe he was holding a plugged in hair dryer that he would chuck into the shower stall. Or he might have more hydrochloric acid that he could dump over the top of the shower. The possibilities were endless.

What should I do? Was he calling my name to figure out which stall I was in? Considering the fact that I was the only one taking a shower at the moment that shouldn't be too hard for him to deduce.

So pretending I wasn't there was not going to work. I decided I had better see what he was up to. I stuck my head out of the stall around the curtain.

"Yo," I said. Jeff was standing there. He had no gun, no hair dryer, no acid – just some books and a jacket.

"I'm leavin'. You have your key to the room?"

"Uh, no. I forgot it."

"O.K. Then I won't lock the door. See ya." He left.

As I finished my shower, grooming and getting dressed I kept thinking to myself that I must be wrong suspecting Jeff. O.K. Maybe he did threaten to kill Percy, whatever that means. For all I knew, Percy might have just overheard him telling someone that he'd like to kill Percy. Anyone might say that about someone at one time or another. Besides, Percy and the university obviously didn't take it too seriously, or Jeff wouldn't still be here. Right? I thought to myself that I had better check on this.

I called Campus Security and asked to speak with Officer Simpson. I was transferred to him. He was still in the restroom. I could hear running water and a flush in the background as we spoke.

"Officer Simpson, this is Jerry Taylor, from the fraternity? I'm the guy looking into Percy Jordan's death?"

"Oh, yeah, hi. Are you still trying to turn that suicide into a murder?" He laughed. "I'm telling you, son. You're wasting your time. You should leave police work to the professionals."

"Oh, I am," I said. "I'm just trying to tie up a few loose ends – for my own peace of mind. And I was wondering. Does your office have any record of a student threatening Percy Jordan last year? I think it would have been a freshman that might have threatened him. Do you have any record of that being reported?"

"Wait a minute. I've got the file right here in my – office." There was a pause in the conversation and I could hear pages being turned. Then he came back on the phone. "No report of any threats. You really should give it up."

"Thanks, Officer Simpson. I appreciate the help."

I hung up. So if there were no threats reported that would explain why no action had been taken against Jeff. But why were no threats reported? Either there were none, or Percy didn't consider them very credible or serious.

Or maybe he just didn't give a shit. He seemed to have more than his fair share of confidence. Maybe that was it. In any event, this news from Officer Simpson didn't tell me much. Hopefully my visit to Percy's apartment would fill in some holes.

I put the key in the lock of the first floor apartment at the address Josey had given me and it turned.

"Hey Randy, the key works," I said as I opened the door. Randy had been looking through the mail that had accumulated in the mailbox labeled 'Jordan'.

"All junk mail," he said, tossing the envelopes on a table just inside the entryway, but removing a magazine and tucking it into his pocket.

"What was that?" I asked.

"Victoria's Secret catalogue. No sense in letting it go to waste."

We walked into the apartment.

"Jeezus, what a dump. This place would make Martha Stewart turn over in her grave," Randy remarked, looking around.

"Martha Stewart's not dead yet, Randy."

"I knew that."

To call the furniture in Percy's apartment utilitarian would have been generous. The sofa and chairs looked like they had been stolen from a dormitory lounge after many years of use and abuse. They were constructed of orange vinyl, stained and decorated with strategically placed cigarette burn holes.

There were a few coffee and end tables about. They were equally distressed, covered with scratches, bruises and stain marks. Apparently long-forgotten ash trays, full of butts, littered their tops. The linoleum floor was partially obscured by carpet remnants and old newspapers.

The only thing incongruous with the rest of the room was the entertainment system. Along one wall was a large HDTV plasma television. Underneath it, in what appeared to be a custom-made shelf system, was a DVD, CD and VCR system with a Nakamichi stereo receiver and a Bose surround-sound speaker system. There was also an Xbox game system.

Along another wall were shelves filled with lots of games, CDs, videotapes and DVDs. I looked at his material. Lots of gangsta rap audio and death and destruction video materials.

"Look at the crap he liked," I said, holding up some of the CDs to show them to Randy. Randy wasn't paying attention. He was sniffing and grimacing.

"What's that smell?" I asked, catching a whiff of a horrible smell.

"Oh, God. I hope it's not another stiff." Randy wrinkled his nose.

"It's coming from the kitchen. We better take a look." Randy made a face but he followed me into the kitchen.

There was good news and bad news in the kitchen. The good news was that there were no dead bodies – at least not the human kind. The bad news was that Percy apparently had a pet cat – Fluffy according to the name on its food bowl. I guess that when Percy died and the Little Friskies pipeline dried up old Fluffy missed quite a few meals. It looked like Fluffy had licked his bowl clean many times trying to get every last drop of food out of it, but to no avail. Fluffy, the cuddly house cat, was no more.

"Oh, that's disgusting." I grimaced.

"God damn! I think I'm gonna be sick! Look at those pink tails." Randy was referring to the leftover portions of the rat carcasses littering the floor of the kitchen where Fluffy, now a jungle hunter, had left them.

Fluffy sat in a corner of the room, munching on the head of his latest victim, its little pink nose and whiskers still sticking out of Fluffy's mouth. Fluffy glanced up at us briefly, stopped chewing to lick his mouth appreciatively, and then returned to chomping on his meal.

The rats must have come to eat the garbage and food scraps on the dirty dishes littering the kitchen sink and the small kitchen table. Percy was no housekeeper.

"We better let the cat out when we go or he'll starve in here," I said looking around at the room.

"Looks like Fluffy's doin' pretty well so far," Randy said just before covering his mouth and running out of the room. After scanning the rest of the room I followed him out, eager to escape the odor. I found Randy in the living room, leaning out the window, hurling.

"You O.K., Randy?"

"Yeah, I'm fine. I just hate rats and I hate rat parts even more. Especially those skinny pink tails. They give me the creeps."

"Randy, we've got to search the apartment."

"What are we lookin' for?"

"Beats the shit outta me. Just anything that looks out of place, or that might tell us who could have killed Percy."

Randy and I split up. I started in the bedroom and he took the bathroom. I didn't look in the bathroom but I guess it wasn't too clean either because I soon heard Randy hurling again. I hated to imagine what he saw in there.

The major piece of furniture in the bedroom was an unmade queen-sized bed with snazzy red satin sheets. Also scattered around the room were a beat-up old dresser, a large old-fashioned desk containing a very impressive-looking computer among the litter of papers covering it, and another T.V., VCR and DVD combination. There was also a small closet, its door ajar, revealing an assortment of clothes.

I went for the desk first, riffling through the papers that were scattered over its top, then I searched each drawer. Nothing!

From there I gravitated to Percy's dresser. Other than some kinky fishnet bikini underwear, it was unremarkable. I looked through the pockets of the clothes hanging up in his closet. Again nada. I checked under his bed where I found a suitcase. I opened it, but it was empty. Darn. This detective stuff was frustrating.

I was making my last survey of the room, hoping to identify other potential hiding places, when Randy staggered in.

"God damn, you won't believe what I found in the bathroom!"

"A good clue?" I asked, excited.

"Hell, no. I found a big ol' smelly turd floatin' in the toilet and nasty lookin' rat sittin' in the bowl tryin' to munch on it."

"Really? I didn't know rats ate that stuff."

"Think of what we eat at the dining center. There ain't much difference between that and crap. So why not?"

"I guess you're right." I laughed. "What did the rat do when you walked in?"

"He just sat there and gave me a shit eating grin. Then he dove under the water and disappeared down the hole in the bottom of the bowl. Makes ya feel real confident about sittin' down to take a dump, doesn't it?" He and I both shuddered at the thought.

"Did you find anything else in there?"

"Just the most disgustin' bathroom I've ever seen. How 'bout you?"

"Nothing. I've searched the whole room and came up empty."

"What was on his computer?" Randy asked.

"Haven't tried it." I looked at it. I'd assumed that I wouldn't be able to access it without a password so I hadn't attempted to turn it on. But maybe …?

I pressed the 'start' button and when it had booted up I saw the screen listing Percy's name and requesting a password. I held my breath and clicked on 'cancel.' The screen went blue for a few seconds and then up came the desk-top. I was in.

We scanned the icons, looking for a promising program or folder.

"Click on 'games'," Randy suggested.

"Why?"

"He might have some cool ones."

Instead I clicked on the Fleet Bank icon. This was another place where I expected a password to be required but fortunately for me Percy had stored his password. When the computer gave the password prompt it sailed right in automatically and I sailed right to Percy's bank records.

"Holy shit." I looked at the records and blinked, but they hadn't changed. "He's got almost $150,000.00 in his account. How does a graduate student on scholarship who supposedly has no money get that kind of scratch?" I said. Randy scratched his head. No doubt it was my power of suggestion.

"Well, you said he might have been selling drugs. It must be from that."

"Can't be. Look at the records. He was receiving monthly deposits right up through a few weeks ago, each in the same amount – $10,000. If he was getting the money from selling drugs I expect the deposits would vary. These are like clock work." Randy stared at the screen.

"Where do you think the money was coming from?"

"According to these records they're all direct deposits, and look, they're all from the same account! We've gotta find the owner of that account."

I jotted down the account number, then exited the banking program and clicked into word processing.

"How come your lookin' there?" Randy asked as he scanned the computer screen, reading the names of the saved folders.

"Just thought I'd take a look in case there was something interesting."

"You mean like that one?" he said, pointing at a folder entitled 'Blackmail letter 3'.

Excitedly, I pointed and clicked. After a few seconds up came the document. It read:

> *I've decided that $10,000/month isn't enough. Considering what I know and what will happen to you if I tell, I should get twice as much. Starting next month that's what I want. Think of it as the cost of doing business.*

There was no signature and no addressee. The note was dated several weeks before Percy disappeared.

"This has got to be it. He was blackmailing someone and getting ten grand a month. Then he got greedy."

"Greedier," Randy corrected.

"Right, greedier. So he wrote this note and sent it to his victim and his victim decided that the number was gonna keep going up as long as Percy was alive. So it was time to stop paying."

"Yeah. Percy became piranha non grata and the victim killed him so he wouldn't hafta pay Percy $20,000 a month."

"Something like that," I agreed.

"So Jer, where are we gonna find the owner of that other account where the money was coming from?"

"That, my friend, is the $20,000 question!"

# THIRTY-FOUR

"I don't care what you found. I don't think you should sleep in your room with Jeff Bliss until the case is solved," Karen said forcefully.

"But I've worked out the solution. It was the blackmailer who must have killed Percy, to keep from having to pay double."

"And how do you know Jeff Bliss isn't the blackmailer?"

"He isn't the blackmailer," I said in an exasperated voice.

"How do you know?"

"He doesn't have that kind of money. And he only knew Percy from being a student. What could Percy have on him?"

"How do you know?" she said again. I felt like I was talking to the Raven in Edgar Allen Poe's poem. The maddening thing was that although I had a gut feeling that it wasn't Jeff, I didn't know for sure.

"All right. I give up. I don't know. But I'm tired of sleeping on a couch at the house. The lumps and springs are killing me."

"Well I told you I could stay with a friend and you could crash in my room. Why don't you do that?"

"I don't know ..."

"Just try it tonight. If you don't like it you can stay somewhere else tomorrow. Unless you find out the owner of that bank account."

"That'll be tough, seeing as I have no idea how to find out."

"Try calling the bank. Maybe they'll tell you," she suggested.

I got back to my room. It was empty. I looked in the phone book for the bank, dialed the number and asked the receptionist for assistance with an account. When I was connected with a woman in the Accounts Department, I explained that I was doing a credit check on an individual and I needed to verify that the account number which I read to her was active. She confirmed that it was. I then asked her to verify the name on the account to make sure it was accurate on my records.

"What is the name you have on your records?" she asked. After hemming and hawing a few seconds, I told her that I had misplaced my file and I would call her right back. It was about that time that I noticed Jeff Bliss standing in the room, staring at me. I hadn't noticed him coming into the room. I wondered how much he had heard. He let me know.

"Why are you looking up that bank account record?"

I debated whether I should tell him anything or make up another story. But then I decided what the hell? He couldn't have been Percy's blackmail victim. What harm could there be in telling him?

So I did. I told him about my trip to Percy's apartment and showed him the key in my desk. I told him how we had found the letter in Percy's computer and the bank account information. And I told him my theory that Percy had been killed by the blackmailer and all I had to do was find the owner of that bank account and I'd know who the murderer was and I could prove it with the information in Percy's computer.

Jeff whistled appreciatively.

"You're good. That's great detective work. Who'd have thunk it?"

"So now I just need to figure out how to identify the account owner. Any ideas?"

"Not really. But I have a friend who's a real computer geek. Maybe he can find it on line through public records – or he might be able to hack into the bank to get the info. Do you want to leave the account number with me?"

Now that I had spilled all the beans to Jeff, one of my suspects, I decided maybe it wasn't the smartest thing to do. After all, if he was the blackmailer I just told him that I was on to him. And the note containing the account number was my only copy. If I lost that then I lost my source of proof. I could always go back to Percy's apartment and get it off the computer again. But it would be far safer to hang onto it.

"No thanks. I might try some other sources. If I strike out I'll let you know."

"O.K.," he said matter-of-factly.

I put on my suit, then I collected my toiletries kit, a towel and a change of clothes.

"Where are you going?" Jeff asked.

"Oh, I have a pledge meeting, then I'm staying at Karen's tonight."

"Again? Sounds like it's getting serious."

"Don't tell my mother. O.K.?" He held up his hands defensively.

"I won't say a word."

"Not even if she asks you, right?"

"Right."

I went to the fraternity house for my pledge meeting. While we took our usual quiz Toddler inspected our notebooks for signatures of brothers and then left the room with our notebooks.

"What do you think he's doing with those?" Mad Dog inquired. Yaz just shook his head.

"Did any of you guys finish getting all the signatures?" We all shook our heads. "Well, at least we'll all get reamed out together," he said.

Toddler came back, without the notebooks, and collected our quizzes. Then he instructed us to line up, single file, and he gave us blindfolds to put on. After our blindfolds were in place we put our hands on the shoulders of the person in front as we had for the original pledging ceremony. Somehow I thought this activity might not be quite as much fun.

Toddler led us down the stairs to the basement. No humming this time. He knocked on the door and I heard it open instantly. We shuffled into the basement party room and I sensed a lot of people around, although I couldn't see or hear anyone else beside my pledge brothers.

Our line stopped. Then Toddler moved in front of us, turning us so that we were lined up side by side, all facing the same direction. He placed a lit candle in each of our hands and then told us we could remove our blindfolds. Across the room just beyond the edge of the candlelight I could vaguely make out the forms of many people sitting in absolute silence.

"Pledge bothers," Toddler began, "as we told you when you first joined us, your pledgeship is a probationary period. At tonight's lineup the brothers will be evaluating and critiquing your progress to see if your pledgeship should continue."

A wave of panic swept through me! What if they decided to de-pledge me? How would I survive college without being part of this fraternity – without having these guys around to help me out, cheer me up, drive me crazy and do all the other things they did with me, for me and to me? And how would I explain it to my father? On the other hand, my mother and Karen would be happy.

"Pledge Brother Samuel Salvatore Fillippo, step forward," a voice said. Mad Dog stepped forward holding his candle.

"Pledge Brother Fillippo, do you know who I am?"

I could see Mad Dog squinting, trying to see who it was speaking to him from the darkened room.

"No, sir," he replied.

"Maybe that's because you haven't met me and gotten my information or my signature in your book," the voice replied. I didn't recognize it either. It must be someone I missed, too.

The voice went on to identify himself as Larry Tate, whose nickname was "C++" because he was a computer science major. C++ went on to lecture Mad Dog about the importance of meeting every brother if he really wanted to be a member of the fraternity some day. He also admonished Mad Dog about mediocre pledge quiz scores, but complimented him on the successful completion of his project at the Early Childhood Development Center, despite some initial setbacks. He concluded by telling Mad Dog that the brothers had decided to allow Mad Dog's pledgeship to continue, but he better straighten up on his deficiencies or else!

Mad Dog's sigh of relief was audible when he stepped back into line.

"Pledge Brother Bradford Lee Chan, step forward." The voice sounded like Red Neck to me. Buddha hesitated, then took a step forward.

"Which of the founders of our fraternity do you most admire, and why?" the voice asked. Buddha stood there trembling for what seemed like several minutes before he replied.

"Uh, Edward Campbell… sir. He was the founder who left the Pythagoras Society and threw his Pythagoras badge at the officers of that society when they chose to sponsor a bingo night at the local student center to raise funds for a billiard table. It took a lot of bravery to do that and then start his own fraternity.

"And then he saved another founder, Arnold Peabody, when Peabody fell down an elevator shaft. It took a lot of bravery to climb down that shaft and carry Peabody back up on his back. He didn't know that the shaft was only six feet deep when he started to climb down without a rope.

"And in the First World War, he single-handedly captured a German brewery thinking it was an ammunition depo. That also took a lot of courage."

"Very good," the voice replied. Many of the brothers were snapping their fingers in approval as well. Buddha beamed.

But then the voice pointed out that Buddha had missed a number of house clean-ups. It also mentioned that Buddha had failed several quizzes that had to be made up. And of course, Buddha's notebook wasn't finished and he still had not turned in his essay on the history of the fraternity – all very serious offenses.

The brothers made grumbling noises in the background.

"But I'm done with the essay. I can get it from my room and bring it back tonight. And I'm only missing a few names. I can get them done by next week. Just give me a chance," he pleaded.

After some additional lecturing the voice told Buddha to turn in the essay tonight and complete the names in his notebook by next week as he promised or his pledgeship would be at an end. Buddha cringed back into line.

"Pledge Brother Randall Dewhurst Urquhart Bradford. Step forward." I recognized this voice immediately. It was Tuney.

305

"Do you know who this is?"

"Uh… don't tell me. I know who it is. It's right on the tip of my tongue."

He continued to think. After about ten seconds Tuney began humming the final Jeopardy theme song and soon all the brothers had joined in. They got to the end – bum, ba dum, ba dum …, dum …, dum …, batadadum.

"Time's up, who am I?"

"Uh, Sandro?" Randy guessed. Everyone in the room laughed.

"Exactly right," Tuney said. "I'm Sandro the stud. Now, Pledge Brother Bradford, you have done a very good job completing your project and used many of the new skills you've learned to improve the house."

Snaps all around.

"But you are woefully deficient in many areas including your academics – Ds and Cs on most of your tests – not to mention your pledge quizzes and your notebook. Why so poor?"

"Well, as you may have figgered out, I'm not too scholastical. Cheever was helpin' me out with my classes until my project started and since then I've been doin' everything myself.

"And the grades may not be too good, but for the first time in my life I did it by myself without help from anyone else. I earned every one of them grades and I'm proud of it!"

Snaps reverberated around the room. In fact, I started snapping too and so did my other pledge brothers.

"Well, that's very commendable, but we're going to need to see more improvement there. You haven't taken advantage of the brothers for tutoring and you haven't been coming to the mandatory study halls. That's got to change."

Tuney went on to list the other areas where Randy needed improvement, but said for now the brothers were going to continue to allow him to pledge. Tuney also said they had their collective eyes on him and he was under strict scrutiny.

Randy rejoined our ranks. I took a deep breath hoping I was next.

"Pledge Brother Arnold Neil Rosen. Step forward, please." I sighed.

"Please recite the Dorfman Standard." The Dorfman Standard was a standard for membership in the fraternity established by one of the fraternity's founders, Ben Dorfman. Yaz recited it flawlessly.

"No man should be admitted into this fraternity unless he proves himself to be a man who is courteous to others, believes in himself and the ideals of the fraternity, who possesses integrity and honesty, who strives to achieve academic success and who knows at least a dozen uses for duct tape."

"Do you believe that you meet this standard?" the voice asked.

"Yes," he said without hesitation.

"O.K. Keep up the good work. You can step back."

That was it? He wasn't going to get criticized? I mean, sure Yaz was doing a great job, but he wasn't perfect. And I was going to look all the worse following Yaz.

"Pledge Brother Gerald Robert Taylor. You're up. Take one giant step forward." I took a deep breath and took the step.

"What's my name?"

"C.P.?" I guessed.

"Very good. Now, would you tell us what C.P. stands for?" I cringed inside.

"I don't know." Grumbling and a little hissing rose up from around the room.

"Why don't you know?" he asked.

"None of us have been able to figure it out." More grumbling and hissing.

"Don't hide behind your pledge brothers. I'm sure that if I were asking you about one of your successes you'd be taking full credit for it." I hung my head, ashamed that I had mentioned my pledge brothers.

"Well, in looking over your pledge quizzes you've gotten the highest marks in the pledge class, and you haven't missed a clean-up or a study hall. The academic records we received show that you've done very well on your school work. And you successfully completed your project involving Percy Jordan," he continued shuffling through some papers. "Those are all good things." There were snaps around the room.

"We also know that you've been doing some amateur detective work on Jordan's death. Just out of curiosity, where do you stand on that?" C.P. asked.

I reported on the clues I had uncovered at Percy's apartment and my theory that the blackmailer had murdered him. I told them that I still had to find the owner of the bank account to see if it would reveal the blackmailer.

C.P. inquired about my close encounter with the subway train and whether I thought it was related to the blackmailer. I shrugged my shoulders.

"Well, listen. We don't want you taking any chances. You can try to figure out who owns the bank account but then turn it over to the cops. No more doing things on your own without telling anybody. Understand?"

"Yes, sir."

"And you've got until Thanksgiving break to finish getting signatures in your book and figure out what my nickname means. Got it?"

"Yes, sir," I repeated, relieved that I wasn't getting the boot.

After the line-up ended my pledge brothers and I hung around the house for awhile. We were all trying to get as many additional signatures in our notebooks as possible while a lot of brothers were around. I was especially interested in meeting Larry Tate, Mr. C++ himself, to see if he could help me out with the bank account information.

"Let me see the account number," C++ said. I handed him my note containing the number and he studied it.

"This is good. See these digits right here?" he said, pointing to several of the numbers. "These are routing numbers through the Federal Reserve. I think I can trace this down through some sources I have – all publicly available, of course."

"How long will it take you to get me the info?"

"Day or two. Shouldn't be a problem."

"Hey, thanks a lot. I really appreciate the help."

"Not a problem. That's what brothers are for," he said, clapping me on the back.

# THIRTY-FIVE

I got to Karen's room about 11:00 pm. Karen and a reception committee of three other women awaited me. They eyed me speculatively, like chefs eyeballing a cut of meat they are about to cook.

"Hey, glad you could make it," Karen said, looking at her watch.

"Sorry I'm late. We had an extra long meeting at the fraternity house." Karen rolled her eyes and exchanged knowing looks with her friends.

"Well, you're here now. Jerry, this is Becky." Becky was a tall woman with long blond hair tied up in a ponytail. We exchanged greetings.

"I'm sleeping in Becky's room tonight. Becky's room is just one floor down in Room 211 in case you need me for something." Her friends all giggled at that. Karen continued.

"This is Jenny." She pointed to a pretty Asian woman wearing a pink bathrobe who smiled shyly at me and giggled a hello.

"And this is Amy." Amy was an attractive woman with curly red hair, wearing a skin-tight leopard pattern body suit and designer glasses. She held out her hand to me. I wasn't sure whether she expected me to shake it or kiss it. So to be safe I shook it.

"Jenny's in the room right next to mine on this side," she pointed, "and Amy's room is right here on the other side. The bathroom's that door over there. Guys use it from time to time, so you won't shock anyone when you use it. But you better yell in there first before you go in just to make sure you don't upset anybody." I nodded.

"No problem. You forgot I'm experienced." She looked at me vaguely. "You know – Girls' Night Out?"

"Oh, yeah." She laughed. "Well, this bathroom probably won't be as exciting. Here's the key to my room. I changed the sheets for you. What time are you getting up tomorrow?"

"Uh, 8:00? Is that O.K.?" I replied.

"Yeah. That's fine. I just need to get back in the room by around 9:00 because I have a class at ten."

With that she and her friends left me. I went in her room and shut the door. It felt really weird to be staying in Karen's room. I saw the photos of her family members placed around the room. It felt like they were staring at me, waiting to see if I was gonna go through her underwear drawer or something.

I resisted the temptation, and changed into some flannel pajama pants and a T shirt. I made my way to the bathroom and called in. No answer. I quickly entered and did my business, then returned to Karen's room, locked the door and settled into her bed. The sheets felt and smelled fresh like she did. I fell asleep wishing she were in the bed with me.

The next morning I woke up to the sound of a strange alarm clock. I kept batting at the spot where my alarm clock would have been but nothing happened. Then a feeling of panic overcame me for a few seconds as I realized that I wasn't in my room and before I remembered where I was. Finally my memory banks kicked in and I reached over to shut off Karen's alarm. The clock read 8:05 am.

I got up, grabbed my towel and toiletry kit and walked down the hallway to the bathroom. I listened at the door and heard no sounds. I pushed the door open slowly and called in. There was no response.

I entered, used the toilet and brushed my teeth. Still no one else had entered. I walked over to the showers.

Each shower was in a separate stall and attached to each was a small changing room. There was a curtain that covered the entrance to the changing room stall and a shower curtain that separated the changing room from the shower. The changing room contained a small bench.

I entered the changing room, pulled the curtain shut and undressed. I hung my towel on a hook in the changing room and laid my pants, T shirt and toiletries kit on the bench. Then I turned on the water, adjusted the temperature and got in the shower, closing the curtain behind me.

I immediately noticed that the showerhead came out of the wall about the level of my belly button. That made it easy to wash the lower part of my body, but it was murder rinsing the soap from my arm pits and my hair. I had to try to squat down in the stall, but there wasn't much room and I lost my balance, causing me to fall against the shower curtain and hit the bench in the changing room.

When I finally finished my shower I discovered that I had knocked my pants and T shirt off the bench and onto the floor of the changing room. And by moving the shower curtain out of place I had allowed a lot of water to drench the changing room and my clothes. I was thankful that I'd hung the towel. It was still dry.

I dried off and thought about putting on my soaked pants and shirt again. But they were cold and clammy so I decided against it. Karen's room was just down the hall a short way and no one had come into the bathroom since I had been there. My towel was a standard dormitory issue postage stamp-sized towel, but I figured it would be sufficient to sort of wrap around my waist while I crossed the short hallway and jumped into Karen's room.

I hung my wet clothes up to dry in the shower stall and wrapped the towel around the front of me as best I could. Then I opened the bathroom door and peeked out into the hall. No one was there.

I threw open the door and hopped the few feet to Karen's door, grabbed the doorknob and pushed. Nothing happened. The door was locked. That's when I remembered that I had left the key in the room.

"Fuck! You're such an idiot!" I said to myself. If I had had a whip I would have begun self-flagellation at that moment. But since I didn't I used both hands to hold up the tiny white piece of cotton that was covering up my crotch and maybe one quarter of my butt. What was I gonna do now?

I was still pondering the situation when I heard a door opening and there in the hall stood Amy, still in her leopard body suit. Instantly I tensed up like a deer caught in the headlights.

Amy looked me in the eyes but then I saw her eyes lower as she surveyed the situation. I heard a sound come out of her that was a cross between a low growl and a purr.

"Now isn't this an interesting predicament?" she said in a husky, sexy voice. I gave her a little half smile.

"Forgot the key," I said.

"So you did," she said, eying me again.

"Any idea how I can get the key?"

"Well, we could go find the advisor, she'll have a key. But there aren't supposed to be any guys in the dorm. If we do that Karen might get into trouble."

As she said this she walked around me, trying to get a better look at my butt. I turned, keeping my butt to the wall as best I could.

"No, let's not do that. I don't want to get Karen in trouble. Any other suggestions?"

"You know, you've got a cute little ass." I gulped.

"Uh, thanks. But about the key ...?"

"Well, hows about we go into my room and you show me what's behind that towel? And after a while maybe I can go find Karen. Then Karen can tell the advisor that she locked herself out of the room and get the advisor to open the door. That way everyone can be happy."

Having sex with Karen's next-door neighbor this morning, with Karen about to arrive at any time, was way up there on my list of things to do. It fell right between having a proctology exam and getting disemboweled with a butter knife. What was I going to do now?

I was incredibly nervous and upset at the situation I was in. So it came as a real shock to me when I found myself getting an erection at that moment.

I tried thinking of horrible non-sexy thoughts to arrest the rise, but there were really no more horrible things that I could think of than the situation I was in. So all I could do was to try to squat down and bend over to keep it hidden.

Of course my bending over caused the towel to pull up off my ass even more, so it was like a full moon rising the more I bent over. It was quite the dilemma I was in.

Although I had the best of intentions, my maneuver was not entirely successful. Amy could see that I was aroused and a wide grin curled her lips.

"I see that your little friend likes my idea," she said coquettishly.

"Little? What do you mean, little?" I asked angrily. I was still sensitive from my ill-fated liaison with Bridget.

"It was just a figure of speech," she said defensively. "I didn't mean anything by it."

"My penis is not little," I said through clenched teeth, standing upright, removing my towel and letting it all hang out.

Unfortunately, that was the moment that Karen chose to walk into the hallway with Becky and several other women. Their mouths dropped open. I wanted to attribute that to their shock at the massive size of my member, but I was more realistic than that.

"Uh-oh," I said, and clutching the towel to me, I immediately returned to my bent-over squat position, hoping that I could just hide. That was not meant to be. In fact, I became an even greater attraction.

"Hey everybody, come on out here and see Karen's friend butt naked in the hallway with a hard-on," Becky yelled. Doors flew open in response. Flash bulbs started going off all around me. Camcorder lenses were zooming in on me. I was the biggest entertainment to hit that dorm in ages I guessed. I looked around for Karen and saw her standing to the side, a shocked look still on her face.


I attended my classes that day but I couldn't concentrate on school. My relationship with Karen was definitely in the shitter. I did my best to explain the situation, and Karen's resident advisor certainly accepted my explanation, but I guess it was hard for Karen to overcome the image she saw when she arrived. I tried calling her between classes and I got through to her a couple times, but as soon as she heard my voice each time she hung up.

As I thought about it, it occurred to me that she thought I was coming on to Amy and she must have been jealous. I guess that was good. It meant she thought more of me than us just being friends. But then why didn't she want to go out with me?

The more I thought about it the angrier I got. She had no claim on me. We weren't dating each other, and that was her choice. So why was she getting so upset just because I was standing outside her room almost buck naked with a big hard on, talking to her hall mate? I just didn't understand women.

By dinnertime, I had tried calling her a few more times and I had been spurned each time. All right. If that's the way she wanted it, I could play that game, too. I would just ignore her and see how she liked that!

I got to the Dining Center and the table where we ate was full of excited brothers and pledges when I arrived. Beeker and Randy grabbed me as soon as I sat down.

"Guess what?" Beeker said.

"I don't know. What?"

"The house where Percy Jordan's apartment was located just burnt down. The police think it was pyrotechnology," Randy blurted out, unable to contain himself. My mouth dropped open.

"You're kidding me, aren't you?" I said, looking from one to the other.

"No. I heard it from one of the chemistry grad students. It just happened this afternoon," Beeker said authoritatively.

This was an unsettling development. If the computer was lost my proof that the blackmailer killed Percy was gone.

"What happened to the computer? Was it saved?" Beeker shook his head.

"Don't know for sure. But I doubt it. I was told the entire apartment was gutted."

"How could this happen?" I asked, holding my head in my hands.

"You didn't tell anyone about Percy's apartment and what we found there, did ya?" Randy asked.

Instantly I started to do mental head banging. What an idiot I was.

"Yes," I said despondently. "I told my roommate, Jeff Bliss." I hung my head.

"That wouldn't be Jeff Bliss, the kid who threatened to kill Percy, and one of the murder suspects? Would it?" Beeker asked, incredulity in his voice.

"Yes," I said in an anguished voice.

Randy put his arm around my shoulders and said, "That's O.K., Jer. I've been known to do some pretty stupid things, too. But that one's a real humdinger!"

I guess that was intended to console me. It didn't.

"But how could Jeff be a blackmail victim? It just doesn't make sense. And he doesn't seem like the murdering type. I mean, he has so little initiative to do anything. How could he be the one?" I reasoned.

"What does a murderer look like?" Toddler asked from across the table.

"Like me," Sheik said, winking at me.

"Maybe your roommate isn't the blackmail victim. But maybe he's working for the victim," Kim Chee suggested.

"I know. It's like 'Murder On The Orient Express' where everyone who hated Percy got together and they all killed him. Your roommate was one of them. The blackmailer was another one. The mafia guys from the North End and all his jealous girlfriends are in on it, too," Buddha said excitedly.

"I don't know if it was your roommate or not. But it does seem like too much of a coincidence that he's the only one you told and the apartment suddenly gets torched," Waldo said. "You aren't staying in your room with him overnight, are you?"

"He's staying at his girlfriend Karen's, aren't you Jer?" Randy said.

"Well, not exactly." I told them my woeful tale, which elicited howls of laughter from them.

"Jesus, you should be giving lessons to Elrod and Sandro. More women throw themselves at you than anyone I've ever met," Beeker said, knocking the salt and pepper shaker off the table when he gestured.

"Well, the gypsy woman in the North End said I was going to start getting some action. Maybe she does have 'the gift.' But I'll tell you, it hasn't been very satisfying. Karen's the one I'd like to go out with and she won't even talk to me now."

"Aw, she'll get over it. Give her a chance. I once dated a woman who I accidentally spilled a whole container of sewer water over when I was doing a lab experiment. And she forgave me after a few months and started dating me again," Beeker said.

"Are you still going out with her?" I asked.

"Uh, no. I accidentally knocked her over the rail of the deck on the house and when she got the casts removed she told me never to see her again. But, hey, that was under different circumstances. I'm sure your friend will forgive you."

"Well, I think you should stay at the house again tonight," Waldo said, more as an order than an invitation.


I stayed at the house that night, finding a new "Little Couch of Horrors" to sleep on. It was no better than the earlier choice.

The next day, between classes, I called Officer Simpson to see if he knew anything about Percy's apartment. He didn't. If it was off campus it was a city police matter.

I tried calling Karen again. I know I said I wasn't going to do it, that I was gonna let her squirm without me, but I couldn't resist giving her another chance. She didn't want it. I would try to catch her at Tae Kwon Do class. But I'd be sure to wear a double cup having experienced the fury of her scorn before.

I had an early dinner with Buddha and Randy. I was just getting ready to head over to my room to get ready for Tae Kwon Do class when C++ walked into the Dining Center. He gave me a confident look, so I assumed he had some news for me. I waited while he got his dinner and then he parked himself in the seat next to mine.

"I've got some news for you," he said smugly.

"Do you know who owns that bank account? Did you get it?" I asked eagerly. Buddha and Randy also looked at him expectantly.

"I did. And I can tell you, it wasn't easy."

He started to regale us with the story of how he got the information without first telling us who owned the account. Whenever we tried to interrupt him to get the name of the account owner he held up his hand and said he was getting to that. After ten minutes of listening to what was to me complete techno-mumbo jumbo, he finished his story.

"… and that's how I got the answer." He beamed at all three of us.

"So who is it?" we all said in unison.

"Oh, the account you gave me is owned by Ronald Harnash."

# THIRTY-SIX

"Harnash?" we all said at the same time.

"That's right. Isn't he a professor here or something? I think I've heard of him," C++ asked.

"Yeah, he's Jerry's and my chemistry professor. And he was Percy Jordan's supervisor," Randy replied.

"He must be the blackmail victim, if that's his account. But what could he be blackmailed about? His wife knew about the women he was boffing," I said.

"Then it must be something else," Buddha suggested.

"I guess. But what could it be?" Everyone shrugged their shoulders.

"Well, it's not your problem. Turn it over to the police and let them investigate it. Understand?" C++ ordered.

"Yeah. Right," I replied.

"I'm serious. You heard C.P. at the line up. You're not supposed to do anything but get the account owner and turn it over to the police. This isn't a game."

"I understand," I said firmly.


Buddha, Randy and I left. As we walked across campus we talked about it.

"Are you gonna do what the brothers said and just turn it over to the cops?" Randy asked.

"If I do that it'll go nowhere. The police still think it was suicide. I can't prove otherwise. If I told them it was Harnash who killed Percy they'd laugh at me. I don't have any evidence that he was paying blackmail – especially now that the computer is torched. And Harnash could just say he was paying wages or something like that."

"So what're you gonna do? You'll never get any evidence – unless Harnash confesses. And why should he do that?" Buddha asked.

"He wouldn't. So unless I get more evidence, I'm dead."

"I'd use another expression if I were you," Buddha said, smiling. I smiled back but I didn't feel happy.

"I wish ol' Percy would come back as a ghost and haunt him. That'd fix him good. Maybe if he was scared enough he'd fess up," Randy said wistfully.

I thought about that for a minute and then something clicked.

"Randy, you're brilliant!"

"I am?" Randy said. Buddha looked at me like I was ready for a trip to a room with padded walls.

"Sure. Think of it. I look enough like Percy to fool most anyone. And remember how Bridget was trying to call back Percy from the dead at her stupid séance?

"What if I dress up as Percy the friendly ghost and I confront Harnash – accuse him of killing me. I can ask him why he did it and try to get him to explain the motive. Maybe I can even find out how Jeff Bliss is connected to him and whether anyone else was involved in the murder.

"And you guys can have a tape recorder or camcorder going – you know, the way the brothers did it when I played Percy at the Chemistry Dept. dinner. It'll be perfect. We'll get a full confession on videotape and put him away."

"There's just a couple problems. First, how do we get him to come to the place where we're set up to record? Second, what if he's not a murderer and there's some reasonable explanation for the payments? And third, what if he doesn't believe in ghosts?" Buddha asked.

I thought about it awhile.

"Well, maybe we can use the Chemistry Dept. Faculty Lounge again. It shouldn't be too hard to get him in there. We can come up with some pretext – maybe send him a note from a gorgeous woman who wants to meet him there for a little nookie. That should get him there.

"And if I do a good job with my Percy impersonation I should be able to convince him that I'm Percy. He may not think I'm a ghost, but maybe he'll think he failed in his attempt to kill me. All I need to do is create some doubt and I can get him to sing. And I'm positive he's the killer. But if he isn't we'll find that out as well."

"Shouldn't we tell the brothers we're gonna do this?" Randy asked.

"No. If we tell them they'll tell me not to do it."

"Well, we should at least tell Yaz and Mad Dog. They can help out," Buddha urged.

"O.K. We'll let them know. But no one else."


Buddha and I skipped Tae Kwon Do class so I didn't see Karen. I'd have to try to speak to her another time. My pledge brothers and I met later that night and worked out our plan to trap Professor Harnash. It was now Tuesday night. We decided to set it up for Thursday night, because Harnash had office hours on Thursday so he'd definitely be around. And we figured the Faculty Lounge wouldn't be occupied at night.

Mad Dog knew a lot about videotaping from doing training videos in the military. Using information from Randy and me he was able to fashion a trash barrel videography blind. Randy would hide in the trash barrel and do the taping through a hole in the barrel. Mad Dog drilled Randy in the use of the camcorder so Randy wouldn't screw it up. I would also have a Dictaphone on me to record what was said as a back-up.

Yaz had a gorgeous female friend whom he said was sure to appeal to Harnash. He'd get her to flirt with Harnash and pass him a note stating that she wanted to meet him in the Faculty Lounge Thursday night for some 'private tutoring.'

Buddha was going to help me dye my hair and get me made up to look like Percy again. He, Yaz and Mad Dog were going to run look-out to make sure no one came into the lounge. They and Randy would have walkie-talkies so they could warn Randy if someone was coming. If necessary Randy could warn me as I confronted Harnash.

We went over everything one more time to make sure we hadn't missed anything. Satisfied that we had everything under control, we split up to work on our projects.

I returned to the house to crash that night. I was tempted to call Karen again, but I decided against it. If she refused to talk to me then I wasn't missing anything. If she did speak with me, then I'd be tempted to tell her what I had learned and what we were about to do. She wouldn't approve. I'd let her know when it was over.

# THIRTY-SEVEN

Wednesday was spent in preparations between classes. Yaz met Randy and me just before our chemistry class. He brought his friend. She was a strikingly beautiful woman with medium length chestnut hair, a firm athletic body and a sexy Southern accent. Harnash would be drooling over her.

"Guys, this is Reggie. She's gonna help us get Professor Harnash to the Chemistry Dept. Faculty Lounge tomorrow night. Reg, this is Randy and Jerry," Yaz said.

"Hi there," she said flashing us a remarkable smile.

I returned the greeting. Randy just stuttered, unable to generate speech. This caused her to smile even more widely.

"Y'all sure are brave trying to capture a murderer," she said, her eyes twinkling. She had a sweet voice, made all the sweeter because of her accent.

"Uh, we don't exactly know for sure if he is a killer. We're just trying to find out," I said.

"Aw, shucks, he's definitely a killer, and a dangerous one, too," Randy jumped in, laying on his most exaggerated Texas accent. "Why there's no tellin' how many folks he might have done in. But dangerosity is my middle name."

"Where is this desperado?" Reggie asked.

"There he is. There's Professor Harnash," I said, pointing him out.

"He sure looks harmless," she mused.

Reggie took a seat up front where Harnash was sure to notice her. It was a particularly boring lecture, even for Harnash. But Reggie gave the impression of being enraptured with every pearl of wisdom cast by him. And it was fun watching Harnash attempting to give a lecture while his mind clearly was more focused on Reggie than his notes.

After the lecture ended most of the students began to get up and shuffle out of the lecture hall, but Reggie remained seated, playing her big tuna. Harnash tried to appear as though he was busy organizing his papers but it was clear that he was eyeing Reggie over the top of his bifocals.

Reggie got up leisurely and walked over to him. It was about that time that Yaz nudged me and motioned for us to leave. I guess we were a little obvious, too. We vacated the lecture hall and loitered outside the back doors.

About ten minutes later Reggie came out, tucking in her shirt.

"I do declare, that man is a groper."

"Did you do it?" Yaz asked, excited.

"Of course. Easy as pie. We have a date in the Chemistry Dept. Faculty Lounge tomorrow night at 7:30. Ronny wants to show me his Bunsen burner."

"Sweet!" Randy and I said, jumping up and down.


Thursday was a tense day for all of us. Mad Dog had fabricated the trash barrel blind and got the camera ready, but Randy was having a hard time getting the hang of using the camera in such a confined space. He kept cutting off the picture, dropping the battery pack, not focusing properly and doing a hundred other things that were driving Mad Dog crazy.

Mad Dog was going military on Randy, which was making Randy all the more nervous. I just hoped Randy would get it straight before Mad Dog used him for bayonet practice.

Buddha and I went to Buddha's room to get me ready. That required my dressing in Percy clothes again, cutting my hair and dying it. I had some trepidation when Buddha came at me with a pair of scissors, by eventually I let him have a go at my hair and his trim wasn't too good.

"Don't worry. Harnash won't notice. He'll just think they have lousy barbers in Hell," Buddha said, trying to mollify me.

Fortunately, the dye went a little more smoothly. When it was finished I placed the glasses on my nose and admired myself. As best I could recall I looked a lot like Percy again.

"I'll definitely fool him. Remember, he hasn't seen Percy in a long time either."

"And now, for the finishing touch?" Buddha said.

"What finishing touch. I'm finished."

"Just one more thing." He came at me with a big powder puff. I drew back.

"What are you doing?"

"I'm powdering your face."

"Why?"

"So you look like a ghost."

"How do you know what a ghost looks like?"

"Well, they always look white in the movies."

"Yeah, but this isn't the movies."

"Well, I'll just put a little on. If you don't like it we can wash it off."

I let Buddha powder my face and hands and I looked in the mirror. I certainly looked like I was dead now. I debated awhile then decided to go with the Casper look.

I checked my watch. It was now 6:00. We had agreed to rendezvous at the Chem Building around 6:30. Yaz, Mad Dog and Randy were gonna reconnoiter to make sure no one was roaming about the Faculty Lounge. Once it was empty they would get the place set up.

Buddha and I set out about 6:15. By this time of year it was already dark at 6:15, so we were able to travel without anyone seeing me too clearly. That was good because I didn't want Campus Security to come after me with the padded ghost busters wagon.

We arrived at the Chem Building and were met at the door by Yaz, who quickly shuffled us into an empty classroom.

"We're screwed right now. There are a couple grad students in the Lounge. They've been there awhile. If they don't leave we can't get set up," Yaz said. Just then Mad Dog came strolling up.

"The Lounge is now vacant," he said nonchalantly.

"Really, let's go," Yaz said.

"I'd wait a few minutes," Mad Dog replied.

"Why?"

"To clear the room I dropped some poison gas in there. It cleaned the grad students out in a minute." We all stared at him in horror. How could he have gotten access to poison gas, even in the military? Didn't you need a security clearance to get access to weapons of mass destruction? And was he really nutty enough to use something that dangerous on people?

"But where? How?" Buddha asked, aghast.

"I had stuffed cabbage for dinner. I just went into the lounge pretending I was looking for someone and let 'er rip. Those grad students were out of there before the echo had even died down."

Relief flooded over all our faces. We waited a few minutes then went into the Lounge. There was still a slightly unpleasant odor permeating the air. Mad Dog sniffed appreciatively, apparently pleased with the virulence of his combustion by-products.

We all worked swiftly to get the room set up while Buddha played look-out. The trash blind was placed in a strategically located spot where Randy would have good coverage of most of the room. Mad Dog gave Randy one more set of instructions before sequestering Randy in the hopper with his camera and a walkie-talkie.

We lowered the lights to a romantic level, one that would make it more difficult for Prof. Harnash to see me too clearly, and I took a position hidden behind some bookshelves. Mad Dog and Yaz left to take up their lookout positions with Buddha. I practiced speaking like Percy so I would be in good voice when Prof. Harnash arrived.

I was anxious, trying to rehearse in my mind what I was going to say. "Hey Professor, I've been dying to see you again?" No, that wouldn't work. "Professor, you slay me?" Try again. "Professor, it's been deadly dull where I've been. Too much time to kill?" Nope. "I bet you've been dying to know what I've been up to?"

Just then I heard Randy's muffled voice coming from the trash can.

"Get ready and be quiet. They said he's coming."

I tensed up and waited. Then I remembered the Dictaphone in my pocket. I turned it on. I hoped Randy remembered to turn on the camcorder. A few minutes later the door creaked open and peaking through the bookshelf I saw him come into the room carrying a bouquet of flowers.

"Reggie, my little rose petal, it's me? It's Daddy Long Leg. Are you here? I've brought something for you," Professor Harnash said, scanning the room for her. I took a deep breath and spoke in my dead Percy voice.

"She had to leave professor. She didn't like my company. Said I was too deadly dull." I stayed behind the bookshelf when I said that.

Prof. Harnash immediately cowered, looking around the room.

"Who said that? Your voice sounds familiar? Do I know you?"

He held the bouquet of flowers out in front of him as though it was a sword ready to fend off an attack.

"Oh, you knew me very well. I used to work very closely with you."

"Did you retire? Are you Prof. Margolis?" he asked, still cowering and searching the room to find me.

"No, I'm not retired. But you might say I've departed."

"I know. You must be one of my former students, come back to harass me. Show yourself."

"I'd say haunt is a better description," I said, stepping out from behind the bookcase so he could see me. He stared at me as though he had seen a ghost.

"Is it …? Is it you, Percy?" he asked, his voice trembling.

"What's left of me, after you killed me," I replied.

"Why are you here? What have you come back for?" he asked, his whole body shaking.

"To find out why you killed me?" I replied. He stared at me wide-eyed, then shuffled over to the door. Uh-oh, I thought. He's gonna run out of here to get away from me and this whole exercise will have been a waste. What'll I do to keep him here?

"Wait," I yelled. "Don't leave me if you want to live." That must have worked because he didn't leave the room. Instead he shut the door and then locked it.

Then he turned to me. But now he wasn't shaking. And he was no longer wide-eyed. In fact, he didn't look at all frightened of the ghost of Percy.

"Oh, I'm not about to leave … Mr. Taylor. And I'm not the one who is in danger of not living."

He flipped on the light switch and then began to unwrap the flower bouquet. Clutched in his hand among the flowers was a small but potent looking handgun which was now pointed right at me.

He took one more look around as if to assure himself that no one else was around. It took all of the self-control I could muster for me to not look at the trash barrel containing Randy. I figured that Randy would inevitably jump out and startle Harnash at some point, so I should keep my cool, keep Harnash talking and be ready to pounce on him when Randy emerged from the trash can.

"How did you know it was me?" I asked.

"I was going to ask you that question myself. But I'll go first," Harnash replied. "I deduced that something was afoot when I saw you and several of your cronies speaking with that voluptuous creature in my classroom yesterday. That young lady was quite striking and I noticed her immediately when she was still with you.

"And I found it strange that she would identify herself as one of my students when it was quite obvious that I had never before seen her in any of my classes. When she invited me to join her here, though flattered and aroused, I knew that something nefarious was afoot. So I came prepared with my body guard here," he said gesturing to his gun, "and here we are.

"As soon as I heard the voice I knew it was someone pretending to be Percy. And I had noticed the resemblance between you and Percy the first time I saw you in my class earlier this year. As soon as you came out from behind the bookcase I penetrated your disguise.

"By the way, I'd cut back on the powder next time. Makes you look like a rather unattractive geisha without a fan."

I took that as a sign of encouragement that he was saying there would be a next time. Maybe he wasn't a murderer after all? Maybe the gun was just for self-protection?

I was quickly disabused of that notion when he began to speak again.

"Now, you were about to tell me how you figured out that I had killed that miserable whelp, Percy Jordan?"

"Uh, yeah. Well, I was able to track down Percy's apartment through one of his old girlfriends. She gave me the key and I searched the place and found his letter saying he was blackmailing someone and he wanted to double the monthly payments.

"And I saw his bank account records which showed the money transfers from another account. I had someone track down that account and it was yours. So I figured he had been blackmailing you for something and when he got greedier you decided to kill him."

"Very astute detective work, Mr. Taylor. As I'm sure you've learned, Percy was sub-human, a parasite that didn't deserve to live. I made the mistake of taking pity on him and letting him continue working for me when I should have expelled him from the university. The complaints I received about him from students were extraordinary. And the sexual harassment claims had begun. But I tried to give him a second and third chance and he repaid me by blackmailing me. By that point I couldn't expel him."

"But how could he blackmail you?" I asked, genuinely interested. "Your wife knew about the women. She didn't care."

He stood there staring at me for about ten seconds, then a tired, resigned look came over his face. He sighed.

"In the movies the villain – that's me by the way – the villain always has his prey captured and then, instead of killing his victim, he toys with the victim. He tells the victim everything the victim wants to know, figuring that the victim will soon be dead anyway, so what's the harm? And then the victim escapes or gets rescued and the villain finds himself captured.

"I always say to myself, what an idiot that villain is. Doesn't he watch the movies. Just kill your victim and be done with it before something goes wrong. And of course he never does and that's his downfall.

"Well, my gut tells me that I should just shoot you and be done with it. But I know that the door is locked and we're three stories up so no one is going to rescue you. And I chatted with Percy before the end without consequence. So I suppose that I can tell you what happened. It's the least I can do after all your hard work."

"Thank you," I said.

"Percy and I were working on a project for the Dept. of Defense. It was a very lucrative project for the university and for me personally. But we were not achieving the goals and milestones that had been set for us on the project. There were a whole host of legitimate reasons for this, but the lack of success was going to jeopardize the project. In time we would reach our goals but we would never get to that point without reaching the milestones because the project would be cancelled.

"I also relied heavily on those research funds to maintain my household, my lifestyle, my wife's lifestyle and to fund some of my more intimate acquaintances. I could not see losing this project and its funding. So I fabricated some of the milestone results in order to keep the project extant.

"Percy Jordan found out and threatened to expose me unless I paid him every month. I couldn't fire him or expel him and he became even more brazen in the way he treated other people, including his students, and the disrespect he showed to other faculty members, his fellow graduate students and me.

"I would have fired him in the blink of an eye if it were just me, but if he reported this it would have had wide repercussions. It would have brought disgrace to our noble institution, to the department and to my family. So I paid that parasite and tried to ignore his excesses."

"Jeez, that's amazing."

"And as you correctly surmised, when Percy demanded that I double his monthly payments it became clear to me that this must not stand. Now he wanted double. In a few more months he would demand even more. His greed was boundless and he would never stop unless he was stopped by me."

"So how did you do it?" I asked.

"Oh, that part was quite simple. I asked him to meet me in my office after hours when the building was empty. I knew that he had a proclivity for British beers so I had some of those chilled. I also had an ample supply of tranquillizers which I used to lace his beer. The India Pale Ales have a medicine after-taste which masked the taste of the tranquillizers.

"He drank heavily and when I saw the tranquillizers begin to work I helped him to his feet and half dragged him to the room where you found him so he could ostensibly sleep. I gave him a few more pills and then just before he nodded off, when he was quite unable to resist, I gave him an additional drink – this time of acid.

"It woke him up quite nicely, allowing me to tell him what I had done and that he would plague me no further. I enjoyed watching him suffer after all the suffering he had inflicted on me. Then, when he was dead I typed the suicide note and placed it by his side to be found by you."

I had felt somewhat sorry for old Harnash originally, but hearing his confession made me see him for what he was – a certifiable fruitloop of the highest degree. It also made me realize that if something didn't happen to save me he was gonna kill me for sure. I wondered whether Randy had fallen asleep in his trash can. If possible I would have to give it a good kick to wake him up.

"Were you the one who burnt down Percy's apartment?" I asked. He chuckled.

"Oh, yes. That was rather a smashing blaze as Percy might have said. That was me. Reminded me of the days when I was a kid playing with my first chemistry set. I created some terrific chemical fires back then – all inadvertent at that time."

"Why torch the place?"

"To eliminate any evidence, of course."

"Did Jeff tell you where the apartment was? Was he working with you?" I asked.

"Jeff? Jeff who?"

Uh-oh, I thought to myself. If he doesn't know Jeff then Jeff didn't have anything to do with the murder or the fire. I spent all of those uncomfortable nights on spring-loaded sofas for nothing. What a depressing thought. But I better not tell him who Jeff is or he may go after Jeff to silence him after he finishes me off.

"Uh, Jeff … Jefferson. A friend of mine. I mentioned that I had heard where Percy lived and I thought he might have told you."

"I overheard an undergraduate chemistry major, Mr. Flintlock, mentioning it to a couple graduate students. I had been looking for that apartment for a while precisely because I thought there would be some evidence linking me to his death. Unfortunately, he had recently moved without notifying the department of his new address."

"You're very thorough," I said.

"Have to be in my line of work," he said proudly. "Of course, I wasn't too thorough when I tried to kill you."

"You tried to kill me?" I asked.

"Don't you remember on the subway? That was me." Again, the pride in his voice was palpable.

"Why did you try to kill me? And how did you know I'd be there?"

"After meeting you in my office it was obvious to me that you were going to be troublesome. I could tell you were a bright and determined young man, and that you stood a good chance of figuring out the truth. My assessment was obviously correct. So I determined that if I got the opportunity to kill you, I should take it.

"Then a few days later I happened to be taking the subway to Filene's Basement for their Brooks Brothers suit sale and there you were, standing there. You looked almost moribund, like you were ill, so I decided to use the opportunity to eliminate you as well. I moved in close behind you and just before the train pulled in I gave you a shove, hoping that you would fall beneath its wheels and that would be the end. But I didn't stick around to see what would happen because there was some lunatic following me around, trying to study my head. He kept calling me a cyborg."

"Did you ever try to kill me again?"

"No. Unfortunately, I had no other opportunities… until now, that is."

"So what are you going to do with me?" I asked, weakly.

"Oh, I'm going to have to shoot you. I'm sorry but there's no way around it. It is a pity, though. You have a lot of talent. You're bright. You had a very good future until you got mixed up with Percy and me. Why didn't you just leave it alone? Everyone else thought it was suicide. Those mental midgets at Campus Security had closed their files as had the Cambridge Police. It would have been so easy and peaceful for everyone if you had just kept your nose out of it and not meddled."

"I guess I've just got an inquiring mind. That's how I got accepted into this school in the first place."

I tried to think of something else to say to keep the conversation going.

"Mind if I sit? My legs are a little weak."

He shook his head. I walked over to the trash can where Randy was supposed to be hiding, almost certain that he had fallen asleep, and sat down on it. I gave it a good kick as I sat there.

"Well, I think we've chatted enough. I have to get back home to watch Mystery on PBS. I've got to kill you now."

"Uh, wait. Just one more question. Tell me how you're going to get rid of my body and get away with killing me when other people knew I was coming here tonight to confront you?"

He smiled and shook his finger at me.

"Naughty, naughty, naughty. Telling people you were coming here and why. But I anticipated that. I am actually going to shoot you in such a way that it makes it look like suicide. I'm going to leave your body here with the gun. And I am going to prepare a note that demonstrates that you had lost your faculties, believing yourself to be poor dead Percy Jordan, to the point of dressing like him, cutting and dying your hair, powdering your face to make you feel like a ghost and then killing yourself. It should be very plausible under the circumstances."

I stood up. I had to move out of the way so that Randy could (and hopefully would) jump out. It seemed like I was at the end of the road here and if something didn't happen soon I would be well-ventilated. I shuffled a little to the side.

"So where are you going to shoot me to make it look like I did it myself?" I asked, hoping he would have to get close to me to do it and I could make a grab at the gun.

I tried to think back on what I had learned in Tae Kwon Do, but I didn't feel competent to deliver a kick or punch quickly enough to not get shot in the process. So I wasn't feeling terribly optimistic at this point.

I concluded that Randy must have asphyxiated in the trash can and I wasn't going to get any help. Prof. Harnash moved a little closer to me.

"I'm going to shoot you in the head. And I do have to get closer to do it properly. I don't want any heroics because if I do it properly you won't feel a thing. But if you make it difficult for me I'll have to shoot you in other places that won't kill you … immediately, giving you plenty of time to suffer. So just hold still."

He inched forward a little closer and was starting to raise the gun when I heard the shattering of glass. I looked in the direction of the sound and saw Sheik and Mad Dog, swinging on ropes and crashing through two large picture windows. Each of them carried knives, clutched between their teeth like pirates.

Prof. Harnash fell back, startled, but quickly recovered and began to raise his gun to point it in the direction of this new threat. But before he could get the gun fixed on Sheik and Mad Dog, he was distracted by a loud explosion which came from the other direction.

Immediately I turned to see the door to the lounge blown wide open and the soot covered face of Beeker as he charged into the room followed by Yaz, Buddha, Sigmund, Waldo, a large number of the other brothers and Karen!

I did a double take. What was Karen doing here?

Prof. Harnash turned to face the new onslaught. He started to raise his gun but Karen was already up in the air in a flying side kick that caught him square in the chest. He fell back but still had the gun in his hand. Sheik and Mad Dog were on him in a flash and had him disarmed and unconscious on the floor a second later.

Just at that moment, Officer Simpson, gun blazing, came tearing into the room.

"All right. Campus police. Everyone put your hands up."

# THIRTY-EIGHT

"Officer Simpson, you've solved the murder. Congratulations," I said walking over to him, my hands up in the air.

"What murder?" he asked, puzzled.

"Percy Jordan's murder. Prof. Harnash confessed. I have it all recorded on this Dictaphone. Can I put my hands down now?"

He looked at me and nodded. I pulled out the Dictaphone, rewound a little and played it back. His eyes widened as he listened.

"Where is he? I've got to put the professor under arrest," Officer Simpson said, looking around.

"He's right over here, taking a little nap," Sheik and Mad Dog said, pointing down to the unconscious professor.

"Can everyone else put their hands down now, too?" I asked. He looked around dubiously but finally nodded. Then he walked over to Harnash and handcuffed him before calling for backup on his radio.

I went over to Karen and gave her a big hug. She hugged me back.

"What are you doing here? How did you find out about this?" I looked at her still disbelieving that she was standing there in front of me.

"Amy told me what really happened, that she was the one coming on to you and that you'd just been locked out. I felt terrible. And then I ran into Randy, and he told me what you lunatics were up to. So I insisted on being here.

"And Randy told me that the fraternity brothers didn't know anything about this. So I contacted them and they wanted to come too. I guess they aren't as bad as I thought. They're actually a pretty nice bunch of guys." She grinned sheepishly.

Waldo walked up to me, looking severe.

"I know I wasn't supposed to do this, but I didn't want him to get away," I said defensively before Waldo could say a word. Waldo's face cracked into a smile and he gave me a pat on the shoulder.

"You're O.K., Sherlock. But next time do me a favor? Let us know what you're up to so we can protect your backside." I grinned back at him.

Buddha came up to me.

"Hey Jer, where's Randy?"

"Oh, shit. I forgot about him. He's still in the trash."

We rushed over to the trash blind and tried to remove the top. It was stuck. Sheik and Mad Dog came over and helped Buddha and me to pry it off. Randy stood up. He was a little wobbly.

"Randy, what happened?" I asked. "Are you all right?"

"I'm a might cramped but O.K. That god-damned lid was stuck, Jer. I was gonna jump up and surprise that son-of-a-bitch Harnash, but I couldn't get the top off. Sorry. But at least I got it all on tape."

"Not a problem, Randy. It all turned out great."

Then Sheik and Mad Dog came over to me. I thanked them for dropping in at a critical time.

"My pleasure," the Sheik said. "It reminded me of the old days smuggling goods across the border. We were always rappelling down mountains and swinging on ropes. I'm just glad that we were in time. It took us awhile to find the ropes and get up on the roof. But I thought they'd come in handy."

Officer Simpson came up to us with another man, whose uniform brass indicated he was a big cheese.

"This is Chief O'Shaunnesy. He wants to have a word with you," Simpson said to me nervously and then backed away.

"Simpson says you discovered that Percy Jordan had been murdered and that Prof. Harnash was the murderer. That's incredible detective work. I want to shake your hand."

"Well, you really should be shaking the hand of Officer Simpson. He's the brains behind what turned out to be a complex solution. I was just helping to track down some of the evidence for him. He solved it."

I glanced at Officer Simpson, whose jaw had dropped. He was gaping at me like the village idiot.

"Is that true, Simpson?" the Chief asked, probing him with his eyes.

"N, n, no, sir."

"Oh, he's just modest. He doesn't like to take the credit. It was all his idea. I did very little," I said.

The Chief looked from Officer Simpson, to me and then back to Officer Simpson. He shook his head.

"Well, it doesn't sound like the Simpson I've known, but you have no reason to lie about something like that, young fellow. It must be true.

"Simpson, there's more to you than meets the eye. We've got to move you back to a real office. And maybe think about promoting you to detective."

The Chief started leading Officer Simpson away. Simpson gave me a quick glance and I winked at him. He winked back and a tear ran down his face.


Our Thanksgiving break was scheduled to begin the next day and the fraternity decided to host an impromptu party to give thanks for everything that had occurred: the successful resolution of the Percy Jordan murder and bringing Prof. Harnash to justice, with no one getting hurt.

It was a wildly successful affair, in no small part because the newly promoted Inspector Simpson of the Campus Police had taken the chapter under his protection.

The big secret that Waldo had learned from the Dean, but couldn't say to anyone, was that the university administration had decided to crack down on fraternity parties. Now when a fraternity tried to hold a party, Campus Security would be there shutting it down in no time. But not at Sigma Epsilon Chi. Inspector Simpson saw to that.

So now there was no fear that the party would get shut down, and the house resembled a waterfront saloon when the fleet is in port.

Everyone was relaxed and happy. Classes were over and wouldn't resume again until after the break. There were no academic pressures for the present. And there were no fraternity pressures now. My pledge brothers and I had completed our projects and we had completed getting all of the missing signatures in our notebooks. Our complete contentment was marred only by the fact that we still didn't know what Fred Burdick's nickname, C.P., stood for. But we figured one of the brothers would loosen up at the party and we'd get the answer that way.

This party was especially great for me because of one particular guest at the party – Ms. Karen Kim. That's right! When I invited her she readily accepted my invitation. It was her first fraternity party ever and she seemed to be having as much fun as everyone else, eating, drinking, dancing and celebrating in general.

She and I took a break from our frenetic dancing to Springsteen's "Born To Run" and sidled up to the bar. Cheever, resplendent back in his butler uniform, greeted us from the other side of the bar.

"May I provide you and the young lady with a refreshment, sir?"

"Thanks, Cheever. I'll have a Harpoon and Karen will have a glass of white wine."

"Very good sir." He set about preparing the refreshments and my roommate, Jeff, came over to us grinning broadly.

"I was just speaking with one of the guys and he was telling me you were staying away from our room because you thought I murdered Percy?"

"Well, Karen learned that you'd threatened to kill him last year, so we didn't know. We just thought it best to play it safe." Jeff roared with laughter.

"What's so funny?" we asked.

"Percy and I both happened to be in a squash tournament last year and I was scheduled to play him. I had told him that I was gonna kill him in our squash match. I guess it got a little distorted over time."

"Yeah, like my butt, from the springs on those old couches I was sleeping on instead of my nice comfortable bed," I said.

Cheever served our drinks and we continued mingling with people, enjoying the evening. After awhile I felt nature's urge and excused myself for a bio break. But when I got to the first floor bathroom there was a long line of women waiting to use it.

I skipped up the stairs, two at a time, destined for the second floor bathroom. I found the same situation and my bladder was beginning to churn in anticipation of the relief.

I started running upstairs to the third floor where the last bathroom was located, but ran into Randy coming down the stairs, a distressed look on his face.

"If you're thinkin' about drainin' your dragon up there, you're outta luck. Someone plugged up the toilet and the floor is flooded. They're gonna halfta call a plumber."

"Damn. The bathrooms on the first two floors are jammed up," I said.

"I know. That's why I was up there. I'm gonna just go outside and piss in the bushes," he said and started down the stairs. I followed him.

We went out the back door of the house into the moonlight and we were greeted with a freezing wind. Neither of us had put on our coats because the trip was intended to be short, but almost immediately I was regretting it, freezing, especially my nose, ears and hands because of the biting wind chill.

We walked around, looking for a promising set of bushes to water. After a minute we found the ideal candidates, a little off the beaten path and not open to the moonlight. So the risk of getting arrested for exposing ourselves was minimal.

We lined up next to each other, unzipped our flies and then proceeded to whip them out. We both winced from the feel of our freezing hands.

"Ouch ..." Randy said. "My hands are cold."

"Burrr. So's my dick," I replied.

Randy laughed.

"What's so funny?"

"You said burr, my dick's cold.    It reminded me of Fred Burdick."

At that moment I had an epiphany.

"Randy.  You've solved it."

"What?"

"Burdick is C.P."

"Huh?"

"Think about it.  Burrr – dick.  Cold …"

He looked at me and then I saw understanding spread across his face.  We both grinned and said it simultaneously.

"Burr Dick.  Cold Penis."

# THIRTY-NINE

I was awakened from a heavy sleep early the next morning by my alarm clock. My head was pounding from overindulging the night before. It had been a great party and a great way to blow off steam after the stress of the last few days. But now I was a hurting buckaroo. As I lay there in bed I vowed never to drink again.

I tried to get my mind working. What did I have to do today? As I thought about it, I recalled that today was the day I was returning home to Seattle for the Thanksgiving break. Randy was heading back to Texas and the night before he told me he had rented a stretch limo to take him to the airport. He'd offered to give me and Karen a ride to the airport in his limo and we had accepted.

Now what time was the limo supposed to leave? I thought about it, trying to get the RAM of my brain to kick in. I recalled walking Karen back to her dorm room and her reminding me to set my alarm for 8:00 am because the limo would leave at 9:00 am. Had I kissed her goodnight? No, I recalled thinking that I should let her give me a sign that she wanted me to kiss her first, but she hadn't. She had just said 'goodnight' and gone into her dorm.

I sighed. Things seemed to be back on track between us now after that fiasco outside her room, but I guess we were still just good friends. Maybe romance would never be in the picture.

I looked over at the clock – 8:15 am. So I had plenty of time to get up, shower and …Oh, no. I remembered that I hadn't bothered to pack yet. I was going to do it the night before but I had blown it off when Yaz, Mad Dog and Buddha had stopped by my room to pick me up before the party. Now I had to do that as well as my normal routine. I had to move.

I began to get up, but felt a freight train running through the middle of my brain. Must be the same one Springsteen had encountered when he was on fire, I mused before collapsing back into my pillow.

After a few minutes I tried again. The headache was still there along with a heavy fatigue, but I willed myself out of bed, stumbled to my closet and dragged out my suitcase. Then I fell back into my bed to rest up and let the pain in my head subside for a few minutes.

On my next trip out of the bed I took a few aspirin and began throwing my clothes into the suitcase. Clean clothes, dirty clothes – I threw them all in together without discrimination and without folding. I could sort them out when I got home. For now, I was just happy to have them in my bag.

I collapsed on my bed again and rested, hoping that the aspirin would kick in soon. I looked at the clock – 8:30. I'd give it another five minutes and then drag myself to the shower.

By 8:54 I was dressed, had my suitcase and I was heading out of my dorm. I reached the sidewalk, sat down on the curb and waited with my eyes closed. I still had a headache and my stomach wasn't feeling real well, either. I desperately needed more sleep.

A few minutes later a white stretch limo with bull horns on the hood slid quietly to a stop in front of where I was sitting. I heard a door open, looked up, and there was Cheever, looking fresh as a daisy despite the fact that he had worked the party the prior evening and had gotten as little sleep as me.

"Good morning, Master Taylor. I've brought you something." He opened the rear door of the limo, reached into a cabinet and removed a tumbler. He shook it a few times then poured the contents into a tall glass which he handed to me.

I looked up through bleary eyes.

"What is it?" I croaked.

"A restorative, sir. Please consume it. I'm sure that you'll find it quite satisfactory."

I sniffed. "What's in it?"

"Ah, I'm not at liberty to say, sir. A secret family recipe. But I can tell you that it is all natural and guaranteed to invigorate the tissues."

Oh, what the hell, I thought. It can't make me feel any worse than I already do. I chugged it down.

My first sensation was a burning feeling in the back of my throat and in my nostrils as though I had just consumed a piece of sushi that had been slathered with a particularly large glob of wasabi. It was very unpleasant initially but it was soon followed by a warm glow and a new-found strength that moved to all the parts of my body. Suddenly I was wide awake, my headache was gone and I felt refreshed and energized. I hopped up.

"Cheever, this stuff is amazing. You should sell it," I exclaimed excitedly.

Cheever just nodded and smiled slightly.

"I'm gratified that I have been of some assistance, sir."

I now became curious about Randy, whom I hadn't noticed in the limo.

"Where's Randy?"

"Ah, Master Randall also was suffering the ill-effects of last evening and he has declined to leave at this time. But he asked me to send you his warmest regards for an enjoyable holiday with your relations and he will look forward to your renewed society when classes recommence."

"But won't he miss his plane if he doesn't come now?"

"Master Randall's father possesses a Lear jet. I took the liberty of canceling the scheduled flight and arranging to have the jet modify its destination so that it can collect Master Randall later this afternoon. So there is no need to be anxious on that account. Now, shall we depart to rendezvous with Miss Kim?"

Saying that, he picked up my suitcase, deposited it in the trunk, and held the door open for me. I got into the back and sank into the luxury of the plush and spacious seats.

We traveled over to Karen's dorm. She was waiting outside and Cheever assisted her into the rear of the limo. She looked stunning to me.

"Hey, where's Randy?" she asked upon entering.

"I guess he was too hung over, so he decided to go home later."

"It was nice of him to still give us a ride to the airport!" she commented. I agreed.

"By the way, I'm surprised <u>you</u> look so good," she said. "You were tying one on pretty well last night."

"I'm never gonna drink again," I replied. "Actually, I was in terrible shape until Cheever gave me some mystery drink. He wouldn't tell me what was in it, but boy, did it fix me up." I laughed.

We continued to chat all the way to the airport. We were both looking forward to getting back to our respective homes, seeing our families, and just hanging out. Karen told me how nice it was to come back home after being away at school for so long.

Upon arriving at the airport, Cheever collected our luggage and handed it to us. We exchanged our goodbyes with Cheever, and then Karen and I walked into the airport ticketing area together.

We were both taking Northwest Airlines, with Karen going to Detroit and me to Seattle. We checked in, passed security and then walked down the concourse together. Her flight left about twenty minutes before mine, so I waited at her gate with her. It felt nice being with her and enjoying her companionship while we waited.

At last, her flight began boarding and I got up to go.

"Well, this is it. I hope you have a good vacation. Don't eat too much turkey," I said.

"No worry about that. We'll have Korean food for Thanksgiving. My Mom doesn't know how to cook a turkey."

"I still haven't tried Korean food. Would I like it?" I asked.

"I don't know. We'll have to go out for Korean food when we get back to school after the break. It'll be an experience for you."

"Great. It's a date," I said.

"I thought I told you, I don't date frat boys," she said, suddenly looking serious.

Was she goofing on me or did she really mean it? In light of everything that had happened, I'd assumed that she had gotten over her closed-mindedness about fraternities and me. I looked at her closely. She definitely wasn't smiling. I must have been wrong.

I sighed. I had been feeling so great and now, with that one comment, she had dashed my hopes and ruined my good humor. I was depressed.

"Oh yeah, I forgot. Well, I guess we'll just be friends getting together for dinner," I replied, my eyes downcast. "I'll see ya," I said dejectedly, still not looking at her and I started to walk away.

I had only gone a few feet when she called to me.

"Hey, Sherlock. Aren't you forgetting something?"

I turned around and looked at her, puzzled. She walked up to me, put her arms around me and kissed me. "There. I've been waiting ages for you to give me one of those," she said, looking into my eyes and smiling broadly.

"Believe me, I've wanted to."

"Well, then why haven't you done it?"

I looked at her sheepishly.

"I was afraid you'd slug me if I did. And I preferred not to experience that again."

Just then Karen's row was called and she picked up her bag.

"That's me. Well, have a good one and I'll see you in ten days," she said, waving and flashing me a glittering smile.

"Yep. And when we get back we'll go on that date, right?" I replied, grinning.

She laughed.

"Maybe, fratboy. Maybe."


## THE END